**FRONT PORCH**

A Novel of Life Lessons

✿

*Reflections of Five Generations of Redemption*
*"It was gon take more than prayer to bring them through"*

Layla Patrice

A Black Pearl Literary Perspective
Generations Series

**FEATURING AN EXCLUSIVE EXCERPT FROM THE AUTHORS UPCOMING GENERATIONS SEQUEL**

**DOWN SOUTH SUMMERS**
*"Where Seeds Were Sown"*

A Novel of Confessions

This book is a work of fiction. Names, characters, places and incidents either are products of the author's imagination or are used fictitiously. Any resemblance to actual events or locales or persons, living or dead, is entirely coincidental.

Registered Copyrights © 2022 by Layla Patrice. All rights reserved. No part of this publication may be reproduced, distributed or transmitted in any form or by any means including photocopying, recording, or other electronic or mechanical methods without the prior written permission of the author, except in the case of brief quotations embodied in reviews, and certain other non-commercial uses permitted by copyright law.

Visit the Website at: ABlackpearlliteraryperspective.org for more information about upcoming novels, discussions and podcast

ISBN – 979-8-84220-959-0

All Photography by Layla Patrice
Poem "Ancient" Written by Layla Patrice
Front and Back-of-jacket design by Layla Patrice

First Edition

***The Generations Series***

*The Generation Series is written specifically to honor the relevance and role of all family members within the context of community. Life is fully captured and understood from the perspective, experience and voice of past, present and future generations.*

*Welcome To*
*"A Black Pearl Literary Perspective"*

The use of African American Vernacular English (AAVE)
is a conscious choice.

*In Memoriam*

*Ernest and Harriette*

*Emmanuel and Nancy*

*James and Callie*

*Robert Daniel III*

*Miciah*

*and*

*Forever Twelve-Year-Old Jaden Christyana*

# ACKNOWLEDGMENTS

*To My Lord & Savior Jesus Christ*

*In Dedication to:*

*My older siblings that selflessly wrapped themselves around me*

*My children*
*that taught me to keep loving, striving and praying*

*My grandchildren*
*to the sixth generation and beyond that keep on*
*breathing life back into me.*

※

*To my childhood friends and covenant relationships*

*To the teachers who showed me the way*

*To the neighborhoods that raised me*
*and the streets that somehow protected me*

※

*To the generations of saint's past and present*
*that allowed prayer to travel through them*
*spoke a good word over my life and imparted wisdom.*

*A Special Acknowledgement to:*

*My Jurisdictional Prelate*
*Bishop Ocie Booker & First Lady Mother Jean Booker*
*for preaching the gospel, leading souls to Christ*
*and pressing the battle all the way to the gate.*

Layla Patrice the youngest of seven children is a Christian Writer, Poet, and Playwright. As a young adult, Chicago's Bronzeville provided the perfect blend of community, arts, culture, education and exposure.

As a student of Haki R. Madhubuti, Founder of Third World Press, Poet, Editor and Educator that sowed seeds into the lives of his students, she had the privilege of reciting her poetry at the Historic Geri's Palm Tavern under the watchful eyes of the late Poet Laureate, Gwendolyn Brooks and the late Dr. Margaret Burroughs, Founder of the DuSable Museum.

The Black Writers Conferences held at Chicago State University brought young writers in the room and to the table with the greatness of Amiri Baraka, J. California Cooper, Mari Evans, Useni Perkins, Sonia Sanchez, Val Gray Ward and many others.

A series of classes in Columbia College Fiction Writing department with Shelia Baldwin, and Elizabeth Yokas gave her wings to write and produce her first play, *Movin by His Power*. In 2000, A. Okechukwu Ogbonnaya of Urban Ministries contracted her to open the "*Christian Pastor Leaders & Educators Conference.*" The play ran at the Chernins Center for the Arts and was later staged at the DuSable Museum's Harold Washington theatre with a full house.

These are just a few memories alongside the Thursday evenings spent at the Historic Sutherland enjoying Malachi Thompson's jazz bands; all of which help change the trajectory of her life. She went on to complete her education earning a Master of Arts in Community Counseling from Roosevelt University and a Doctor of Education from Argosy.

After playing supporting roles in workforce development and other employment venues, she returned to her love of writing to begin a series of novels under *A Black Pearl Literary Perspective,* her website, blog, podcast and Utube Channel. *Front Porches & Corner Stores* is her debut novel for the Generations Series to be followed by its sequel, *Down South Summers*.

# INTRODUCTION

*"In the beginning was
the Word, and the Word was with God, and the Word was God."
– John 1:1*

*A Black Pearl Literary Perspective* strive to capture the fluent expression and the close relationship between times, places and emotion through the use of imagery and episodic memory. It calls to mind life's spiritual lessons within the context of prayer moving simultaneously with the good and the bad; linking the two and shifting outcomes. A phenomenon commonly known as, *"Prayer Changes Things."*

It is in this spirit that *A Black Pearl Literary Perspective* book is written and to be fully enjoyed. The writer will always be found in her stories being honest in words, events, experiences and character development. Exhausting senses and remembering the simplest of things to capture the nuance of fleeting moments.

Remembering the winter of '67 that dumped 23 inches of snow in 29 hours. Cars and buses looking like big lumps, like giant strangely shaped snowballs in the middle of the street. People getting out their cars and walking. CTA bus drivers parking buses, pulling their skull caps down over their heads, snatching jackets off the backs of seats. Looking at passengers, getting off with unpunched transfers in hand and walking away. Saying nuthin. Figuring if they had good sense, they'd get off and do the same thing before it was too late. Like racism the snow did not stop, it kept on coming down.

Remembering the sadness, anger and the courage of Thursday, April 4, 1968, just after 6pm. When black and white televisions announced the death, the murder, the killing, the assassination of Dr. Martin Luther King Jr. Remembering how black families mourned in the projects from behind caged balconies, assembled in doorways, stood on stoops, huddled on corners, and sat in pissey stairwells, crying, reliving the tragedy, and the loss of hope. Stuck in disbelief, how they shook their heads and held their babies just a little bit closer that night.

Remembering how enraged teenagers boldly galvanized and took to the streets to express their hurt the best way they knew how; destroying what was within reach in their own communities that would never belong to them.

Remembering black boys shipping to Vietnam in packs. Remember the sound of the Temptations, *"Don't Send Me Away"* and *The Monitors "Greetings this is Uncle Sam"* hauntingly playing nonstop from a transistor radio from an apartment window on the 9th floor where a girl cried for her boyfriend who was drafted to die.

Remembering her six-year-old eyes following the search light that rode across the sky over Saint Ignatius with the Friday Night Late Movie in the background to the tune of Dave Brubeck's *"Take Five"* from the 2nd floor window of Robert Brooks extensions.

Remembering how her voice was being made with every vibration of vowel sounds, the moment her 1st grade teacher placed a tuning fork to her chin. Remembering how she fell in love with syllables, diphthongs, consonant' sounds and blends that somehow when formed and shaped made words that liked to come out to play and tell stories the way she wanted to tell them.

Remembering how anxious she was to learn to read, spell and write. How she was excited by freshly sharpened pencils, and the sound of crisp notebook paper. And enchanted by a mysterious black woman, *Ella Jenkins* that somehow appeared in her 1st grade classroom strumming a guitar, helping children learn to sing songs together.

Remembering the move from the projects to Roseland. Rushing home with armfuls of books from the Pullman library to find the perfect spot to cozy up and journey. Remembering the parties *Whine N Down* and *Jackin* her body to Reggae and hours of house music. *Steppin*, skating, singing, and dancing.

Remembering when her conscious was pricked and her heart turned when she discovered the generational anchor of Holiness, prayers, and the faith that was always working, always somewhere moving in the background; steering, guiding her away from sin and leading her to God's ordained destiny for her life. Remembering the reoccurring dream of chasing the train to heaven and being pulled aboard by the saints of God just in the nick of time.

# PART ONE

# CHAPTER ONE

❧

## *Leaving*

*"Father God in The Mighty Name of Jesus! My Sweet Lord. Please Sir! If it be thy pleasure and if it be thy will. Let this bitter cup pass. Tear it up from the root that this family may walk with you down through the generations all the days of our lives. Amen."*

It just wasn't right to see or hear such a thing in a sanctified house. God wasn't nowhere in it. A father and son standing toe to toe hollering at each other like wasn't no love, like wasn't no God in em. It was dangerous like judgment coming. They never forgot that night Mother Howard turned her face to the wall, refused to stop praying to the Lord. Anted up the score for the life she lived before HIM. Told HIM how she raised her children in His Will and in His Way. Called HIM on His promises like she knew HIM. Held HIM to His word, gave it back to HIM. Told HIM she wasn't letting go His unchanging hand. Put her foot down on it and wouldn't back up off it. Told HIM though you slay me yet will I trust you the more. Told HIM how much she loved, needed, leaned and depended on HIM. Walking through her home speaking in unknown tongues. Touching and anointing the walls with holy hands. Stomping her foot, raising her arms, reaching and grabbing like she was snatching something out the air. Quickening, that's what she was doing. Shouting every scripture with a rumbling in her voice stirring the spirit in her soul. Igniting the power of the Holy Ghost. JE had a praying mother
    Raised along the Great Ohio River, just north of its convergence with the Mighty Mississippi. Where the Cairo Mississippi and Cairo Ohio River steel truss bridges joined Illinois to Missouri and Kentucky. Where Villa Ridge was seated in Pulaski County on 470 acres. Where Native mounds, earthen formations like flattened hills and mountains were replaced with development and farming. In a segregated Mound City, Illinois, late winter early Spring 1961 James Earnest Howard came home to leave.
    Prayer like time never stops, it keeps on traveling. That night when

it was all falling apart, Mother Howard turned from the wall, pushed her way out the screen door onto the front porch, looked up to the heavens knowing it was done, she uttered Amen. When she went back inside the house was burning like a fire. Conditions were already breaking and like a curse they broke. Daddy Howard was down on his knees pouring out, crying long and hard. They aint never heard that type of cry come out a man before. There was a howling like a wounded animal. A groan and an agony underneath it that went way down deep in his soul and when he hit the floor with the palms of his huge calloused hands shock waves went through the whole house and the foundation shook.

No one knew till then. Mother Howard said it was God's promise. Said it was a God decision. Said He whispered in her ear, told her, "This one is mine, this one you love unconditionally." Said he was a good righteous man. That he was afflicted and needed *tending*. She married, sanctified her unbelieving husband and lived a life of holiness before HIM that both their souls might be saved. She was his second wife and JE was not his first son.

Mother Howard stood still, reverenced the salvation of the Lord and told Addiemae, "Stand back; let him be!" She said it was happening, that God was purging him from the bitterness in his heart when he blamed HIM for the loss of his first wife and first-born son. And blamed HIM for the beating he endured as a child from his stepmother. And blamed HIM. And blamed HIM. And blamed HIM. God was blamed for everything that hurt in his life. Time and chance was happening to him. Deliverance had come.

Mother Howard retched down, anointed his head and neck with handfuls of blessed oil. Laid the dingy white oil-stained prayer towels over on his belly. The ones pulled out when she came against the spirit of death, the ones prayed over by anointed men and women of God at revivals. The ones used to swaddle, shroud and cover souls in the midst of a healing. She finished ministering, tied a white handkerchief around his neck, and watched over him like an angel with a flaming sword.

As he laid there in the floor writhing, twisting and turning, JE ran pass and out the house in a sudden summer gust of wind that slammed the door, "Bam!" He took off running like an extension cord had hit him dead in the middle of his back. He tripped and ran from the front porch right into the Navy, where he was stationed overseas on sinking ships had to box white racist men in the hulls and left the child of a black man behind. When that was over, he joined the Army and was sent into wars trying not to come back home. He couldn't stop running, and he couldn't stop hearing his momma's prayer moaning in his ears convicting him of his wrong.

She prayed, "God, hold on to him, make him hate sin and withhold yo peace. Give him long life. Don't take him till his soul be worthy of eternity." The devil wanted to kill him dead, but God wouldn't let it be. He honored Mother Howards' prayer. Kept on sparing his life, kept tapping on his heart, kept a hedge of protection around him and brought him back home safe with a few thorns in his side. Wasn't gon be no more ripping away, not this time it wasn't. The Lord, Mother Howard and Addiemae was gon see to that.

Poor sky. It wanted to greet him like the warmth of the sun he played under on hot muggy summer days when he was a boy but had no choice in the matter; it was ordained to be there during the bad times covering the sadness that was allowed to visit his life. It knew him by name, by deed and watched faithfully over him with no recognition of its goodness or its purpose.

The tired old town saw him coming a mile away hoping he'd brought something new to its memory to justify its existence. Remnants of hard dirty snow from January's winter awaited his arrival finding their way into the tiny crevices of the pine posts of the chicken wired fence he built; resisting the pleasant 54-degrees that crept in to thaw the ground for Spring. In April, there would be plantings of small fruits and vegetables. Wild blue and blackberries would instinctively grow to become the pies and preserves his momma made.

The red faded wood frame house sitting amongst a grove of white oaks on ten acres presented somewhat stately for land owned by its sharecropper. Geese wandered freely across the dry rigid road near the remaining mounds he climbed to play games of Kingdom, right where the Central Illinois railroad train tracks laid. Where Maggie their swaybacked horse agitated by his coming and going stood lazily near the barn slowly swishing the skirt of her tail reminding him, he was home.

The wide-open front porch wrapped her arms quickly around JE; soon as he put his foot down on her landing, she embraced him remembering the times they were alone together. Times he sat, whined and whispered to himself trying to figure things out that confused him. Times he felt misunderstood, lonely and shed tears that fell sweetly from his innocent eyes melting into invisible stains that never washed away. The time he tripped, that night he ran and she yielded herself just enough to splinter, securing a piece of evidence for remembering. His soul bared witness to the moments; he paused and paid homage. Before entering the house, he turned and looked suspiciously at that winding road that kept leading him back home with a quiet knowing.

The welcome was different from when he came home on leave; this wasn't no leave. Three terms, twelve years, honorably discharged; JE was home for good. An expectation hung over heads that something was coming, something was gon happen. He sat there still in his Army uniform long after the fanfare lifted like he just came home. Like he just got picked up from the train station in Cairo. Like everybody was gon run greet him all over again. He'd been home for three weeks but every day he got up and dressed in his uniform as if he was leaving.

Black families had been leaving for decades. Migrating, getting outta the south making their way up North to the Midwest and the West the best way they knew how. Stuffing hopes, dreams, wishes children, everything that belonged to em in cars, buses, and trains and headed to Chicago in search of the life advertised in the *Chicago Defender* newspaper. The one Addiemae snuck out his suitcase and passed around to anybody sitting on the front porch after dinner that wanted to see. She could tell he'd been reading; it was crumpled up, had a phone number and a name scribbled on it that read, "Franklin."

Night fell. Mother Howard stood at the kitchen sink washing dishes. Rocking, humming gospel, hushing and shooing away memories that wanted to steal peace. JE's stomach was full, but his heart was empty. He couldn't find nuthin there, not in Mounds he couldn't; it made him anxious looking into the darkness that looked back like it had eyes, threatening him since he was a boy. No matter what they said, JE wasn't nowhere near crazy, something caught his wrist. He grabbed, yanked it, broke free, pulled back a rope with a loop and a running knot at the end; a noose. There was somebody out there. He had a bloody imprint in the palm of his hand where the rope burned clear cross his lifeline to prove it; making him think he was gon die early. Wasn't no secret. Black boys coming up missing. The southernmost part of Illinois didn't wanna let go its slaves.

Ever since it happened when night came seem like he couldn't stop getting outta bed, running to the middle of the field in his pajamas, checking to see if it was gon happen. If they were waiting for him. If they were gon come try to grab him again. You couldn't see him, but you could hear him yelling.

"Aint nobody tying my hands. Aint nobody taking my freedom!" Punching the air, feet shuffling, hopping, shoes beating thirsty ground. JE was out there boxing with his big heavy 10-year-old fists. Fist like his daddy Ernest. Swinging, fighting against the darkness like it was a person, against what he couldn't see; it was one reason he left. JE took no issue saying. "Aint nuthin in Southern Illinois but memories of slavery and the fear of dying." Said he wasn't gon be nobody's slave and he wasn't bout to die. Not in Mounds he wasn't.

He came back a grown man with a strong voice. He got a taste of life in the military and spent hours entertaining his buddy's that never left Mounds with tales of New Finland, Japan, Germany and France. He told them black soldiers contributed to its liberation, that they marched along the Avenue des Champs-Elysees and the Arc de Triomphe. Although he left home at fourteen, he stood up proudly and spoke like a true scholar. Told them every black man should know what the streets of Paris felt like on the soles of his shoes. Told them when he was off-duty, he sat, crossed his legs, sipped coffee, ate croissants at cafe-bars and people-watched just like the Frenchmen.

JE had been places; even the dark places of racism where he felt the torture no man should ever feel. And he been places that didn't see him as an oppressed black man. Said the French was color-blind. Said if it wasn't for Honey and the children, he never woulda come back state-side, he woulda stayed overseas and made a life for himself. Said it so certain they listened with an uneasiness hoping Honey didn't hear. they figured wasn't no way JE was gon stay married. They could hear it in his voice, see it in his eyes, his walk, and the way he strutted with his chest stuck out. He had a worldly freedom about him. A freedom a married man couldn't have. Truth was, JE was ready to square off with the past. It wasn't gon be no more telling him what and when to do. Time was getting tight and sooner or later something was gon bust right through the good feelings.

Addiemae saw it clearly she looked straight through him knowing in his heart he wanted to do right but couldn't even if he tried. Not without the Lord he couldn't. He'd been gone too long, seen and done too much wrong to do right. He had a war going on inside him; a fight between good and evil.

Mother Howard stood in the doorway listening to his discontent. Eyes closed, arms folded across her body, swaying side to side knowing trouble done followed him home; that he needed *tending*. She ministered to him through the screen door. Told him he was a good righteous man. Kept saying how proud she was he come home to his wife and children, building his faith she came against what his daddy already knew. He was the same way when he fought in Korea and World War I with the 370$^{th}$ Infantry Regiment in France. A regiment so fierce the Germans called them *Black Devils*. They were relentless, they kept coming, they would not stop. He saw that same spirit of fight and freedom walking up and down in JE. Same way it warred inside of him, when he served. Every time JE came and went Daddy Howard said coming home for good was gon whip him bad. Said he was full of pride. Said being on leave was one thing but staying for the long haul was yet another. Said one day he gon have to take that uniform off, put on a suit of clothes, go to church, bow down and meet the Lord for himself.

JE was choking. Addiemae saw what he was thinking caught in his throat. Being home with his wife and children three weeks not even a month was too much. He couldn't take it.

"Let me see that paper, Addiemae. Franklin been up there in Chicago six months, he sent it to me. Said he got a job waiting if I want it. Just wasn't sure if I was gon follow through." He said matter of factly with a stern face as he swallowed deep, let the toothpick hang from his bottom lip and sucked the dinner meat from between his teeth. Addiemae wanted to hear what was caught in his throat. Tired of waiting she pulled it out.

"Seems to me like you should JE. I already know this not home no more, not for you it aint. Probably aint never been. Everybody done moved to Chicago Detroit and Indiana. But you still here like you don't know how to let go. Like you don't know how to stop coming back down that road out there." Addiemae rose up slowly from her seat, pointed toward the road and turned around to him frustrated. She had her mother's spirit but different. Hers was a righteous indignation that cut just beneath the carnal surface of the skin between hidden intentions and the truth that triggered a response. She cut deeper.

"What you waiting for JE? What you afraid of? I see you getting restless. I see that demon crawling all up yo back and Honey don't even know it. Wasn't for disability, can't say I'd be here either. But you done married that girl, tied her up with those children knowing you weren't gon be able to settle down. Yo heart good but your mind not right JE. You running like hot coals under weary feet. You simmering like a pot coming to a boil full of pressure, boy you bout to blow! Got her believing in you like momma believe in Jesus. Believing you gon come take her and them children to the top of the mountain. Still playing Kingdom looking down on the world. Well, this here aint no game. I know you been talking that sweet talk. I oughta know I heard it all before. A black woman gives up her life and for what! Don't you do to her what already been done to me. Lord knows it aint been easy, she got dreams too JE and the day she wakes up she gon speak her heart. And you best take it like a man cause you got it coming. If you don't do nuthin else get Honey outta here. Get her outta this South so she can make something of herself. Maybe be somebody. My God JE! What you bout to do!"

She already knew what he was bout to do. He was gon leave with or without his family. Same way Luke left when she had the stroke. Had the nerve to show up and plead his case. Brought her back to Daddy Howard on his knees. Crying, talking bout he didn't want no limping woman on his arm, that she couldn't keep up with him no more. Then he left out the door with his head hung down like a jack-legged preacher caught laying in the bed of his sinful act.

Wasn't a week went by he was drunk in the juke joint, got to talking mess to a well-dressed man with a fine woman on his arm. The man ignored him. Luke got mad and touched his woman's behind on the way out the door. She let out a shriek and the man turned around to deal with him like he aint never been dealt with before. Luke never had a chance, never even saw it coming, it was one swift smooth graceful move; a demonic dance. He dropped his lit cigarette to the ground smashed out the fire with his red wingtip shoe, tilted his Stetson back off his forehead, spun around and slid a shiny switch blade from the inside pocket of his tailor-made suit jacket. Within seconds Luke's face and arms were sliced to the white meat. Veins were cut and blood poured out him so fast he was swimming. He was shaking and his eyes were rolling up in his head trying to see where he was. Poor Luke didn't know if he was living or dying. The man told his boys.

"Scrape that negro up. Put him in my pickup truck and take him home to his mammy!" They threw him on the front porch bleeding like a slaughtered hog. His mother came out slipped in the blood and screamed hysterically. Addiemae said it wasn't no better for him or her. She blamed herself for listening to his promises and turning her back on the Lord to run the streets. Nuthin came to none of em on the altar that night that left the Lord.

It broke her heart knowing. They all knew, JE was gon leave Mounds backslidden. Aint no way he was gon stay and it wouldn't be long fore he left, that's rean she brought that paper out there in the first place, passed it around hoping he'd make good and follow through on the offer. She knew he was thinking bout it, pretending not to know; she wasn't the only one either.

Everybody that knew JE saw it coming every time he came home on leave big shotty. Leaving Honey pregnant like he had money to take care all them babies. Took her out that big house away from her family for his momma and daddy to keep an eye on while he did what he wanted to do, where he wanted to do it. Then dropped in like a hero. Long as he was government property, he aint had no worries. Now that he was a civilian all hell done broke loose cause Daddy Howard was gon ask about his plans to take care the family he made. He didn't trust JE's heart when he didn't get the Holy Ghost. When all he had to do was give up and give over to God. Everybody else gave over to HIM.

## CHAPTER TWO

### ♣
### *The Holy Ghost*

*"Son! Wasn't no visitation, the anointing aint fell, and JE you still aint saved. Lord have mercy on yo soul. Come back tomorrow get on this altar and don't you leave till the Holy Ghost come!"*

JE never did.

The organist was so full of the spirit he left his body. His fingers were running up and down the keyboard moving. Pushing repetitive rhythms higher and higher on top of the saints of God incessantly chanting, *"Power Lord!"* Tossing the song from one side of the room to the other for hours. The minute one person stopped singing another one started. The momentum was so strong, they couldn't stop, they were locked into a sacred space in time that ushered in God's presence like a lion was in the window ready to roar. The church got caught up. Young people were zealous. Ushers barely had time to grab enough sheets to cover long legs under short dresses with no stockings. They fell out under the anointing and when they came to themselves, they cried, ran, and gave their lives to the Lord.

The pastor was preaching hard. Sweating like he was driving a jack hammer straight through five miles of concrete busting up fallow ground. Snatching young souls from the gates of hell, throwing em over on the altar. Deacons were struggling to wipe his brow and keep up with him. Missionaries were holding backs and bellies in hands, whispering in ears, "Say Thank you Jesus! Thank HIM outta yo belly! Give up to HIM! Hold on to HIM!" Church mothers were walking, guarding the alter floor with intercessory prayer. Stooping and rising, stooping and rising. Arms lifting in praise like angel wings. Quickening, pulling down and casting out everything that wasn't like God.

The Pastor. The Good Sheppard sent by God was so hungry for young souls he could taste it. He wanted them all saved. He kept on preaching cause he saw what was coming down the road.

"I gotta cry loud. And spare not. I gotta lift up my voice. Like a trumpet. I'm just a dying man, trying to preach to a dying people. Tell a church. With itching ears. What it doesn't wanna hear.  Tell a lost soul. You got to be saved. Is there an Amen? In the house. Uh huh. Romans Chapter 7 and Verse 19-24 says.

*For the good that I would I do not: but the evil which I would not, that I do.*

*Now if I do that I would not, it is no more I that do it, but sin that dwelleth in me.*

*I find then a law, that, when I would do good, evil is present with me.*

*For I delight in the law of God after the inward man:*

*But I see another law in my members, warring against the law of my mind, and bringing me into captivity to the law of sin which is in my members.*

*O wretched man that I am! who shall deliver me from this body of death?*

"I believe I got a church. Uh huh. I said it's time to get right. With God. Tell the Lord you sorry. Ask HIM for deliverance. From this body of Death. While you still. Have a chance. While you still. Have blood. Running warm. In your veins. You see. Tomorrows not promised. And today. Is already gone. If you want. Something from the Lord.  If you want. The pow—er of the Holy Ghost. You got. To be saved. You got. To have. A clean life. And a glad. Spirit. The only thing that's gonna save you, is the blood of Jesus, and the power, of God. Say yes. Yessss. Yes Lord!"

The sermon concluded with, "The Holy Ghost is a Keeper for those who want to be kept." It was *Friday Night Tarry Service*. The Spirit was high. The kinda high that made you forget yo troubles and love everybody. Lord it was so high, you could envision yourself letting go everything carnal. Yo feet becoming spiritually coordinated, yo body give up to an unlearned holy dance and sounds would gush right outta yo mouth. Seven of the eleven Howard children rolled on the floor, ran like their feet were on fire, shook uncontrollably, some even spoke in unknown tongues; got the Holy Ghost right there on the spot.

Not JE. When he confessed the Holy Ghost, he didn't do nuthin. Said it didn't take all that. Stood almost proudly, without so much as a flinch. Daddy Howard walked up on him, right pass the preacher, something he aint never did. Looked him in the face and gave a firm rebuke. "The devil is a liar!" and JE cried. When they got home from church he pleaded.

"Momma, you know I wouldn't tell a story about a thing like that. I did feel something momma. Something different. Something I aint never felt before. I don't know what it was, but it was something. Something happened to me Momma. It did! I swear to God it did!"

"I know baby. I know what you felt. Same thing happened to me when I was yo age. You felt *A Touch* from the Lord." She lifted her hand, touched his nose softly with her finger.

"A *Touch*?" he asked timidly.

She did it again and asked him. "Do you know what that mean JE?"

"Nawl momma. What that mean?"

"That mean, the Lord see you, that mean the Lord know you, and that mean the Lord got His hands all over yo life. Momma's praying for you baby and she aint gon let you go. Now how bout that!"

JE eyes got as big as his smile. Mother Howard shouted, "Hallelujah thank you Jesus!" Held his face in her hands, peered into his eyes and spoke to his soul. "Baby them prayers gon catch up with you one day. Keep seeking the Lord and when it's time, He gon fill you with the Holy Ghost. If you think a *Touch* was something, just wait! Son it's mightier than anything you ever felt. It's gon lead guide and protect you. The devil uses good people to do bad things. He's gon work what's good in you and give you the power to do what's right, watch what I say! And when you need HIM, you can call HIM, stir HIM up, He'll be right there inside you. And the devil in hell can't tell you nuthin different. Don't you never ever forget that. You hear me son!"

JE looked in his momma's eyes captured by every word she spoke. "Yes, Ma'am Momma. Thank you please." He said in his childlike way in his desire to be sure to use good manners.

# CHAPTER THREE

♣

## *Letting Go*

*"Mother Howard these children don't know nuthin but church on Sunday, now what we gon do bout that? Ooh Wee! Lord knows they sho gon miss Sundays Momma!"*

JE swore fore God he wasn't gon let his daddy provoke him to anger again and his momma wasn't gon have to cry out to the Lord the way she did that night. Memories rushed in; taking him back. It was time to leave fore he wore out his welcome. He could feel it, just like soldiers them old blues wanted to march up from inside, but he humbled himself.

Honey slept, JE stayed up and Addiemae was right. It took everything in him not to kill Luke when he brought his beautiful sister back home damaged like a worn-out tire, he couldn't use no more. Said he was wrong as two left shoes. Said he did good not to bleed out and die but he was sho nuf gon bust hell wide open. Even though it was in him, JE didn't wanna do wrong. He got up early the next morning to catch his daddy at the breakfast table. Put on civilian clothes, grabbed the newspaper from the nightstand and went downstairs in a good spirit. Sat at the table shaking inside hoping to get the words out that tried to back up in his head. Snapped through the pages, put enough bass in his voice to be heard. Spoke matter-of-factly as if they'd already been in a conversation. His daddy watched tones of voice; he was careful to mind his tone and braced himself respectfully.

"Daddy, this here newspaper from Chicago." He stopped talking, raised the newspaper, offered it to Daddy Howard and waited for his reach. Once he reached, he started back talking again.

"It says there's opportunity, good schools for black children, and industrial jobs. I can't buy property yet but they building three new buildings sixteen stories high, with affordable rent in a black community. I got an Army buddy up there he's the superintendent of the workmen. Said he got a job waiting for me if I want it. Me and

Honey gon take advantage. Y'all done helped more than can be expected, God knows we thankful. But you raised men that take care their families so it's time we be bout our way. A man will never be a man in another man's house."

Addiemae was listening from the kitchen holding her breath, helping him ease out every word. JE made him know despite everything he still had respect, believed in the Lord and the power of prayer. He took a deep breath figuring it wasn't nowhere for his daddy to take what he said but inside and wrestle with it. But he didn't. He had long since been delivered, he was a changed man and wasn't gon push it or pull it. His silence eased JE. Gave him permission to speak as a man in his daddy's house. JE stood up, stepped away from the table and told his momma.

"We gon miss you ole lady! We gon get on that Green Diamond and be on our way." Fore he knew it he scooped her up in his arms like his daddy's. Arms that hung heavy like two sledgehammers on the sides of his body but gentle enough to hug his momma while she giggled like a teenaged girl. They didn't notice his civilian clothes till he stood up and was Godly proud of what they saw.

JE's black slacks hung perfect. Wasn't no pulling in his belt, it sat right above the pleated waistline the way well-made pants supposed to fit a healthy body. The legs rested on the front of his black spit-shined Stacy Adams with exacting length, the cuff rested at the heel seconds from the floor and a white shirt tightly tucked complemented his five feet eight medium build. He was military alright. Wasn't a seam or stitch outta place. JE's black wavy hair was cut short, tapered along his broad forehead to his temple's; every strand was intact. The spitting image of his father. He inherited the Howard's dark smooth skin, long brow, brown almond eyes, thick lashes, strong jawbone, keen nose and full lips that yielded only to a sly grin. JE was fine!

"Gone hug them babies, me and Honey moving to Chicago next week! You betta go ahead on now momma. Addiemae! Come on out here."

He knew she was in the kitchen praying. She didn't like confrontation especially since the stroke, she came out the kitchen with a wet dish rag in one hand smelling of strong bleach same way she did when Luke acted a fool or a stranger was at the door; it was a weapon. Addiemae said everything was a weapon you just had to know how to use it. She wiped her free hand down her apron acting surprised, with a silly grin on her face.

"Did I hear my brother say they moving to Chicago and taking my nieces and nephew from me? Is that what I heard him say? He just got home didn't he momma!" She asked as if she didn't encourage him to leave.

"Sho did! Why so soon son? We barely got a chance to look at you good." She grabbed his hand. "Come on, sit back down with yo daddy and have some breakfast. You hungry aint you?"

Mother Howard eased over to Addiemae looking at her with *have you lost your mind eyes* and discreetly pried the rag loose from her tight grip. She went in the kitchen, came back and placed a platter of fried eggs, hominy grits, salmon croquettes, toast, and a jar of her blueberry preserves in front of JE. She offered him coffee with a stroke of his ego.

"Coffee JE? I know you been drinking coffee in the Army out there fighting them wars and carrying on. How you take it son, black or with cream?"

"Cream momma." He replied before bowing his head to bless his food and the hands that made it. Pleased with his manners she stared but Daddy Howard didn't bother to lift his eyes. He quietly sipped his coffee and flipped through the newspaper.

JE broke the silence. "And what y'all talking bout so soon? My family been here taking up space, eating daddy's food, worrying y'all. Look at them big ole girls." He pulled one into each arm. "They eight and nine years old. They can't swing on my arms like they used to do. Fore we know it they gon be teenagers. We got these stairsteps, one right after the other. We gon bring em back down south summer when school out so y'all can see em grow. We leaving but this is home, this is where we heal."

Honey made her way downstairs with a baby coming due in her stomach and Angie straddling her right hip; legs dangling in white Buster Brown walking shoes. Big brown eyes sitting between two thick long ginger wavy braids, roaming the room. The granddaughter of a black Mississippi Choctaw she took on the height and features of her tall mulatto granddaddy. Born with light brown eyes and blonde hair; they named her Honey. The short hair worn close to her face accentuated her high cheekbones, earrings and the ancestral jewelry that adorned her long neck. JE said her breast were good for feeding babies and her hips made carrying em easy. Seem like she been pregnant most her life, almost every year since high school. Honey sat down and sighed.

"Lord have mercy, my husband done came home with big dreams! That's what traveling in the military done to him. Y'all forgive him bragging but that's what I love about him. JE not afraid of nuthin and nobody and he'll make you believe he can do anything. Can't he?" she petitioned.

Mother Howard and Addiemae looked at each other saying nuthin. Thought she put too much faith in him, like idol worship. Daddy Howard raised the newspaper higher, covering his face, removing himself from the conversation as the room fell a shameful silent. No one agreed but it didn't matter, Honey smiled anyway.

Blessed to come from a family of dreamers wasn't no reason for her to believe different. The Spence family arrived Mounds in a dark blue soft top *1939 Opel Admiral*; a luxury car when most people didn't have a car. Pulled up to a big house and ran their own business when most couldn't find work. They were a grateful and optimistic people. Caroline, her momma, traveled with a band singing, sending home large wooden crates of clothes to cover being gone. A beautiful woman, she inherited grandma Josie's features. Fair skin, oblong face, long ginger wavy hair, a prominent nose, high cheek bones, sharp chin and full pouty lips. Her children loved to listen to her tell stories and hear her sing. Singing ran in the family. Josie made a jingle for them to sing outside the barbershop to bring in business.

*"Shave and a haircut six cents, who's the barber Ms. Spence."*

Daddy Howard didn't like Spence for no good reason. Said his high yellow skin, grey eyes and curly blonde hair made his way easy. Said he looked like a white man's son sitting up in a Baptist church with his Indian wife dolled up in furs, broaches, fancy hats, and gloves. High-minded he called em. Thought maybe that's why the white man he worked for gave him a car, a big house and a barbershop. Said he had everything handed to him, didn't have to work for nuthin. Thought maybe he was his son. Son or not, he went back to being black when he gambled his money away, lost everything but what he had in Mounds. Left Charleston Missouri with his wife and three grandchildren in tow. Said he had a nerve to act big shotty coming from the top of the Mississippi Delta. Said Mrs. Spence saw JE in his uniform and sent Honey chasing after him, figuring he was a better catch than what she already had. Daddy Howard told him not to marry Honey. Said they were unequally yoked, wasn't gon never twain become that one flesh the bible talked about. Honey knew he didn't walk in agreement with her but it didn't stop her from talking.

"I know one thing, we gon miss y'all. Mother Howard these children don't know nuthin but church on Sunday, now what we gon do bout that? Ooh Wee, Lord knows they sho gon miss Sundays Momma."

※

There was much to remember putting everything they could muster into the children and Honey. She thought about how she taught em *The Lord's Prayer*, how to help on the farm, preserve jam, and food for the winter. Taught em not to be afraid of the rooster when he bristled up, the chickens that chased them and how to get eggs out the coop. Had to tell the older children to behave and not fight amongst themselves. Honey having babies so close together made em anxious. They didn't get enough time alone with her and had to be responsible too soon. Honey was pregnant when Caroline passed. The sadness made the baby come early wasn't a full year between two of em. When she tired of waiting on JE, Addiemae had to breathe a word of prayer over her before she left out the door to hang out with friends.

Then she warmed thinking of Sundays at church, girls in pretty dresses, pressed hair, ribbons, and a three-year-old Myles in his black suit, white shirt and tie. How he carried his bible under his arm and marched proudly down the road with his head thrown all the way back, pretending to be the preacher. When they played church, girls wanted to be ushers and church mothers. Boys, preachers and deacons but Myles, he wanted to be God. She thought about how they chased the train and how the nice conductor tossed sticks of *Juicy Fruit* and *Spearmint* gum onto the tracks to reward them for following.

Thoughts coursed through her mind as she covered them in prayer, touched and anointed the unborn child in Honey's womb. Grieved about the news, she retched over, took Angie from her arms into her own, held her close in her bosom. Angie, a momma's child, gazed at Honey like she was in love. They said she was an old soul, a serious child that didn't laugh or do much smiling, maybe cause she took sick unto death when she couldn't keep food down. Afraid they were gon lose her, Mother Howard called *Red Cross* to contact JE and told him come home quick. Honey wouldn't talk, come out her room or touch the child. Said she couldn't stand to see her baby die.

JE called home. Told Addiemae. "Buy a dress, a pretty one. Put her hair in two braids like Honey fix it, and a nice crisp ribbon on each one. Get Honey out the bed, dress her, do her hair like she like it, make sure they look good and take a picture with her sitting on Honey's lap." Told her he was on his way then asked to speak to Mother Howard.

"Momma, wrap her up in yo prayer towels like you did us when we were sick. Hold her tight in your arms till I get there. Tell daddy to pray I don't lose my mind. I got to talk to God, I need HIM to tell me what to do."

The Army flew him in the next day. He came in the door with a shaving bag in one hand and a brown grocery sack in the other. Never bothering to take his uniform off, he went straight in the kitchen, made a concoction of peaches and cream from goat's milk. Held and fed the baby all day and night every day as much as she would take till her appetite came back. A week later, she gobbled down peaches and cream; ate like she was hungry. Then he gave her soul food from the table, juice off the greens, mashed potatoes, let her suck on chicken bones to draw out the broth and she held weight. She turned into a little round butterball overnight.

JE got Honey out her bed, tied a scarf on her head, washed her face, brushed her teeth, carried her downstairs in her night gown and sat her on the sofa. Put their greedy baby back in her arms, watched tears come down, rubbed her cheek with the back of his hand and left.
When he stepped out on the porch, he looked up and thanked the Lord.

Mother Howard reminisced quietly, waiting for Daddy Howard's counsel. He took the last sip of his coffee, got up from the table, grabbed the newspaper and stood in the doorway. Peering out the wooden frame screen door at the farm he studied the ten acres passed down from two generations of sharecroppers. His mind traveling the miles of his life knowing nuthin but God, hard work and providing for family. He squared his shoulders, and right before he pushed the door open, the words came sharper than a two-edged sword.

"Take yo own children to church. God gave em to you it's yo duty.

I believe it's time y'all get on out there and see what you got." Then he said in a solemn tone of voice. "A good son does himself well to listen to his father, and follow him as he follows God.

Daddy Howard set the record straight. "I know all about Chicago, we got deep roots there; family. I lived and was stationed there before you were born. Just know our prayers go before and follow after you. Walk with Rufus and Cousin Emma they know the way, they live a blessed life. They not stacked on top each other. They own property in a good black community. Reach out to em soon as you get there, they'll help you look well to yo going."

Then he spoke directly to Honey. "Daughter, life aint big dreams, big talk and traveling. Don't put yo faith in nuthin and nobody but Jesus. Life is simple. Serve God and take care yo family. It aint gon always be easy. It aint gon always be what you think it should. It's gon be some heartache and disappointment just know God will see you through."

He never called Honey daughter till that day. What he said told her something deeper, he was preparing her for the journey. She hugged him long; knowing she shoulda drawn closer sooner. Daddy Howard stepped out on the front porch sat down in his sitting chair with the *Chicago Defender* in his hands. He snapped and looked through the pages as if he could read.

# CHAPTER FOUR

♣

## *Chicago*

*"All Around My Goose Is It, Red Light Green Light and Red Rover, Red Rover Send Donna and Debbie Right Over"*

Southern families arrived bringing values with them. Maybe it came from the South, maybe the Motherland, but whatever it was it was there. A closeness, a sense of belonging. A way of being that permeated the projects, transforming them into African villages where children was raised by communities. Where a warmth lulled them to sleep for generations. Where they thrived amongst the poverty. Where children didn't know they were poor because everybody was poor. Their world was as far as feet and the CTA bus could take them. ABLA, the sum total of Jane Addams, Robert Brooks, Loomis Courts and Grace Abbott Homes. A group of projects that housed more than 17,000 residents within a surrounding community of Italians, Jews, Greeks, Hispanics and Asians that barely touched except when money left their hands. The main event was the tradition of black children going back down south for the summer to stay connected to family.

Time kept the tempo, holidays and events brought in the rhythm. The beat was in the pulse of everything that happened, every nuance that made a difference when time and chance happened to them all. School started in September and ended in June. Time was measured punctuated by seasons, the beginning and ending of the school year was the constant reminder that time was passing. It was how life transitioned. Every day and time had its own unique flavor. Daily routines were similar if not the same in every household.

Mornings began with bowls of warm *Malt O Meal* in the winter, boxes of Corn Flakes in the summer. Working men hurried off with lunchboxes of last night's dinner in hand and a metal coffee thermos. Black and white televisions were turned to Channel 9 for children to watch *Garfield Goose* on their way out the door to school. Babysitters stood wait in doorways for toddlers not old enough for Head Start. Gorgeous stay at home mothers with shapely bodies that fashioned dusters, hair styled like Diana Ross and the Supremes, with made up faces like they were going somewhere, smelling like Avon's *Unforgettable*; ready to receive and care for babies like aunties. They laid them asleep on living room sofas when they cooked and cleaned. They bounced them on laps while they watched "*As the World Turns*" with soap opera music cascading in the background. Modestly dressed church women walked the building like warriors ready to do battle witnessing in breezeways and knocking on doors offering prayer knowing the devil was always busy trying to see what he could kill steal and destroy.

Afternoon smells of fresh picked collard greens bubbling in salt pork. Well-seasoned meats graced the air throughout the building. Smothered pork chops basting in mushroom sauce. Chicken rolled in flour and corn starch fried crisp, sitting straight up in huge black cast iron skillets full of hot sizzling lard in time for dinner.

Open campus gave children a chance to come home to eat lunch. A bowl of *Campbells* S*oup* with oyster crackers. *Hostess* donuts pies and cakes were a treat with a tall glass of *Borden's' Dutch Chocolate* milk. They rushed home from school and fights and threats to have eyes blackened at 3:15. Visited friends and sat up in front of televisions watching *Dark Shadows* with Barnabas Collins. Dipped vanilla cookies in thick white cow's milk. Spread peanut butter and jelly on sliced white *Wonder* bread.

Evenings ended with *WVON* Motown sounds on the radio. Hidden parent request slips, homework, dinner, ironed clothes, baths, pink rollers in thick black hair, *Vaseline* on arms and legs. Red containers of *Crown Royal* hair grease with sharp silver lids that cut fingers. Baby doll pajamas, gossip, talk about boys. Language with honey baby, honey baby chile, rolling necks, hands on hips, popping hips, backbones slipping, popping fingers and watching the Friday night Late Movie to the tune of Dave Brubeck's, "*Take Five*" in an off-kilter 5/4 rhythm as the searchlight rode high across the sky on the Near Westside of Chicago. West of the river, across the street from Saint Ignatius where Robert Brooks Extensions were built, and Layla was born.

In the Congo, Prime Minister Patrice Lumumba was assassinated. In the same month on the same day Harriette Tubman died; Layla Patrice arrived. There she would experience black pride, black power, love community and embrace seasons. Have good feelings about mittens, hats, scarfs, and boots. Make snowballs and ice skate at Fosco Park. In the Fall she savored the smell of leaves burning in the trash cans near the rowhouses and learned to camp at Marcy Newberry.

In the summer when school was out, she walked with her sisters to 12$^{th}$ street beach hugging a beach ball, wearing red beach shoes that snapped and popped against the back of her heels, flowered petal pushers, ruffled cropped tops and greased hair, brushed, and parted unevenly into three thick nappy braids. Stayed with white families on farms. Threw water balloons off balconies, popped firecrackers. Played games in B15 and the fire lane. *All Around My Goose Is It*, *Red Light Green Light and Red Rover, Red Rover Send Debbie and Donna Right Over*. Bought *Black Cows, Chick-O-Sticks, Pepsi Cola*, and took a letter to the corner store to get a pack of *Pall Mall* cigarettes for her momma. Shopped at *Zayre, A&P*, ate *Jew Town Polishes*, Italian beefs and Italian ice. Piled in station wagons, and went to drive-in movies. Was placed on tabletops to do the Twist. Hid behind the sofa at black light parties. Bopped. Did the *Jerk*, the *Twine*, the *Funky Four Corners* and screamed, "Yay!" when the sun went down, and the lights came up at the same time on all sixteen floors of all three buildings while her sisters hung out the side window talking to boys.

Eyes watched, ears listened, and hearts felt. Behind closed doors every unit had a situation and a circumstance. The first to know was the maintenance men. JE, Layla's daddy was the maintenance man.

♣

Maintenance men like good beauticians and skilled barbers had a way about them that was endearing. They knew how to work their craft well. A part of the perceived ease, they maintained the village, had the trust of community and management. They were everybody's friend, brother, cousin, and confidant. They were respected, often desired by women and loved in more ways than one. Women teased greeting them with pretty smiling faces, ample switching behinds, full breast, shapely legs and reminders. "JE sweetie, don't forget to drop by and get you a hot plate of my fried catfish, spicy spaghetti and juicy greens."

Recipients of friendly hugs, sneaky kisses, lude inferences and long lunch breaks, reciprocated with favors and promises they ought not keep. Their wives and children were known throughout the buildings. They enjoyed a level of rent-free comfort in the largest unit directly over maintenance rooms for convenience. But JE's persona preceded him contending with his faith. He took pride in his appearance, his authority, being needed and went above and beyond his call of duty. Raised in his daddy's house with a praying mother, he was grafted into Christian principles. Polarized, he melded a deceptive intelligence, a sinful righteousness that blurred the lines of right and wrong and people got hurt. The pressure was great and the trust was gone. JE's weakness put Honey at risk. A desperate half-dressed resident knocked at the door looking for him in the middle of the night. Claiming, she needed to see him. Claiming, something needed fixing. She stood there with one hand deep in her pocket, a longing in her breath and tears of despair welled up in her eyes.

JE's obsession with running horses at the racetrack coulda cost his life twice and landed him in jail for murder. He bet the big-time with pimps, politicians and gangsters. Had a gun put to his head when he played a hundred-dollar trifecta box with four horses and couldn't put his money where his mouth was. Got angry when he won big was robbed at gunpoint, knocked out and left to die. That's when he started driving his *1965 White Cadillac DeVille* with red interior; strapped. Kept his *45 long Colt* with custom fit white pearl grips tucked underneath the front driver seat and had Porter riding shotgun.

He ran across the guy that robbed him, stalked him till he got near an alley. Swerved, pulled up fast so he couldn't run. Jumped out the car and pistol whipped him bloody. The devil told JE to take his life. He pulled the hammer back cocking it to the rear but stopping short of pulling the trigger when the man got on his knees looked up at him blood streaming down begging, pleading for his life filling JE with conviction. He de-cocked the gun, hit him one last time and told him. "Ima let God deal with you." Got back in the car and burnt rubber pulling off. Wasn't no church on Sunday, nobody said the Lord's prayer at night, and no one watched tones of voice.

♣

*"Good ole days? Man, what you talking about! We were in a war trying to stay alive. Praying to get home. We still in a war."*

Franklin knew JE needed to reminisce to get his mind off everything going down. He sat, ate hog head cheese with crackers and halfway listened to what he called a black man lecture he was tired of hearing. Franklin pulled the dog tags out his shirt and jingled them to get his attention.

"Don't forget these. They not nuthin more than modern day chains; brother they owned us! Wanted us to die for a country that didn't wanna call a black man a soldier. You gotta kill that slave mind JE. That's why I sent that newspaper to you and Porter so we can get out the ditch together. Save money, find better jobs, pool resources, get our own so we can do for self. Mattie not gon have to clean another woman's house." He said angrily.

Stuck in his own selfish thoughts, all JE heard was clean another woman's house. "What you say man? Mattie cleaning houses?"

Ready to defend what he hated to admit, he replied firmly. Yeah! That's what I said."

Franklin paced the floor with his hands in his pockets. Not wanting to say it no more than JE wanted to hear it. His patience for everything was gone. He didn't like JE's attitude, how he and Porter rode around like gangsters, gambled and carried on with the women in the building. It had to be handled, he led up to it talking about his and Mattie's plans.

"We figure in another year or so with both of us working we can get outta here. Mattie gon come home and take care her own house. I start work at the steel mill next month. I told you and Porter to put that application in, it was a sure thang they only hired veterans but you didn't follow through. What you and Honey gon do? Y'all got plans?"

JE smarted, knowing he didn't have a plan. He fired off. "Oh yeah, we got plans alright. But look here man, I understand you down for the cause and all the black stuff but don't be talking about what you told me to do. You can ask, but you don't tell me to do nuthin. I'm a grown man. Understand me!" he said smugly thinking that was gon be it. JE swung both his feet on top of the metal office desk and crossed them. Let the toothpick hang from his bottom lip, sucked the hog head cheese from between his teeth, washed it down with a strong sip of his *Pepsi*. Blowing off steam, he misspoke and kept talking. "Look here man, my momma aint never worked outside the house. Ima work this job and I don't need nobody riding my back not even you."

Franklin walked over to the desk knocked JE's boots off with his hand. JE stood up and they faced off. Neither one of em backing down, both of em frustrated for their own reasons. Ready to get it on.

"Stand down Joe!" Franklin commanded. "For what it's worth last time I checked I was the C.O. here. Don't talk that jive to me. If I didn't have yo back, you would've lost this job a long time ago. Do you understand! You aint got no business messing around with the sisters in this building, brother. I thought you had sense enough not to squat where you eat. You'll work this job as long as they let you work this job. And yo mother never worked outside the house cause yo father built her a house with his own hands and its sitting on ten acres!" JE didn't flinch. Franklin stepped off of him and came back, raised his hand, put ten swollen fingers in JE's face and told him.

"Count em up! Ten!" Then he slammed both his hands down hard on the desk and leaned in. "Thumb yo nose at that if you want. He owns land and produce food. What we got JE? What we got to show for fighting another man's war. Nuthin! Not a dog gone thing but mind sickness! Now you do what you wanna do with it. But those right there, those facts for yo head brother. I'm talking bout doing for self."

JE stayed on his feet. "What you getting at Franklin? You wanna fire me?"

"Fire you from what? This? The plantation? You worried about Massa firing you from the plantation? You see a piece of straw stuck in my cap JE? I aint nobody's straw boss. Brother you can slave and run game as long as you want."

"Hey man don't you look down on me, you aint got no children. I got the whole world on my shoulders. Honey's job is at home."

"I see. You still mess with heads, yeah, you into playing them head games with the women like you did overseas. You think Honey came up here to stay in the projects JE? What you do? Bring her up here to lose her? Is that it? Well, let me tell you, rent free not free my brother when it cost you something that's gon blow yo mind!" He placed his fingertips to his lips and blew JE a kiss; provoking him.

"What you mean lose Honey? Why you worried about my business?"

"Worried about yo business? Brother are you blind? You think Honey don't see what you doing? She on the phone crying to Mattie every night you gone. That's what makes it my business, she got my woman upset! What's wrong with you man? Got a half-naked woman showing up at your door in the middle of the night crying with a gun in her hand. Got struggling sisters singing yo praises cause you give em something out the garbage! I don't even recognize you. Awh man, you got this all-wrong brother. I tell you what black man. Ima get off yo back like you said. You don't want yo woman, be man enough to let her go." Franklin sweetened his voice and started talking slick. "Ima tell you now that half breed Mare won't be out there long. I know a few good brothers with money that would have no problem raising yo family and putting Honey up real pretty, just waiting to step up to the plate. So, when you swing, make sure you don't miss." He winked his eye. "Just so you know, they watching, wondering why you sleeping on the job my man. And since you want everything free, this piece of advice don't cost you nuthin. It's on the house."

JE stared at Franklin with a glazed look in his eyes, the thought of losing Honey never crossed his mind; he couldn't handle it. Talk about Honey and another man taking care his family made him grit his jawbone. He kept nodding his head real slow. Franklin felt threatened got loud and aggressive.

"What! What difference do it make? You don't want her! You mad now? You gritting yo jawbone staring at me like you wanna do something. You want this JE? Oh, you think I'm right in the head? Like something in me don't want to kill somebody. Man, we trained to kill. We gon die today JE? You know aint nobody walking outta here alive if we do this thang. We taking it all the way to the wall like old times. Cause that's what we been programmed to do. Kill! We killing machines, only difference is now we killing each other."

Franklin got in JE's face, started hitting himself in the head hard. JE heard the metal plate and stood down. He forgot his friend was wounded in the war and backed off.

"Man, you aint got to do all that. Beating yourself in the head not right. Aint nobody dying today either. Why you talking like that man?"

"I got to! My brother sleep and I'm trying to wake him up. Shake yourself man! You think I don't feel it. You think you the only one struggling to keep it together! Brother sometimes I can't even breathe. I feel like a ticking time bomb about to explode. Like one more thing gon break my back and Ima snap! At night I sweat. My woman constantly changing sheets like I'm a baby wetting the bed. Holding me when I'm shaking like a drug addict and I never smoked so much as a cigarette a day in my life nor put whisky to my lips. Man, I don't even eat swine and I'm shaking? Now you tell me why that is! You still think they aint did nuthin to us?

One night Mattie got up walked around my side of the bed to go to the bathroom. I thought I heard something moving in the bushes. Jumped up on both feet, got in standing position, got my aim right and drew down like I had my M-1. My body was so pumped I could feel a kill. I squeezed that trigger to blow her brains out! Yelled pow so loud when I came to myself Mattie was standing there shaking. Man, my wife was peeing on herself. I scared her half to death."

He leaned in, raised his eyebrows and whispered like he had a secret. "JE you betta be thinking brother, they aint got to put up with this crazy stuff we brought home man!" Then he groaned. "God knows what else I've done or said in my sleep she aint got the heart to tell me. If it were a real gun I woulda killed my wife JE. My wife! And I woulda took one to the head cause I aint here unless she here. That's why I don't keep no guns at home, I'm liable to kill." Then his voice changed from a groan to a sharp tight-jawed threat when he said. "You understand me, on that! So don't talk to me about riding yo back having the world on yo shoulders and not having children when you out here slumming. That woman in my bed done lost babies helping me come through. So, watch yo mouth before you make me shut it permanently. I love you but my head aint right. I just assume take you out yo misery." He eased, smiled and calmly said. "My brother."

Franklin sat down, took a deep breath and laughed really loud while he spoke. "What makes me angry JE. What really gets me is brothers like you!"

"Brothers like me huh?" JE replied knowing he was wrong. It scared him when he heard the metal plate and how hard Franklin was hitting himself in the head. He was ashamed.

"Yeah man I got a plate in my head but you the one with a short memory. I'm talking bout brothers like you that forget who pulled em out ditches and carried em on their backs. I risked my life getting you home to the woman you said you loved. Any one of us coulda been left to die but we pulled together knowing it was the only way out. We left no man behind. I thought that's what this was JE. I see it's not. Now you can fall in or you can fall under soldier! But know this. You and me, this here our last rally point. Think on that! And get yourself together brother it's enough pain out here to go around. We don't need to be spreading it amongst our own people."

♣

Like most veterans JE and Franklin had covenant, the bond didn't break it got stronger. Septembers and Junes came and went like graduations, summers, and Christmases. Years later. Six years. the summer of '67 all hands were on deck loading the moving truck while Mattie sat in the passenger seat seven months pregnant with their third child, a son. Miciah.

Honey stood outside the window excited. They talked, promising to visit. Layla and Mina spent their time running around in circles, jumping over guard chains, playing in what was left of grass. Franklin hugged JE, said goodbye a couple of times, did the long version of the soul brother handshake twice. Got behind the steering wheel and kept talking not knowing how to pull away. He couldn't bring himself to leave. He called his daughter. "Come on Mina, come on babygirl, we gotta go now. We gon come get Layla next weekend."

Honey graciously asked. "You sure y'all wanna be bothered that soon Mattie?"

"She not no bother Honey, we family. Besides it'll help me out. They can keep each other company so I can get things situated." Mattie didn't want to pull away either. She broke down and cried. "All y'all come by as much as you can. Frank, I don't want them in this place!"

Franklin tried to break the heaviness that was overcoming them. It was a bittersweet moment. They were glad to be leaving, but it hurt leaving JE and Honey behind. "They not gon be here much longer Mattie. What's all this talk? We only going to South Shore not more than twenty minutes from here. JE know where to find me." He said, knowing twenty minutes was a world away.

JE manned up. Hit the side of the truck twice with his hand hard. Snapping Franklin outta his hesitancy. "Alright man y'all worked too hard to be doing this." He firmed up, raised his voice like a command. "Pull off! Soldier! That's an order!" As soon as the word *order* fell from JE's lips, Franklin automatically turned his head like a robot and pulled off. JE waved at the back of the truck, and mouthed "my brother." He took his family back in the building. Grieved.

♣

*"It's over. I don't need it JE."*

Seemed every weekend moving trucks came and went. Porter moved back to Arkansas. Said he had enough of the big city and took his main squeeze with him. JE was promoted to superintendent but wasn't no glory in it, by then Black consciousness rose and people demanded more for themselves. While JE and Honey argued, things came down around them and backs were against the wall.

Families got desperate to get out, and new ones arrived from other projects, bringing with them rivalry, crime, gangs, and drugs. Pregnant teenagers gave birth to the next generation of project dwellers and public aid recipients. Maybe it was the condition of the people, maybe it was the master plan but whatever it was it took life before it came out the womb.

The village transformed into jail cells. Where balconies became cages, and children were held hostage in a blighted community where grass refused to grow. Where snotty noses ran wild holding too big pants tightly with hands full of trying. Where raggedy shoes flipped and flopped and ran to possess kingdoms of torn pissey mattresses. Where there were desolate playgrounds with no swings, basketball courts with no hoops. Where nobody thrived and children knew they were poor. Cousins lived in one building on the 3rd floor. Aunts and uncles on the $8^{th}$ floor of another building and war was waged one against the other.

Welfare came with stricter rules that separated husbands from wives, pushing for single parent households, labeling capable women that helped raise good children, welfare mothers; shaming them. Fathers were frustrated with income limits, income monitoring and losing eligibility when another dime came in the house. They left and snuck in like thieves in the night to see their families till they could get them out.

Racetrack gambling kept JE broke, he claimed his hands were tied. Arguments grew shorter and colder, no matter the issue he told Honey.

"You and the children have a roof over yo heads, clothes on yo backs and food on the table. Get off my case!"

The next time Honey suffered the indignity she spoke her heart.

"It's over, I don't need it JE. You think you can justify a woman coming to my home in the middle of the night half-dressed, crying ready to shoot somebody with these children in here! Wasn't fore Mother Boyd praying next door she probably woulda blew both our brains out. Telling me you don't want me to work while you gambling away the only money we have and raising yo voice to me like you talking to a broad in the street. I made my peace JE. Don't stand in the way of me taking care the children. Gone on with yo life. I'm not in yo way. I'm not gon fight you. I'm not gon argue and I'm not gon lose my mind."

※

People were losing minds. Children gathered, watched, and laughed while Ms. Madison walked up and down the fire lane in the summer in a fur coat, long ball gown, and high heeled shoes swinging her handbag. Looking side to side saying thank you and waving like Ms America on the catwalk. Wig on backward, eyebrows drawn in an arch that went up to her forehead, and red lipstick smeared pass her lip line up to her nose. Windows filled with faces sixteen stories high, fingers pointing blame, and mouths yelling mean things. Thank God someone was kind enough to call for help.

A man, a dignified black man, a resident of the building came down in a suit of clothes to talk to the white policemen when they pulled up in the paddy wagon. He convinced them to watch, said she didn't mean no harm that she was sick in the head. One police pulled out his Billy Club and started tapping it in his hand with a dead look in his eyes, itching to hit her, to throw her down on her stomach, cuff her, dehumanize her publicly. But the one in charge. The big burly, red headed sergeant with a mustache turned up on both ends like a smile shoved him hard. Stood boldly in his face and commanded him to stand down.

When Ms. Madison walked back in their direction the sergeant stepped forward, smiled, took his hat off his head, bowed, and reached for her hand like a gentleman to help her aboard. She batted her eyes like she was being courted, curtsied, graciously walked inside, and took a seat on the metal bench along the wall like royalty. The door came down like a moving truck loaded with furniture as she turned her head and started motioning like she was talking to somebody.

Honey said she used to be a model, that the fur was genuine mink. The handbag, snakeskin and the wig handmade. The misdiagnosis was given in the emergency room, the ball kept rolling downhill and the children adapted. They knew the molester and the Raper man, they were friends of the family, lived in the same building. They knew not to be alone with them, not to sit in their laps, not to take gifts and not to get in their cars; they became street smart.

They knew the prostitute who treated them kindly and gave them money to buy penny candy. She was someone's beautiful cousin that came up from down south, full of beautiful dreams. She had a beautiful body and kept them in awe weaving beautiful stories of a beautiful life she wasn't gon never live. And they cried when she died from being beat to death and because of her lifestyle no one looked for her. On his way to turn on the incinerator where rats ran out when the heat fired up, JE tripped over the mangled body and got sick with flashbacks.

Layla was six. No one prayed. Honey filed for divorce. JE went down south to heal and school started in September.

# CHAPTER FIVE

♣

### *Leaves on the Family Tree*

*"Now kick it in cruise and she'll take us all the way. Don't pump the brake you got to let her ride. Let the windows down, turn my music up. There you go Honey. Keep it just like that."*

It was like love; her first time behind the wheel of the Cadillac. It hugged the road and all he had to do was lay back and ride. Driving with JE beside her felt safe but then again it always did. She trusted him that's why it hurt so bad when she couldn't. When there was love he took her on long rides before they went to bed to help her sleep. There he was again taking the lead, the way she liked. Guiding her through like ole times, she fought the urge to believe in him. He came back to himself, and they felt good together. JE leaned over the armrest to observe her while she drove with the sly grin on his face that won her heart. He knew she was tired. He gently touched her cheek with the back of his hand and they warmed; the attraction was still there. Wasn't no denying it. It had been a long time since they were alone together. He teased her. "Look at me, I'm riding with an independent woman."

Honey was uneasy about the comment, it was a point of contention. She warned him, "Gone now, JE don't do that it makes me nervous." She triggered him.

"Good!" He asserted. "You need to be nervous. Going up there with all that mouth and tough talk about what you not gon do. That kinda talk turn a man right off." He relaxed back in the passenger seat leaving her to her thoughts. Miles and miles of road was behind them. The Blues testifying in the background, made them think and feel. Ten miles and ten minutes later Honey got up the nerve to ask.

"Is that what I did JE? Turn you off? Asking for what I needed turned you off?" Hurt by his cheating, she wanted to know.

JE sounded more serious than ever. "Honey, you have the right to ask for what you need and some of what you want. You're my wife, the mother of my children. But you don't demand nuthin from me. Don't nobody have that right. I do for you cause I choose to, no other reason" He asserted his man voice. "Honey, don't fool around here and hurt yourself trying to raise a grown man; be careful with that."

His words cut deep and she went silent. He never said that before, not that way. Never used those words, tone of voice, issuing a firm rebuke that she may have earned. Honey wondered if that's what she did. Tried to raise him. Wondered if that's where it went wrong. JE reached under the dashboard close by her knee and she jumped. He popped out the 8-track tape and put in another one. They drove an hour with Motown love songs serenading them in the background. She resisted the words to the songs that spoke, begged, pulled and drew them closer. Not willing to break down, she disturbed the groove.

"What you doing JE? Trying to put me to sleep. If you gon play something, put on something that's gon keep me alert."

He threw his hand up. "Never mind that! Get ready to pull over."

"Why?"

He asserted again, spoke to her like he used to do. "Don't ask me no questions woman." She liked it when he called her woman. "Pull over at that diner coming up on the next two exits. I'm hungry. Aint you hungry?"

She knew JE was working on her. "Yeah, I'm hungry but I don't want no trouble. Don't be messing with my head. I made my peace now Jay. You free to stay on out there in them streets. We done moved on. I'm sorry about what happened to you but coming home aint changed nuthin far as you and I go." She said, convincing herself not realizing she called him Jay. That's what she called him when things were good. And he heard it.

"That's yo problem girl. You talk too much." He hadn't called her girl in years. He went silent and thought about how he hurt her. Recalled the moment he got frustrated with himself and turned his back on her. Thought he couldn't please her, that Franklin was right, another man woulda been glad to change places with him. Honey was harder to please than other women. It didn't take much for them. They didn't want nuthin and if they did, they knew better than to ask. JE made it a point to tell em; side women didn't have no rights, only pleasure. Told em it was fine if they could handle it but to leave it alone if they couldn't. Told em he was a married man, it wasn't gon be no divorcing; that he didn't believe in it.

Honey wanted the world, demanded and went after what she wanted. Felt entitled and refused to live beneath her privilege. That's what attracted him to her; she was a dreamer. That's what made it hard to leave the Army and come home. He served three four-year terms afraid of not being able to provide and have stories to tell to hold her interest. Now he was nuthin more than a maintenance man, in his mind she was outta reach. Watching her leave the children with a babysitter to go to work and school made him angrier. She was making good money at the post office, it embarrassed him, challenged his manhood. but coming home he came to himself, and he didn't make it easy.

When they sat down at the diner, he winked at the flirting waitress and she came over to the table. He told her to bring a little of everything; something he always did. The food was good, and he fed Honey well. On the way out he called the waitress over, stood in her face and said, "Thank you baby." And tucked a twenty-dollar tip deep in the cleavage of her low-cut shirt real slow. She smiled at him and he walked out. But Honey stayed. She hung back long enough to give her an evil eye. The waitress dared and matched her stare. Layla backed out the diner never taking her eyes off the waitress letting her know she meant business. She stared her all the way down till she got in the car. Then waved bye to her with a smile.

JE had taken the wheel, adjusted the seat, the rear-view mirror and told her to relax. He pulled off fast, putting his foot in the tank picking up the speed bragging, "Feel that? The Cadillac is a road car; you don't play with em you drive em." He said letting her know he was the better driver, then he redeemed himself for making the purchase. "That's why I bought her, to bring the family down south for the summer. By the way, since you so independent, co-pilots don't get to sleep."

JE knew she would fall asleep. She didn't know how to kick back and enjoy the drive; it wasn't her pleasure; she was a rider. He saw the tension in her shoulders, how she sat up stiff as a board close up on the steering wheel. Soon as he put her in the passenger seat, she eased. She was tired and hadn't noticed the bird's chirping, how the big city dropped from beneath them taking worries with it. Enough breeze came from the driver's side, she rolled her window up and looked out from behind the glass. The colors in her hair scarf contrasted against the green leaves. Honey put on her shades closed her eyes and dozed off as JE cruised.

Three hours later, her earrings dangling against her face jolted her and she woke up to see the road passing. Just when she missed his attempts to engage, he reached out with welcomed words. "You were sleeping pretty good. You alright over there co-pilot?" He teased knowing it was his intention to put her to sleep. They drove for almost two hours listening to jazz skipping around in the background, Myles Davis' *Kinda Blue* came on when they were just about there. Honey rolled her window down, and a hot breeze swept across their faces. When the sound of the trumpet, piano, bass and drums queued up, they caught glimpses of down south summers. JE reclined his seat, stretched his arm out and steered with a light touch of two fingers.

Honey thought about sun dresses with spaghetti straps, bare feet, open fields and lazy days when he came home on leave. Full of stories to tell like Caroline, he created an atmosphere to let her mind travel. He planned how he would take her away from where she was to where she wanted to be. Stopped along the way to purchase items not sold in Mounds for the lunch basket he would make. Found the perfect spot away from the house behind the barn further into the acreage where they couldn't be seen as he evoked country fields in France.

He longed for her to visualize the villages, green vineyards. See the rolling hills, pastures, lakes, canals and tree lined country roads. Soak in the smells of lavender, yellow sunflower and red poppy fields. Touch and ride the parked bikes sitting alongside cafes with baskets filled with herbs, cheese and bread.

He spread a blanket out before her, copped a squat. Cut slivers of earthy aged Comte cheese, placed them on thick olive oil crackers and fed her. The freshly picked blackberries and a container of mushrooms from the fridge complemented the cheese, crackers and wine. He filled their two glasses with *Cabernet Sauvignon*, kept her laughing at his silly jokes and read her poems from Gwendolyn Brooks' "*A Street in Bronzeville*." Honey remembered how she felt pretty, strong and liberated with his hat on her head smoking his *Marlboro* cigarettes fantasizing about Bronzeville like a faraway place.

The blue sky and the warmth of the sun greeted them. The little taste of Tennessee Whiskey he took at the diner before he got back in the car made him mellow. He bobbed his head to the music spontaneously opened up and extrapolated about the sky.

"It's something about this sky. We know it's everywhere but down here it's quite different, its bluer in the morning and dark enough to count the stars at night. It's different from Chicago's sky hindered by skyscrapers, you never got to see how blue the sky could be. Different from the sky overseas that was much too foreign. But no matter how far away we were from each other, when I got under my blanket at night, we were sleeping under the same sky."

Honey peered helplessly across at JE knowing she was captured, and it would only be a matter of time before she forgave him, again. The car cruised down the road to the sound of the instruments introducing themselves, heightening, blending rising to a crescendo, into a moment of euphoria where everything familiar welcomed them. JE was glad to see the mounds he climbed still standing. The corner stores buzzing with business. Farms producing and the red, green and black colors that rivaled the inside of a watermelon everywhere.

Green rind skin like grass, red sweet juicy fleshy fruit like painted farms, black seeds like rich black fertile dirt. Neighbors working, front porches with sitting chairs, noisy tractors plowing to mix and make sure the sun reach the deep soil, fresh air filled with scents of cut grass and loose dirt where car tires left tracks that led to the house. Mid-summer July 1967, JE and Honey came home to heal.

The red house popped sitting on green grass amongst a grove of white oak trees boasting a head full of leaves. It was summer the way they remembered it; awaiting their return, captured in time. The front porch was ready for sitting, listening and talking. Mother Howard had burlap sacks of pole beans ready to be snapped and froze. The trellis hung heavy with leaves and more pole beans hiding underneath. Wild blue and blackberries sat around in deep dented two-gallon metal buckets with wooden handles. Maggie stood in the shade of the stall looking out. Blue, the farm dog ran around in circles barking. They could see Daddy Howard pushing the tractor across the field followed by thick dust clouds.

Soon as the car door slammed shut Mother Howard and Addiemae ran out on the porch. She rushed to get to him. He rushed to get to her. JE tripped on the board that splintered that night he ran. He paused for a split second; flashing back. Mother Howard reached for him and pleaded. "Oh, my Lord, be careful son." She asked, "You alright JE?" They laughed and hugged long and hard. She patted him firmly on his back signaling her release.

"I'm fine momma! It's good to be home. Some things need fixing around here starting with the porch and the fence posts. I see daddy out there on his tractor."

"What else he gon do but work? He's a Howard, that's how they are." she said casually. "They don't know nuthin but God and work. You gon be the same way. But don't worry about him. He'll be in when he ready. Come on I just finished making lunch."

Mother Howard stood gazing at them. "My goodness. My arms not big enough to hold you both at the same time." She fussed.

"Momma, look at Honey! Don't she look citified." Addiemae said thinking she was paying Honey a compliment.

"Nawl chile, she still a country girl. Don't pay Addiemae no mind. But I do see something different and its sho not city. Uh, come on over here Honey." She reached her arms out, hugged her tight, kissed her cheek, stood back, looked at her again. She saw something. She held both Honey's hands.

"You just as pretty as ever. Y'all come on in. Did you stop by the house yet to see Spence, or did you come straight on here? I know y'all got to be tired driving all that way. Come on inside."

JE blurted out "Nawl momma, we came here first. We plan on resting up before we see Spence. Honey wanna look extra special when she sees him." The comment agitated her and she pushed back.

"Gone Jay! I said I want to look fresh when I see him, that's all I said. You know how he is. Soon as he sees me, he looks me up and down to make sure I'm alright. Bad enough he didn't want me to leave. I'm not giving him no reason to question nuthin. He don't understand why it took six years to make a five-hour drive. I just assume deal with that tomorrow."

"Well, aint no need in worrying. Spence gon think what Spence gon think. You can stop fretting about that, he's yo granddaddy, that's what they do. But I was disappointed when you said the children weren't coming. I guess we'll have to wait till next summer huh."

"I know, I'm sorry Mother. JE and I needed to step away for a minute."

"Well, aint nuthin wrong with that. I aint complaining, only glad to see you is all. Guess who else stepped away for a minute?'

"Who Mother?" Honey asked wondering.

"Cousin Emma and Rufus. They bout here. I thought y'all was them pulling up."

Honey relaxed. "I guess we finally gon meet."

Mother Howard was shocked. She thought they met already. "Finally, gon meet? Y'all aint met yet? JE, you aint take Honey and the children to meet Emma? I was sure y'all were getting along fine by now. Nobody said nuthin different. JE you know yo daddy told you to reach out to Emma and Rufus when you left here."

"We didn't have a chance momma with the children in school and both us working."

Mother Howard interrupted, looking at him sideways. "Haven't had a chance? In six years, JE?"

Addiemae got nervous, to break the tension she changed the conversation but Mother Howard didn't budge, she wanted an answer and she wasn't backing down. "Honey, I heard you went back to school and work at the post office. Something I always wanted to do. Get my own job so I could have my own money and have my own place. But that's water under the bridge now. Seem like my stroke took most my strength. I do good to get around this house."

"Addiemae don't go changing the conversation. I wanna know why JE didn't listen to yo daddy. He told you that for a reason. If you weren't gon listen, you shouldn't have wasted his time. Son, did you think he was talking idle?"

"Nawl momma. I just didn't follow through."

She mocked him. "Just didn't follow through. Uh, well that's yo choice and that's yo business. They coulda saved y'all a whole lot of time and trouble getting situated up there. But like I said, that's yo business. One day y'all gon realize that man has a way of seeing things fore they come up the road. If only you grown children would only listen sometime…"

Honey never heard Mother Howard fuss. She hurried to confess. "You right Mother. He gave us good counsel fore we left. I wasn't sure what he meant but since we been gone not a day go by that I don't understand. We haven't been to church but his words minister to me more than you care to know."

Shocked at what she heard her voice raised, "Jesus! Haven't been to church! Y'all haven't been to church? In six years?"

JE didn't want Mother Howard to know, he shewed Honey off. "Baby gone get you some rest. Momma don't need us bringing all that Chicago talk back down here." He said cutting the conversation.

"I done told you JE!" She snapped in an angry tone.

"Told me what! He snapped back."

"Told you I don't want no trouble!"

Mother Howard's head went side to side like she was watching a tennis match. Standing in the middle of confusion in her own home.

"Wait a minute! Y'all alright? JE? Honey? Y'all alright?"

JE tried to smooth things over, "Yeah momma we fine. Only tired that's all."

Honey confessed. "No we not Mother. We not alright that's why we came home. We in a real bad way."

"I see that baby. But you home now." She sat on the sofa to collect herself. "Everything gon be just fine. JE take the luggage on upstairs. It's been a long ride, get Honey a good bath and some fresh clothes. Get that smell good bath oil off Addiemae's dresser. Put some over in the tub and run the water deep so she can sink down in it. Y'all been driving for hours you bound to be cranky."

They went upstairs. Mother Howard and Addiemae looked at each other *with big eyes*. Addiemae kept blinking wondering if she should say something.

 "You thinking?"

Before she could get the words out her mouth, Mother Howard stopped her. "I aint thinking and you not either, we gon leave that alone. Too much thinking gets you in trouble just like too much talking and not enough praying."

JE came back. "Honey gon get her bath first." He said trying to act normal but Mother Howard couldn't hold her peace, she lit into him for a good thirty minutes.

"See what I'm saying JE. That's rean yo daddy put you in Rufus and Emma's care, but you didn't listen. Told you that wasn't no idle talk. Y'all aint been to church in all this time?"

"Nawl, I know momma. I know."

Honey came back downstairs refreshed thinking things had moved along. "JE you can get a shower and take a bath later. It's plenty of hot water." She said as if they ran out of hot water at home. Mother Howard kept fussing.

"No, you don't. If you knew so dog gone much you woulda did what he said. That's alright Honey, JE gon wait. We gon talk fore yo daddy come in his house. Y'all make me tired with all this fussing. Let me tell y'all grown children something, we not gon have no confusion in this here family. Me and yo daddy didn't make it on our own, it takes the Lord and a good pastor. One sent by God that love people, pray for em and look well to their going. You can think church is old fogey if you want to but that man out there…"

Mother Howard pointed out the door. "Raised eleven children.

Spent many a night grieved, prayed over y'all and you act like it don't matter, aint made a bit of difference in yo lives. Like prayer aint nuthin but some uttered words till trouble come then you want us to get a prayer through. Y'all living on prayer fumes cause it aint obedience and it sho not no goodness, of yo own the way you fighting. Coming in this house divided like oil and water. Arguing across me no sooner than you get in the front door. Actin like you aint got no home training, sense enough to keep yo business to yourself or have the fear of God in you.

Well, that spirit getting cast outta here, it aint welcome. I prayed over every one of you, but you won't pray for yourselves. Don't be looking at me funny I'm telling you what God love. All these many years, I aint brought no trouble in this man's house and no danger to his door. Our children go out here knowing better, do what you big, bad and grown enough to do then come back home busted up and don't know why! Ima say it cause it need to be said. I mighta stopped yo daddy and spared the rod too much. He told Addiemae to leave Luke alone and look what it got her but I thank God every day I wake up for His mercy. I rather the stroke than her life."

"You right momma." She agreed quickly.

"Addiemae don't push me past my thought's telling me I'm right. If you thought we were right you woulda listened. I'm saying something! You didn't listen either Honey. He warned you. Told you y'all were unequally yoked. But you took offense turned a cold heart to him, lived under his roof, ate the food off his table and buried yourself in babies trying to prove him wrong. Thought he was saying JE was too good for you when he was telling you his lifestyle wasn't gon suit you. He couldn't settle himself, worried about a child overseas he may never see."

"Mother Howard…"

"Honey, sweetie, baby when I said don't interrupt, that meant you too. JE look real good, can tell you stories that take yo mind away but he his daddy's son. He's protective of his family that's rean he moved you in the house with us while he was gone. Now how you spect him to be alright with you leaving the children when he aint seen his own momma leave the farm. He'll put his foot down when he's tired of talking that's why y'all fighting and can't walk in agreement; you see his foot down. Howard men are real men. You not gon run em and you aint gon control em; they'll walk away fore that happen. Deal with em right you got a good man they'll give you their best. But you gotta tend to em like a garden. Thorns and thistles and weeds done choked out his goodness. He not straight so the whole family crooked. I can see that from all the way over here. That's why I prayed for them babies fore they left here. The Lord said it wasn't good that man be alone and gave him help. Formed the beast and fowl out the ground. You aint come out no ground, you came outta him. He pulled you from his rib and called you woman. Be a woman! If you not ready to help him, be a man, acceptable in the sight of God fore he leaves this earth; you aint did him, yourself nor yo children no good. Aint nobody benefited."

"But momma..."

"JE I'm still talking. I said I aint finished. And you aint done no better. You knew how Honey was raised. She used to expensive things. She's social, used to flitting around free like a butterfly, doing busy things. That's what you liked about her. She wasn't no stay-at-home woman when you met her. She's an enterprising woman. Spence raised her that way to help him manage that barbershop. Fore she turned twelve she was driving his car, taking care business, and handling money. Honey is full of virtue a wise man could mine, but you took her up there to less than what she already had, sat on her like a toad and blamed her for how she was raised. JE, you took a wife and didn't have nowhere to put her. If you don't do nuthin else put her in a house and see don't her goodness, come forth. Son she's yo wealth. Why you think daddy said go and see what you got? Neither one of you knowed what you had.

She laughed. "Hah! but I think y'all done found that out. You can't raise grown people, that's already been done. Now you come home fighting, biting, hurting each other and aint neither one of you in yo bible standing on the word of God. See this wasn't no cakewalk. Good Looks and muscles may make babies but they don't make no marriage. What me and Mr. Earnest got we earned. It took counsel, prayer, patience, love, kindness even when we weren't worthy. Understanding, acceptance and a whole lot of forgiveness. You don't get the big years with no trouble baby. If somebody told you different, they don't love you. Sure as we walk in this sinful flesh, we gon have trouble in this body. Mistakes gon be made, you can expect that unless you Jesus and I'm living to meet HIM. Blame yourselves for the mistakes. Both of you get down on yo knees, forgive one another, come against the problem together; don't turn in on each other. Fix it! Till the hurt go away, till the anger subside and time make you wanna come together again. That's how you do that."

Mother Howard eased. "I tell you living in a big city will kill a horse, it'll try yo soul. That's why yo daddy come back down south to heal. That's why he told you to walk with Rufus and Emma. I'm done fussing cause what's done is done. We glad you came home. We gon get with the pastor, get some prayer, and get this figured out the right way. Oh, we gon get some supernatural blessings on this here marriage. But right now, we got to get lunch on the table y'all. JE gon see bout yo daddy, he got ears and eyes like a hawk. Don't let that noise from the tractor fool you, he saw you fore you made it to his road. Honey, help Addiemae fore Rufus and Emma get here. And just so you know I invited Deacon Saint Clair."

"Momma I asked you not to meddle."

"Chile, I just bout brought a Sunday sermon and you aint heard a thing I said. Walking round here talking much about nuthin. Going on and on and on bout the stroke. Giving glory to the stroke! Praising the stroke! Claiming it! Calling it yours! Hallelujah to the stroke! Addiemae, you had a stroke the stroke aint had you. It aint stopped Deacon Saint Clair from dropping by on Sundays to look in yo face and I aint either. What you pose to do Addiemae? Shrivel up and die cause you had a stroke and yo husband walked out? You a good woman, you the one sees yourself a victim. So what you got a limp. The Good Lord bless you to keep on living you might have more than that fore it's over. And how you gon get better sitting around here like you older than me and yo daddy. That aint a testimony you want baby. Aint no glory in that."

"Momma, long as Luke living, I'm still married. I aint got no business lookin at nobody."

"Hah! Still married! Chile what you talking bout? Who done put you in that prison? "

"That's what that evangelist told me."

"What evangelist?"

"The one that came to town when I went to church right after Luke and I got divorced."

"You aint told me nuthin bout it."

"Wasn't nuthin to tell momma."

"Wasn't nuthin to tell? The devil is a lie! What you mean wasn't nuthin to tell! You running round here believing a bald-faced lie. Where all this happen?"

"After the service when we were outside talking in the parking lot. She said the Lord gave her a word for me. That Luke was coming back and to wait on him."

"Jesus Addiemae Lee. I don't believe what just came out yo mouth. Long as you walked with Pastor Jones. You mean to tell me you took what that woman said in yo heart. When you got a good pastor. Did yo pastor tell you that? To wait for Luke to come back? Did he?"

"Nawl momma."

"Well Addiemae, why on God's green earth would you letta out-of-town one-night wonder whisper in yo ear. That's a disrespect to the pastor. He the one watch for yo soul, not no visitor. I bet it was; after the service. Out there giving out parking lot prophesies. God told you that?

"Nawl."

"So, she the only one with the witness. I think He'd clued you, me, Luke and the pastor in on that one. I bet you didn't tell him, did you?"

"Nawl, I didn't."

"I know you didn't cause he woulda got that straight right quick. She never woulda got back in his pulpit misleading his members."

Lunch was ready when Rufus pulled up in a brand new *1967 Green Cadillac Fleetwood Brougham.* Everyone ran out the house to greet them. Honey's eyes were fixed waiting to see Cousin Emma. Seem like time slowed as he opened the door for her to step her foot out like a movie star. She was younger and prettier than Honey envisioned.

Regal, like a taller refined Addiemae. Blessed with the Howard's dark skin, oval face and brown almond eyes. She wore a short Dionne Warwick Bob, pitched high in the back and tapered on the sides. A full bang swept her right eye. She enjoyed brushing it out the way with her long-manicured nails. Rather than approach the porch, she stopped, slid her shoes off her feet to walk barefoot in the grass with pink painted toes and oily legs. She sauntered when she walked. She looked beautiful sporting a Kelly green, pink and yellow floral linen dress that buttoned down the front with a wide belt separating her narrow waist from her round hips. Honey's nose caught the flowery smell of Wind Song perfume. Emma climbed the stairs, took in a deep breath of fresh air and shamelessly yelled.

"Thank God, we made it Dd! We'd been here sooner but Rufus had to stop at every *Waffle House* and diner on the way. For him traveling aint no more than an eating trip."

Mother Howard looked at her. "Chile aint nuthin wrong with that, let the poor man eat, he got you here didn't he. And in style may I add. That man done spoiled you rotten. I tell you Howard women something else." She laughed extended her arms while Honey looked on.

"Come on give me a hug and grab an apron, we got a lot of snapping to do fore we sit down to lunch. JE and Honey here too. I pulled enough pole beans for everybody to take back home." She reached alongside her, caught Honey by the hand and showed her to Emma.

"Come on Honey, aint no need being shy faced. This here yo Cousin Emma."

It had been a while since Honey sported fine clothing, intimidated by her appearance, she went closer and gave Emma a limp hug. "Nice to finally meet you. I been hearing yo name since I came to the family, saw pictures too."

Emma stepped back and looked at Mother Howard confused. "What I do to her? Why she giving me a fake hug?" Then she turned back to Honey. "Don't you do that to me." She smiled, "Girl you betta give me a real hug. We family. And this family get up and get down together, so you can forget about that shy stuff." Emma grabbed, hugged her tight, released and looked at her.

"Uh huh, I already know what this is. JE sho got his hands full with this one Dd. You aint nuthin but a doll baby. Chile where you from? Don't tell me Mounds either, I already know that. You got some stuff mixed up in you from somewhere else."

Honey wasn't used to a bold pretty woman with a loud voice and answered timidly. "My grandma a black Mississippi Choctaw."

Emma yelled. "Oh! I knowed it was something with them high cheek bones! But what's all that pretty wavy blonde hair about?"

"My granddaddy's daddy is a white man." She admitted like a child in trouble.

"Oh, I see they mixed you up good that's why you exotic-looking!

Don't you be shame, you be proud of how God made you, He aint made no mistakes and He ain't surprised about nuthin." Then she laughed hard. "Where JE at? I know he having a stone fit trying to keep her. That's what he gets with his fine self, a fine wife. Hah!" She laughed again. "If that don't beat all. God got a sense of humor, HE got him good! Well, here I am in the flesh, Cousin Emma and it sho feel good to be home!"

She grabbed an apron off the hook, tied it on, sat down in one of the sitting chairs, stretched her arms and legs out at the same time, wiggled her toes, took in another deep breath and yelled.

"Will you smell that dirt and that fresh cut grass! If they bottle it, I'm buying!" She went on. "My God! I can't go to Africa, but I swear fore God this got to be the next best thing." Emma was a mixture of laughs, praise, song and good counsel. Seem to Honey like she couldn't stop laughing. "Ha, Ha! Lord Jesus been good to me! Been good to y'all too! You betta gon thank HIM! Ha, ha!"

Honey was learning how to take her; Emma had a way with conversation. She fully engaged, even broke out singing if the spirit moved her and the laughs weren't necessarily laughs; most were unction's, spiritual expressions. Honey was in for a surprise. Mother Howard went inside while they snapped beans and talk woman talk knowing Emma was gon get the both of em straight. She was loud but the tone of her conviction bared Christian witness. It drew people and Honey wasn't no exception fore she knew it she was acting like they'd been friends for years. Honey talked as she dropped snapped beans in the bowl.

"Addiemae, I think you outta give the deacon a chance." She suggested casually, wanting to hear what Emma was gon say.

"Don't start Honey!"

Emma jumped right in. "Start what? What she talking bout Honey?"

"Mother played match maker. She invited the deacon at church to lunch and Addiemae don't like it."

"And I told momma like I'm telling y'all, he not my type!"

"Girl what she say? He not yo type? Well Addiemae what exactly is yo type?"

"Have you talk to him Addiemae?"

"Not really. I told you I'm not interested Honey."

"How you gon know if you aint even talk to the man?" Honey

asked.

"You still aint said what yo type is cause I'm itching to hear it."

"Well, Emma you met Luke." She said as if meeting him explained things.

Emma retorted. Yeah, I met him."

"Something like that. You know a man that got looks, flair."

"Something like that? You said that like I'm supposed to be impressed. Aint no buzzard ever impressed me. Honey get ready to pull me out cause I'm bout to fall off this chair over in this sack of pole beans. Did she just tell me about looks and flair when I asked about a type? A type Addiemae, not a look."

"I said the same thing, Emma." Honey agreed.

"I don't know about y'all but I'm too old to bite my tongue. Ima tell you what God love. We family, we gon get along and we gon fall out. Addiemae, you limping around acting like you older than me talking bout a look. Girrrl, you betta wake up! You aint had no stroke. He drove you to a stroke worrying you like the devil from hell. Mighty funny he aint had one. You ever wonder why that was?" Emma didn't give her a chance to answer, cause she aint want one. "Nawl, you didn't. Then he brought you back home limping and you gon talk to me bout a look!"

"Emma, you don't know the whole story." Addiemae contended.

"And you do? So, what part did you miss? I don't need to know the whole story. He brought you back home. That's end of story right there when a man brings you back to yo daddy aint nuthin left to say. So, I'm looking forward to meeting the deacon. What's his name?"

"Saint Clair. Deacon Saint Clair."

"Is that his first or last name?" She asked not really wanting an answer. "Never mind it don't matter. Saint Clair, that's who I wanna hear about. I'm done with Luke. He may not be limping but baby he sho nuf walking round here maimed for life, I can tell you that much! God don't like ugly and he not too fond of cute. He best be thanking and praising God for his life. The way that man cut him every which way but loose, threw him on his momma's porch bleeding like a pig and left him for dead. And you weren't married long enough to get social security if he died. So, he wasn't no good to you dead or alive."

Honey chimed in. "Addiemae let me tell you, looks and muscles not all it's cracked up to be. Give him a chance. Get to know him don't push him away. You never can tell."

"What's wrong with the man y'all? Do he look that bad? Ya'll act like he an alien."

"Nawl Emma, he not no alien, he just don't appeal to me that's all."

"That's cause you after a look. The look you want Addiemae is the look of doing right by you. You can tell if a man doing right by a woman; she looks like it." Emma stood up and paraded herself around the front porch.

"Look at me, all bright and shiny, fun, full of myself! That's cause Rufus take care of me. He don't beat me down and worry me. He takes all the trouble on himself and make sure I have time to do what I need to do to be beautiful. And he not no jealous man either. A good man wants his woman happy and looking good. You mess around here and get one of them scalawags, you really be in trouble then. A scalawag don't take care his woman. He keeps her dull, scared to talk. She bet not have no opinion cause if she do, he'll beat it right out her. He can't love her cause he don't love himself. You see women like that, walking round looking timid, scared to open their mouth. Getting embarrassed in public. Soon as I see that, I look right at the husband. I give him that look that let him know I know what's going on. Talking bout how you doing Evangelist Turner. Evangelist nuthin. I see you devil!"

"You too much Emma!"

"She been that way all her life Honey, and she not changing."

"Don't put that on me. Telling me I'm too much. I aint too much, y'all just too little. Say what ya'll wanna say. The same man that treated a woman wrong will treat another one right. You betta be too much too. See young women complain about stuff that can be fixed. If he don't know how to dress, for God sake dress the man. What difference does it make, help him look good, he'll appreciate you. Baby the man can be as ugly as sin but if he loves the Lord, he can love you right. And don't let him make no special request and pray for you, you'd be surprised. God will give that man what he wants and you won't know what happened, fore you know it that man will start looking good to you. God will put the spotlight on that brother! You'll be doing double takes thinking, hey he don't look half bad. Don't act like you don't see it every Sunday. Physically challenged brothers married to beautiful sisters. And sisters that may not appear attractive, but know how to pray the house down, got the right heart, right spirit can get a prayer through and know how to help a man. The Lord will give em good looking prosperous husbands another woman couldn't pull away if she tried cause they know what side their bread is buttered on. Any who, poor man, I can't wait to meet him. I don't think he that bad. Like Dd say he may need *tending*."

"Who's Dd?"

"Momma, that's what the family call her, its short for Deannie." Addiemae said.

Honey's mind drifted. "Oh! Deannie, like *Splendor in the Grass*. Natalie Wood played a girl named Deannie."

Emma stayed focused and kept talking. "Men need *tending*. You got to study em. Learn how they work, how to deal with em. But aint no need in you *tending* to nobody if you don't tend to yourself first. Believe me, you. We all got something to tend to. I can tell you some *storays*." Emma shared her testimony and by the time she finished Honey was all ears.

"How long you been living in Chicago Emma?

"Forever. After Earnest served in the Army, he'd come down to Mounds telling us stories about Chicago. We had family there, but for some reason, daddy wouldn't let me visit. He talked him into letting me move with him to finish high school and I loved it! But when he lost Adeline and Junior, he nearly broke. He came back home and took over the farm. By then I turned eighteen, had graduated and moved to a nice respectable boarding house where I met Rufus and the rest is history."

"The Howards sure can tell a story, I see it run in both our families. My mother traveled a lot and came home with a mouthful of stories. Listening to her made me want to travel. Closest I got to traveling was listening to JE tell me about the places he'd been. Anyway, I'm glad to be home too. The city helped me appreciate small town life. I'm not saying I wanna come back, but I wouldn't mind something in between Mounds and Chicago. You know not too rural but not too city. Lord knows I needed this. Seeing my family doing my heart good. Ima spend the whole day with my grandparents tomorrow. JE just like my family; he can make you believe anything that's why I put all my eggs in his basket. Never in a million years I woulda thought…" Honey paused, stopping short of complaining.

Emma picked it up. "Never woulda thought what? That it wasn't gon be no heartache and disappointment?"

"Yeah. I never woulda believed it. We weren't just married we were friends." Honey's mind drifted again. "I hope you know you sound like Daddy Howard."

"That's cause he taught me to be strong, keep my integrity. You can't rock and be steady at the same time. He's my older cousin. His father and my mother; sister and brother. We took him in when his mother died. His stepmother was crazy, she didn't wanna treat him right, but we were glad to have him. That man no matter what happen kept on going. I leaned on him when my parents died. He aint nuthin but a rock you can stand on and a bridge you can cross over."

"I aint surprised. But I missed out; I didn't want to listen. Thought he was too mean, too hard on JE. It wasn't till we got ready to leave I got an understanding about him." Honey admitted.

"That's alright, long as you on this side of the dirt it aint too late to fix it. He was tough on JE cause JE just like him. Don't make the mistake thinking a father don't know his son and take his side when he wrong. You talking bout a mess. You betta let him take that chastisement. You been made a monster can't nobody deal with and cost him his soul. He'll lift his eyes up in hell five miles down. A woman supposed to help her man get closer to God, not pull him away to his own devices. Do that and you'll be the dark side of his past when he gets himself right with the Lord. He was mad at God when he lost his first family. You couldn't tell him, but he was. He woulda denied it to the end. When he met Dd, he said he knew who she was to him and why she showed up. She told him about himself, he got back in church and married her. When she had JE, he didn't want to leave the farm to do nuthin. Long as he could see her and JE sitting on that front porch, poking round on the farm, he was happy. Then she gave him a bunch of children, maybe trying to make up for the loss. Somewhere in his mind he wanted to make sure everybody met up in heaven. So, he was gon force us even if we went kicking and screaming. Wasn't no such thing as a personal choice."

"I remember what he told me before we moved."

"I already know but what he say?"

"He said what you said. It wasn't gon always be what I think it should, it wasn't gon always be easy, its gon be some heartache and disappointment, but God would see me through."

"That's the Word, that's Earnest. I know he said serve God and take care yo family?"

"He did. Yep, he said that too."

"That man been saying that as long as I can remember. When I got down in my spirit, I didn't even bother to call him. He let me know wasn't no running back home. If I came Rufus had to come with me and he didn't get in our business either, he waited us out. Said you can't solve a problem if you don't have both of the parts. In other words, wasn't no one person to blame. There were times when I got so mad at Rufus, I thought I would bark like a dog. I tell you if it wasn't for the prayers of the righteous, I woulda walked out the door!"

She pointed at the front door and said it again. "You hear me! Right there. I'm pointing at that door but you know I mean my door at home in Chicago… right. Chile, I done stood with my bags packed at the door ready to go! Keys in my hand and the Lord wouldn't let me leave. All I could do is stand there cry and look ugly. And guess what?"

"What?"

"Rufus did too. He came from a sanctified family; he just didn't go to church. His brother is our pastor. When we moved in the Greystone, he brought the prayer team to pray in our home. Rufus wanted to leave more than once and got angry when he couldn't. He'd walk out the door, turn around, come back slam the door so hard I thought it come off the hinges. But I stayed out the way, I didn't say nuthin. The devil wanted me to argue with him but that was between him and God. He came back, sat at the table and drank shots of *Jack Daniels Black Label Tennessee Whisky*. Then he'd start talking crazy. Smacking his lips after each shot rambling on about how smooth it went down knowing he had to go to work the next day. Then he told me he couldn't leave cause the Howards had him under a spell. He forgot his brother was the one that came and prayed. Then he fell asleep on my designer sofa. Next morning, I gave him tall glasses of water to hydrate him, lots of orange juice and made his favorite breakfast. A plate of pancakes with strawberries, bananas and syrup to help boost his energy so he could go to work. Cause he had to go; you do what you gotta do to make sure yo man can work. After that, we sat at the table like civilized people and ate. Neither one of us said a word. We went on like nuthin happened. That's how we were taught. Don't argue everything, let it ride sometime, choose yo battles or lose yo peace. And it aint gon always be no resolution but if yo heart right you won't have to say a word, you'll find forgiveness in each other's eyes. I tell you this thing called marriage will have you singing the gospel."

Emma started singing. "*Just Another Day.*"

She stopped and laughed. "Uh huh! Honey them songs came from somebody that went through something, lived to tell the story and they can get you through too. We call those deliverance songs."

"To look at you it don't seem like you been through nuthin. I saw them pictures, y'all got it together. A Greystone in Bronzeville. That's a fairytale. JE used to show me pictures of Bronzeville in a book."

"Yeah, Bronzeville definitely had its heyday but far as me and Rufus having it together, chile please. A house! That aint nuthin but brick and mortar. We don't put no faith in that. I told you he slammed doors off the hinges. Both of us were ready to walk out the door when we got to acting a fool. Good things can be an albatross around yo neck when you aint content. Everything we have is by the grace of God, and it took HIM being in our lives to appreciate what he gave us. We weren't always in church Honey. I used to clean that Greystone."

"Clean it?"

"Yeah, I was the housekeeper."

"Really."

"Yeah. Wasn't no shame in it either. More than ten years I cleaned that house. I know the place like the back of my hand. I knew it better than the owners. But guess what?"

"What?"

"I was faithful. Every day I cleaned it like it was my own house and loved doing it. Living in a kitchenette wasn't easy. Everything was in one room. We were sleeping across from the stove. Till one day Mr. Goldston came home told us they were moving to New York and he wasn't gon sell to nobody but me and Rufus even if he had to finance and set us up on payments. I knew it wasn't nobody but God. I was tired of that kitchenette. Things got so bad in that building, it turned into a slum. Aint no way in the world a housekeeper and a security guard could afford a Greystone, payments or not."

"So how y'all get it then? "

"God turned the neighborhood black. He parted the Red Sea, so what's a neighborhood. We told Rufus's brother and the prayer team prayed. Honey the next day that man walked up the stairs in our building where you rarely saw white folk unless they were coming to collect late rent. You hear me? He came to us didn't even sit down. Signed the deed over with a bunch of other legal documents his lawyer drew up that we didn't even understand. Put a file in our hands and gave us the keys. Told us to send him what we could, when we could and paid me till I found another job. Don't you tell me it aint no good white folk and that God don't hold hearts in his hands and turn em."

"Are you kidding me?"

"I'm talking bout what God can do! Aint no trick in living right. Yeah, you may suffer for a minute but you coming through every time. when it was said and done, we paid him all of about five hundred if that much."

"Five hundred dollars!"

"Yep. Five hundred dollars. A couple months later, Mrs. Goldston called and told us not to send another dime. He died and left the Greystone to us in his Will. God rest his soul; we been there ever since. All we pay is taxes. Honey if it's a house you want ask for it. You have not cause you ask not."

"I needed to hear that story. I been wanting a house for the children?"

"That's not a story Honey that's a testimony. This conversation shoulda been had in Chicago six years ago but JE didn't listen so the Lord called us down here together. JE's not listening don't stop God's plan. What else could it be? Why else we sitting here talking?"

"I don't know. Maybe cause we visiting."

"That's what you think? We didn't know you and JE was gon be here. Last thing we heard was Earnest telling us y'all was gon call and come by the house and that was six years ago, y'all never called or came. And we haven't been down here since God knows when so go figure. Honey let me tell you about this Howard family you done married into. We got so many prayers out there traveling it aint funny. And talk about a corporate blessing, whoever you touch gon benefit. One day all of a sudden answered prayers just gon start hitting you all upside yo head."

"Well, aint nuthin wrong with that. I feel blessed right now. I'm glad we came."

"I'm glad all y'all came. I feel better. I haven't been able to talk like this in a long time. I feel strength coming back in my legs enough to throw this cane down!"

"That's good but wait till the deacon come because we'd be hard pressed to get you up off the floor. But let me tell you this Addiemae, if God didn't allow it, it wouldn't have happened. Things come in our lives to force us forward. Otherwise, we would never move. You heard preachers say He set you back for a come up?"

"Preachers? Baby, momma the one always saying that."

"If you believe it give it to Jesus and watch HIM, give it back to you better. Addiemae, you not just yo legs, yo hair, yo teeth, arms and eyes. You're not parts, you're a whole being. You're a spirit having a human experience."

"For a long time, all I could think about was how low I felt and I gave up on myself."

"Well, you been through a lot but you don't have the right to feel less than what God made you to be. And yeah, I called Luke a buzzard. You know the tree by the fruit it bears. Buzzards swoop in and take what Eagles leave behind. You just so happen to be in a condition to be taken."

"What you mean I was in a condition to be taken?"

"Ha, ha, there it is. You weren't all there. Thank you, Jesus, for the revelation. You were straddling the fence, dibbling and dabbling. Yo yay wasn't yay and yo nay wasn't nay. You didn't have a made-up mind. So, he swooped in on you."

"You right. I never thought about it like that."

"Oh, I know I'm right cause the Lord dropped that in my spirit. You wanted something out there and you weren't gon stop till you got it, so He let you have it and everything that came along with it. But He didn't let it consume you. Hallelujah thank you Jesus and that aint everybody's testimony. Somebody got outta here backward and died in their sin."

"Momma always said, if we want the devil to leave us alone give his stuff back to him."

"Then give the devil back his stuff. You got something that belong to him? God not gon force you to do nuthin, He too much of a gentleman for that. He gave you free will."

Addiemae got silent, closed her eyes, nodded her head in agreement and confessed. "I know what I got that belong to him. I know what I gotta do and I'm doing it right now. Y'all excuse me. I need to go get myself together fore lunch."

"It's alright. Take yo time baby." Emma said.

"Yeah, Addiemae take yo time."

She left the porch. Honey couldn't wait to chime in. "Wow, I don't know what to say but I know you just blessed her."

"I didn't bless her, God blessed her. She already knew what she needed to do; she was just ready to hear. How about you? You ready?"

"I aint gon lie cause you gon tell me something I don't wanna hear and not willing to do."

"I appreciate the honesty. That's yo truth but just because its yo truth don't make it true."

"Excuse me?"

Emma repeated herself. "Just because it's yo truth don't make it true. It's only one truth and that belongs to God. Experiences influence what we believe but at the end of the day, it's no more than smoke and mirrors. That's why you gotta get outta yo head and get in the Word. The bible says, *"In all thy ways acknowledge Him and He shall direct thy paths."* Paths, that's plural, that's how we walk through life. We walk Paths. When we make decisions without checking with the Lord, we mess up and then call it our truth to justify a bad move. You married James Ernest Howard, didn't you?"

"Yes, I did?"

"Uh huh. Why?"

"I guess I loved him."

"You guess. And I'd be willing to bet you don't understand it's something wrong with what you just said."

"Why would you say that? I thought we were being honest. Just talking."

"We are just talking but aint no need in idle talk. You said something worth knowing so Ima talk to you about the Howard men since you married one. And Ima give you an example of the best and the worse reason to marry since you spoke in negatives, past tense, guessing and carrying on."

"I said that cause I don't feel that way anymore."

Emma didn't like what she heard. "Lord, we need yo help." She pulled her chair closer to sit in front of Honey, held both her hands, squeezed them tight. She could feel the pain. She dropped her head offered a silent prayer while tears fell from Honey's eyes. She looked up and spoke.

"You a wife. You married a Howard. I can talk to you naturally about Howard men. I know the father and I know the sons! They all good men but their wives pay for that goodness and it aint coming cheap. They don't come into your world; they create one and put you in it. Aint no need to debate or go into a big deliberation so just indulge me. The Howard men build around you in a way that after God, you're their foundational structure. I'm trying to say this in a way you can embrace it so I hope I'm making sense. Am I making sense to you?"

"Yeah, you making sense. I'm listening." Honey said shaking her head slowly.

"One thing I do not do, is play around with God's people. But you don't have a pastor, so Ima help you out till you get one. You an intelligent woman but more important than that you a hurt woman and that's urgent. I see you hanging in the balance so Ima take my time and be led in my approach; God wanna do something in yo life."

"And I need HIM to do something in my life."

Emma took a deep breath. "Thank you, Holy Spirit. The other part of being foundational is that they tend to have an unspoken unconditional expectation. Despite everything, they expect you to help them get to God. They expect you to know when to hold, fold, play dead, turn a blind eye, appreciate their success, and pray them through transgressions. They got good hearts and they know they not always right. You're a Help meet, help him meet God's standard. That's true for all men, Griffins, Daniels, all of em. The name don't matter. The only name that matter is the name of Jesus. If you can do that, you're all in."

"Turning a blind eye is a bit much. I don't know about all that. JE just sat up and flirted with a waitress right in front of my face. I don't think I can do it."

"You right, it is a bit much. You gotta have a strong commitment to righteous living. You gotta love the Lord to be able to do that. Scripturally speaking its setting yo face like flint, being resolute, unshakable, determined. You can't let his foolishness move you. You know, interfere with yo salvation. Ask Dd she'll tell you. She married to his daddy. Best believe there were times when she had to go inside herself and find some more strength. Said when she couldn't say a word, all she could do is wave her hand. Sacrificing to do what's right in the sight of God, takes a special anointing, it's a gift most don't want but it runs in her family. When she met Ernest, she was on her way to college to become a teacher. We called meeting him her *Road to Damascus* but that's a story for another time. Anyway, she prayed, married him and never looked back to wonder. She said it was a God decision, more than anything she wanted his soul saved. Her parents never argued the point."

"She put him before herself and her education?"

"So it seemed. Seemed like she gave up her dream of teaching, but she didn't. She teaching on a much higher level. She taught me, she's teaching you and she'll be teaching till she leave here."

"She sho nuf teaching."

"I know she is. She teaching what God love. What matters. Now look at Addiemae desiring a man based on his looks."

"And they both had experiences that changed their looks!"

"Now you got it. It's like riding a bike, look at you! See people think spirituality aint practical but the Holy Ghost is intelligent. Most of the women in our family married men that do right by them and sacrificed to some degree. We're not silly women, we know aint nuthin perfect and you don't get the big years without trouble."

"I did that. I sacrificed. I gave JE a family and waited years for him to come home and he didn't do right by me."

"Maybe there's more work to do."

"I'm sure it is but I don't think Ima be the one working. Not right now. I been through too much that's why we're here."

Emma put her hands up. "That's yo flesh kicking and yo decision to walk that path. But when you get in yo bible, its gon open yo eyes. There's an answer to every question. There's a time and a chance for everybody. I pray one
day you'll hear the preacher cause what I do know is that we not no more than a bunch of leaves on a tree that's gon blow away just like the song, *"After while it'll all be over."*

Chile don't get me started. But that's how Dd sees life. Spend some time talking to her, she's yo momma too. She'll tell you, it's not how long you stay here, what you have while you here and all that other stuff y'all doing. Life is living in a way that prepares you to leave and live forever. People spend too much time seeking everything carnal, investing in everything except our souls. Now how intelligent is that?"

Emma thought about it. How prayer always prevailed. She laughed. "Ha, ha. All these prayers hanging round, it just aint no telling, you can't begin to call it. But I wanna see you and the children saved. When we get home come by the house, get close. Spend time with us. Let us help you."

"I'd like that, Emma."

"And bring the other leaves when you come."

# CHAPTER SIX

### ♣
### *Seeing Down the Road*

*"Everything was suspended in the midst of a miracle, none of em noticed Addiemae walking not even Addiemae."*

The pastor gave wise counsel. He had the gift of seeing down the road. JE and Honey would not divorce, Addiemae was free to move on with her life and all three were at peace. Hung over from the prayer they sat and listened to the choir rehearse and left drunk in the spirit as they walked down the road to the house. Evening fell and the fireflies came out for the night. For some reason, even though their spirits were quiet Addiemae sang out loud. They saw Daddy, Mother Howard, Rufus and Emma sitting on the soft amber lit porch resting from the day. There was a peace they dared not disturb. They let it linger. Addiemae finished her song and sighed. "It sho is a sweet spirit in the air."

JE agreed, "Yeah, but more than that. The Lord touched us tonight."

Mother Howard saw em walking toward the house and heard the sound of Addiemae's anointed alto voice singing *"Sweet Holy Spirit"* from afar off; she hadn't sang like that since she was a teenager. "Lord have mercy, will you listen to that girl singing like an angel! If I'd known fussing woulda made em act like this, I'd done it a long time ago. I guess they heard something good huh Emma?"

"Nawl Dd. It looks like they got what they needed. I can see the healing. Look closer, Addiemae is walking. She not limping. Aint no cane in her hand. The Lord done healed her body!"

Mother Howard stood up again and cried out. "Oh my God Earnest, she is. My baby is walking! Look at her! She walking Ernest!" She could barely stand up straight for praising the Lord.

Daddy Howard let her go on for a while then he said, "Leave em be y'all. It's a sacred time, the Lord still healing. Come inside fore they get here, get to talking and quench the spirit. Come on Dd we need our rest." He reached for Mother Howard's arm to help her along. As they started walking, he looked back, "Rufus, you and Emma too."

By the time they made it to the house the porch was empty. Addiemae hugged them, said goodnight, went inside singing, climbed the stairs without a struggle and the cane the pastor took away. Everything was suspended in the midst of a miracle, none of em noticed Addiemae walking not even Addiemae.

JE and Honey copped a squat on the stairs butting themselves up against each other like childhood sweethearts. The hush that came over them after prayer had em speaking in soft whispers that lightened their hearts. Honey looked up at the sky. "I wonder what the children doing?"

"Why? You worried?"

"Nawl, not really. Just wondering. It's such a beautiful night. I wish they were here with us"

"Remember how I told you I felt close because you were sleeping under the same sky?"

"Yeah, I do."

"Well look at it that way; it helps. At least until you get back home. And if I know anything about Mother Boyd, she took em to bible study and if I know anything about our girls, they ready for their momma to come home. They had enough structure by now. But they're fine."

"I know. How about you. You gon be alright JE?"

"You worried about me huh?"

"Nope, I aint worried. I just aint been without my man in six years."

"Listen to you. Yeah, you worried. I'm worried about you too. You a good woman, a good mother and a good wife Honey. The Lord touched us tonight and I believe he gon give you what you want."

"What make you say that?"

He faced Honey and touched the tip of her nose with his finger. "Cause the Lord see you. The Lord know you and the Lord got His hands all over yo life. That's what momma told me. I ain't never forgot it and I'm fool enough to believe it."

"You know I can't remember the last time you had a chance to sit still. Always working like yo daddy busy doing something ever since you were a boy. Since the Lord gon give me what I want, guess what else I want?"

"What else you want?"

"I want you to heal. You deserve to heal and get everything you want.

A good life. You fought for this country and this family. Take time for yourself, don't think about nuthin else and heal JE. My God, you been through so much. I'm sorry you found that girl's body, Lord knows you done seen enough death. And I apologize for making you feel less of a man. Honey spoke through her laughter, "Ha, ha, and if I tried to raise you. Forgive me."

"Awh girl, you didn't know no better. And yeah, you did try to raise me, maybe because I was acting like a child, but I forgive you if you forgive me."

"I do"

"Pinky Swear!"

They joined their pinky fingers and thumbs." Ok, now that that's settled let me tell you, the women didn't mean nuthin to me but they didn't deserve to be hurt either. I wanted to hurt myself, not you or them. Momma was right about the way Spence raised you. He gave you a good quality of life I couldn't. It did something to me, I couldn't see the light in yo eyes. Seemed like you stopped looking at me the way you did when I was in the service, when I came home on leave. I liked the coming and going because it made you glad to see me. We were always new. That's why I didn't want to come home for good. Afraid you'd get tired of seeing me, I'd be a loser and that's how I felt, like a loser."

"JE, Spence is my granddaddy, you're my husband. I was glad you came home to me. I knew the temptation. You had a woman and a child out there. You didn't have to come back but you did, you kept yo promise, that's all I needed. And you got us out this South like you said you would. I didn't get to travel but I'm grateful."

They made peace but when the morning came, JE stayed in Mounds and Honey rode back to Chicago alone. The pastor advised them to separate as long as they needed before making a final decision. Told them to take their time.

Honey reflected while she rode home with Emma and Rufus. She noticed their disposition, their kindness and consideration of one another. How he tended to her needs as he drove like JE did her. Although cheating was a good enough reason to divorce, it wasn't the only reason. When Emma questioned why she got married, she was ashamed that her desire to leave the South and travel influenced the decision to marry JE. They both had a lot of healing to do.

JE's healing began with Cassie, his daughter in Germany. JE thought he would never hear from her but the pastor encouraged him to write. By then, she was old enough to understand. As it turned out, she was looking for him too and wrote back. Meanwhile, he and Daddy Howard worked side by side on the farm. They saw forgiveness in occasional glances and the hard work brought them together without discussion. Then they hung out with Spence at the barbershop. Daddy Howard was shocked at what they had in common. Turns out Spence never had nuthin handed to him. In fact, he suffered indignities and the shame of being an illegitimate, mulatto child. The stories he shared broke their hearts.

After staying on the farm nine months, he was ready to put the Caddy on the road. He drove to Arkansas to see Porter. He was doing well. When they saw each other, they did a long version of the soul brother handshake then they stood back and checked each other out.

"Man, look at you!"

"Look at me? Look at you! I thought you weren't never coming back South."

"I thought I wasn't either, but things happen you know."

"Yeah, I knew me and Chicago wasn't gon make it. Man, all them buildings and people piled up on top of each other like sardines, I had to get outta there. As you can see, I'm a big ole country boy!"

"You gotta be sitting out here on all this land." JE said looking as far as his eyes could see. "Man, how many acres do you have?"

"Ten." Porter pointed in another direction. "My youngest brother have ten over there." And another direction. "My sister have ten over there." He pointed in the same direction but further out "And my momma and daddy have forty over there behind hers. They dividing that into smaller parcels for the grandchildren. They make sure everybody got some land. Man, up from slavery that's just how they think. As soon as a baby is born, they get two acres and a mule."

JE smiled. "Check that out! That's alright. Your family sitting on seventy acres. Why you leave?"

Porter laughed. "Would you believe I didn't want to live this close to my family? Didn't want to deal with land. But guess what I found out. Aint no place like home. And aint nuthin like having yo own."

"No, it's not. Especially when the family own this much land. You got enough land between you. It aint like y'all were sitting up under each other. You can build a neighborhood, a whole community and still have space"

"I know man. When we pulled up and Brenda saw all this land, she thought I was crazy for leaving. She didn't know she hit the jackpot. That woman couldn't be happier she didn't judge this book by its cover. It aint like I was a good-looking, muscle-bound man like you."

JE laughed. "And that aint never paid the rent."

"I'm messing with you. But check this out, half her family done moved down here. They said it got so bad up there in them projects they thought they were gon end up in jail trying to stay alive. Hey man, her sister Gwen and her twin brothers Daryl and Durrell came down here; they doing good. Working, got southern wives, started families. Our parents done fell in love with each other. Come to find out they from Tupelo and Jackson, Mississippi. Every summer they come down here, staying up all night sitting on the porch talking. I told em they might as well put a double wide over there."

Porter pointed to an area near a bunch of trees. "Them trees coming down next month, the timber already sold. They don't know it yet, but we gon use that money to get em here fore it gets cold. Man, ole folks aint got no business up there like that in all that cold weather. They can't take them winters and Brenda got to be close to her momma, they be on the phone everyday all day. She can visit as much as she wants and won't have to leave the property."

"That's alright. Seem like y'all got it together."

"Nawl, we got a little way to go. It's gotta be official, we gon get married and she gon give me some babies. My folks real funny about that. They believe in keeping things in the family."

"Babies?"

"Yeah man. She already knows, we talked about it. She came to me with two children. The deal is, she gon give me at least three."

"You know you crazy!"

"Man, that's real talk. I don't mind taking on the two she already had but I gotta have some of my own too. I'm not nobody's fool."

"I understand. You gotta have that blessing on yo life. A man aint nuthin without family. Speaking of family, lemme get outta here. It's been good seeing you, Porter."

"You too man, what you getting ready to do?"

"Go get the kids and bring em down south for the summer, let em hang out. You know get em out the city."

"Yeah, you do that man, it's getting bad. I'd hate to see em stuck up there like that."

"Nawl nawl. Long as we got land that's free and clear, they not stuck nowhere. And I'm moving back. I bought a house out in Indiana not too far from family."

"Is that right? Check that out. Right on! Hey, you know you aint said nuthin right? Last time we talked, you were doing yo thang so I gotta ask you, how Honey doing?"

"Honey doing fine." JE laughed, "You act like you were scared to ask."

"I was. Man, the way we were clowning, I wasn't sure if I should. I still got them southern manners. I wasn't trying to be offensive and bring up bad memories. You know what I'm talking about, it aint like we were saint's we did some real crazy stuff. I'm just glad we didn't hurt ourselves too bad. Who knows where we woulda ended up?"

"Not a day go by it don't cross my mind but thanks for asking. We not together but that don't mean nuthin. I still love that woman and we still married so who knows; just keep us in yo prayers. Would you believe Franklin and Mattie is doing real good; living the *"Life of Riley."*

"Yeah? Franklin! That brother! I was scared he was gon get assassinated the way he spoke truth to power like he was ready to die."

"Well, aint none of that changed. He's all about Black power. The way I see it, we get out here one way or another. Might as well leave here believing in something."

"Sho you right! Now all you got to do is believe you gon make it out this neck of the woods and back to Chi Town in one piece."

# CHAPTER SEVEN

### *Climate Changes*

*"Girlfriends gave out sex like candy. Like it was an opportunity to get pregnant and leave the remnant of a young soldier that would surely die."*

The winter of '67 came dumping 23 inches of snow in 29 hours. Cars and buses looked like big lumps, like giant strangely shaped snowballs in the middle of the street. People stopped driving got out their cars and started walking. CTA bus drivers parked their buses, pulled their skull caps down over their heads, snatched jackets off the backs of seats, looked at the passengers, got off with unpunched transfers in hand and walked away. Saying nuthin. Figuring if they had good sense, they'd get off and do the same before it was too late. Like racism, the snow did not stop; it kept coming down.

Thursday, April 4, 1968, just after 6pm. black and white televisions announced the death, the killing, the murder, the assassination of the *Drum Major for Peace*, Dr. Martin Luther King Jr. was dead! Nina Simone cried out *"Why? (The King of Love is Dead)"* in her tribute. Black families mourned in the projects from behind caged balconies, assembled in doorways, stood on stoops, huddled on corners, and sat in pissey stairwells, crying, reliving the tragedy, and the loss of hope. Stuck in disbelief they shook their heads and held their babies closer. Enraged teenagers galvanized to take to the streets and express their hurt the best way they knew how. Destroying what was within reach in their own communities that would never belong to them. There would be no recovery from the destruction that reflected the pain of the loss of Dr. Martin Luther King, Jr. Not in Chicago it wouldn't.

The summer of '68 was hot, hazy and blurred with the steam of frustration. The Black Power movement was rising high. James Brown released, *"Say it Loud, I'm Black and I'm Proud"* and it rang out like a black national anthem through the ghettos. Teenagers cut perms and processes from their hair. Guys stopped doo-whopping on corners and became soldiers, armor bearers, messengers of truth vigilantly standing at the ready, cracking atoms, handing out literature shaped by black intelligentsia, poised to educate the masses, and protested for equal rights like Malcolm X said, *"By any means necessary."*

After the assassination of Dr. King, summers were synonymous with racism. Young people, high school students, angry teenagers actively led political and racially motivated riots in the big playground, where *Seay Dog* sat under the basketball hoop playing his bongos till he was drafted and shipped away like a package to Vietnam. Stokely Carmichael spoke of identity, liberation and empowerment. Fed up with prejudice, inequality and living conditions, there was nuthin to lose but a life of oppression that wasn't much worth living.

Black people everywhere adorned themselves with huge afros, cornrows, dashikis, red black and green tee-shirts, black shades, black leather jackets, black berets, taught black children how to raise their right fist and say black power. Greeted one another with my sister, my brother, my man. Ending conversations with "you dig" and "dig that." Smoked good weed freely and got down with the get down.

Conversations were about black people and more power to the people for God's sake. What was once acceptable was no longer tolerated. Consciousness was reflected in art, music and dance, putting the world on edge, pushing racism back on its heels, on the brink of a reckoning, channeling a societal change. Discontentment with the government was the status quo; it wasn't gon be no peace. Racial tensions loomed over heads like dark heavy clouds full, waiting to burst, to pour down. People were locked and loaded ready to pull the trigger.

Black mothers stopped buying white dolls. Black Panthers attended assemblies, posted up at entrances, called black children little black sister and little black brother, and passed out bag lunches in the little playground. Young men were drafted through the lottery system. Parents agonized at the thought of fighting a war doomed from the start. Girlfriends gave out sex like candy. Like it was an opportunity to get pregnant and leave the remnant of a young soldier that was gon surely die. Throwing caution to the wind before boyfriends shipped to

Vietnam, like they needed to get pregnant, like they needed, like they needed to get, to get. Pregnant. Like it was the end of the world while the Temptations, *"Don't Send Me Away"* and The Monitors *"Greetings This is Uncle Sam"* played nonstop from the raspy sound of a transistor radio from an apartment window on the 9th floor where a girl cried knowing her boyfriend wasn't coming back home.

But for some who made it back, hoping to be well received, there were no celebrations for sacrificing lives, limbs and minds. There was no coming home to dedicated girlfriends, baby love and love child's. They were stigmatized for their troubles. Traumatized, called crazy and addicted to psychedelics, LSD, mushrooms and cocaine, heroin and marijuana. Drugs. Just trying to be normal. Trying not hear the sounds of helicopters, tanks, automatic weapons fire, and explosions. They tried to even drown out the rain and the thunder, trippin on their high. Listening deeply to Jimi Hendrix, guitar whine, scratch and scream out, *"All Around the Watchtower"* and *"Purple Haze"* reminiscing about danger and death. Missing heads, arms and legs. Remembering how desperately they wanted to get home but couldn't. Left to suffer the consequences of what was conceived; like babies in the womb of a dying nation.

But after the snow and the rain. After the pouring down of hatred, after the breaking asunder of the will and ways of oppressive powers, the community got out from under its slumber, and woke up from its sleep ready for a change. Children rose up singing Nina Simone's *"Young Gifted & Black."* Little babies' with barely a voice recited Dr. King's, *"I Have a Dream"* speech. Meantime, on the backend of the movement where a nation of people was empowered, drugs flooded the community. Conscious music disappeared. Disco showed up with hypnotic spinning balls, flashing lights, long repetitive vocals, and reverbs that dulled senses, and kept people dancing like puppets on a string. Like puppets. Like strings. The children went down south summer with JE and school started in September.

♣

Troubled by the war, the political climate, separation from Honey, and his children growing up in hell, JE rose up on a Sunday morning. He put on a suit of clothes, went to church, walked down the aisle, and bowed down at the altar to meet the Lord for himself. Daddy Howard raised his arms in the air to give praise and one by one every minister, every deacon, every man walked forward to kneel down beside him; surrounded by missionaries to pray and bring him in. Mother Howard could not contain and offered up a very soul deep, "Hallelujah Thank you Jesus!"

# CHAPTER EIGHT

### ♣
### *A Change*

*"Calling the trump suit.*
*Three Uptown, "Three Downtown, Three No Trump."*

Apollo 11 landed on the moon and JE got his life together. Midsummer 1969, JE came home to a small house in a small town in Indiana. Daddy Howard sent Blue; said he'd keep away the lonelies. When he moved in the house Emma and Rufus blessed it and anointed every room. When he settled, he dropped in on Franklin and Mattie to reminisce and the children stayed on weekends.

A very nice lady lived across the street who was anxious to become friends. She had no husband, loved to cook and bake. After several waves and passing words, she made her way to his door with plates of food and insisted upon baking him a cake. She presented herself the same way the women in the projects did with food and it angered JE.

On a Saturday morning she came by unannounced again, this time the children answered the door. JE sent them, knowing it was her. She found herself staring into the faces of children. "Daddy there's a lady at the door to see you." Layla hollered.

JE came and greeted her, noticing the shift in her behavior. "Morning!" he said.

She stuttered, "G…G…Good morning, I see you have company." "No!" He replied firm and swiftly. "I don't have company. These are my children and this is their mother's, my wife's house." He said with the same sly grin he used to flirt. Only he wasn't flirting this time.

"Oh!" the lady said, standing there with a plate in her hands waiting as if an explanation would come. "Well now. I got up early this morning, made a big breakfast and thought I'd share some with you." She tried to laugh, "I guess it wouldn't be enough for you and the children. I feel kinda foolish." She admitted still posturing for an explanation but JE did nuthin to ease her shame allowing the silence and discomfort. Angie pushed her way to the front of the door.

"How nice of you to bring our father a plate of food." She said standing in front of JE. "We appreciate it but our mother taught us how to cook for our father "she said leaving her speechless. Layla stepped in front of Angie. "Mommas on her way, would you like to stay for breakfast?"

"No no no…thank you!" she said turning, running and nearly falling down the stairs trying to get off the front porch.

JE yelled after her. "Thanks for thinking about me! "He closed the door, laughed and confessed. "Angie, I know why you did that."

"Daddy I'm sorry but we tired of these ladies always coming around pretending to be nice when all they want to do is steal you from momma."

"I know, but you don't have to worry about that. I learned my lesson. I'm a married man. The only woman welcome and the only woman coming in this house is yo mother. This is her house, that's why I let you answer the door for her." He smiled. "I gotta tell you I thought she was about to faint especially when Layla mentioned momma. I been avoiding that lady since I moved here but I think this did the trick. Thanks!"

Myles chimed in. "You can thank us by making breakfast cause I'm hungry. That food smelled good, you coulda gave it to me. And since when did Angie start cooking?"

♣

It was summer, school was out and Honey's route expanded to include Bronzeville where Emma lived. They visited during her lunch breaks and at the end of their talks Emma always said, "With the Lord on yo side what can't you do? You have not cause you ask not."

After a few visits, Honey sat in the mail truck and prayed for the first time since they moved to Chicago. Emma told her not to worry about having the right words, to just speak her heart.

"Dear Lord, I know I haven't prayed, been to church, haven't done nuthin your way so I don't feel worthy to ask for anything. But I am a mother trying to raise my children, the best way I know how. The children deserve a better life, a better chance and I need yo help and guidance. Because if I don't know nuthin else; I know if you don't do it, it can't be done. So, I'm begging you to get us out these projects."

Honey sat still. Hearing the words come from her mouth broke her down to tears, she came from the bottom of her heart and talked to God. "Lord my husband not here with me, it's getting dangerous and I'm scared. Scared for our lives. I don't know what's gon happen to us. I'm not begging for me; I'm begging for the children." She doubled back before ending her prayer. "And Lord help us. Help me and JE forgive one another. Make things right between us. Amen."

*"Honey baby you should have saw us at the Club DeLisa. I tell you we were something else. We were quite the envy back in them days. And it wasn't long ago Rufus was getting down doing the James Brown split, the Funky Chicken and everything. Don't tell him I told you. Now that he's a dignified Elder he just sits in the pulpit."*

Emma's conversations were lessons. She delivered stories like Honey delivered mail in a way there was no shame. Separation wasn't easy and Honey needed strength. Emma shared stories about mistakes and bad decisions in humorous ways that ended with a message; one she needed.

"I remember me and Rufus thinking we had it together. We found a new set of friends to hang out with. Friends that like to party, work buddies. We'd get together, walk the *Stroll* decked out, sharp as a tack. You couldn't tell us nuthin. We drank, danced all night, got up and went to work hung over. We thought we did something moving out the boarding house to a kitchenette. See how sin can make a fool outta you?"

Honey laughed but like Daddy Howard, Emma could see down the road, she knew temptation was at the door. After Honey prayed, things moved fast, people came quick. Night school was ending, the backlog at the post office kept her working, pulling overtime. One day the bus was slow and a very nice man, with grey eyes reminiscent of her granddaddy Spence, a co-worker noticed her waiting on the bus stop. He pulled over, gave her a lift, offered to keep picking her up and dropping her off; he became her boyfriend. Casual conversations with business owners became lifelong friendships. A young Jewish lawyer impressed by her desire to purchase a home for her children promised to close the deal for her when she was ready.

The owner of a clothing warehouse extended her credit holding postdated checks until the money was in the bank and the job service lady referred her for a desk position at her office after graduation.

Blessings were coming down like the Chicago snow at Christmastime.

Children and parents stood in the cold marveling at the State Street department store windows while they stood in the cold; it was a treat for Layla and worth the winter bus ride with Myles. She watched the mechanical lily-white doll dressed in a crimson red coat with red green and blue plaid trimmed collars, velvet buttons, a matching tam, white cable knit tights, and black patten leather shoes standing in glistening snow.

Myles eyes followed the moving trains as they traveled over bridges, frozen lakes, pass bakeries, around glittery church steeples, through little towns lined with frost covered cottage homes, black lamp posts with red light bulbs and twinkling trees where little white people carried armfuls of wrapped gifts, caroling. Pine, gingerbread, and cinnamon smells filled the outside air.

Colorful lights that looked like Easter eggs lining hundreds of windows greeted them as they walked from the bus stop to the building. It was the holiday season and it was spent with everybody cozied up on the sofa and in the living room floor under blankets watching *Miracle on 34th Street, A Wonderful Life,* with intermissions of *Suzy Snowflake, Hardrock, Coco and Joe*; in front of their black and white television sitting on a wheel cart near the aluminum Christmas tree. It was trimmed in green red and blue glass ornaments with a spinning light that made it turn colors.

Honey was home. She had vacation time and cooked for two days. Ham with pineapple, glazed with spicy cloves, macaroni and cheese, dressing, cranberry sauce, collards and mustard greens, dinner rolls slathered in butter, candied yams, baked cakes covered in homemade chocolate made from *Hersey's Coco* mix, coconut frostings, and a gang of *Milnot milk* drenched sweet potato pies they ate in huge slices with a glass of eggnog for breakfast; Christmas was coming.

One second after twelve, Layla was pulled from the bunk bed to open gifts. There was a *Tippy Tumbles, Chatty Cathy* and *Christie* doll, toys, games, *Spirograph, Etch a Sketch, Monopoly,* house shoes, and pajamas. Myles had boy stuff. A train set with black metal tracks, trains, engines, caboose and scenery. An orange plastic racing strip with battery-operated cars, buckets of Army men complete with barracks, corrals, cots for wounded soldiers and barricades to set up a war scene.

The teenaged girls ripped open bags of clothes. There were a bunch of skirts to be shared; all plaid. One pleated skirt with red green and blue with a huge gold safety pin. Another black red, gold and white with two black velvet buttons on the front. Another green, blue, black and white with fringes around the bottom. There were crimson red, hunter green, navy blue, and gold turtleneck sweaters and Dickies. There were hats, tams, gloves, fluffy mittens, and long matching scarfs. Layla opened a bag to find cable knit tights in every winter warm color. She pressed them against her face to smell the newness and feel the warmth.

Honey sat on the sofa alone for the first time watching the children enjoy themselves, missing JE but not the arguments. She felt blessed to provide a good Christmas. She grabbed a garment bag from the closet. "Layla come here, lemme see how this fit, she said pulling a coat from the bag. It was a wool crimson red hooded duffle coat with red, green and blue plaid lining, front toggles with black leather loop fastenings and a red matching tam. Just like the coat in the window. Plaid was in style.

♣

Spring 1970, it was Honey's place. Friends, food fun jazz and booze. Rules relaxed, curfews lifted, secret boyfriends surfaced sitting low narrow and nervous on the living room sofa, watched closely by Honey and a bunch of giggling girls.

Coworkers flaunting postal uniforms came over Fridays after work pulling in the parking lot in a parade of cars. A gang of em piled out of a turquoise blue 1969 Pontiac Catalina, a gray and black 1968 Buick Skylark, and a 1970 powder blue Chevy Impala with a white convertible top. They marched boldly to the building carrying restaurant food. Shrimp and crackers, pork rinds with packets of hot sauce inside, sacks of hamburgers, six packs of *Budweiser* beer, brown paper bags with a purple box of *Crown Royal*, *Jack Daniels* wrapped by itself tightly inside another brown bag with chasers. *7Up* and *Coke Cola*. Decks of playing cards, and jazz albums to play and skip around in the background while they partied.

The apartment eased, laying all the way back to accommodate connoisseurs of jazz as they sat, tapped their feet, and bobbed their heads, drinks in hand, sipping with extended pinky fingers, feeling mellow as a cello listening to Lonnie Liston Smith, Charlie Parker,

Wes Montgomery, and the Jazz Crusaders' *"Way Back Home."* Talking, laughing, friendly, fun-loving, hardworking black men. Longtime friends calling one another pet names like Chap, Puppy, Sweetheart, Silk, Scratch Daddy and Feather. Playing Bid Whist all night long, partnering up, calling the trump suit. Three uptown, three downtown, three no trump. Strategizing, bluffing, making books, reneging on bids, slapping cards down hard on the table with every winning hand, while long ashes hung miraculously on tips of cigarettes till they were tapped off into the big thick orange glass ashtray in the middle of the table.

It was an artform, a language like barbeque slang sliding off the pink inner layer of the lips of big smoky blues men skillfully shouting out orders. Hats cocked and perched on heads, sightly tilted over eyes. They looked cool and commanded the space where they stood with their hands extended with 20-dollar bills in em from the back wall of the crowded corner rib joint. "Hey hey sweetheart, baby!"

For some reason the lady behind the counter could interpret every request perfectly and gave them back as good as they gave. "Let me have a half order of them tips, fries, coleslaw with mild sauce on the side. Thank you darling Thank you honey!" She'd holler back, "Ima put some extra sauce on them tips for you sugar" And bellowed. "Next!"

Men and women looked like movie stars. Ladies popping long painted fingers to Jimmy Mack. Loud, boisterous confident women that drove their own cars. Made their own money, talking to children, calling them *Chee Nee Poo*, baby names. Interested in what they had to say. Pinching cheeks with liquored breath, cigarette smelling fingers handing out crisp dollar bills for no good reason. Uninhibited they sat on the laps of their men, fed them food while they played cards, and made contorted body movements to syncopated rhythms in the background. Life was different. Layla heard a familiar tune and stopped putting rollers in her doll's hair, expecting to cry but couldn't cause it wasn't sad this time. She heard it before. It was the tune her daddy listened to when she visited and he sat in his let back chair with his cap pulled down, resting his eyes. It had no words, it was a guitar playing, Wes Montgomery's version of *"Down Here on the Ground."* Instead, she hummed, ate hamburgers, drank the *Coke Cola* chaser and put the rollers back in the pretty purple velvet bag with the gold rope.

*"Finish school, go to college; get the highest degree. Then you won't have to break yo bodies down laboring. Be over-qualified."*

    Honey graduated. The small ceremony for families with frappe and cake at their own tables gave them time to be together. She encouraged them to stay in school and announced she had a desk job helping people find work.

    When they left the ceremony, they came home to a surprise party. The smell of rib tips, fries, baked beans, and the sound of loud music met them in the breezeway of the building. And he was there to greet Honey. Her friend. The man that picked her up and dropped her off from work. The man she talked to like they were best friends. The man that was so smooth they called him Feather but she introduced him as Evans her co-worker.

    A week later, they pulled into the parking lot in a White *1965 Ford Mustang* blowing the horn; Honey had a car. Then a new living room set. Then a new kitchen set. The apartment transformed overnight making them forget they were in the projects, except for the cinder block walls where the shadow box hung with the glass figurines. And the corner wall that led to the back of the apartment where two pictures of Jesus hung hauntingly. One with HIM hanging on the cross, a crown of thorns on His head and blood streaming down. On the other picture, He stood with His foot on the world. Layla always stopped to stare at the pictures, closed her eyes and held her breath before she ran pass; every time she went to the bathroom.

    It was the summer of 1970 school was out, Honey sat behind a mountain of papers; pen in hand. Every time her lawyer nodded, she signed. The deal closed and he placed the keys to her house in her hand.

# PART TWO

# BRANCHES

# CHAPTER NINE

♣

## *Better Off*

*"I felt led to end the service with that beautiful selection, "Accept What God Allows." I'm sorry y'all but I'll say it again and again. Can't nobody sing that song like Evangelist Emma Turner sing it. And with such conviction, the song just comes up right outta her belly! You got to know something about it to sing it like that. Glory, glory glory. The song says, You're Better Off Anyhow. Uh huh. How many of us know now that we betta off without what we thought we wanted? Oh, help me Holy Ghost. I betta stop I feel my preacher waking up but God already blessed. Get up on your feet raise your hands and repeat after me. What I say unto one I say unto All. Watch as well as pray. Amen. You're dismissed."*

The service was high, the church went up when Honey and the teenagers walked down the aisle. Emma sat in the choir stand; eyes full of tears the entire time. Seeing Honey and the children fill a pew gave her shouting fits when she thought about God's goodness. The organist didn't make it no better, his fingers got loose and a praise session started; when he broke out and the church followed singing, *"When I think about Jesus."*

Everybody shouted. Musicians tried to let the song go but each time somebody let out a holler, it ramped back up again. Even the church mothers couldn't keep their cool. Mother Turner tried to stay seated but every few minutes she leaped from her seat, lifted both hands, threw her head back, her hat flew off, somebody picked it up and she sat down only to jump up and do it all over again.

Pastor Turner got happy and told em, "Don't quench the spirit, gon and praise HIM. Never mind the program, this God's church." He got to dancing and they shouted till church was over. The family received new bibles and Carl introduced them to the young members. One of the junior ministers told Angie about the young worker's class. Layla was introduced to the Sunday School teacher. Carl, Myles and the other musicians hung out in the pulpit playing instruments till the last minute.

On the way there it weighed heavy on Honey's mind. She wasn't sure she wanted to surrender, to give up her ways, and stop what she was doing. Being away made coming back hard but she knew the moment the preached word went forth and the gospel rang out she'd be convicted and give over. She remembered how Emma never let her go, kept walking with her, calling, encouraging and talking to her about the goodness of the Lord. Had her testifying about how He blessed her everyday leading up to the service. She told Honey, "Call and tell me what the Lord did for you Honey." Honey called with a testimony. Emma would say, "Chile, look at God working in yo life. Call me again when He do something else, I don't care what it is or what time it is. Call me, I wanna hear about it." She was winning her soul. Before Honey knew it, she got excited testifying about the goodness of the Lord. She remembered Emma saying how sin could make a fool outta you. It wasn't much to ask; the Lord was faithful; he brought her out the projects. Pastor Jones was clear; the separation was not for adultery so walking away from Evan was a small price to pay. A clean break that needed to be made.

JE would be the only man welcome in their new home, and since it wasn't the party spot: the friendships withered up and died. Soon as she got the keys Rufus and Emma came over to bless the house, prayed, touched and anointed every wall.

*"Lord, God break every curse every stronghold, everything ordered to come against her, the marriage and the children's lives. Lord, we cancel the assignment of the devil in the mighty name of Jesus. Lord break the backbone of the enemy that seek to destroy these precious souls. Now Lord, make provisions and we thank you in advance for providing, that there will always be a roof over their heads, clothes on their backs and food on the table, that there will be no lack because we know you God are the great provider and there is none like you. And we call upon your protection that you be that hedge around them to keep out all harm, hurt and danger. And Lord, for Honey, when nights are long and cold and loneliness gets her down in her spirit, Oh God we ask that you wrap your loving arms around her. Let her know that everything already alright. Give her comfort*

*give her peace. Let the family find happiness here. Make good memories here. Lord you are welcome here. Make this house your home. Keep it clean, keep it sacred, keep it sanctified. And Lord, at your appointed time move Honey forward in purpose and put her on point that you may have the glory in all their lives and all things concerning them. Now Lord we ask that you forgive our sins, wash us in your precious blood and deliver us that we may be found worthy of eternal life. Oh God, we love you, we place no one above you. You are the Prince of Peace, you are the Mighty Counselor, you are the Everlasting Father. You're mighty everywhere and worthy to be praised. We love you Lord and we'll be ever so careful to give you the glory, the honor and the praise. Thank you, God. Thank you, Lord, Wonderful Jesus. Amen."*

The prayer went on and on and on; it was hard to stop. Emma's prayer lingered in the air. They anointed her bed, and a calm came over Honey. She felt no loss. She watched Emma. A woman of God that spoke sang prayed and counseled in everyday conversation. She wasn't imprisoned, there was much she could do that was good and right and acceptable in the sight of God. The women at the church looked well, were prosperous, and enterprising. They were creative women of God. Spiritual was practical. It made Godly sense for Honey to make the decision, she had teenagers to raise, and it set her free to do what needed to be done.

Promises to visit and remain friends were real. Boyfriends helped them move; making sure they weren't left behind. A small convoy of two cars and a moving truck pulled outta the parking lot for the last time. Friends chased and waved at the Howard's as they looked out windows, drove down Blue Island past Marcy Newberry, Smyth school and made the right turn onto Roosevelt Road; they were on their way. Headed East to the Dan Ryan expressway past *Jew Town*, the pungent scent of sweet onions made them reminisce.

It was hard to say goodbye so full of memories. Honey noticed before they hit Interstate 90, the cars were buzzing with talk about what they were gon miss; poverty had become a close friend of the family. Up the ramp, pass *White Sox Park*, they looked out the back window and for the first time noticed the mass of skyscrapers and smog. The buildings blocked the sun. The further South they drove, the sun shined brighter, leaving the coolness of the lake sent hot breezes through the open windows.

Honey took the scenic route, exiting the expressway at 111th. The new neighborhood had to be properly introduced. She led them through the historic Pullman community where green grass and bushes made the red brick rowhomes pop like the farms in Mounds City. The decorated front porches were perfect for sitting chairs. Honey told the story of the *Pullman Porters* then slowed down at Palmer Park. The environment changed, imaginations soared, and the conversation subliminally elevated; when they saw better. Nice clean basketball courts surrounded by benches in the middle of the grass, baseball fields with fenced strike zone, tennis courts, a swimming pool, field house, playgrounds, and up the hill on the corner of State Street, White Castle.

They pulled in the parking lot to buy hamburgers. The guys were eager to get out the car to see the pretty girls working behind the counter in blue uniforms and white hats. A young man their age polished stainless-steel and shared information for employment as they waited. They returned to the cars with sacks of hamburgers, waving applications in their hands as the old neighborhood lost its grip.

They drove down State Street to 107th and West to Wentworth. Myles spotted the moving truck parked on the side of the last house on the corner. He yelled, "There it is, that's our moving truck!" As Honey pulled into the driveway to a garage that looked like a house he asked, "Ma, can I have the garage too? Where the keys at?" He pushed his friend that came along on the shoulder. "Come on Dae Dae, let's check out the garage!" Honey pressed the remote and the door lifted. "Awh man, a remote! It's going down right here!"

She was glad to see her son excited, knowing how difficult it was being the only boy in a houseful of girls. Overweight, he hid in the shadows, behind mixing bowls full of cereal, was pushed around, made fun of and disappeared into quiet spaces away from the family. This time he had a church, Cousin Carl, karate class and the space he needed to express his masculine self. JE made it a point to be present. He dropped in privately to visit Honey. Cruised the community. Even showed up at church from time to time.

A car full of screaming teenaged girls pulled up and piled out not knowing what to do first. They ran in the house to fight over bedrooms, there were three but only two to choose from. The third one was Honey's. Windows on every wall of the house bathe the rooms in warm sunlight and created a cross breeze that made sheer curtains blowy. The view from the front and the side of the house was perfect for talking to friends from windows when it was too late to be outside.

Honey stood on her front porch grateful, haunted by the danger they escaped. She never told em about the drug addict that shot up near their back door, how she almost stepped on a used needle, the used condoms on the stairs, the harassment by two guys after JE moved out, being chased by dogs delivering mail, disrespected and when she fell down a flight of stairs but afraid to miss a day's pay wrapped her foot in a plastic bag to bring down the swelling to keep on going. Nor did she tell them what it was like to work in the heat of the summer and the cold winter. The thought of being inside a controlled environment, sitting down at a desk was a blessing.

She walked down the stairs looked back at her property and up the block. Families took pride in their homes, cut grass, and trimmed bushes. Children played in their own yards, visited friends over fences. Women walked from the corner store in high heeled shoes, carried groceries, greeted one another as they passed with a head nod; like Emma she lived in a good black community.

♣

*"Don't y'all go no further than the front porch and the corner store"*

Sunday was church. They sang in the choir, repented, got happy and shouted in aisles. But Saturday was a strong contender. *The Soul Train* rode into the hearts of teenagers on television. Beautiful black teenagers dressed stylishly, brought in the latest trends, dance moves and music. Singers sang and bands played. The girls ran in the den soon as they heard the announcement and participated right through to singing the *Afro Sheen* commercials that made black children feel like African Kings and Queens.

Myles waited for the bands. He practiced at church. One Saturday he broke out in a tabletop funky drum rendition with the drumsticks Carl gave him. Myles had chops! A hidden talent. He used the table as a drum set, tapped and kept up like he was part of the band. The girls screamed not knowing he and Carl funked up church songs and had people shouting to "*Killer Joe.*" Pastor Turner gave a public rebuke and put em on a month's suspension outta the pulpit.

"Ma, come listen to Myles!" They couldn't believe it, Myles was good! He was so good; Honey gave him the money for a drum set and the use of the garage to keep him inspired and out of trouble. He formed a garage band called *Undercover Funk* because they liked mixing funk with everything, even gospel."

June came, school was out, and they were jamming. Hot summer Friday night concerts; the yard was packed. Myles and his friends dressed in their Karate Gi. The garage door opened to the driveway where people gathered as they banged out a fusion of funk, R & B and rock. Word got around. Teenagers came in droves, from other blocks, down the hill, other school band members wanted to sit in. *Soul Train* was on the block.

For years, good church boys rocked band clothes. Big fros, shades, crosses hanging on naked chests peeking from behind open long-sleeved shirts with loose dangling cuffs, tee-shirts, vests with no shirts, apple and flop hats, tight wide legged jeans and platform shoes. Gerald walking the baseline was a hit until he sported the white captain's hat start slapping the bass doing his Larry Graham thang. Feather went to work behind the *Fender Rhodes* bending and blending sounds wrapping around instruments mastering the groove. Patrick was Jimi Hendrix all by himself with his colorful clothes and scarf tied around his fro wilding out. Malcolm stood raptured in the sound of his saxophone. Myles sat in a sea of symbols, bouncing. off his seat behind the drums, slapping sticks, sprinkling occasional open high-hat variations phasing into a funky drum solo at the end of every set introducing band members. The girls were all about that Chaka Khan look. Long fros, wide legged hip huggers, tube, belly and halter tops, hot pants, long feather earrings, red lips, big smiles and platform shoes to show off pretty well-oiled legs.

Junior year Myles mastered the trumpet for the school concert. He brought the house down with "*The Flight of the Bumble Bee*" solo and the band grew. He invited guys from other bands and fused in jazz.

Carl and a few guys from church fell off but Gerald stayed.

Myles was an updated version of JE. Standing 5'10 a solid 220 pounds, sporting a large fro with Sly Stone sideburns and eyeglasses that made him look like the nice guy but he wasn't nuthin nice. Like JE he was weak for the women. He pulled girls from every venue, church, school, in the neighborhood from off the block and broke hearts.

# CHAPTER TEN

♣

## *Grow Up Layla*

*The voice on the radio asked.
"Do You Know Where Your Children Are?"*

Nope. And wasn't nobody looking. Until curfew came. Even then the fun didn't stop. Layla and her friends across the way ran off their front porches to the middle of the street and beat each other with pillows until the next car came. Growing up she found out sticks and stones break bones, words hurt but prayers were always somewhere moving in the background.

School started in September and Layla went to eighth grade. By then wasn't no such thing as staying on the front porch, going no further than the corner store or attending church on Sunday. By then everybody was grown or almost. Honey was an easy win, puberty came, but she was too busy working to notice.

Teenagers traveled in groups. Spent Saturday at the Show watching karate flicks and walked home kicking at each other. Precinct Captains handed out jobs and when Wendy managed *White Castle* everybody in the neighborhood worked. Good money was spent on Army jackets, fatigues at *Herman's*, *Chuck Taylors*, *Right On magazines*, hot glazed donuts, steak sandwiches with cheese, hoagies with oil and oregano, *Pepe's Tacos*, corn beef sandwiches, Mr. Browns sherbet, albums from *Metro Music* and skating the midnight ramble at *Rollerena, The Loop, Skate City and Markham*. Skaters protested in front of the DJ booth until they put on *"Stealing Watermelons, JB's Monorail or Play that Funky Music White Boy"* so they could gang up on the wall to gangster walk, do the crazy legs, big wheel across the floor or kick off their skates and start *Steppin* in their socks.

A group of teenagers that weren't afraid of trouble stayed in trouble. The finest ones. The guy's quiet girls dreamed about. The fast girls that enjoyed intimidating awkward boys. Rather than go in the school, they hung outside looking cool. Sitting in windows during class, *mackin* between class periods. *Steppin* in front of the building, in restaurants, sitting in beauty shops getting their hair permed, buying old wing tipped shoes and vintage clothes from resale stores, handing out *Pluggers* to basement sets and *The Dungeon* to make sure there was a crowd.

Down the block close to home without being seen from the street, good kids, not quite ready to do bad things, sat on deep steps inside the red brick walls of the Seventh Day Adventist school, "*Shakin and Bakin.*" Turning their fingers purple, mixing White Port with grape Kool Aide, sharing a 40 ounce of Ole English 8. Bad kids hustled to get five on a dime bag of weed to get eight people high. Sitting around in somebody's half-finished basement, burning huge incense sticks from the Chinese store, listening to really loud Earth Wind and Fire. Analyzing the lyrics of "*Reasons.*" Trippin on failed attempts to hit Phillip Bailey's high note. Standing face to face giving shotguns. Guys taking fire in their mouths, girls receiving not only breath but smooth streams of mind-altering smoke till eyes closed, inhaling till heads shook and minds blew. An acquired skill, the most intimate thing they could do with clothes on and dared not choke on the smoke.

Getting high, coming down to Brothers Johnsons "*Strawberry Letter 23.*" Heads bobbing in agreement. Scarfing down snacks and taking naps before parents got home. The next day, they showed up for division ready to cut again and dropped out when they were finally demoted.

Coming-of-age on the Southside of Chicago, Roseland, the *"Wild Hundreds"* mid 70's everything crystalized for Layla. Life happened and things changed. Myles and the band members sat on the front porch when they weren't playing and Layla hung around comfortably. At fourteen she thought nuthin about an older boy sitting between her knees to get their hair braided, and they came six deep like a beauty shop. Everybody knew like poppa don't take no mess, Honey didn't take none and JE cruised gangster style in the wings liable to pull up and check trouble. They sat on the front porch for hours fully engaged. Clowning. Acting a fool. Only the strong survived. Those that couldn't handle it best leave once the signifying started wasn't no way out. Jokes were embarrassingly funny, close to the truth funny. They really weren't jokes. The laughter was so loud it was ignorant. Coughing gagging ignorant.

Yo Momma jokes were the worst leaving friends in tears ready to fight. Arguments were settled with slap boxing matches or sparring in the front yard. After the indignation they kicked off shoes exposing raggedy socks. Afros moved as they ducked, dodged, bobbed and weaved. The louder the slap the bigger the insult, the Ooh's and the Awhs. It ended respectfully when someone tapped out, asked to be let out of a choke hold or up off the ground to save face. Stories were raw; they couldn't do nuthin but lean in, listen, shake their heads, and say stuff like. "Awh man! For real? You lying!"

Male energy pumped but there was always. "Be cool you fool's Babygirl is out here you dig!" Layla didn't mind, most of em played and churched together they were family. Pastor Turner was glad for the new members that followed Myles and Carl to church and their talent. The front porch and the pulpit stayed full of musicians.

After school the guys strutted down the street pass the front porch sporting the huge afro Layla made; pimping in platform shoes with their girlfriends on their arms. They offered a soulful head bob, a wink and a "What's up Babygirl?" Layla gave em back the language they taught her. "Everything's copasetic my man!" She liked older guys. They knew how to engage, referred to her as Babygirl, began and ended sentences with *Dig, dig that or you dig!* Especially the one she nicknamed Feather after Honey's old boyfriend.

Summer came. The summer of graduation. School was out. They crossed the stage. Wasn't a quiet block in Roseland. They lived outside from sunup to sundown. Piled on porches, walking down the block, courting, learning to kiss, smoking, rapping and stealing lyrics from the Commodores, *"Just to be Close to You."* Older boys practiced till they got it just right. Even though the girls knew it was a song; it was hard to resist a fine-looking brother with a strong rap. Especially if he had a head full of curly hair and rode around on a mini bike.

Grammar school kids courted in groups, crushed on the same boys on the same block at the same time. Leaving the block was reserved for high schoolers; They hadn't started high school yet. They weren't ready to leave the block but over the summer everybody grew.

Boys grew taller and had to put on deodorant, nurse peach fuzz on faces, smacked on too much *Brut* aftershave lotion, picked out unshaped afros, put creases in jeans, kept gym shoes clean, kept a pair of *Thom McAn* dress shoes for special occasions, had trouble keeping hands to themselves, and said stupid things that embarrassed girls that were trapped at the back of the line on the way to the school lunchroom at lunchtime.

Girls grew body parts. Had to wear brassieres, panty girdles, shave underarms and carry purses to be discrete during what mothers called that special time of the month that wasn't special. Girls were traumatized and walked like statues. If there was one slip up, a girl could never live it down or so she thought. That's where sophisticated big sisters came in handy, they knew the ropes and how to navigate feminine waters.

Layla thought her body was taking its time, but it wasn't, it did something different. The assumption was she worked out at the gym, she looked athletic, and her physical abilities peaked. The guys noticed, avoided her like the plague, and refused to let her braid their hair like she did something wrong. Feather was the first to blurt it out.

"Babygirl! You know you not gon be braiding our hair no more, right." It hurt her feelings. Front porch conversations paused till she left, and horsing around stopped. Looking for attention elsewhere, she dressed up to hang out at the basketball court. Walked out on the front porch and the guys stared at her hard. Feather reared all the way back with flared nostrils, inhaled deeply scrunching up his nose and examined her from head to toe with a mean look on his face. Raised one eyebrow, snatched her by the arm, and pulled her aside.

"Babygirl, you getting kinda thick. You growing up now. You can't be running up and down these streets hanging out with the guys like before. You gotta slow down. Spend time with yo big sisters they'll get you right. You understand what I'm saying Layla? And when was the last time you been to church?" Then he pushed her arm almost shoved her and yelled.

"Hey Myles, look like we gon have to tighten up some young pimple faced freshies next year man!"

Layla rose up. She never saw Feather look at her that way and didn't like it. He was angry. She fired back.

"Y'all not gon have to do nuthin. I don't want no stupid freshman!"

Feather stepped backward pointing at her with both index fingers. "See that right there? See what I'm saying Myles. Hear that mouth?" He walked down the stairs turned around and shouted.

"Hey Layla! Don't hurt nobody! Myles man, you got yo hands full big brother. I gotta split. See you Sunday and bring yo little sister to church before she mess up something!"

Layla yelled at him. "Well gone then! Aint nobody holding you! Talking about when was the last time I been to church. The only reason y'all go is to flirt with girls and show off!"

Myles grabbed her by the arm, she snatched away. "Layla what's wrong with you hollering like that. Girl you betta go in the house and calm down somewhere!" He shoved her. "Ima tell momma you were out here acting crazy."

"So! Tell tell go to hell. I don't care. Feather needs to mind his own business he not my daddy and you not either. Acting like y'all big stuff." She was hurt.

They didn't know she daydreamed about them. The guys she grew up with. She liked Myles' friends. Musicians. Guys that went to church, listened to music, and laughed but her attitude changed. She got fussy and emotional and snapped at people. Trips to the basketball court by the train tracks where the cute high school boys hung out got tired.

Ms. Cole, the tall yellow lady who lived across the street from the court in the brick bungalow watered her front lawn early in the morning. Sat on her plant-filled porch in a green metal chair on a colorful cushion, windchimes faintly tingling in the summer winds, rollers in her hair covered with a silk scarf, always looking and judging. Sometimes she laughed when they sat around the fence watching the boys. When the basketball rolled in their direction, they were anxious to pick it up and toss it back to get attention.

But the only girl caught their attention was the one who played. And she wasn't afraid to play. Wasn't worried about being cute either. She kept her hair in cornrows and played ball like a boy. She hustled, dribbled, ran, jumped and slam dunked in their faces and laughed. She didn't trip when they slapped her on the behind because she did the same thing to them. Layla walked to the court alone. She sat against the fence watching but when she thought about what Feather said all the boys started to look stupid.

The boy that used to be cute yelled. "Hey! Hey you. Shoot that ball back over here." No please, no thank you, no nuthin for the times she and her friends ran to get loose balls. Fed up Layla stood up to walk away and hollered back.

"Get it yourself!" No sooner than the words left her lips she slapped her hip hard enough to hear it, worked her wrist up in the air over her head, spun all five of her fingers, flicked her wrist around giving him the forget you hand twirl on steroids.

Ms. Cole jumped up from her chair almost knocking it over, clapped her hands and hollered loud from across the street. "There you go! That's right Babygirl don't be nobody's flunky! They not no good no way, they be out here drinking all night. You don't need to be around that. You a good church girl. Gon on back down the street you not missing nuthin, aint nuthin down here. And why you down here by yourself anyway?" She asked not really expecting an answer because Layla never spoke to her. She rolled her eyes thinking to herself. "Why you nosey? And why you talking to me lady?" But dared not say it out loud. He stared as she walked down the block.

Ms. Cole laughed and yelled. "Hah! She a pretty little black girl aint she. Guess she told you!"

The guys yelled at him. "Man, what you holding the ball for? Throw it!" He threw the ball aimlessly and kept looking.

"Layla! Her name is Layla!" Ms. Cole yelled.

"Ma'am!"

"I said her name is Layla while you standing there looking at her. She been trying to get yo attention for the longest. I guess you see her now that she done told you where to go huh!"

He repeated her name. "Layla. Thanks Ma'am! She live around here?"

"Uh huh, down the block. First house on the corner across the street."

"Thanks!" he said walking back to the court. He sat down, propped himself up against the fence. His friends yelled out, "Man you gon play or what?"

Ms. Coles reared back in her chair, flipped through her magazine and laughed to herself. She thought. "Aint that just like a man, they aint interested till you walk away."

❦

Summer was cooking with emotions and Donald Morgan had a growth spurt. Already tall he grew two more inches. Cute but unpredictable; she didn't like that about him. He kept girls swooning like Myles did. Tall, lanky, large round fro, the closest thing to a Jackson Five on the block. Bummy and raggedy but cute. Gym shoes old and dirty; he was disheveled. Layla didn't like the boys at church her age. She stopped going and played softball Sunday mornings across the street behind the church on the corner.

Angie got on her case. "What's wrong with you? Look at you Layla. Running around here like a wild banshee. Just wait till you get in high school you gon see."

"See what. They my friends, and it's our last year to be wild banshee's before we graduate."

"More reason. Momma not gon force you to go but you need to. You gon get enough out here playing ball on a Sunday. Never mind that when I come home Ima show you how to wear yo makeup. You cute so you don't need that much. Just some mascara and lip gloss close to the color of your lips. You not old enough to be wearing no color yet."

Layla thought, "She had a lot of nerve; she wasn't no better than Myles. Only reason she was at church was cause she sang in the choir and was courting one of the junior ministers." Angie stayed glammed up even when she went to the corner store. Like she was gon meet a movie star, be discovered or something. Layla hated how it took her forever to get ready to do nuthin. Angie kept criticizing.

"Think about how you want to look for high school. Momma gon give me the money to take you shopping cause you not gon embarrass me! And we not buying no stupid gym shoes and desert boots so you can just get that out yo head if it's in there. You can wear yo cornrows they look cute but they'll look better with some hoop earrings. And you gon get at least one dress and a skirt." She concluded on her way out the door for church.

She didn't notice Layla had on clear lip gloss, mascara and bought hoop earrings; they just weren't big. And she already had dresses she hadn't worn with tags still on em. Her cornrows were just done in the Egyptian queen design that framed her face and fed back into twelve long braids. The braid girl gave her baby hair and she paid extra for silver beads with her own money, Angie didn't give her no credit for doing that.

Layla kept dressing. This time, she reluctantly put on her small hoop earrings. Pulled the tee-shirt she made carefully over her head. The blue green colors and burst of white from the tie dye matched her straight-legged *Jordache* stretch jeans. She looked in the mirror at the bump in her tee shirt and how her thighs and calves pushed through the legs of her jeans. She sat down on the edge of the bed, pulled on her burgundy high-top Chuck Taylors, strapped em tight enough to stay on but loose enough for her jean leg to sit inside. Same way she did her skates.

Layla looked as fine as her sister. They weren't playing softball they were walking around the block. Something they didn't usually do on a Sunday, it felt wrong. On the way she had thoughts. "Maybe I do need to grow up and stop hanging on the block." She got closer. "Maybe I should turn around and go to church." She remembered. "This is our last summer at *V.V.* Besides, nobody made up their mind where they wanted to go. *Corliss, Julian, Carver.* We may not see each other that much." She walked up, the group was complete, and they strolled.

# CHAPTER ELEVEN

### *Enough*

*"Hey Layla, I bet you can't kick me in my private!"*

For some reason they stopped at the basketball court by Ms. Coles house, it was empty. Even the ballers had sense enough not to play basketball on a Sunday morning. They walked inside the fence, Donald Morgan turned around and started walking backwards in front of Layla, playing. Singling her out. Boys did that when they wanted to assert themselves to a particular girl. Her friends seemed surprised. She was the tomboy. Layla was surprised they were surprised. The girls egged it on. "Uh huh girl he like you." One of em teased like it was something wrong with him liking her.

She listened to the strange sound of his changing boy to man voice saying nuthin with suspicion. Then he opened his mouth and something stupid fell out. She blinked her eyes twice thinking she didn't hear him right, "What?" She asked.

"I said I bet you can't kick me in my private. I'm too fast for you." He concluded with a blank look on his face almost as if he didn't say it.

She thought he sound stupid. "Why on earth would you dare me to kick you in yo private? And why on earth would I want to kick you there? Don't you think that would be painful?" That was one reason liking older boys made sense. They wanted to rap or steal a kiss; not ask you to kick em in the private. And why was he talking about his private anyway she wondered. She couldn't believe where the thought came from let along doing it. But he wouldn't let it go. He was fixated. He jumped in her face. A boy never did that before and she didn't like it. It made her furious.

"Nawl, it wouldn't be painful cause you wouldn't be able to get a kick in. I told you I'm too quick girl."

Layla looked around at her friends, then at his buddies. They looked like wild children, like Angie said. All of em were bummy. Looking like they got out the bed and came outside without washing up. She never noticed before. Maybe never cared. They were her friends but she felt alienated.

"What's going on? Y'all acting like it's a fantastic idea."

The girl that started the uh huh he like you chant had a smug look on her face. Frowned up like she smelled something bad. She put in her two cents.

"It is a fantastic idea. If he stupid enough to ask you to kick him in his private, then kick him in his private!" She rattled off like it made perfect sense.

They weren't her friends. They didn't look or sound like her friends, not the ones she enjoyed and defended; they were estranged. She looked at the girl, it was the twilight zone. They were goofy, dirty, and the girl wasn't frowning she always looked that way. Now that they weren't friends, she could see them clearly.

The perm had eaten her hair, it was gone around the sides and the back of her head, but she still made a damaged three-inch ponytail in the top and tried to curl it. Layla caught a glimpse of his brother Willie. He had a light face full of red acne pits, a lop-sided fro, knocked knees and pigeon-toed feet. He put in his two cents.

"What's the big deal? You not gon get a kick in." He said with a high-pitched voice that cracked.

Everything happened so fast, they musta planned it. They musta talked about her like a dog behind her back before she got down the street. She could feel the jealousy. They wanted her to take the dare. She was already hormonal and ready to fight at the drop of a hat. Layla got ticked off and reasoned. "Maybe it's not so crazy, it's not like we don't do dumb stuff."

They did do stupid stuff. They beat their knuckles with click clacks. Walked to the Show together to see, *Fist of Fury, Five Fingers of Death, Enter the Dragon* and did round house kicks on each other all the way home. Took nun chuck challenges, knocked themselves in the face with wooden sticks and everybody was into *Kung Fu* fighting, it wasn't a big deal. She took the dare.

"You said you wanna test yo speed, but it's mine you wanna test. Don't get mad when I kick that thang off yo dirty body!" She said figuring she had nuthin to lose. Since he didn't like her, she didn't like him. JE told her plain and simple, "If a boy don't like you, don't you waste yo time liking him. Leave him alone!" So, she didn't waste time.

"Get mad? Girl you crazy if you think you got a chance. See what

I said she thinks she halfway tough, sparring in the yard with her brother and them old dudes. He not the only one that know karate. And he aint nuthin but a white belt. My cousin is a black belt."

"Hah! You think he a white belt cause he wears a white Gi when he's playing with his band? How dumb can you be? Big dummy, all Gi's are white. His Obi is black. Since you know so much check him out. Bring yo cousin and his black belt to spar with Myles and em."

"I'm not challenging nobody to spar, I dared you."

"You rather dare a girl? Maybe you need me to kick you in the private!" If looks could kill she woulda been dead. He had a hateful expression on his face. She made the commitment.

"Ok, but like I said, don't get mad."

"I told you it aint ever never gon never ever happen." He said in a petty tone.

They moved back to give them space. The girls boasted about her skills fueling the fire.

"She do know karate." One girl called out.

Ms. Cole was on her front porch watching. Layla had been agitated for weeks. Too much was going on with her body changing, boys, sisters, and brother. Everybody had something to say but nobody listened. Now Donald Morgan wanted to challenge her all because he was jealous of Myles. She thought the whole idea was stupid. Thought about her fresh hairdo and the money she spent on an outfit trying to look cute to walk around the block with a gang of wild children that really weren't her friends. She stooped down, tied her gym shoes, stood up and initiated the REI. He didn't have a clue how to do it correctly. He came up with a trumped-up version, frustrating her more. That's the first thing she learned. Myles wouldn't teach her nuthin till she learned to bow perfectly and it took time.

Oohs and Ah's hovered over their heads. Ms. Cole stood up from her chair and yelled from across the street.

"Don't you fight that girl!" She called her son. "Michael come out here, this boy out here trying to fight Layla!"

By the time Michael came out Donald Morgan was walking around in circles, doing stuff he saw at the movies. No technique. Fake threatening moves, posturing as if he was gon take her down.

"Don't worry momma, this not going far. Let's see what happens, I don't know what he doing, but she does. Layla is Myles little sister. Mrs. Howard's daughter." He said confidently.

"Mrs. Howard, the job lady?
"Yeah"
"She's nice. I know one thing, he bet not hurt her. If he put his hands on her you betta beat him down good Michael and I mean that!"

Her buddies faked concern. "Hey Donald, you know this for fun, right?" A girl called out with a *Blow Pop* in her mouth that made it yucky and red with her stomach peeking out from under her shrunken tee shirt.

Ms. Cole asked. "Aint that them boys over on the other block. Ms. uh, uh." She couldn't recall the name.

"You talking about Ms. Richards. Two of the boys her foster children?"

"Yeah, Ms. Richards. And them boys not no foster children those her grandsons. Her daughter done ran off and left em on her. They get social security checks and they always in some kinda trouble. Out here acting a stone fool on a Sunday morning. They gon mess around and take em from her!" She mumbled. "She aint taught em nuthin! Won't even buy em new clothes." And them girls know better, Ms. Young take good care of them, they aint got no business looking like that, they just wanna be trifling.

"Don't worry momma. I aint gon let him hurt her besides if he did, the whole family would have to move out the neighborhood."

One of his buddies yelled out. "Nawl nawl, she took the dare. Let's see what she can do!"

It was a setup, that's what she felt when she was walking down the block having second thoughts. They never walked on Sunday; they played ball. The pastor of the church said he'd rather see em playing than getting in trouble even though church was going on. He knew Pastor Turner and looked forward to talking to them about the Lord when church was over.

Layla didn't know Donald Morgan watched them in the yard sparring She wanted to call it off but knew it was too late. He didn't like her. He wanted to shame her not knowing she knew enough to protect herself, Myles and the guys made sure of it. She thought about how Angela Mao ran scared turned around and whipped three guys at a time. Good thing she had on her stretch jeans it made moving easy. She jacked em up in the thigh to get ready. If nuthin else she could break him down long enough to run home.

She thought, "He not gon mop the court up with me. I got one shot aint no tapping out. Myles said the fastest way to end a fight was to take that knee! I got to get that knocked knee. I got to incapacitate this big goofy." Layla was ready until Donald Morgan put his left foot out, leaned back on his right leg, turned his body slightly left, extended his left arm and raised his right with his fingers out. She saw the perfect opportunity to sweep him and take his knee out.

She thought, "Is he offering me his fingers and his knee? Didn't he see *The Way of the Dragon?* That's the same form that took Chuck Norris out the game! I'm not gon do it. I don't wanna cripple him. I'm just gon kick him in his private and be through with it."

Ms. Cole eased to the edge of her chair while Michael stood vigilant, ready to cut across the street at a moment's notice. She knew exactly what to do. Stay loose like they did in the front yard, like Bruce Lee. She hopped in one spot, watched him, followed him with her eyes turned slightly while he moved around. She remembered, "Bruce Lee never wasted energy; he was wasting energy. Ima watch and wait like Bruce Lee, like Myles and em. They waited for the opportunity to strike." She anticipated him.

Layla gave him the right side of her body, watched him then she struck. "E-Yh!" she kicked him once uprooting him, knocking him off his square, then she went to work with her right foot tapping his private with her brand-new burgundy Chuck Taylors three times in a row. You could hear it all the way across the street. "Thump thump thump!" The last time he leaned into her foot. She kept her leg extended pushing him off with a final thrust like a bag of garbage, made a wild animal sound and went instinctively back to form.

Everybody yelled, "Whoa!"

A boy in the group hollered, "That was a bad move!"

Ms. Cole leaped from her chair almost knocking it over, hopped around like she knew karate and yelled, "Yeah! Kick his behind Babygirl! Kick his behind Layla!"

Michael gasped and bent over like he was kicked in his private. "Awh man I felt that myself! This not gon end good. I think she hurt him. Best thing she can do now is run before he gets himself together. If he gets himself together. He's down. I heard that all the way over here!"

Ms. Cole could care less. "Well, that's what he gets, trying to fight a girl!" She hollered again. "She kicked yo behind didn't she. I bet you leave her alone now! Y'all betta gon on home fore I call the police on yawl bad behinds!" Layla didn't hear nuthin. Her adrenaline was pumping, she was angry knowing her so-called friends waited to see if Donald Morgan was gon annihilate her. But it didn't matter. They didn't know they weren't friends anymore. Her muscle memory kicked in like a reflex. Everything she learned came to her mind and her body. She kept hopping. It was all muscle memory like Myles said. Practice taught her body the next move. She was ready to execute. She waited for him to come back. She forgot about her plan to get him off her long enough to run home. She felt evil, she wanted to take his knee. Cripple him. It played out in her mind up until his body folded in half like a paper doll and all she heard was. "Run!"

She saw Donald Morgan go down in slow motion. Stood over him and yelled, "I told you I didn't want to do it! I told you!" He never answered. When he got the strength, he raised up from the ground looking like the devil coming up outta hell. It was like the *Exorcis*t, a million voices chanted in overlapping unison, "Run Layla run!"

Her track training kicked in like a starting pistol went off. "Pop!" She took off. Layla was out front, out running him, adding insult to injury. They cheered louder. "Go! Go!" They started betting. "She too fast for him I bet he not gon catch her!"

Michael took off running with em on the opposite side of the street. Struggling to keep up, angry at how Donald Morgan was trying hard to catch her. He was gon hurt him if he caught her. Layla's feet were whipping her behind, that's how she knew she was full throttle. Her foot strike was on point, she didn't feel the impact, she leaned forward and landed soft, using the mid-foot strike the coach taught them. But within seconds Donald Morgan was on her trail, running her down. The summer heat washed like waves across their faces making em sweat. Making em compete. Making em run like track stars, with a straight forward lean matching move for move. They transitioned to Hurdle Jumping. Bringing their knees up quick and extending to clear everything in their way. They ran quick and fast and powerful. Skillfully avoiding fences and cars, cutting across the street that led to Layla's front porch. It was Layla and Donald Morgan and she liked it! They both ran track.

Eyes focused squarely on the screen doorknob; she ran up on her front porch at breakneck speed. Heard Honey's music playing in the background. She was safe. Like she slid into home plate, and the umpire swung his arms and yelled. "And she's safe!"

Michael fell back panting. He stopped running. She made it home. He watched from the corner. Bent over catching his breath. Then he thought. "Don't tell me this dude gon run up on the front porch after her!" No sooner than the thought crossed his mind it happened and it was too late for Michael to stop him. Her reach for the doorknob was crossing the finish line. She slammed the right side of her body into the porch wall trying to make the sharp turn into the metal screen door. Caught a glimpse of his blown-out fro in her periphery. Moving like a Ninja, he swerved around the door. A calm quiet wind dropped down around her on all sides like a blanket, then a violent rush like a Tsunami; he released all his size 12 black and white dirty Converse gym shoe into her narrow back thrusting her inside. Layla hit the living room floor hard. "Bam!" the floor shook.

For a split-second silence ushered in a conscious moment of reckoning. She looked over her right shoulder at him from the floor. Hurt. He looked back with empty. Eyes. The screen door closed breaking their contact. "Click click!" She got up quickly. He walked down the stairs slowly and over to the estranged group that stood watching, waiting to see what was gon happen.

Michael walked up on him furious, anxious, wanting to swing on him. Stepped dead in his chest breathing hard, pumped, walking into him with his chest, pushing him back threatening him. "Hey man! I saw what you did to Layla." Donald Morgan was scared; he moved back as Michael walked into him. Then he turned away trying to avoid eye contact.

"I aint got no beef with you." He said sheepishly.

Michael smashed his finger into his temple, pushed his head so hard it made his neck jerk. "Beef with me! I'm the least of yo worries. You think you got away with something! Myles gon pay you a visit! And you betta hope JE don't come looking."

"I don't care." He said shrinking down knowing he was in trouble again.

"You will care! I outta kick yo behind myself Punk!" Michael motioned and balled his fists up like he was gon hit him. Got back in his chest and swelled up in his face. He raised his fist. "I oughta fic! On you right now! Chump! "Donald Morgan cringed, closed his eyes like he could disappear. Then Michael looked at the rest of em and asked.

"What y'all looking stupid for? Layla was the only friend y'all had and y'all wanted to see her get hurt. That's alright, y'all can forget that friendship and these dudes aint gon be around here long." He told em, putting the fear of God in em. "Rather than be grateful yo grand momma took y'all in; y'all wanna fight and stay in trouble. The State gon take y'all from her. So what! She didn't buy y'all no new clothes, at least she family, the house safe and she didn't beat y'all."

They looked scared knowing if a police report was made, there would be trouble. He wished he woulda stopped it and made her go straight home.

The needle on the stereo skipped when Layla hit the floor. Honey heard the noise and rushed in the living room. "What's going on out here!" A Pepsi in one hand and a raggedy bleach filled dishrag in the other. If there was trouble somebody was going to get slapped clean across their eyes with that towel. Layla knew it. Honey almost blinded a guy in the projects when he tried to rob Myles. Layla kept her composure.

She didn't tell. "Nuthin momma, we were racing." She talked fast to make it believable. Honey stood poised to address the matter. She kept talking. "Me and Donald Morgan were running, we couldn't stop and ran up on the front porch." Then she lied. "He said he sorry Ma."

Honey stared with suspicion before she restarted the album and left the room fussing knowing something had happened. She came back. "I bet not find out nuthin different Layla. Y'all know betta than that, come running up on my porch. If my album scratched, he gon pitch in and help you buy me a new one I know that much!"

Layla agreed quickly and didn't tell. "Ok Ma. I'm sorry. You got anything you need me to do?" She asked knowing she wasn't fit to do nuthin but go in her room breakdown and cry.

"I need you to stop all that foolishness that's what I need you to do. You getting older Layla. You don't need to be out here racing these hard-legged boys."

Relieved Honey didn't need her to do nuthin, she walked to her room pretending not to hurt, closed the door and crumbled onto the bed, wondering what was wrong with him? Why her friends betrayed her? Her back was throbbing, she undressed, put on her robe and tucked a pillow under her back; it started to contract and cramp really bad. She wished she followed her mind and went back home or church. She thought about how she was so angry she wanted to cripple him and felt guilty. She closed her eyes in pain while Al Green's

"*Simply Beautiful"* played in the background, making its way into her cellular memory. She had enough.

♣

*"And what if Mal was interested?"*
*"Then I wouldn't have nuthin to do with it."*
*"Then don't have nuthin to do with it then"*

September came again. Layla graduated, went to Corliss, tried out for track made the team and turned it down. It was too much. High school was too new. The school was too new. Kids all over Roseland came, a sea of faces she'd never seen before. She did her usual, made friends with people that had things in common. Friends that ran track, liked to *Step* and skate.

Donald Morgan went to *Corliss* too. First quarter he was constantly fighting. He got beat up bad by so many guys the counselors got involved. It was obvious Donald Morgan was provoking the fights. He was assessed, diagnosed with a behavioral problem and transferred to what they called a bad boy school. Layla remembered the emptiness in his eyes the night he kicked her in the back and was relieved she wasn't to blame. Whatever it was, made him do and say things that got him into fights; he couldn't help himself. She wanted to reach out but didn't.

The first day of school explained things. It wasn't a school; it was a fashion show. The hallway was the catwalk. Every day students dressed like models. Girls in high heeled shoes and makeup. Guys in three-piece suits. Some even sported large brim *Fedora*'s until security made em take them off. The guys were popular cause they looked good, dressed well, was in the band, and drove cars. High school was exciting but not what she expected. The population jumped from 500 to 1500 teenagers. Layla wondered if she made the right decision.

Having her own routine helped. Midnight Rambles and *Steppin* at *The Dungeon*. Wednesdays after school she practiced with her friend in the living room. The wood floors were perfect. It was the only time she put on high heels at home, it made sliding and spinning easy. Layla liked her music loud so she danced close to the stereo. Smooth was helping her with turns and taking her through a series of spins. Lost in the music they cruised from Smokey Robinson's *"Virgin Man"* into James Brown's *"Funky Soul."* They noticed Myles and his friend watching, decided to kick it up a few notches and gave them a show. When they stopped Myles walked up slapped hands with Smooth, smiled laughed and told him.

"You a bad man." Turned to Malcolm and said. "Mal, this is my little sister Layla and her *Steppin* partner Smooth. She's a freshy at Corliss. As you can see, she thinks she can *Step*." He said casually in a condescending tone. Malcolm looked at Layla while he slapped hands with Smooth.

"Yeah, dig that. Nice to meet you, Layla." He said with a serious tone of voice.

"You too." Layla replied trying not to look too long thinking he was fine. He thought she looked good too. Malcolm caught himself distracted and tried to recover.

"What's up my man! Yeah, right well Myles your sister can definitely *Step* she can do that. I'm just wondering if she got the right partner."

Not knowing why, he said something that bold, he laughed and placed his hand firmly on Smooth's shoulder before he took offense. "No disrespect my man. You know I'm joking right? It's the first time I've seen y'all up close and personal. I checked y'all out at *the Dungeon* a couple of times. Y'all look good *Steppin* together."

"Is that right!" Smooth replied with a hard stare.

"Yeah, maybe I need to take a few lessons." he added still attempting to recover from his rude comment, but it was too late, offense was already taken.

"Maybe you aint said nuthin but a word. The only thing I turn down is my collar. I teach a class at the park district every Thursday evening I got a few slots open. Ten dollars a lesson with a four-lesson minimum. Come holler at me."

"Word?"

"Wordup. Then you can practice with Layla! Look here partner. I'm not her man. I'm not in yo way so you aint got no beef with me."

Myles and Layla watched the intense exchange of crafty words. Myles broke in. "Hold up, is that testosterone I'm smelling Mal? Man, you just walked in the door; what's up with that? Got yo shoulders up. All tense." He rubbed Malcolm's shoulders laughing.

Smooth looked at Layla smiled and gave her a hug letting her know it was all good. "Layla keep practicing and use the doorknob like I told you. You gotta come out those turns a little smoother so you can be where I need you to be when I come back. I can't be looking and waiting on you. You need to be right there. Remember, one unit one movement. We got to be seamless. I got another session I'll see you later Babygirl."

He looked at Malcolm and spoke louder. "Brother I'll see you Thursday 6PM!"

"Straight up and down man!" Malcolm confirmed feeling challenged.

"Straight up and down and bring yo money, chump!"

"Yeah, I got yo chump!" he replied

No matter how much time Layla spent around the guys, Myles treated her like a child, like what happened went over her head. She knew what she was wearing and how she was looking when she walked out on the porch that day Feather got mad and left. She was tired of being ignored but didn't know it was gon break their friendship.

Smooth was used to guys like Malcolm it happened all the time. Guys that wanted to talk to Layla thought they was kicking it since they danced well together which couldn't have been further from the truth. Layla wasn't his competing partner, she was too young, she couldn't get in regular clubs. He was training her to work toward competing; how to win contests. If they saw how good Layla and Smooth *Walked* together, they woulda freaked out about their closeness. Myles looked at Mal, then Layla. He questioned him. "Mal you getting ready to do this? You trying to get up with my little sis man? Is that what you doing?"

Before he could start in on Mal, Layla stopped him dead in his tracks. She had enough. "Myles! What is yo problem? Why you gotta embarrass me in front of yo friends. Everybody always telling me to grow up. I'm growing up. When you gon grow up huh? When you gon get out my business and mind yo own? And for yo information I know guys older than you. Smooth is older than you. Guys not following me around *the Dungeon* asking me how old I am. They just wanna have a good time *Steppin* with people that know how to *Step*. Maybe create some new moves, that's it, that's all. They not trying to get up with me Myles. You act like I'm slow. What? You gon treat me like they use to treat you. Or did you forget what that felt like." She paused as if she was waiting for a response. "I thought so. And what if Mal was interested?"

"Then I wouldn't have nuthin to do with it." Myles conceded.

"Then don't have nuthin to do with it then. What you need to figure out is why you got to run through girls like the days of the week and stop worrying about me. Just because they accept yo disrespect don't mean I do. Excuse us Malcolm. I'm sorry you had to hear this, but it stops today. Myles do this to me all the time in front of his no-good friends and I'm tired of it. Real talk Malcolm, you the one that overreacted. What? Watching Smooth dance with me had you catching feelings? He's my friend. If you interested in learning how to *Step* take his class. If you interested in me don't insult my friends and come correct." Layla walked away fussing out loud. "As if he know how to treat somebody, got them silly broads fighting over him like he a rock star. He not nobody."

Myles tried to save face. "Sorry Mal, but I can't have my little sister out there like them chicks with all that mouth."

Malcolm took offense to Myles. "Say man, she not out there like that. She carries herself very well. And what's wrong with you calling yo sister a chick?"

"Man, you don't know, I had to hear yapping all my life. You live with a houseful of females then talk back to me. I aint never getting married man. Never! I aint trying to hear all that noise."

Myles and Layla fell out. When the guys came to the house, she had nuthin to say. At school when Feather tried to talk to her, she kept walking like she didn't hear him. Myles graduated high school and boot camp, she missed both ceremonies. Honey was tired of it.

"Let him live it down Layla. How long you gon stay mad? Forgive him. He's your brother, you betta keep that in mind. You gon miss him when he's gone. And how did you get so dog gone stubborn? I hope you know God aint nowhere in what you doing. Better yet you taking your behind to church Sunday, that's what you gon do. You getting beside yourself. I'm clipping yo wings."

## CHAPTER TWELVE

### *What If's*

*"I was crazy about Feather. It scared me when I saw how he turned out. What if I woulda got up with him?"*

Honey said the neighborhood was slipping. She was a hawk when it came to neighborhood decline; it was time to go. She rented the old house moved into a new one and transferred Layla. Attending the neighborhood school had perks. Leaving out at the last minute, coming home for lunch to sing Patti LaBelle songs with friends, and hosting basement sets. Layla and Mina spent sophomore year skating before Franklin and Mattie sent her to Savannah to get ready for college.

It was 1977, a new group of friends and Peter Brown's, *"Do You Wanna Get Funky with Me"* was playing at sets and skating rinks. Shoulders snapping and hands in the air in front of faces. Somehow a hop skip and a jerk got mixed in, creatin a shuffle back and forth across the dance floor like popping choo-choo trains. They were doing the coolest dance on the Southside; the *Errol Flynn* at Mendel an all-boys Catholic high school across the street from Palmer Park.

 Saturday night they walked in droves from all over Roseland dancing their way in the door. Music was heard from far away like gospel on a Sunday morning and it got down in their souls. Beats slowing down, picking up louder and stronger heightening the frenzy, compelling them to keep dancing. They danced all the way home. Sleeping bodies vibrated with beats throughout the night.*"*

College, The Northside, the *Warehouse*, where bodies *Jacked* to house music nonstop. Reggae at the *Wild Hare* had Dred heads, girls with a beer in one hand, bookbag purses on their backs, mouths blowing the whistle and hips *"Whine N Down."*

Self-expression came with the cost of an education on college campuses. Conferences brought forth seasoned black writers, poets and scholars. Black activist that intrigued young minds, took tender hands and taught them to be wordsmiths. Taught them to send out profound messages. Taught them to used their writing to provoke thoughts and compel movement. Open mike poetry sessions ignited at coffee shops bringing truth and consciousness back to the heart of black communities. Villages were rising on corners and neighborhood coffee shops.

Leaving *Churches Chicken* on the way home from a spoken word event she came across Feather. She hadn't seen him since they fell out. He was standing outside 111$^{th}$ Street currency exchange high on drugs. He had his hand out begging, sporting what remained of the beautiful fro she braided that made her proud. Her heart sank into her stomach and his head hung as he walked over to ask. "Got some spare change?" Stunned, she reached into her backpack and pulled out a dollar bill. With the same sweet voice, he responded. "Dig that. A whole dollar. Thanks Babygirl."

"Babygirl?" He said Babygirl! She thought he recognized her; she angled her head to capture his eyes wanting to see beneath the ruins. He shied away quietly almost as if he knew and wanted to hide. Refusing to engage he approached another female. Head down, he walked over to ask. "Got some spare change babygirl?"

She sat the bag of chicken and a five-dollar bill on the windowsill with his things and took off running down the street as fast as she could. Crying. Wanting to holler but didn't for fear of being looked at strange. None of the poems recited, essays written or dances interpreted captured that moment she never had. She ran and didn't stop till she got home, sat on the front porch stairs breathless. Dropped her head to her knees, and let her mind go.

She thought. "Everybody was babygirl, it never was special." Feather was stoned, he smelled awful, his light-skin turned ashy and his nails were filthy, so unlike him. She felt bad being away so long and losing touch over a stupid argument. She went to her room, grabbed her pen, notebook and wrote vehemently. Laying bare on paper every thought, feeling, impression, imagination, and misconception till the pen fell from her cramping hand. Once she finished writing, she went back to the top of the page and quickly scribbled the word, "Ancient."

*I know you*
*We met somewhere in the Ether*
*Deeply seeded in the Consciousness of God*
*Long before the foundation of the world*
*Our souls touched and agreed*

*We met in my Mother's Middle Passage*
*It was the longest part of the journey*
*In the womb of a nation dyin to live - struggling to BE*
*You and Me Were*
*Submerged in warm fluids*
*Rich with breath and blood and spirit*
*I swallowed, spat and swam*
*That's why I am!*

*I remember you, we played as children*
*Games I never knew*
*Games of time, chance, and place and being*
*Kings and Queens*
*And you won*

*Somehow you still win*
*Leaving scents of Kush*
*behind every now and then*
*reminding me*
*of my ancestry*

*You are so much bigger than my self*
*Without warning you summon me to greatness*
*When I'm lazy, you get up in righteous indignation*
*When I'm complacent, you send me to war*
*and I am dangerously skillful*

*I feel you simmering like a pot - coming to a boil*
*just beneath the carnal surface of my skin*
*then*
*like hot coals under weary feet, you quicken my broken spirit*
*making my body give in to unlearned holy dances*
*leaving me to lie down speaking in unknown tongues*

*I feel you every day of my life
When I'm unwilling, you come forth
You Mooove me
Standin there breast heaving,
breathing in the air of my confusion
inhaling the funk of my ignorance
believing in me amongst the ruins of cause and effect*

*I saw you, gathering in numbers no man could number
ready to fight for who I AM
I saw a people lookin, sounding, smelling just like me
I saw you waitin for over four hundred years, Centuries
You Are Ancient
Aren't you*

*A peculiar. People. Humble
A musical. People. Playing
saxophones and trumpets
that scream messages from the soul
artists creatin images of God. Man. And Self
depicting stories that could never ever be told*

*I heard poets reciting truths
that break burdens off backs
set captives free
made blind men see*

*I heard singing Zion songs
to the sound of beatin drums
Feet! Shouting the victory
proclaiming one day we will be free!*

*I know you having no name and taking back names
I know you, Kunta Kente
You're a beautiful people, you wore Ndiange
Strong hair, Dreds, Jah's Antennae
Braids, Two-strand twists
Bantu knots, Afros
Bald heads, Nappy heads*

*And big ole church hats on Sundays
back home in the rivers
of the Yazoo Mississippi Delta
I know you, Sanctified Church, Mother
I know you, Beat down Sacrificing, Mother
I know you, That don't know the Lord
I know you, Wayward, Woman*

*You once adored yourselves with crystals and pearls
Cowrie shells, red and gold amber
Black onyx, blue lapis and green malachite
I know you, Queen
in the heat of the day
of the struggle to BE*

*I know you, Baba
I know you, Father
I know you, Hard Working Black Man
I know you, Chief - behind prison walls*

*You wore Bubas, Kufis
Head pieces, Head wraps
Beautiful garments that covered
Beautiful beaten bodies for no reason
Strong, worn, torn bodies
Waitin in the Lord now
Somewhere in the Ether
To begin again*

*I cry for you, sister
You sometimes wore nuthin
I honor you, standing butt naked on auction blocks
Black skin beaming under the hottest sun
Being hated, desired and gazed upon
It's because of you I keep my clothes on*

*And I'll never forget you, my brother
Lookin like strange fruit
Swingin from trees*

*Pants down wearing suits
Dyin to BE*

*I appreciate Rosa's
Sittin on backs of buses
So fed up. They got up
I hear you crying in my ears
African babies
Bellies full of hunger*

*I see you, snotty nose inner-city ghetto child
lookin like you runnin wild
too big pants held tightly by growing hands
full of tryin,
one day you gon be a Man*

*Shoes flipping, flopping
runnin to possess kingdoms of torn pissey. mattresses
just playing.... King and Being*

*I know you, daughter
Mad at, momma
Chasing, old men lookin for yo father*

*I know you, Boy!
arms reaching desperately for a Daddy
who never came
never called you. Son!*

*I know you, Momma
tired of believing sittin up in church sleeping
I know you, Hearts hurting
praying to make it one more day
Crying Lord do it for me
You speak so originally*

*You speak with Ah shays and Yoteps,
Amens and Hallelujahs
Assalamu Alaikum and Wa-Alaikum-Salaam.*

*I know you, Royal people*
*made in His Image*
*You provoke me – to live*
*You never leave me - alone*
*You never - surrender – no matter what*
*You never- go away*
*You keep on coming – through*
*You never end – only begin*
*So we are born again and again*

*Meeting somewhere in the Ether*
*deeply seeded in the Consciousness of God*
*long before the foundation of the world*

*We Are Ancient*
*Aren't WE.*

❧

*"And by the way, we called all the females Babygirl so don't get too busted up over that."*

Myles gone, Mina buried in programs, Layla reached out to Carl. She never called him before then but he wasn't surprised.

"Man cuz, it took this for you to call me? That's kinda messed up."

"I know it's flaky but I needed to talk."

"It's cool. We family. You and Feather the only ones stopped coming to church."

"Yeah, I know. But my head got messed up seeing him like that. Everything came down and I had to get it off me. I start writing to get some peace about it you know?"

"Did it help?"

"It did. I never had so many feelings hit me at one time that hard. I never seen nobody I love destroy themself, you know go down like that!"

"Yeah, well I can't say I didn't see it coming. He had a lot going on from an early age what can I say? You know that girl you used to see him with?"

"I remember a few, all the girls liked him, which one?"

"The short cute one. Caramel complexion, wavy-hair."

He kept searching for descriptions. "The one that wore the pom poms on the side of her head, eyeglasses, nice body. The smart looking one."

He got impatient. "You know who I'm talking about!"

"Carl, I don't know nuthin about a nice body but yeah. I remember the eyeglasses. You talking bout the decent one, she wasn't out there like the rest of them girls."

"Yeah well, I don't know about all that, she got out there enough to have a baby when she was a sophomore. Feather's baby."

"Feather's baby? I didn't know Feather had a baby!"

"Feather was a father at seventeen, living like a grown man. Yeah. His dad's a big-time jazz saxophonist. He took him on the circuit when he was twelve thirteen years old playing clubs. He's smart as a whip can pick up any instrument overnight, can play em all. Read and write music. His mother got tired of living with the night life and divorced his father. He stayed with her but he raised himself."

"Wow!"

"He did good to graduate the way he was pulled out of school; he didn't have no childhood. He grew up on the scene with jazz greats. Then he hooked up with a few friends trying to be boys, that's how he got up with Myles."

Layla sighed. "Maybe that's what it was. The something about him I liked, maybe it was his maturity. But I had no idea how he was living, Myles never said nuthin to me."

"What you mean? He didn't have to say nuthin to you. He knew they was on the low-end playing clubs making money, and running grown women, that's why he brought them to church. For Gerald, it was always business. He grew up in church. He'd play Friday Saturday and came to church Sunday. They didn't take money from the pastor, they gave it. Yeah well, Myles told me you hung around braiding hair. And start calling Greg Feather."

"Greg?"

"Yeah, Feather's name is Gregory."

"How pathetic was I! I didn't even know his real name."

"See that's where things got twisted."

"What you mean twisted?"

"You didn't have to know his name; he was Myles's buddy; those was Myles's friends Layla, not yours. You got involved in his business. And he didn't play with em when it came to you."

"How embarrassing is that. Is it too late to be embarrassed? Carl, cuz, I was straight fantasizing. I never saw them as Myles's friends. None of em. In my mind I was part of the band, a girl that was one of the guys. Wow! I was delusional. Talk about living something down!"

"You were growing up, adolescence aint nuthin but a fantasy. In my mind I was the greatest organist that ever lived and tried to talk to girls' way outta my league. It happens you know."

"I was dealing with them like regular high school guys."

"They were, regular high school guys. Till Feather got em gigs, they made money, bought clothes, cars, then they got popular. You didn't know, it aint like you left the block. I was surprised Honey let you go *Steppin* and skating. I guess she had to let you do something huh?"

"Yeah. And I had the nerve to be mad when Feather walked away from me. He was being a friend, looking out. What if he was one of those low-down dudes?"

"Thank God for small favors right. Myles took the bullet and you wouldn't let him live it down. I heard you didn't go to none of his graduations. You let yo brother go to the Army without saying goodbye. What kinda stuff is that? I outta take yo cousin card. Anyway, since you in college out there *Jackin* yo body, reciting poetry being all philosophical and thangs. When you coming to church?"

❧

*"Aint nobody perfect Layla. You just want a man you can stay with for the long haul."*

Layla fixated on What If's. What if she hooked up with Donald Morgan? What if she hooked up with Feather? What if she moved too fast and hooked up with Malcolm? Malcolm! "What happened to him?" Now that wasn't delusional, that was real. She hoped he wasn't somewhere on drugs and called Carl back the next day.

"Hey Carl, What's up?"

"You got it Babygirl?" He laughed. "Two days in a row. Wow. Check that out!"

"Yeah. You gave me a lot to think about. I was wrong."

"Bet. But you didn't know no better. Now that you know better, do better."

"For what it's worth I love those guys. Still do. I wanna reach out to Feather. I care. Nuthin else."

"Leave that alone for right now. Believe me he do not want you to see him in his condition. Let him save face, you were trippin but to him, you were his little sister. He never got his head right after his big sister got turned out. Let him get himself together first. He will, he got a good family, they know what's going on and its not like they broke. when he bottoms out, they'll be there to pick him up.

"I'm done!"

"What's wrong?"

"That's why he looked at me like that."

"Like what?"

"Mean. He looked me up and down. I'm scared to keep talking. Aint nuthin what I thought. Nuthin. He was scared for me; he didn't want me to end up like his sister and I thought he rejected me and stopped talking to him for years."

"Man, Layla at this point I don't even know what to say. I guess you was trippin like young girls do."

"What about the other guy's Carl? How they doing?"

"Willie, Earl and Gerald? They alright. Still gigging. Last time we talked Willie was married, Earl was still hanging with Willie and Gerald gon always be in church; he not going nowhere."

"At least that's real. But it was another guy I met before we fell out. He was at the house when me and Myles got into it. I…kinda went off on him too. I guess I was going off on everybody."

"You guess! Girl, yo hormones were raging! Couldn't nobody tell you nuthin. Running around with them space cadets. Kicking dudes in the groin."

"What you know about me kicking a dude in the groin? I didn't tell nobody."

"Are you crazy? I know the whole story. Everybody was ready to deal! Y'all was at the basketball court. You betta be glad that Ms. Coles was always watching and Michael was there to tell it all. He made sure he didn't jump on you. So, it wasn't gon be no fight; that was covered. But he didn't think the boy would chase you up on the front porch. Mike called Myles; Myles called Honey. You didn't know but JE was already over there. He left out the back door and cruised that night. Got that dude off the street, put him in the Caddy and talked to him. Ole boy was talking wild, talking bout he was gon do it again. JE snatched him up, threw him out the car and showed up the next day. Told Myles and Feather to take care his lightweight before he send them project boys over there to take him out. Word went out, ole boy got jumped first week of school. They tightened him up every day till they transferred him out. That boy wasn't right in the head."

"My daddy knew?"

"What did I just say? Yeah! Good thing he stopped carrying his 45, he probably woulda popped him. What you expect Layla when you don't listen, stuff jumps off. Angie told you stop running with them kids; they grew up in the street all them boys did was fight. DCFS begged their grand momma to take em. You shoulda been inviting them to church."

"For God's sake Carl, I was in grammar school. I hope you know you making me feel two inches tall, what else don't I know?"

"That everybody had yo back while you were acting out, even the pastor across the street. He was Uncle Chuck's friend. You were running around like you was in Lala Land while the neighborhood was going down. Honey moved to get you outta there."

"And you know this?"

"All this, I'm family. You the one don't reach out unless you need something like now. You spoiled Layla. You calling wasn't no surprise to me. With Myles gone, I figured you would sooner or later. Whether you know it or not, you used to having a big brother."

"As if it's a crime. And if I'm spoiled y'all spoiled me. Everybody kept telling me grow up so I tried; like I was supposed to know how. Now that I'm grown, I find out I been living a lie."

"Oh, you thought you were orchestrating things huh."

"I thought I was growing up, learning to make decisions."

"You were, we just had yo back! You the real Babygirl and will be no matter how old you get; it is, what it is. You been protected from a whole lotta stuff. Grandma Howard prayed for you before you were born."

"And I'm thankful. Maybe that's why I aint never been scared of nuthin, they say I'm just like my daddy."

"Maybe you are but anyway, who else you mistreated Layla? Who was the other guy you were asking about?"

"Oh yeah, I almost forgot. His name is Malcolm, did you know him?"

"Aw nawl. Not my boy Mally Mal that play the saxophone?"

"Yo boy Mally Mal?"

"Yeah, I'm the one introduced him to Myles, he good people. A nice guy. Don't tell me you treated Mal bad? If you did, I know you were bugging! He so cool we call him the preacher."

"What's his story? He know my business too?"

"He don't have no story. And how would he know yo business? Didn't you say you had just met him?"

"Yeah."

"It's not like Honey let Myles bring criminals in the house Layla. He introduced them to you so they would know who you were. You wanna know yo real name?"

"Here we go. Yeah, I wanna know my real name."

"Yo real name is *Myles Little Sister*."

"You kidding right?"

"Nope!"

"You know my foundation been shook."

"I wouldn't say all that. Just don't be running up on people like you know em. So, what you wanna know about Malcolm?"

"Is he normal?"

"What kinda question is that? Is he normal? Come on now Layla. Are you normal?'

"I'm doing what you told me. I'm not running up on people. You know what I'm talking about."

"No, I don't know what you talking about."

"Is he on drugs, out there in the street. Stuff like that?"

"Why? You interested?"

"I don't know! I only met him that one time and I wasn't delusional."

"That's not what I asked you."

"I know what you asked me. How I'm supposed to know when I only seen him once."

"You know."

"Know what?"

"Stop with the games, Myles told me y'all liked each other day one. That's why you said you weren't delusional. You were just too young but I shouldn't tell you nuthin. You didn't get me no play with Mina."

"How was I supposed to do that? She moved to Savannah, she's still in college."

"You coulda called and told me she was moving. That woulda gave me a reason to go see her; I coulda saw her off. I told you I liked her. I was like Malcolm, waiting around for her to grow up."

"How was I supposed to get you some play Carl? She moved at the end of our sophomore year. You were grown and in college."

"Never mind. Give her my number. That's how you do that."

"That I can do. She probably not coming back no time soon."

"That's cool we can be phone friends, pen pals. Aint nuthin popping no way. I'm talking to somebody but who knows where that's going."

"So, you gon tell me or what?"

"About the guy you not interested in? You need to stop playing. Malcolm is a grown man. If you interested act like it."

"Dag Carl, you worse than Myles. Stop beating me I got it already!"

"Make sure you do, cause you don't get no more passes here. But it's funny you asked, Mal just moved back to Chicago. Oh, I wanna say about five months ago."

"Really?"

"Yeah yeah. He just graduated. He was down at SIU. Anyway, he got up with Gerald and em. They call themselves the Jazz Masters and play the Velvet Lounge sometime. He's not married and he's not on drugs. When I find out where he playing, I'll call you. Who knows, even though you were acting like a crazy person he might be glad to see you."

"I might be glad to see him too."

"Bet."

"Thanks. So, Carl, what you been up to?"

"I aint trying to be funny but you sound phony. So, Carl what you been up to? How fake is that, as if you interested."

"Didn't you just tell me to do better now that I know better. I'm trying. You gon let me live it down or what?"

"Only if you make it right with Myles. You were wrong cuz!"

"So now I know. I love my brother, Ima write him today. I owe him an apology. I owe everybody an apology. Ima get up with him."

"That's better!" He sighed, "So what have I been up to? Nuthin much. Going to church trying to do the right thing. Helping my uncle with his music department. I got a little girlfriend that went through some family stuff, lost both her parents in a car accident."

"Awh man Carl. That's gotta be hard."

"It's hard for both of us. Truth be told I aint that into her and I feel bad about it! I wasn't trying to get serious but when it happened it wasn't like I could quit her. We went to college and church together and she stays up under my folks."

"Yeah well, you got good folks, I'd probably do the same thing. Wow, that's complicated. Maybe talk to the pastor, you know tell him how you feel."

"My uncle? And tell him what? Our business? Nawl nawl, I aint about to do that!"

"I guess not huh."

"And you know how my peeps are. They took her under their wing, just about moved her in the house; she's always around. I can't even bring a girl home. I think she more into my parents than me."

Carl found himself drifting deep in thought and had to snap out of it. "That's all! That's enough about me. And aint you a trip telling me to talk to the pastor. I asked you when the last time you been to church and you went drop dead silent."

"Nawl, it's not like that. I just didn't think it was time to go into it."

"What's with all this nawl stuff. Everything is nawl. Wasn't time to go into what?"

"Into the church talk."

"But you had time to go into the guy talk?"

"See I knew you were gon take it like that."

"Layla. Plain and simple you need to find time for your family. It's bad when the pastor's own family don't come to church. At least think about it."

"I will. Carl?"

"Yeah?"

"Did they hurt him?"

"Hurt who?"

"Donald Morgan. Did they hurt him?"

"Oh, you went back to that. No, they didn't hurt him. He got help. At the rate he was going, it probably saved his life. You gotta be sick to tell a O.G. you gon to hurt his daughter to his face and plan on living. You know you changed the subject again right."

"No, I didn't. I'll see you Sunday!"

🍀

*"Layla, aint no perfect people. Take yo time, and see what you got."*

Talking to Carl led to more talking. Layla never talked to her family not even her parents' not about serious stuff anyway. On her way to bed, she stopped in Honey's room. Sat at the foot of the bed talked about Feather and ended with how she felt when she met Malcolm.

"Lala, I'm sorry You grew up so fast right under my nose. I don't know where my head was, I guess I was trying to provide, figured you were safe and having fun. I didn't think to talk to you about girl stuff.

I thought you were talking and learning from your sisters; that was my mistake."

"Thanks Ma. I didn't think I needed to hear that from you, but I guess I did. I talked to Carl and found out things I didn't know so don't be too hard on yourself. Even though you were busy working you had me covered. Everybody had me covered. All the time I thought I was growing up and making decisions, y'all had my back."

"I know growing up not easy. I was just glad you didn't have to grow up in the projects. We had a house, a front porch to sit on, you hung out with Myles, the guys, yo friends. And you had your own room. I gave you what I couldn't give the older girls. I probably gave you too much freedom."

"Probably? You did but I know why. You didn't wanna force us to go to church because of what daddy went through growing up. And after being stuck in the projects you wanted us to be free. Moving to Roseland was safe. You didn't have to worry about nuthin. We could walk to the corner store, the park, and hang out in the backyard right up until the neighborhood started changing but then you got me out before it went bad. I don't have no complaints. Far as I'm concerned, I had a great childhood. You didn't know we were doing bad stuff but God covered and kept us safe. It wasn't like you could protect us from everything, somethings we had to go through on our own. I can't speak for the rest of us. I don't know about the bad times like they do. Maybe it wasn't for me to know."

"I guess I didn't do too bad" Honey smiled, "Seem like you got your head on straight to me. Lala, we all got our own tears to cry, secrets and stories to tell. We just gotta tell the truth even when it hurts how else you gon know yo daddy was the finest man I ever seen."

"Awwww. Listen to you!"

"Yeah, listen to me! I'm telling you something so you can learn. I mighta missed adolescence but I'm not missing womanhood and you need to know. Woman to woman, that man could hang a military uniform like nobody's business, that's what caught me and my grand momma's eye. But better than that, JE had a way about him that commanded respect and you could tell he had good home training. Sharp from head to toe, still is. Look at him when you see him. Even in his maintenance uniform, he was clean and smelled good. That's why the women kept messing with him. He had a weakness for women. He aint never been nuthin perfect but when that man came home and saved Angie's life, he was my hero. If he didn't do another thing that was enough. I'll never forget how he put her back in my arms. And I don't think he know, cause I didn't. I didn't know he was always more than a uniform or a way to travel and see the world through his eyes. And when he spoke, he made you believe he could do anything."

Honey laughed to herself. She was getting clear about her life. "I dropped outta school, left my family and my boyfriend to be with him. I thought it was because I wanted to travel but realized later it had everything to do with who I became when I was with him. How I felt when I was with him. How we were and how we dreamed together. I felt alive and safe. I remember how scared I was thinking we were gon lose Angie; but he didn't flinch, he turned to God. Who wouldn't feel safe with a man like that? I think it's about time I told him."

Honey went deep. Layla couldn't believe her ears. Her mother was still in love after all the years of separation. Until that moment Honey wasn't nuthin more than a mother, she was finally meeting the woman.

"We all have regrets Lala, aint no perfect people. I regret a lotta things. I regret we didn't stay in church. I didn't force church on y'all. I told myself it was a decision of the heart, a personal journey but it was my duty to lead you and I didn't. Daddy Howard warned us. Told us it was our duty. I know one thing, walking with the Lord will save you a whole lot of trouble. It'll help you make right decisions for your life and the lives of your children. We prayed you would get yo life in order before you made serious moves especially about marriage. The last thing you want is to be unequally yoked."

"I've heard that all my life. What exactly does that mean. Unequally yoked?"

"Committing to someone that don't share yo beliefs and that's on many levels, not just spiritual that's why you have to take your time and like Daddy Howard say, see what you got. Don't jeopardize your future, more importantly don't jeopardize your soul. If you have to walk away from a relationship, walk away. If it gets to a proposal, make sure it's somebody you can stay with for the long haul. Don't just accept any proposal because at the end of the day, you gotta love him enough to stay And if it's something lurking in the past when it surface, just forgive it and keep right on going. Don't let the devil rob you of your life with discontentment, fussing and unforgiveness. I'm glad you got a lot of questions. Just let the Lord in your life. Keep talking that's how you learn, call yo daddy, get a man's perspective. while I'm going to sleep, I got to get up in the morning."

❦

*"You got a lot of questions Babygirl!"*

Layla called and he came. When he pulled up, she jumped in the car and gave him a big, needy hug like she didn't want to let him go. "Whoa tiger, what's all that about?" He said allowing the hug to linger. "You alright?" He asked. Wondering why she was so happy to see him. She let go and wiped the tears from her eyes.

"I'm good daddy." She saw him through a new lens. Thought about what Honey said about him saving Angie's life, how he suffered racism in the Army and the Navy. How he had to walk away from a daughter in Germany. Then she thought about how he protected her from Donald Morgan. They sat in the car and talked. When he spoke, she felt it, what Honey said, the reason she fell for him. She listened and when it was over wasn't no tears, her eyes were wide open. It was straight talk. Different from a mother and a daughter. He strengthened her. She met the man, a well-traveled black man. Like Honey, he walked away from a relationship but had to leave a child, an older sister she never met. He coulda lived a different life but wasn't willing to stay in Germany and his daughter's mother wasn't willing to come to the states. He said every time he tried to stay, he couldn't. He had to come home. Said he missed the sky.

The next time on leave his brother introduced him to a girl named Honey that dreamed of traveling the world. He said he liked how she believed in him, how he held her interest when he told her stories about faraway places. How he could take her mind away, how it felt like she was traveling with him and he fell in love.

"Don't get involved with someone else if someone's in your heart. If there's not a woman in his heart and there's not a man in yours, you free. You want a man that can hold your interest. Take yo time, see what you got. See if he's worth the long-haul. The man you talking about is older, don't fool yourself, he been through some things. Maybe got some regrets, we all do. If you love him don't let that get in the way. Hold on and deal with it together. It aint gon always be easy. It aint gon always be what you think it should. It's gon be some heartache and disappointment just know God will see you through. All marriages have challenges. You don't get the big years without trouble. Babygirl, I can see you got a lot on yo mind talking about marriage."

"I do. I'm grown and when I think about the things that was going on I didn't know about, it scares me. And like you I aint scared of nuthin, not even the devil."

JE smiled. "You just like me but I'm not gon lie, I spent most of my life scared. I grew up in a different time and suffered a lot of things. I didn't know if I was gon make it one day to the next. So, Babygirl as much as I'd like you to think I wasn't scared, I got to tell the truth. I'm a man, men don't wear feelings on their sleeves, somethings you may never know. When you talk about getting married be ready to do the work. Get to know the man so you'll know how to help him. Understand me?"

"Yeah, daddy I understand."

"Good! Now, what you have is courage. You can be afraid and still have courage, that's what you saw in me, but it didn't come from me. God the one gives us courage to do the things we're afraid to do. My momma put prayer in us, it traveled right on down to you. It's in you and you'll pass it on to your children."

"I know. I always felt it. I didn't know what it was but I felt it."

"What happened you stopped going to church Layla? Hold on, strike that, don't answer that question. Let me put it to you this way. You trust me?"

"Yeah, daddy with my life!"

JE leaned over the armrest. "If you trust me with your life, why not trust God with it, He's greater than me. He gave you to me. You wanna feel confident in the decisions you make. And feel good about what you do. That's yo ticket. And aint nuthin spooky about HIM. I remember you used to run past those pictures yo grand momma gave us. Ever since you were a little girl you were captured by those pictures of Jesus hanging on the wall. They scared you, it was only an image, but it made an impression."

"You remember that daddy?"

"Aint much I don't remember. Layla, I think the Lord may have touched you."

"Touched me?"

"Yeah. You don't have to be at church to be touched and He can touch you in a way that make you wanna come closer to HIM. You think you ready to stop being scared of God. You think you might want to get to know HIM?"

"I do. I think I ran long enough."

"I think so too. I'd be proud to lead you to the Lord through prayer. All that means is that you gon tell the Lord you sorry, that you want to do right, that you gon stop doing wrong and that you gon follow HIM You think you ready for that?"

Layla thought about it again. "Yeah daddy, I'm ready for that." She said with certainty.

"I asked you a couple of times, didn't I?"

"Yeah, you did."

"That's because it's got to be your decision and based on what you been saying, it's what you looking for. It's what you need to get rid of that fear and we not gon wait for Sunday. The devil been tried to step in and change yo mind. We gon do this right here and right now. Raise both yo hands and repeat after me.

*"Lord I thank you for dying on the cross for my sins. God I'm sorry. Forgive me. Come into my life. Make me yours and teach me your ways. Amen."*

Layla repeated the prayer and said Amen. JE shook her hand. "Congratulations. Now go to church Sunday, don't make a big deal about nuthin, it's already done. You saved. Let Pastor Turner know and he'll take care the rest."

"That's it?"

"That's it. Don't you feel better?"

"Actually, I feel the same, but I know I've been coming to this point for a while and I'm here and it feels like I'm getting it done. Like I finally made the commitment."

"That's what it is. That's what you did, made the commitment and it'll grow deeper. Layla you like music and dancing aint none of that gon change so don't be surprised if you start shouting in church."

Layla laughed. "I won't daddy."

"One more thing, this is just a touch, when you get the Holy Ghost its gon be mightier."

"The Holy Ghost? I been hearing about the Holy Ghost all my life. I'm still not sure how he works but if he's gon make me mightier, I can't wait to get it.

"Ima leave that to Pastor Turner to explain. Just know you'll have a closer relationship with God and He'll lead you in the right direction."

Layla smiled. "I like that. I need to be led in the right direction. Thank you, daddy, for listening.

"JE gave her a hug. "You think I can peek in on yo momma now?"

"Yes. And I think she might be glad to see you."

"She always is. We spend time Layla. We never stopped."

"Well excuse me Mr. Howard."

"Babygirl, she still my wife. If you think I stayed away from that woman all these years, you crazy. She couldn't get rid of me if she tried. But that wasn't none of y'all business. That was between me and my wife. Now later for us. I want you to tell her the good news. She'll be glad to hear it from you and don't let nobody make you doubt yo decision. You God's child, understand?"

"Yes, sir daddy. I understand."

# PART THREE

# LEAVES

# CHAPTER THIRTEEN

❖

*Who Are You?*

*"He could have done like my dad. He was honest with my mom day one. She never had to go through junk mess and garbage."*

Mecca sat on the windowsill cupped her head with both hands and whined. "I'm not gon be watered down and I'm not gon be minimized. Who is he? Why couldn't he just be honest. And why am I dealing with dumb stuff? Girl I'm too old for this!" She spun around from the window after peering out over the Chicago skyline; it was getting dark. She looked at Jules as if she knew what was going on in her head. Snatched her locs into what could be a ponytail before letting em bounce back down around her dark brown oval face.

She resembled Layla but had Malcolm's height and features. Exotic like Honey only darker. Wild bronze locs that turned blonde in the summer. Soft arch less eyebrows, sensually deep, almond shaped light-brown eyes, long straight lashes that gave her a stye when she was little. High cheekbones, a keen nose leading down to her small well defined pouty lips, a sharp chin and a long slender neck that sat her head high and royal.

People were intrigued, sneaking glances trying to determine her origin; where she was from. Wild and strong, no one could quite figure out what she did to look such a way. Always polished but free. Never perfect but naturally pleasant to observe. Her granddaddy's genes graced her with an athletic appeal. She inherited her dancer legs from Layla. Sculptured thighs that pushed through jeans, large calves and slender ankles. The rest of her body was quite deceptive, no one thing dominated the other. There was enough of everything. Enough breast to be busty and enough bump of a behind. Enough height to be tall and five six could be pretty intimidating in three-inch heels.

"OMG Mecca, please tell me this is not another Malcolm and Layla perfect marriage episode." Jules complained. "Mecca, Mecca!" she called trying to get her attention. She left her chair to smooth the cushion on the chaise. "Ok girl, we not doing this. What is this talk about being minimized? Did you come over here complaining about my brother? I don't appreciate you talking about him behind his back. Besides, we both know you the one trippin."

"Yeah, right, I'm the one trippin. And he's only yo brother because I married him my sista and don't forget that." Mecca teased with a roll of her neck. Jules thought they were perfect together. Mecca flopped down on the chaise Jules made smooth. The one she claimed made her feel like a client and laid back as if she were in a real session.

"Jules, I know you think I don't have nuthin to complain about, and that I'm doing too much. But I do. I'm just saying, we may need marital counselling."

"Marital counselling! Really Mecca?"

"Yes, really Jules."

"Uhm. Ok then I guess I betta get ready to listen. I invested too much money in this marriage and I'm still paying for yo wedding gift from the last one. Why you acting like this Mecca? What's wrong now?"

"That's a good question."

"It's' only been two years come on now! Y'all wrecking my professional flow!"

"I'm not wrecking nuthin, he's wrecking yo flow. Yo so-called brother act like he don't have to put forth an effort to keep this love alive. He thinks it's in the bag. Walking around like a dead man. Like he in a trance or something."

"Girl what are you talking about? A dead man in a trance? What's going on? Why you talking like that? A dead man in a trance Mecca? What is that supposed to mean? Is Jahi depressed? He not depressed, is he?"

"No. He not depressed. He not nowhere near depressed but he showing me who he is. If I believe him, he gon be depressed, because that's a deal breaker."

"What's a deal breaker? Ok, ok. Wow, that's what's up huh? The ole deal breaker. What happened to the long haul the Howard family always preaching about? What's up with that?"

"How would I know. Speaking of preaching I aint been to church in a month of Sundays. Ima backslider. He taking me for granted. He knew what this was when he came to the table."

"Mecca! For the last time what are you talking about? Let me give you what you giving me. Jahi is a dead man walking in a trance and you're a backslider. I don't know what you talking about and I'm really not trying to read between the lines. I can't, I cannot, not today."

"Did I ask you to read between the lines? In case you haven't noticed I'm frustrated am I allowed to be frustrated? I listen to you when you frustrated."

"Yeah, you allowed. And you do listen to me. Be frustrated. But wouldn't it be nice if you told me why you frustrated so we can talk about it. You know, maybe be frustrated together. Obviously, you want to talk Mecca. You didn't drive to the city for nuthin."

Jules knew Mecca needed special attention and tried to lighten up. If she were honest, she'd admit she wasn't in a good place herself, and hadn't been for weeks. Not since she got the news. She collected herself. "Ok my love, I got you girl. Come on. Give it up. Spit it out. What's going on honey bun?" That's what they called each other when they needed love and support.

"So, you know me, right?"

Jules sat up straight looked her boldly in the eyes teaming up. "Better than anybody in the whole wide world." She boasted.

"You know I'm not trifling?"

"And I know you not petty either!"

"See that's why you my girl! You understand it's a Howard thing. Check a person out and see what you got. I pulled out all the stops when we dated. I left no stone unturned getting to know him and letting him know me. This husband number two Jules I aint got no games to play, understand? This is it; I'm not doing this again."

"No. Yeah, I understand you don't get no argument from me; you definitely didn't leave a stone unturned, I thought it was overkill."

"And you thought right. It was. It was intentional overkill, I'm not where you learn. I'm not the trial-and-error station. What I can't understand is why my husband perpetrated a fraud, he knew how high this ride was going."

"You got that right. Wait a minute, did you say perpetrated a fraud? Girl don't tell me he got another wife somewhere!"

"Jules, I didn't say he was a bigamist. I said fraud. Lying about who he was and what he wanted in a relationship. He had me thinking we were on the same page, like we wanted the same things, that we were equally yoked. Apparently, we not. Equally yoked that is."

"I thought y'all was all good. You telling me he changed? How much changing could the man do?"

"You mean, how much lying could the man do!"

"Lying?"

"Lying girl! How bout he knows I don't eat meat, neither did he. All the time we spent together. Jules, we been married for two years don't forget we dated for two. That's four years I never saw the man eat meat. Nev-ver! Not only is he eating meat he sucking down pork!"

"Swine!"

"Oh, I'm not done. Slick yo edges back. Exercising together, reading in bed, socializing, going to church on Sunday. Bae Be, that's out the door!"

"Jesus take the wheel! Jahi don't exercise? That man is a gym rat."

"Yeah, right. Now he's a house pig! Gut hanging over the top of his pants. He got a man muffing Jules, a man muff--fin! What Ima do with that? Jahi aint lift a leg, cracked a book, don't want to go nowhere and aint been to church since Jesus came and left and he know how I feel about church. Momma Howard in Mounds speaking in tongues probably bout to give up the ghost! A Howard not in church. Girl, that'll get you killed in this family. And I'm not calling her to give me the spill about *Tending*. I not trying to hear that right about now. I'm *tending* to myself that's the only person I'm *tending* to. Me! I need *tending*."

"I can't hear you. I cannot. I went deaf. I can't wrap my mind around what you saying. I'm dying. I'm dead! I'm dead Mecca! Bury me before I start stinking. "

"And you think I can? And he looks at me like. What?"

"As in. What you gon do? "

"Nawl girl like a thug. As in what you gon do about it. And it aint a question. He laying in the bed looking like a dread man. Girl it's like a stranger done broke in my house and sleeping right next to me."

"Stop! Ok Mecca we got to stop. Both of us. This aint nuthin funny. I can't in good conscious be over here calling Jahi names with you. It aint ethical. How I'm supposed to look at him the next time we get together?"

"What next time? Did you hear any of what I said? We not getting together, he don't wanna do nuthin!"

"Ok, ok, ok. Gotcha. Let me run this back because I'm thoroughly confused. Is he going to work Mecca?"

"Yeah. He going to work but how hard is that when you teach music Jules. He spends time with his friends, hang out at his parent's house, buy clothes, bring in greasy bags of *Harold's Chicken* with mild sauce on the side and offers me some out of courtesy. Depressed people don't do that Boo Boo."

Wasn't nuthin Jules could say halfway listening. She had her own problems. She couldn't wrap her mind around leaving Chicago going back to Savannah to work let alone deal with everything else that was left behind. Mecca venting wasn't helping matters at all. A man was the least of her worries.

Mecca called Jahi her thinking man. A professor of music, a jazz guitarist that had outside interest, things he loved to do, things he couldn't do without, things that made him whole. He played his jazz and she read her books. Never infringing on one another's space. They spent regenerative time together on the weekend. She kept her agenda he kept his. Two-years later, the thinking man stopped thinking. Stop bringing his uniqueness, who he was to the table, the things that made her want to see him, be with him, do things with him like read books in bed and hang out at the gym. She loved hearing his views and opinions. He lost his swag and start fault finding like a old cranky man. She found herself night after night looking at the back of a sleeping dreaded head. He was thinking too much. His rational was unless issues were resolved wasn't no greetings in the morning. Then he stopped trying.

"Mecca, he trippin on something. What you do to that man? That aint Jahi. Did you sit down with him and ask him what was wrong? Don't nobody change overnight like that. He playing you girl. Somethings going on!"

"I'm not asking him nuthin. Playing me? Uh, he can. He can trip, he can play me but Ima keep doing what I do how I do it. Ima stay on my game while he trying to make a point. He telling me by example it's some new rules in the game, some he didn't run pass me. He gon do what he gon do how he wanna do it. Emphasis on he and that's fine good and great. And I'm telling him by example, I'm not going and when he finish killing himself, when his blood pressure shoots through the top of his head, when his heart turns around and attack him, sugar diabetes cancer and arthritis wreck his health, he betta have somebody to take care him cause I aint that one. This right here, this is new; we don't have forty-three years under our belt. Jahi knew what this was. He knew he had no business coming in this marriage laying down like it wasn't gon be no thang. He not nuthin but a scam artist,

I see you laughing at me Jules but that's alright too." She snipped.

Naturally Jules didn't know what Mecca knew. Mecca knew a very different Jahi. She wasn't talking about the, *that's my brother Jahi.* Not him. She was talking about the one, women had no business knowing. The one who when driving had a distinct way he peered at her from behind his sexy shades and spoke with a voice that sound low and soothing like a mellow wooden instrument. The one whose face was much too strong and powerful for her hands when she cupped it to issue controlled good-bye kisses. The one who came around to the passenger side of the truck to help her from her seat and had a way of positioning himself so she would fall into a brief intimate embrace just before he lowered her down to the pavement. The one with earthy smells. Passionate controversial points of view. The one sometimes too busy, not necessarily available to talk but got back with her later like he said he would. The one that got caught up with his buddies hooping, played ball like a high school boy, blasted music, and had an out of this world rap when he stood there talking to her and all she could focus on was the beautiful bow in his thick legs and the sweetness of his smile. The one that was insatiable with conversation, endless knowledge, on top of that look like a black prince and on occasion had absolutely no problem telling her no! Which quite frankly was a turn on from time to time because sometimes she needed to hear no! The one that took her in the mornings before work to start their day right. That one! While Jules laughed, she really did want to know what happened to her man! Where did he go? She wanted him back and was willing to fight but not at the expense of losing him.

"I'm not laughing at you"

"So why you got this silly smile on your face, you sho not crying. What you smiling for Jules, look at you. You can't even hold it in!" Mecca pulled her mirror from her handbag to show Jules her face.

"I'm not smiling Mecca and get that stupid mirror out my face and don't be getting jazzy mouthed with me, I'm thinking. And calling my brother a scam artist is too comical. What he gon be next Mecca? And you expect me to keep a straight face, listen to what you saying. You done called the man a scam artist.

"He gon be what he gon be and yes he is a scam artist."

"You too serious for me. I don't know how we came up together. When did I miss all this seriousness? Was that a social work class? Did they teach you this in school Mecca? This stuff is so funny you should laugh but you not. You too stubborn and you aint gon stop me from laughing. I need a laugh right about now and this aint even no thang. Ok, for the sake of argument. Did you think talking about yo expectations and this fully engaged stuff was gon fly forever?"

"I didn't have reason to think it wouldn't. I was upfront I was clear about the direction I was going, and he led me to believe he was on the same page."

"Girl stop! Mecca listen to me please."

"I been listening. I was listening while you were laughing."

"And I'm gon keep laughing. Somebody gotta laugh. All I know is in the beginning you and Jahi was having fun doing things you both liked. Correct me if I'm wrong, but did I hear you say, the direction…you were going? And that's a rhetorical question. I know you said it cause I heard it. That right there!"

"That right there where?"

"You taking Jahi in the direction you going. That aint never gon work. Who told you that worked? You think yo mother taking yo father in the direction she going? Girl please, that man is at home because he got peace in the valley, that's it, that's all. But since I love you so much Ima tell you what really happened. You wanna know?"

"Yeah, right and for the record truth be told he is going in the direction she taking him. Believe that Honey baby! What Lala wants Lala gets. But go ahead and tell me, tell me what happened since you know so much."

"Ima leave that alone, but do you really wanna know?"

"I know you gon leave that alone unless you wanna talk about yo momma and yo daddy. And yes Jules! I really wanna know. What kind of counsellor are you anyway? Is this how you treat yo clients? You got me batting my eyes scared you gon attack me. Who are you?"

"Who are you Mecca! You not my client Ms. Ma'am. And flipping and flopping around on my chaise not gon make you one with yo impossible self. You need to stop clowning you know you aint nowhere near scared. Ima keep it real counsellor that's who I am, that's what you need. You the one broke me down and told me to keep it real. To heal myself and stop taking crap. I listened. Now what? You back peddling? This too real for you? You want me to lie?"

Mecca was bucking her eyes like she was taking punches. She thought, "What was all that stank? Where all that come from?" That wasn't Jules usual response. They were going at it more like a fight than girl talk. Mecca sat with the remark. She focused on the impossible self comment, she didn't like it. Wondered what side of her neck it came from. It caught her off guard. Not willing to damage the friendship she let the comment go on a dismissive note.

"Yeah yeah yeah and all that, whatever else you said. Ok! So, in yo super extra professional wholistic highly experienced estimation what happened. Cause I already know. I'm not the one who need help."

Jules none the wiser. Unaware of Mecca's dismissive sarcastic response and how she was coming across to Mecca continued her insults.

"Mecca what had happened was what always happen. See you read the other book, *Act Like a Woman Think Like a Woman*. You know we don't think alike, don't you? Ima answer that. You know, you just don't wanna accept it. And you using honesty as the culprit."

"What! How I'm using honesty as the culprit?"

"I asked if you wanted me to tell you what happened so listen Lisa."

Mecca batted her eyes again. She thought. "Oh, so now I'm Lisa. I guess Ima be Karen and Felicia before it's over. Something is wrong with this chile right here; this aint Jules, I'm not even gon trip." She listened.

"It's not a question of honesty. He not a scam, con artist, and he not a dead or whatever you called him, a dread-man walking in a trance. Get yo hands up so you can catch this it's in the air coming yo way!" Jules yelled out, "He was in love!" She jumped up from her seat, laughed and motioned like she threw a football, caught the football and made a touchdown.

"Get my hands up so I can catch what? Girl what you talking about? Is that something you learned at a seminar? I'm listening like you gon tell me something and you talking bout get my hands up. I don't see yo point Jules."

"I know you don't, you don't see nuthin but what you wanna see." Mecca took a deep breath. She thought. "Oh no she not. Lord help me not go in on her. Let us get out of this conversation and this office still friends. Lord, we been together too long."

"Jahi wanted to marry you. Did you think he was gon risk losing you? Did you think he was gon let you walk out his life because he wouldn't eat Tofu or make fresh juices with you in the morning? How about this, did you think at all? Newsflash! I doubt he wanted to read

*Sula, Black Eyed Susan's* and them other books you had him reading. He did that for you! At least tell the man thanks. Please and thank you is always in order. Mecca you can't call all the shots." She emphasized, "All of em? All of em Mecca? All the shots? The Mecca I know is not so insecure that she must control everything; I don't know that Sista. She not a part of my tribe. She not even on my front row."

Mecca's eyes got big. She thought. "This girl spewing venom like a wounded serpent trying to blind me. Knowing full well, I'm the one talked her off the roof when some trifling dude, some *Weak Willie* played her for a fool. Whose side is she on? Throwing out words like insecure, being a part of a tribe and not on her front row. I'm the one who taught her game. I'm the one schooled her about front rows and tribes when she could count her friends on one hand and three out of the five didn't even know her whole name. Somethings wrong. Now she jumping me with my own words?"

Jules continued her offhanded attack while Mecca looked at her with a head full of internal dialogue going on, trying her best not to react.

"That's what I meant when I said you were thinking one way and he was thinking another. Now should he have handled things this way. No Boo. He should have been up front and took the risk. He was wrong so now he's rebelling like a spoiled child."

Mecca's facial expression was stuck in disbelief. She thought. "No she didn't just call my man a spoiled child? She don't get to do that. Don't nobody get to talk crap about my man. Help me Holy Ghost!"

Jules went on. "And I think he really wants to work out, eat right, go to church, fully engage you, all that good stuff. And I know for a fact he loves you."

Mecca thought. "Oh, now she knowing stuff for a fact. How she knowing anything when she aint been in a relationship since she was 16 years old."

Jules was on a roll. "Good benefits come in time Mecca. Trust and believe yo parents did not get there overnight. Neither did my grandparents, don't be naïve and we not gon talk about my parents we both know that's a hot bubbling bunch of who knows what. We're one, I'm with you. It'll happen, let go let God. Then you can run around here saying. Won't He will and stuff like that and mean it.

Girl go get you a testimony. For God sake Mecca, suffer through something."

Mecca was stunned. She felt like Jules threw shade, spilled tea, threw the kitchen sink at her and felt like a fool for discussing her business. Exhausted, she looked up and Jules was standing over her. The only thing she didn't have was a dagger in her hand. Mecca popped up off the chaise more than ready to go. Grabbed her *Birkin* bag, gave Jules a fake hug, threw her head back, strutted to the door, as if she didn't want to be there in the first place and couldn't get out fast enough.

Jules wouldn't quit. "Yeah, girl gon on home Jahi waiting for you. He may be playing sleep when you get there but he woke. If I was you, I'd enjoy the evening with my man instead of all this complaining."

Mecca offered a disingenuous smile and thought. "I bet you would but you not me and you aint had a man since Sophomore year in high school. And he was a boy."

"Hurry up Mecca I gotta go. My house alarm waiting for me." Putting her out.

Mecca wanted to end on a rational note. Knowing Jules was having an outta body experience, she changed the subject turned around looked at her in one last attempt to connect.

"And Ms. Lady while I'm telling you all my business and you putting me out yo office, how bout I heard you were moving to Savannah and you aint said nuthin to yo girl?" She said trying to lighten things up.

Jules dismissed her. "We'll talk, as if you don't have enough on yo plate as it is. It'll give you somewhere else to visit. Come see me with yo husband. And I'm talking about the one you have now. Anyway, how else I'm gon make money. Don't none of y'all pay. Come up here flipping and flopping around on my designer furniture."

Mecca almost got in her flesh. They were definitely gon have to have a real heart to heart later on to get beyond the funkiness but that was it! She had to say something. Mecca laughed and blew her off.

"I hear you girl, you right let me stop all this complaining and go home and enjoy the evening. You know flip flop around with my husband. Like you said he waiting on me to get in. But look here girl, make sure you text me so I'll know didn't nobody kill you on the way home and that you made it in safe. O.K. Gotta. Go. Smooches!" And she was out the door.

The dig was intentional but Jules really didn't notice. Her mind was on what she had to deal with, so it didn't matter. It was a waste of Mecca's breath. On the drive home she couldn't get it out of her mind.

None of what Jules said made sense, it was out of character, she never met that side of Jules. And since when did money become a problem. Jules's dad owns the building. She worked for him and he paid her whether she got clients or not. And if family and friends didn't hang out, she had a hissy fit and Mattie would question why you haven't been visiting. Feeling worse than when she came, she called Momma Howard and asked her to pray for her marriage and for Jules too.

"Good evening, Momma Howard, I didn't wake you. Did I..."

Night dragged and morning came and Meccas eye's popped open. She sat up in bed did a few neck rolls. It was always tense its where she carried stress. It didn't help that Jahi hadn't massaged it in weeks. He'd make her lay on her back, hang her head over the edge of the bed cup her neck in his hands, have her do chin tucks and massage away all the tension when she lifted her head.

The thought of it was relaxing, she missed it, needed it. He felt the bed move, flipped his body over in her direction still asleep with dried slob tattooed across the top of his cheek. She sneered at his face; she didn't think he look peaceful stuffing himself full of crappy food. She thought. "That's why he slobbing, eating that swine. If he weren't clowning so bad, I would have treated his scalp with the tea tree and nettle oil treatment I made. I probably woulda brushed his beard too." She noticed it was starting to look nappy.

She looked at him again, cringed like a chill ran up and back down her spine but left their bed pleased with the thought of another day. Mecca loved daytime, especially before sunrise. She grabbed her housecoat, slid her feet into her house shoes as she wrapped and tied the belt of her favorite housecoat that felt like a sweater around her body. Walking pass what she considered Jahi's lifeless body and over to her armoire she placed special items into her woven basket as if she were at the health food store shopping for products. The basket, lined with a yellow and red African print cloth she bought at African fest the same year they met. She could smell a combination of essential oils, and incense that leaked onto the cloth, creating a fragrance she loved smelling but couldn't replicate.

Mecca pulled selections for the day considering her choices wisely. The mint body scrub would be the perfect pick me up but then again Dr. Bronner's peppermint soap would make her body breathe. She giggled and covered her lips as she remembered how it once was between them. She blushed and remembered loving the fact that he had no finesse, his bumbled attempts to be romantic and join her in the shower was hilarious, it wasn't his natural approach. He got in like a friend pushed him from behind and said. "Man get in the shower with yo woman!"

He opened the shower door so wide the burst of cool air made Mecca scream. They almost argued when she rushed him to hurry up and shut the door. Oh, and the time he washed his face with her peppermint soap in an unmarked container and blinded himself. She had to help the yelling giant. Knowing he was adorably clumsy in that way made her love him more. He didn't need finesse that wasn't the attraction; he knew how to stimulate her intellectually, fully engage her senses and warm her heart. She was tired of being angry.

It was Saturday. Malcolm and Layla's anniversary Saturday. She loved Saturday morning as much as she did daytime when she didn't have plans, she could take her time and go through an entire wellness routine. She got up early to take food and other items to the cultural center before noon. Remembered how Jahi used to join her and missed stretching together, it was fun. Her whole body felt constricted. She took her basket and went into the family room to begin the routine.

Took out her Yoga mat, the one with the yellow happy faces, rolled it out on the floor and began. She stood up straight reached her left arm up, behind her head and down her back, bending her elbow covering it with her right hand, pressing down the elbow for a full stretch pushing her hand down towards the middle of her back and released. Reached her right arm up, behind her head and down her back, bending her elbow, covering it with her left hand, pressing down the elbow for a full stretch pushing her hand down into the middle of her back. She repeated that movement twice on each side. Sat down into the Lotus position, straightened her back, placed a hand on each knee, pressed her chin into her chest without rolling back into her hips stretching the thoracic area, the spine. Placed her right hand behind her back close to her spine, fist to the floor, left hand over her right knee, she turned her neck to the right looking over her right shoulder as far as she could go and repeated the movement on the left for two repetitions.

Mecca stood with a limber body to perform what she called, *Look Down Go Down.* Standing with her feet a fist width apart, she allowed the weight of her arms to take her body down, slowly, one vertebra at a time, slowly came up back up into a standing position for a sun salutation and took a deep breath. She went into the bathroom to begin her cleansing routine. Starting with her face, she applied a Bentonite Clay mask mixed with olive oil for moisture.

She sat down on her teak wood shower chair, dry brushed her body, and buffed her feet with Ginger and Clay Epson salt. She reached for her peppermint soap, suds up, stepped under the warm pulsating shower, washed away the salts and soap. Relaxed, she placed her locs under the shower head to allow the water to run down her face and through them. Then performed her breast examination, it was the last part of her routine. She took a deep breath knowing all was well outside of her regularly scheduled mammogram when the landline rang. She called out, "Jahi please get the phone."

There was no answer. She listened for movement, called out again louder in increments. "Jahi! The landline is ringing. I'm trying to finish my shower. Please answer the phone."

It had to be his mother. She was the only one that called the landline and if it wasn't for Malcolm having a pacemaker, they wouldn't have one. Still no response. Mecca snatched the towel from the rack, wrapped herself, ran out the bathroom past the bedroom door where Jahi was still sleeping; feet oily, she slipped, fell and slid across the wooden floor. By the time she crawled to the phone it had stopped ringing. She looked at the caller ID, it wasn't his mother, it was Jobari. She wondered. "Why is he calling the landline?"

Mecca sat in the floor. Trying not to get tense, she took deep breaths to calm the nerves it took an hour to unwind only to become frustrated again. She uttered a simple prayer request. "Lord, help us Jesus."

# CHAPTER FOURTEEN

### *Something In the Past*

*"Now we can't have that can we. The men in this family don't intimidate women."*

Mecca dressed and returned the call. Diamond, Jobari's forever fiancée answered the phone crying. "Good morning. Sweetie, are you crying? What's wrong Diamond?" Soon as she asked, she cried harder. Not wanting to hear anything ridiculous. She said.
"Never mind. Can you please put my son on the phone?"
Diamond stopped crying and like a bad girl licked her tongue out at Jobari, smirked, handed him the cell phone and whispered. "Yo mother wanna talk to you."
He took the phone and whispered back with a tense face nodding his head. "It's like that huh?"
She replied with a snappy, "Just like that!" and walked away. Jobari sat in his office, laid the phone on his desk, put it on speaker. "Hey Ma, what's up?" Knowing it was coming and it did. Mecca let him have it.
"What's up? You tell me what's up with Diamond calling here crying. Why am I getting this kind of call in the morning when I'm trying to relax myself and start my day? Jobari, you already know but Ima remind you. I invest a lot of money buying what I need to relax and spend a lot of time doing it. I buy soothing music, incense, yoga and breathing DVDs to relax myself. I do this about 45 minutes to an hour every day. I get up early to get it done. I'm telling you this so you can fully appreciate why I'm about to snap all the way off. So, what I need you to do is explain to me why I'm getting yo business in my ear, first thing in the morning Son!"
"Man bros, it aint nuthin. I don't even know why she did that. And she just walked off laughing, aint nuthin wrong with her Ma. Diamond be playing them games."
"Man? Bros? Son, I told you. I'm not a man and I'm not yo brother. You don't have a brother, I'm your mother. Ima really need you to

watch yo language."

"Right right right right right right right. Sorry Ma, my apologies. You know I didn't mean it like that. Dude got me messed up that's all."

"Dude? Would you be referring to Diamond? Jobari what is the problem?"

"The problem is basically I yelled at Diamond. God forgive me, I yelled."

"Ok. I got it, everything with this generation starts with basically. So basically, you yelled at her? Who are you? What did I do so wrong that got you yelling at a black woman? The mother of yo children. Jobari what have you seen me do all yo life? For God's sake, I'm a social worker, I protect women and children mostly from men. What's going on with you? You know what Jobari, never mind. I got stuff and things to do. Ima have Pops call you, it's about that time. I tell you what, when Diamond wakes up and get fed up with yo trifling behind giving her babies, dragging her along with all these fake phony proposals, wasting her time with no real intentions of marrying her, I won't have to locate a shelter, cause she got plenty of property. Since you holler at women, I'll holler back later."

Mecca released the call, hit Malcolm on speed dial and told him Jobari yelled at Diamond. "Hey dad. I'm sorry to bother you on your anniversary but that knuckle head grandson of yours act like he losing his ever-loving mind. Can you call and talk to him please? We over here trying to get over there."

"Yelling? When did you talk to him?"

"Earlier this morning. Why?"

"Aint no need to call him, he walking through the door now carrying Cherish, Diamond got CJ and they look burned up." Malcolm let out a sigh, knowing he had to deal with Jobari. "Let me get to him before he trips yo mother's radar. Oops, too late. She saw him, he's headed this way, let me get to him first."

"Thanks daddy. Give that talk about how he come from a legacy of lovers."

"Mecca, I don't need you telling me what to talk about. Work on what you got going on over there so you can celebrate another anniversary, I got this handled. Let me get to him before Lala."

Malcolm put his phone away, headed in his direction but Layla reached her arms out from across the room. Walked toward him making sure he came straight to her. Malcolm winked his eye signaling Jobari. They met halfway. She wrapped her arms around him.

"I'm so glad to see my baby. How's Lala man doing?" she kissed him on the cheek. Jobari hated walking into Layla knowing his business was out, he returned the hug.

"I'm fine Lala." He said with no confidence assuming he'd been the topic of the morning.

Layla stepped back, looked at Jobari and spoke in a cool, stern tight-lipped tone. "No, you not son. You not fine. Why you think I beelined over here. I saw you and Diamond's facial expressions when y'all walked in the door looking beat up on my anniversary day around my friends. Ima ask you again and be careful with yo answer son." She repeated herself with the same nice smile on her face. "Now how's Lala man doing?"

"Not good Lala." He admitted.

Not knowing she didn't know what happened. She asked why in a sweet tone of voice. "And why is that baby?"

Jobari hated to repeat it. It seemed like he'd been saying it all day like a criminal pleading guilty. "I messed around and yelled at Diamond this morning."

Layla grabbed her neck, stumbled backward as if she were falling down to her death. "Oh!" She blurted out in a disgusted tone making a face like she saw something bad. Then she leaned in and looked at him with *eyes like he was crazy*. She repeated what he said as a question. Making him say it again. "You yelled at Diamond this morning?"

He said another shameful, "Yes Ma'am."

She stood back and sized him up. Looked him up and down. composed herself and said in her sophisticated voice that sound British, somewhat scholarly. "Awh, I see. Now we can't have that can we?" Using hand movements suggesting they were not on the same level nor engaged in a good conversation. Malcolm watched knowing what he was going through and almost laughed.

"My dear child, the men in this family don't intimidate women. Your granddaddy never raised his voice to me." She emphasized her comment ushering out a firm, quiet, tight-lipped. "Nev--ver! Then she modulated her voice. "Let me go back over there." She turned around and pointed her pretty fingernail showing him where they were as if he didn't know. "And check on Diamond and the children."

Layla shifted her focus to Malcolm and asked sweetly. "Mal would you talk to yo grandson… please? I don't know who he is, and I don't think he knows either." Then she rolled her eyes at him. Layla's response and expressions made Jobari feel awful. He got desperate.

"Lala, but you didn't hear my side of the story." He pleaded. She ignored him and directed her response to Malcolm politely. "Mal sweetheart, when you talk to yo grandson would you please explain to him that he don't have a side of the story. Not to tell me, he don't."

He knew Jobari didn't have a chance; he couldn't take the heat. Malcolm wrapped his arms around Layla, strolled away and started rapping to her.

"Babygirl, now you know you looking too dog gone fine to be letting this mess up yo day. I got this handled momma. You go enjoy Diamond and yo grandbabies; they need you. Look here, gon on over there and teach Diamond how to handle herself like a real grown woman. You know, put on that poker face, keep her composure, her dignity. She don't need to be coming out here in the public putting all her business in the street like that; making all them faces, carrying on and thangs." Then he laughed. "You know you something else, don't you? You too much for em baby."

Layla laughed at herself. "I betta be too much. You know if wasn't nobody around I woulda took this red bottom shoe off my foot and bashed and knocked him all upside his head so hard he'd seen stars. I'll beat him down in the floor like a fool in the street, I don't care how old or how big he is." Catching herself, she calmed down, kissed Malcolm and walked away mumbling "No grandson of mine and on my anniversary too. Ima get him. Ima get him good."

Malcolm went back over to Jobari laughing. "Ooh Wee! Boy had I known yelling at your woman woulda got Lala to stop fussing at me, I'd yelled at her myself."

"Pops!"

"Pops nuthin man. Oh, you gon learn today messing with these women. She been on my case all week drudging up old stuff. Never mind that. It's simple. Don't raise yo voice and don't talk sharp to women; you lose every time. A real man don't want his woman scared of him. How you gon sleep in the bed with a woman that's afraid of you. And it don't matter why you yelled. Don't do it again! You got that!"

"Got it Pops."

"That's all. Good. Now let's move on!

Not feeling heard he asked. "Pops can I say something to you?"

"Yeah, you can say what you wanna say but it aint gon change nuthin. I done already told you Jobari."

Malcolm was ticked off with Jobari disrespecting the family. Shacking, having babies outta wedlock. One was enough but he went and got another one. Everybody was so busy coo cooing the babies and being impressed with their accomplishments didn't nobody say nuthin and he went unchecked. This was an opportunity to get it off his chest. Jobari was relieved thinking he was gon be heard. He led in boldly with an unjustified complaint.

"Pops, I was tired of Diamond accusing me of cheating. Ever since we had Cherish, she come to bed. If she come to bed any kinda way. I wasn't complaining till I got tired of seeing her like that, when I said something, she hauled off and slapped me. Before I knew it, I yelled. I told her not to put her hands on me again, I don't play that Pops. That'll make me walk out the door, I don't care how many kids we have. She was wrong but I apologized. I wasn't raised that way."

Malcolm tried to digest what he heard but Jobari sound like a fool. The first thing came out his mouth was. "She was wrong? Dig that!" Then he calmed down and expressed his concern. "Watch that knee jerk reaction son you coulda hit her."

Jobari kept pushing. "Nawl nawl. I already know Pops and she do too. That aint never gon happen that's why she can't be putting her hands on me either. We not doing none of that!"

"I'm glad to hear it. I mean you talking about you weren't raised that way. Exactly how were you raised? It's hard to hear my grandson talk to me about how the mother of his children looks when she comes to bed. Man, that's disrespectful. You should be ashamed to even open yo mouth to me with that kind of talk. Son, you not my equal. You aint paid the cost. You stealing. What you on man? What you smoking? Jobari, you blowing my mind. Son, you sound like a street thug. Where you coming from with this? Y'all aint married! You talking to me like you got rights! Talking about how she come to bed. Neither one of you got rights! You living fowl son. Aint no honor in what you doing. So, what we talking about here? You aint got no business with her in your bed for that matter. Not married you don't,

I don't care how many children you have, you still not married! You weren't raised like that either. What you doing? Picking and choosing values you gon stand by? Get yourself together!"

Jobari was learning his grandparents. And they weren't no joke. They never came for him like that before.

"Nawl Pops. I'm not picking and choosing. But when she put her hands on me, ran called momma and laughed like it was funny it made me think about pumping my brakes on signing up for the long haul. Whenever I think about getting married; here we go with the shenanigans."

Malcolm heard it loud and clear. Jobari was scared to commit. Any excuse would do. He pushed him further. Challenged him. "Don't you think it's too late for pumping brakes Jobari. Whether you realize it or not you already in for the long haul. You got two children, seem like to me you playing some games of yo own. She didn't have the option of not pushing yo babies out when you did something silly. It was game on when you got her pregnant. Twice. Deal with that and talk back to me black man!"

Jobari was caught trying to find a reason not to get married when there was no reason. His insecurities showed up instead. "I know you right Pops. I was frustrated. You should see how she walks out the door looking like *WOW BAM POW*. Like a celebrity. She goes out, do big business but when she gets home, all bets off. The public getting more than we getting. It's like home don't matter."

Malcolm knew there was something Jobari wasn't willing to admit and brought his comment back to him. "What you mean home don't matter?"

"I mean like home don't matter. She busy with everything else."

It dawned on Malcolm. They were having the father and son talk he hoped to have with his own son till Layla shut down on him. She told him she wasn't having no more babies after that night he got caught up. He knew the feeling. Jobari was feeling insecure.

"Jobari, Ima take a shot and tell you what it is. I know. I been down that road, I took that trip man you don't want that smoke. The problem is. You feel like you don't matter. Not the house, not the children. Forget all that public getting more than we getting. Man, that aint nuthin but trash talk. You trippin, it's you Jobari."

"Nawl Pops that aint it."

"Yeah, it is Jobari. Wanna know how I know?"

"It's not but yeah. How you know."

"Aint nuthin new under the sun man. Same game new players, I felt like that before. I told you I been on that road trip. Ima tell you this much, you can only string a woman along for so long or take her through so much before she starts looking at you different. It's not the best analogy but kick a dog long enough and he'll bite you. Corner a cat and you gon get scratched up bad. We men. We make mistakes we not perfect we feel like the next person feel. We hurt and we cry. That's why you don't drag things out too long. Listen to an old man. Get married while the woman still crazy about you. She already knows you not perfect, you the one don't know; walking around here looking for perfection. Now, you told me yo side of the story can I talk to you about the woman' side?" Malcolm asked not wanting Jobari to mess up his life.

"The woman's side? I don't know what you know about it but sure Pops. I guess it can't hurt nuthin."

"Jobari, if Ima take time out my day to talk to you, you betta wanna hear it. I got 15 more minutes then I'm done. I gotta an anniversary to celebrate, one I earned with blood sweat and tears son. You aint cried yet. That's yo problem. But you gon cry like Lenny Williams if you don't listen. Come over here and let me holler at you for a minute young blood."

Malcolm took Jobari to a table off in the corner to talk privately. "Jobari my man. Do you think I don't know nuthin about intimacy?"

"I wouldn't put it that way but I don't want no mental picture either. I don't need no private thoughts crossing my mind you feel me? Obviously, you and Lala had y'all differences back in a day but still loved each other. Like GGMa Honey and Big Pops. Nobody said nuthin but we knew she wouldn't talk to you for years. You were like a stranger in the house, I knew that and I was a shortie."

"Well then, you should know shortie's pick up on stuff. That's why you don't raise your voice at yo woman in the house or anywhere else for that matter. Your job is to protect."

"Yeah, Pops but what was that about? I heard she moved out the bedroom. All kinda stuff. What you do to get her that mad?"

"Contrary to what you heard it wasn't years o.k. and it aint none of yo business how we slept, son. I'm trying to help you out but you not digging that far into my business."

Malcolm recovered from his embarrassment and began the story awkwardly. He started in the middle. "Back in a day I was pretty fly. That's what we called guys that had girls running em down. You know. Interested."

Jobari interrupted. "Oh, you were the stuff, huh Pops? You had the shorties waiting in line!"

"Dig. If that's what y'all call it now? Yeah, but I didn't say I had em waiting in line Jobari. Don't embellish my story, just listen."

He tried again. "As I was saying, I was an up-and-coming musician. I came home from college formed a group with some cats from high school, we called ourselves the Jazz Masters. We had mad skills and were booking gigs hand over fist."

Jobari interjected, "Y'all musta been some bad boys, huh."

"We were Jobari. We were some bad boys." Malcolm conceded using Jobari's expression.

"One day we played the *Velvet Lounge*. She strolled in, sat down, and stayed till the last set. I thought she was attractive and she musta saw something in me too because we kept eye contact all night. The set ended and people came up to tell us how much they enjoyed the music. Everybody was standing around chit chatting it up. Finally, she walked up grabbed my hand and started *Steppin* with me. She didn't say nuthin just spinning around using me like a doorknob and I'm thinking oh wow, check it out; this Myles little sister. I hadn't seen her since she was a cute little freshy, now here she was a fine grown woman. When she finished dancing, I said you're Myles little sister and we laughed. I asked her how she found me, she said Carl told her I was gigging there and she came because she owed me an apology."

Apology? Apology for what?"

"Man, that's another story. We had a brief encounter when I played with yo Uncle Myles band. He brought me in the house and she was *Steppin* with this cat. Myles and I watched, waiting for them to finish; seem like they were dancing for hours; I figured they were performing for us. What freaked me out is I had seen her *Steppin* at this spot we called *the Dungeon*, she was younger than me. I just turned 18, Myles age and she was 15. I couldn't say nuthin. All I could do was dig her from a safe distance. On top of that, a buddy of mine asked me to help him setup for track tryouts and there she was again, trying out for the track team. Man, she was moving, the girl could run!

"Check that out Lala could run! She looks like she can run." Jobari added. Malcolm noticed he was gon have something to say while he listened. He adjusted how he told the story to include him like they were having a conversation to keep flowing so he could make his point teach a lesson and be done.

"Yeah well, fast forward, imagine me in their living room and Myles introducing her as his little sister."

"Like what are the chances right? You seeing and checking her out all over the place. Turns out she's yo friend sister and you land at her house! It don't get no betta than that!"

"You would think. Here I am feeling like I already know her. Unbeknownst to me, I'm Jonesin."

"Jonesin?"

"I had a Jones for her. I desired her ok."

"Check that out Pops. You wanted Lala." He said laughing.

"Anyway, I got agitated watching this cat older than me dance with her up close. He had his hand around her waist, touching her hips to turn her; it was making me crazy. I didn't want his hands on her. I mis-stepped, got outta line, made a stupid comment and before I knew anything she and yo uncle Myles was going at it hard. When she finished lighting into him, she threw me a few choice words insulted my manhood and that was the last time I saw her till she showed up at the lounge. A full-grown woman!"

"Whoa! Like Momma Howard say, look at God! Pops, that wasn't no coincidence."

"No, it wasn't. We sat down and talked. She told me in no uncertain terms she was a Christian woman, she didn't want no foolishness, she wasn't coming back and she was gon take me out the nightclubs, make me an honest man and she did. We hooked up, dated, got married her first year of college and had Mecca. She was into her dancing, performed with a danced company at the college. By the time yo momma was in third grade staying out playing clubs was a strain on our relationship. I was tired of the smoke in my clothes, my hair and the late hours. I was living like a vampire. Sleeping in the day and working at night. She got tired of the flirting women, put me in touch with the college music department, I got hired and came off the circuit."

"Hey Pops, maybe that's where I get it from?"

"Get what from?"

"My passion, my jealousy!"

"Jobari where you coming from with this passion jealousy stuff man? You mighta got that from yo daddy cause you didn't get that from me."

"My dad is a different kinda dude. Passion and jealousy not nowhere in his DNA you can believe that. I got that from you! Now I know where it came from, you! That's what it was Pops, you were feeling a way towards Lala. You called it Jonesin. That's what it was and aint nuthin changed, that's what it is. Don't hide what's in the gene pool, you don't know for a long time I thought it was something wrong with me. I'm like that when it comes to Diamond married or not, she knows it's on and poppin, anybody roll up on her; I'm going ham! I got something for em. I guess you uncomfortable with yo feelings but that's alright that's cool. I see you O G.!"

"O G.?"

"Yeah, back in a day you were a gangster. Now you an old gangster."

"Ok Bari if you say so. Long story short I got myself in trouble. The cats called, said they had a gig and invited me to sit in. I'm talking four five years later. By then I'd been a homebody, working, going to church. I messed around and started daydreaming about what could have been with my music. We didn't do like you young bloods. We didn't get a chance to live on our own, we went from our parents' house to our own house with wives unless we went into the service, college or something like that. But anyway, I was having thoughts. All kinda stuff was going through my head. Man, my mind was playing tricks on me."

Jobari laughed. "You were trippin Pops?"

"Yeah, that's exactly what I was doing. Trippin. That's how you know you getting old, you fantasize about the younger days like they were great when they weren't. You'll see."

"I don't know about that Pops I pretty much do what I do already."

"And that's why you in trouble now. You wanna hear this or not?"

"Yeah, Pops I wanna hear it. I'm sitting here learning about myself listening to you. I'm thinking you were kinda wild."

"I'm telling you so you don't have to think about nuthin. Just try not to interrupt so much so we can be through with this."

"Ok I'm all ears. I appreciate you Pops."

"I'm glad you appreciate me sticking my neck out telling you my business. So, I remembered how the sisters rushed up to meet us after a gig was over. Wasn't none of em marriage material I already had the pick of the litter with Layla that's why I went head on and tied the knot. Not thinking right, I decided not to mention it to her. I came up with a flat-out lie to leave out that night. Fall was coming, it was getting cool outside. To show how backwards I was, I put on my black wool church suit and tried to make it look slick with a old red shirt with huge lapels. In other words, I was outta style. That right there shoulda told me something…right? The cool thing about it was, Lala wasn't even fazed. I swear that woman got a built-in radar. She walked me to the door told me how fine I looked, kissed me good-bye, got a whiff of my cologne, told me I smelled good, that she didn't want me to leave. Gave me that smile I like and told me don't get in no trouble, but she always stroked my ego. She always let me know I was the man; that I was the one. But like they say, hindsight is 20 20. If I knew then what I know now I would've turned around went on back in the house watched TV and took my old behind to bed. One wrong move can change yo life forever. And I had a mind not to go but man when that ego starts hounding you, it aint no joke. I went out there with the intention of being chosen by other women, trying to see if I still had it. Whatever the "it" was. When I got there, Willie Earl and Gerald was setting up for the show."

# CHAPTER FIFTEEN

### ♣
### *The Velvet Lounge*

*"Showing me pictures of that broad. Gon on back to her smelling like my perfume. I oughta run you over; you old fool."*

"Well look at here look at here, ole Malley Mal Baby boy! you look better than ever aint aged a bit did he Willie?" Earl said teasing.

"Not a bit. Every day lovin keep you young and spry. By the way how's that wife of yours doing with those pretty legs. Yeah, it took me a long time to get over that woman taking you from the Jazz Masters. We were at our peak baby boy. But if I don't know nuthin else can't no hard leg compete with a pretty woman and Layla is one pretty woman." He said with a no- good smile on his face that rubbed Malcolm the wrong way.

He cocked his head to the side, squinted his left eye like he was trying to get a bead on him, held his chin and chuckled with offense. "Yeah, uh huh. Enough of that, you know that was made in heaven. I shut that door and it aint been opened since. So, you can cool it talking all that smack my friend." They laughed. Willie was out of line. Malcolm hadn't been around and figured they didn't know no better. Didn't know they were inappropriate with the loose talk and eased up on em.

"Mal! What's yo pleasure buddy, what you drinking?" Willie asked.

He had to think about it. "What am I drinking? Man, I aint had nuthin to drink since I left the band. Except for an occasional red wine with the wife. Give me a cranberry juice with a slice of lemon please."

Malcolm noticed how old the guys looked. They sound the same but look worn down. Gerald was the closest thing to normal. He felt sorry for them.

"You kidding right? Cranberry and lemon? "He questioned disappointed with his selection.

"Willie man. I'm pretty sure I didn't stutter. I said, cranberry and lemon. You got a problem with that?" Malcolm was defensive and shifted the attention from himself knowing being there was a mistake. They didn't jive anymore. They lived different lives. He tried to strike up a conversation. "How the road been treating you cats? How yo wife doing Willie?"

"Man, that broad was gone no sooner than she came." He complained with a deep drag in his voice. "Come telling me she couldn't take me traveling and that it was either her or the music so guess who won?" He bragged laughing until it turned into a chronic cough. It had a nasty gurgling sound like emphysema. Malcolm reared back like he was contagious.

"Whoa, you alright? That cough don't sound too good. Can I get you something, maybe some water?"

Willie fanned Malcolm away lifting his hand like he was shooin away a fly as if he was getting on his nerve. "Man get off me! Nawl man! I don't need you to get me nuthin. I tell you what you can do, you can pass me my drink. I'll be alright. I don't need you checking on me like I can't handle myself. There he goes, good ole Mal. The preacher. Mr. Nice Guy. Baby Boy you aint changed a lick. You used to have the ladies all over you after the show. Remember that? "

"Yeah, I remember."

"Boy you had the pick of the litter. You know Bertha still ask about you when we see her from time to time. You remember Bertha, don't you?"

"Yeah, I remember Bertha. How she doing? "

"Good as can be expected, got some wear and tear on her. Treads worn down but you look close enough you'll see her. It's a trick in it if she not here tonight, she come to most of our gigs. Even sing a song or two. Her voice not like it used to be since she been smoking but she can handle a small crowd on a slow night that's been drinking. The music is good enough they don't care they just wanna hear somebody singing."

"Is that so? It'll be nice to see ole Bertha."

Ole Bertha nuthin. Bertha was trouble waiting to happen. She had a thing for Malcolm. Six two, still weighing a good 220 pounds, rich dark smooth chocolate. Women found reasons to say something to him. Bertha was different, sort of strange, a cloaker, had no problem hiding in the background to wait her turn. She had a problem like a fatal attraction. When Malcolm left and got married, she OD'd trying to kill herself; he never found out.

Earl shouted. "Waitress! Bring this cat a cranberry and lemon, he's a part of the band tonight."

"Sure thing. He bout the only part of the band catching my eye." She politely mentioned as she sashayed over to Malcolm smelling like stale beer and ashes with a big wig perched up high on her head like a wild bird. She leaned over to take his order so he could see down in her cleavage. "Hey baby don't pay these old fools no mind. If you need anything and I do mean anything, just look across the room and Sugar gon be looking right back at you." She said it again like he didn't hear the first time making sure he caught her name. "That's what they call me Sugar, cause I'm sweet."

If he wasn't so dark, he woulda turned red. Ashamed, Malcolm tried to recover with a proper response never heard in a bar, sounding ridiculous he replied. "Thanks Madam Sugar."

The waitress frowned at him and walked away confused. Aint nobody ever called her madam. She wondered if it was an insult. The only time she heard the word madam was in a brothel. But that was in another life. She wondered if he visited and remembered her.

He felt stupid being there and planned to cut out soon as the first set was over. He walked over to tell Willie but he started warming up on the piano playing "*Stella by Starlight*." Earl joined in on the drums and Gerald on the bass. A young lady came to the microphone to sing. Mal put his saxophone to his lips and played hoping to get lost in the music like he used to do. He complimented her when they finished, positioned himself in front of the piano and tried to sound hip. "Look here Willie when this first set is over, Ima split. It's getting late, Layla won't go to sleep without me. You know how that is."

"Awh, aint that sweet. Nawl, I can't say I know how that is." Willie teased. "It's getting late! Since when did a set start on time? We waiting on the crowd, they don't get here for another hour." Willie was perturbed. "Wait a minute negro. Hold up. Man, what you come out here for anyway? What you doing out here in the streets in the first place? Look at you all uptight in that crazy red shirt, man you making me hot." Then he got outta pocket. "Well, I guess I can't blame you. If I had Layla at home, you wouldn't never see me. "

They ganged up on him. Earl chimed in. "Man, you too old to be running home. Sleep without you nuthin. Sound like that girl got you hen pecked. That woman running you. Be a man. Stay till the last set!"

Malcolm got mad. "Hey slick! I done told y'all what the deal was.

After this set I'm outta here. That's it that's all. Can you dig that!"

Willie trying to correct himself got ignorant. "Alright man. We can dig it. You aint got to get all swoll up in the chest. Everybody knows a man gotta do what a man gotta do. We glad you came out. The bet was you weren't coming at all. Seeing how you a church man now, coming in here with that old fashioned church suit. Hey let me ask you this. If yo pastor see you in here, he gon kick you off the deacon board like he did Gerald?" The laughter and insults were too much; signifying like they did on the front porch. He knew he had no business there. And it wasn't what he remembered; he was thankful Layla took him away from that lifestyle. The set ended. He got up, hurrying, he headed for the door without his saxophone.

"Look here cats Ima split."

"Willie yelled. "Don't be no stranger. Hey man! Hey man!" Willie tried to get his attention to tell him he was leaving his saxophone. Malcolm didn't hear him. Gerald hollered back.

"Don't worry about it man I'll take it to him. Leave him alone man. He's gone, he aint never coming back in here."

Not hearing what was said Malcolm hollered out, "I won't!" Lying knowing he had no intention. His head was turned walking toward the door of the smoky tavern that should've been condemned a long time ago. He couldn't believe he went there. It was a nightmare. His suit was full of smoke and he felt dirty. Thinking about it made him break into a run. He spun around, pushed through the door trying to let the night air hit his clothes. He pushed so hard he pushed right into a woman, knocking her purse from her hand. He stooped down apologizing at the same time. Putting the contents back inside without looking up. Talking. "Excuse me Miss, I'm sorry, I didn't mean to… Let me get this up for you."

Malcolm focused on picking the items up off the ground and heard a familiar giggle. He put the last items in the purse. Reluctant to stand up, he let his eyes slowly scroll up from a pair of feet smashed inside black high heeled shoes, to black stockings, to a black mini dress stretched across a bulging stomach, inside a white rabbit jacket. When he scrolled up to her face he saw a short fat jeweled neck, glossy orange lips that opened to a smile sporting two false teeth sucking on a cigarette. A sweaty nose, false eyelashes, thick black arched eyebrows, and a messy head of jet-black hair.

"Bertha?"

He was surprised. She aged like a street woman. She took her cigarette out her mouth, licked her lips and growled with a husky voice.

"Malcolm! Going somewhere again? Seems like you always going somewhere. How you been?" She asked with a permanent scowl on her face.

Malcolm didn't expect to see her let alone looking like she did. She spoke as if she saw him yesterday. He tried to be a gentleman. "So, we meet again Madam." He handed her the purse and she opened her arms. Malcolm thought he would give her a Sunday morning hug but she grabbed him, put her sloppy mouth to his ear and whispered a breathy. "I missed you." Before he realized it, he pulled away and warned her.

"I'm married!"

She released him from her unwanted grip and replied with an eerie calm, a slight push and a gruff tone of voice. "Don't I know it! I was so angry I could have taken my 45 and popped a cap in you!" She caught herself and spoke nicely. "Forget all that, since you leaving, aint no need in me staying. Willie told me you were coming. I came to hear you play that saxophone of yours." When she said saxophone, he realized he left it in the lounge. He figured Gerald would bring it to church. She broke his thought. "I guess I'm late again huh? Ole Bertha late again."

He couldn't believe she still referred to herself in third person. There she was gaslighting, playing mind games, distancing herself. She did that in high school to control and place blame, but it was different. Something was wrong, her mind wasn't right and he wasn't falling for the pity party.

"Well. Like I told the boys it's getting late. Way past my bedtime." He said politely. His response ignited her.

"Cool! I aint mad at you. At least be a gentleman. You still know how to do that right. Be a gentleman and walk a lady to her car, it's right over there." She pointed to an old blue 1983 Oldsmobile Cutlass Supreme that seen its share of accidents.

"For sure, no problem. You shouldn't be out this late either. It's dangerous in these streets."

She waged another subtle attack. "I like a man that's concerned. But you should know, it's a lot of things more dangerous than these streets. And you one of em."

He ignored her comment. She was angry. He walked her to the car, she handed him the keys to open the door. Even though she was from the low end she had a thing about being treated special. She slid inside, before he could close the door. The window came down, and she started fast-talking him. "Hey Malcolm, how you been?" She asked a second time as if the conversation just began.

"I been good. You know I been married going on..."

She interrupted. "Yeah yeah yeah yeah. How many times you gon tell me? You told me already!" She contended then calmed down again. "I know you married yo precious little high school sweetheart soon as she went to college. But it wasn't nuthin like our junior year. Remember that? It was you and me."

Getting frustrated, he blew pass her comment again. He remembered her sneaky controlling ways. "Time fly's when you having fun. We have a daughter, Mecca. She just graduated. She'll be a freshman when school starts in September."

Not interested she slurred. "That's nice. How Layla doing. She still jumping around dancing?"

He didn't appreciate the jumping around remark and corrected her. "Yeah, she still dancing and she look good doing it. Dancing helped her keep her girlish figure. Thanks for asking."

Malcolm reached in his pocket for his wallet and flipped through the pictures, pointing them out. "Look. That's us. There's Layla and our daughter Mecca at her graduation and of course there I am. The proud father."

She mocked him. "Hah, the proud father! I see you got a wallet full of pictures. Now I know you don't think Ima look at all them pictures through the window, it's getting chilly out here. You might as well get in the car." Malcolm walked around to the passenger side, opened the door to get in the car with his wallet in his hand before he could sit down good, he looked up. He couldn't believe his eyes. Bertha had stripped. His mouth fell open. He dropped his wallet and the contents spilled out. She spritzed him in the face with her perfume and leaped on top of him. The safest place he could grab to push her off was in her throat, her necklace made her gag. She thought he was choking her. She got wild. Her arms flailed as she thrashed about snatching and grabbing.

She grabbed and ripped away at his pants till they came down. Layla and Mecca's pictures was on the floor. They scrambled for the pictures. He kicked the car door open with his foot, tried to back out still collecting what he could while she beat him in the top of his head with her fist, and kept spritzing him with her perfume with her other hand getting him in the eyes with it, blinding him every time he looked up to try and stop her. Then she put her black high heeled shoes on him and kicked him out the car to the ground. Screaming at him like a crazy woman. Shaking and hollering at the top of her lungs.

"Showing me pictures of that broad like I'm supposed to care!" Then she whispered real low. "Yeah yeah gon on back to her. Gon on back to her." Then she yelled again. "Smelling like me! Smelling like my perfume!" Then she started gunning the engine before he could get up. "You know what I oughta do, I oughta run you over you old fool! That's what I oughta do." Then she calmed down. "That's alright, Ima get you for what you put me through. Ima get you! Watch and see."

Malcolm rolled away from the car like a stunt man. She sped off spinning on bald tires. The exhaust made him cough. He sat on the curb till he could get himself together. He didn't know what to think. She grabbed some of the contents that fell. There was a business card with his number on it. She called Layla, told her about the relationship she and Malcolm had in high school. How they dated from freshman through junior year, planned to get married till he got her pregnant. Told Layla she never said anything, that he broke up with her, start dating someone else and that their child would have been Mecca's older sister. Layla listened intense and broken as she told her she was sorry for her misfortune. She felt betrayed.

"Jobari, I never sank so low in my life. Here I was with perfume and smoke in my good clothes on my way home to my wife and daughter; jeopardized. Not knowing what I've done. Not knowing the consequences, I would pay. I stopped at McDonalds and tried to pull myself together. Discovered my wallet was half empty, my pants were ripped. She scratched me with her nails right on the spot where I had my appendix removed and on top of that my head was bleeding.

Son, I didn't know what to think or feel. The kind of woman Bertha was anything was possible. I was frantic looking at the picture of Layla Mecca and me. I prayed, God don't let it end like this not over one night and I didn't even touch the woman. I ripped the towel from its holder in the bathroom, stripped and washed my body. No matter how much I washed I could still smell Bertha's cigarettes and cheap perfume on me. What made it worse is that I never wanted her and we never talked about marriage. She was a side chick; a couple of guys had been with her. We never dated. I put my clothes on, stood outside to air my jacket thinking, I shoulda been at home. I never shoulda left. It was a nightmare. I kept hearing Layla say, don't you go get in no trouble. Man, wives be knowing things. It's best to listen to em."

"Pops. That was bougees'. That chick vamped on you. Man, you didn't see it coming? You shoulda known she didn't wanna see no pictures. So, what you tell Lala? That you were showing her pictures?"

"Hey hey hey black man, slow up. You the one insulting and intimidating yo baby's momma. Don't you get jazzy with me."

"Sorry Pops, I don't like what happened to you that's all."

"Fair enough, it's not like I did either but I put myself in that position. And no, I didn't have to tell her nuthin. Bertha had called and told her what I was wearing. Said she thought the pictures were nice. By the time I walked in the door she had already moved out of our bedroom."

"Whoa! That was cold-blooded!"

"Cold blooded? Man, that woman looked at me like I was a germ. Told me she will not be disrespected. She would choose herself over me. She laid down the law like a sheriff in a small town. Told me if I ever lied to her again, we were done! Man, she put so much space between us I was lonely. Talk about insecure, I didn't feel no love. The devil wanted me to get mad and cheat but I didn't. That was my cross to bear and the voice that came outta her, I never wanted to hear that voice again. That night changed our lives. She told me straight out she wasn't having no more children with me. She was so done with me, she gave me permission to go get a child with somebody else, that's when I knew our marriage was in serious trouble. Man, that's when I paid to get Momma Howard up here."

"You sent for Momma Howard?"

"Dog gone right I did and with the quickness! That woman is a miracle worker and I needed a miracle. She stayed, ministered to us for three months straight. Walked through our home praying all day every day. Wrapped us in ole white towels and read scriptures to us out loud with a rumbling in her voice. Doused us with blessed oil. Put us out the bedroom, made us sleep on the living room floor and slept in our bed herself. When Lala could see me without screaming and hollering, she slowly brought us in the same room till we could sit across from one another. Then next to each other."

"Whoa Pops! She went to work on y'all like y'all was possessed."

"She went to work breaking the spirit of death off our marriage! And when it was over, I felt love coming back, Lala could look at me without frowning."

"Pops Pops Pops!" Jobari shivered. "I'm getting chills. Momma Howard, that woman got a real relationship with God. I do not mess with her. One day she said she wanted to pray for me. She didn't say pray she said uh, I can't think of the words she used. Uh…" Jobari couldn't find the words.

Malcolm helped him out, "She said she wanted to breathe a word of prayer over you?"

"Yeah Pops, that's what she said. She wanted to breathe a word of prayer over me. I was still a shortie hanging out with my friends getting ready to run outside. I didn't think nuthin of it. No big deal. She prayed, gave me a hug and I left. Hey, that's what grandmas do right. Man, we got outside ready to do what we do which usually got somebody in trouble. Nawl nawl, I know what it was. We were gon learn how to smoke. We had bought a carton of cigarettes. Camel's. The newbies were gon share packs. Robert and Trell were gon get a whole pack cause they was doing us a favor teaching us. We hid em in the bushes, they were out there for bout a week. We checked every day to make sure wasn't nobody cheating, taking em till we were ready. We had a whole plan before Momma Howard came to visit. I didn't know she was coming; she just so happens to drop by our house with Lala on a Saturday afternoon. Anyway, we go behind Brian's garage cause it was kinda like a club house. Show you how stupid we were; we were ganging up on the carton. Pops! I can tell you now since I'm grown…"

"Grown or not be careful what you say Joe." He called him Joe or Bari when he was serious. He laughed. "Gon with yo story man. I'm playing with you. I'm interrupting you like you were interrupting me."

"You know I'm still scared of you right. "Jobari confessed. "We supposed to be talking man to man. You can't be doing that Pops. You can't be pulling no rank."

"Man, gon tell the story, what Ima do? Whip you? Put you on punishment? It's a little bit too late for all that. I'm listening, you a Howard; tell the story like a Howard."

"Straight facts. Ok. Like I was saying before I was so rudely interrupted. It had to be about eleven or twelve of us. I don't think guys even hang out that deep no more without killing each other. Let me see, it was me, Jacques, Yaheem, Miri, Bo, Brian, Chris, Nate, Randy, Pete and Nick. We were newbies. We start lighting up, dudes kicked back smoking. All a sudden we start choking. All of us at the same time! Even Robert and Trell. Man, our eyes were watering. It was like we fied up *Dago bombs*. We jumped around coughing, eyes watering. Got to looking at the packets like something was wrong with em. We were like man what's up? Started accusing each other of doing something to the carton. Pops, the way that cigarette cut my breath, I aint picked up one since."

"That's a powerful story Jobari, make sure you tell it to CJ. Let him know you made mistakes, it's good for em know parents aint perfect. But that's kinda spooky, that woulda stopped me from smoking too."

"Facts! I never forgot. Let me let you finish. How all that turn out Pops? Momma Howard being at the house."

"Smooth. It was one thing to separate ourselves but Momma Howard putting us out our bed and staying three months made us ready to be alone!"

"I can't see it. Much as we love you and Lala, we not trying to do that. Y'all cannot stay at our house for three months. Y'all cannot stay for three days. Three hours is almost too long! And put us out our bed? Sorry to say, I got tall respect Pops but that. That aint never gon happen."

"Yeah, well it happened to us and we glad it did. One evening after the bible study she made us do every night, she tied these white handkerchiefs around our necks like we graduated or something. I don't know what all that was about. But anyway, a couple of days later we were sneaking, talking to each other at work on the phone, planning to meet up outside the house. You know, we wanted to see each other."

Jobari blurted out, "Ah hah. Look at you trying to be all discrete Pops. Y'all was desperate!"

"Hey man. Don't be ignorant. That's my wife ok; I had every right to miss her; unlike you! You the one, a little criminal. You a thief and a robber. I don't have to steal; that's mine."

"Ok Pops, man I didn't mean to strike a nerve."

"Yeah, well just stop being ignorant. Everything that come up don't have to come outta yo mouth. That aint cool, you need a filter brother. But anyway, she knew what she was doing and did what needed to be done. Don't snooze on Momma Howard. She got them old skills that's older than old school that got us back together. But the funny thing about it, we didn't have a chance to hook up outside the house."

"Why not? What happened?"

"When we got home, she was gone. She had packed up and went back to Mounds. Big Pops took her back home."

"What happened? She didn't say nuthin? She didn't call and tell y'all she was leaving?"

"Nope. We walked in the door. Everything was still. Wasn't nuthin moving. It was quiet, peaceful, warm and it smelled good. We didn't say nuthin, we just looked at each other. We walked in the dining room and the table was set with our good dishes. Walked in the kitchen, and it was a seven-course meal hot on the stove! Momma Howard threw down, biscuits and all. We pushed the bedroom door open, and she had rose petals all over the bed and in a vase next to it."

"Bros!"

"Yeah, she spent some money. It was stuff in there that we didn't have before she came. Everything was different, the furniture was rearranged, silk sheets, a new comforter set was on the bed. The whole Room; the whole house felt different."

"Whoa! What was all that about?"

"You ready for this?"

"I don't know if I'm ready or not. Don't tell me nuthin spooky."

"It aint nuthin spooky boy! She left a bottle of good wine. *Cabernet Sauvignon*."

"Momma Howard left a bottle of wine? What she know about wine?"

"Obviously she knew something. And she left a card"

"A card? What it say?"

"It was a bible scripture. Proverbs 18:22.

*"Whoso findeth a wife findeth a good thing, and obtaineth favour of the* LORD.*"*

"I haven't been reading my bible but that's powerful Pops. That's smooth. That's better than rapping."

"Man, that's the best kinda rap. That's real stuff for yo life! And she left us a message. She told us to recite the 4$^{th}$ Chapter of Ephesians together every day till we commit it to memory. We know it by heart now.

*"Be ye angry, and sin not: let not the sun go down upon your wrath:*

*Neither give place to the devil.*

*Let him that stole steal no more: but rather let him labour, working with his hands the thing which is good, that he may have to give to him that needeth.*

*Let no corrupt communication proceed out of your mouth, but that which is good to the use of edifying, that it may minister grace unto the hearers.*

*And grieve not the holy Spirit of God, whereby ye are sealed unto the day of redemption.*

*Let all bitterness, and wrath, and anger, and clamour, and evil Speaking, be put away from you, with all malice:*

*And be ye kind one to another, tenderhearted, forgiving one another, even as God for Christ's sake hath forgiven you."*


"We spent all this time talking, an hour Jobari. I don't want to spoil our conversation with fussing, so Ima say this. The woman could have been lying like a rug. Who knows, there may have been a baby out there that I don't know about. Whatever happened I can't blame nobody; I brought that on myself."

"Yeah Pops, aint no way around it. You definitely brought it on yourself."

"Jobari! I keep on telling you this not about me. Can you see how you brought what happened today on yourself? Bottom line, the moral to the story is get yourself together! Decide who you gon be with, stay for the long haul and take care yo family."

"I hear you Pops. That mistake probably cost you a son."

"You not gon stop, are you? Still pointing out my mistake to me. No. We never intended to have only one child, but it didn't cost me a son. Cause I got enough to deal with; with yo hard head. And I have

CJ and Ima have some more hard-headed grandsons if the Lord say the same. So don't worry. I got my work cut out for me."

Jobari took a deep breath. "Awww Pops. I already know."

"Diamond love you enough to give you two children CJ and Cherish. Only problem I got with that; she's not yo wife. You haven't married that woman. What else she got to do man? She's beautiful, she's smart. Hey! It don't hurt that she bringing in the big bucks! The money y'all making together is nasty, man! And yeah, she could look better. She can afford to pay a housekeeping service, a nanny and spend time pampering herself but that's not what she wants. Clearly it aint about the money. You want her to look better at home? A woman automatically looks better when you do right by her. That's how they're made. They reflect the man that's pouring into them. She's a receiver, so you gotta make good deposits if you want a good return. You only getting back what you giving. So, look at yourself."

"Look at myself?"

"Yeah! See you not ready for that conversation. You didn't catch me. Let me break it down for you like this, so you can understand. Think about her like an automobile not a car. She's gon help you get where you wanna go in life and death. She's yo transportation. When you take care yo automobile, make sure everything is working right. Shine her up, detail her. You ride better and when you pay her off, she's all yours. That's yo woman, that's why we refer to automobiles as *She*." You gotta take care of em!

"Pops you wild, that's a crazy analogy. But I like it I like it."

"I just bet you do. See I had to give you something you can relate to. You don't ride in a dirty car with low tire pressure, low fluids, busted up windshield, scratches and dents. Jobari, I know how you take care yo cars. But you breaking yo woman down laying up with her, giving her babies out of wedlock, making illegitimate grandchildren. What's wrong with you man? You didn't come up like that, it's disgraceful Jobari, it really is man. Take the pressure off yo woman! You clean up and cook sometime. Do what you need to do to keep the peace. Aint nuthin worse than a woman with a broken heart. Lala still gets an attitude from time to time. She had an attitude all week and I had to suck it up. I done told you stories, read scriptures tried to get you to see the best way I know how, that you hurting that woman! I hurt Lala so bad; my baby couldn't stop screaming. I had her looking at me like I was a monster. By the grace of God, Momma

Howard got us through. But look at what she had to do. Even though she left us in a romantic setting, a cozy environment and we were ready to get back together; she cried all the way through it. You know what it's like to make love to a crying woman. Knowing it's the only way back to each other. Man, we both cried. I violated her trust. A decent woman don't give herself to a man she can't trust. Every anniversary I still have to remind her she's the only woman for me. How sad is that after all these years. Jobari my man, stop acting like a heathen, get married. You don't need babies all over the place with a bunch of different baby mommas. You think you losing yo mind now. Man! You destroying a nation single handedly.

"I hear you. You right Pops. "

"Dog gone right I'm right and I don't need you to tell me I'm right. What you need to do is man up. Grow up Bari. A real man don't take what don't belong to him. You come from good stock. Stop disgracing this family!"

"I got you Pops."

"Do you?"

"Yeah. That's why I talk to you about stuff."

"We gon see about that. Is Diamond a good woman?"

"Yeah."

"You love her?"

"Yeah, I love her."

"You love yo children?"

"Of course, Pops. I love Diamond and my children. I see where you going with this."

"Do you?"

"Yeah. You telling me to marry her?"

"No, I'm not. I'm not telling you to marry her. I'm telling you to make the commitment, propose to her today publicly, set the date and keep it. Y'all been engaged too long, it was a bad joke you played on her. That's what I'm telling you to do. Stop taking what you not entitled to have without the commitment!"

"You serious Pops?"

"Do I look serious? I'm not saying nuthin to nobody. This is between me, you and the Lord. I gotta go, I got guest coming in here and I'm in the corner talking to you. This what Ima do. After the last set, I'll play a solo to queue you in. I'll hand you the microphone but it's gon be yo moment of decision. It'll be up to you to open your mouth and make the commitment before you lose a good woman and fracture your family. If you don't move forward, the DJ is gon play. We gon keep on dancing and I'm not gon say another word about it. You hear me? Ima leave you to do what you do and I don't want to hear another word about it! If you do, Ima straight out coldcock you. I mean that Jobari cause I had enough of this!"

Malcolm got up and walked away calling Layla. "Hey Layla, wait for me, happy anniversary Babygirl! Hey, why we invite these troublesome grandchildren! Jobari over here messing up our anniversary!" He looked back at Jobari, made a mean face, showed him his fist and mouthed, "knock you out!"

Jobari thought for a second about what he said and called out. "Hey Pops!" Malcolm turned around and looked at him. "You know *"If I Aint Got You"* by Alicia Keys? That's Diamond's jam." Malcolm gave a slow nod, a firm look and walked off again. He felt blessed to have had the conversation. It was a pivotal point in Jobari's life; he was the son he never had; he was his grandson.

Malcolm believed every word he said to encourage him and blocked from his memory what could devastate the family. That, he laid down at the altar to stay between him and God.

# CHAPTER SIXTEEN

### *It's Their Anniversary*

*"I promise, you gon be one unhappily married woman until you learn how to surrender."*

They were running late. It was Malcolm and Layla's 43rd anniversary. Mecca was excited, she and Malcolm planned for a year. It hadn't crossed her mind how she alienated Jahi for weeks. She carried on assuming it would be business per usual.

"Jahi, hurry up! It's their anniversary." She grabbed as many containers as she could for him to load in the truck. "I wanna get the food to the center early, you know how momma and daddy's friends are. If we don't get there, they gon start without us." She complained. There was no discussion about the rift between them. Mecca was preoccupied trying to get things done and looked pass what was really going on.

"That's cool. If they wanna start without us they can do that, they know we're coming."

"They know we're coming but we told them we were on the way. On the way mean we're driving in their direction not at home packing food."

Jahi stopped and sat the containers down on the counter and looked at her.

"What you doing? I just told you we got to hurry up." Jahi didn't move. Mecca waited but he said nuthin.

"Awh man, here we go."

"Nawl, here you go with yo mouth like you talking to Jobari. Who you think you talking to Mecca? I don't need you to tell me what, on the way mean. You need to correct yourself."

"All I said was we had to hurry up and get the food to the center."

"You said more than that...it's the way you said it."

"Yes that is all I said. What else did I say Jahi?"

"I know you gon talk to me better than that! Running me down when it's convenient for you. Talking about hurry up let's go."

"I knew you was gonna say that."

"No, you didn't. That's why you buzzing around here like everything's alright."

"Bae, don't be like that. Everything is alright."

"No, it's not and I'm not gon act like it is."

"Jahi, don't be like that"

"Be like what?"

"Like that."

"Oh, like this?" Jahi sat in his chair, reached for the remote, turned on the TV, leaned back comfortably and put his feet up.

"Oh no we not. You know what Jahi? I know you not gon start this right now knowing we need to get outta here. Jahi! Bae! it's not about us today it's their anniversary."

Jahi looked up and laughed. "Hah. Bae? When we get back to Bae?"

"You been Bae and you hear me talking to you. Don't be ignoring me."

"Are you serious right now? Don't be ignoring you? That's what we been doing for weeks. Ignoring each other. I hear you talking to me today."

"Jahi?"

"Jahi nuthin. And that's because you need me to go to the anniversary so you can save face.

"What I got to save face for?"

"For the day. For the anniversary. You want me to act like we all good when we're not. Like everything's everything. Like we been talking and communicating when we haven't looked at each other or said good morning."

"Bae!"

"You can kill that Bae crap. I don't know what kind of game you playing but you not playing it with me. You can forget that. I hope you know you blowing me away right now? And you think calling me Bae, supposed to make me acquiesce to you?"

"Bae!"

"Something wrong with you!" On that note, Jahi got up went in the kitchen, grabbed the rest of the containers and loaded them in the back of the truck within seconds. When he finished, he came back inside and sat back down. Mecca had turned the TV off.

"Why you turn the TV off Mecca?"

"Because we gotta go."

"Go! I put everything in the truck. Jobari can unload it when you get there. Or I can drop you off, pick you up or you can drive yourself. However you wanna do it. Either way, it's all good. The world is yours. Ima be right here doing what I'm doing. And don't turn that TV off again!"

"Is that your way of telling me you not going?"

"I don't need a way to tell you nuthin. Keep doing what you been doing. Keep the attitude from hell."

"Attitude from hell?"

"Yeah. You need me to refresh yo memory? I walk in the room; you go in another room. I turn on the TV in the den you turn on the TV in the living room. You lock the bathroom door behind you like it's a stranger in the house. You hang off the side of the bed about to fall off with yo back turned. You roll yo eyes when I offer you some of my food. And get up before the crack of dawn to make sure I don't touch you. Yeah. The attitude from hell. That one. That's the one I'm talking about. Keep that going!"

"You know what?" Mecca paused

"Nawl, I don't know what."

She walked out the room and came back, still pushing to get her way. "Can we do this later Jahi?"

"I'll be here when you get back."

"That's not what I'm talking about. I'm asking you if we can discuss our issues later when we get back home? Today is not about us. That's what I'm asking you Jahi."

"And I'm telling you, I'll be here when you get back. That's what I'm telling you."

"Jahi!"

"What is it with you that make you think calling my name and calling me Bae is gon change my mind. Keep doing that. You getting ready to make me leave out the house; that's what you bout to do."

"Jahi, it's their anniversary. We should be helping them enjoy it. We can talk but just not right now. Please!"

"Help them enjoy it? Today is not about you, they made 43 years. You sound crazy, we can talk but not right now. It's not about us. If now is not a good time and it's not about us, what we doing then?"

"What you mean what we doing?"

"If everything is more important than us, what we doing together?

Why am I here?"

"Oh, my God. As in what we doing together? Is that what you asking me. Is that the question on the table?"

"That's the question of the year. You heard me the first time. Everything else is more important than us. Why am I here!"

"How I'm supposed to answer that?"

"Like you everything else."

"This don't make no sense. We together because we choose to be together."

"You realize it's a choice?"

"Of course, I realize it's a choice. What else would it be Jahi?"

"The way you running around trying to call shots I was beginning to think you thought I didn't have a choice."

"We both have choices Jahi."

"I'm glad you know that"

"Why wouldn't I know it?"

"Cause you act like you don't know."

"How I act like I don't know Jahi?"

"I'll give you point and case."

"I'm listening"

"Good. When was the last time we did something, I initiated?"

"What kind of question is that, Jahi?"

"The kind you avoid."

"I'm not avoiding nuthin."

"Then answer the question."

"To be totally honest Jahi, since you brought it up, it's not like you initiated anything for a while."

"You noticed?"

"Of course, I noticed. How could I not notice? And I noticed how you systematically took away what we do together."

"Systematically?"

"Yes. Systematically. What else could it be when you withdrew from every one of our routines to the extent of changing yo eating habits. I just didn't say nuthin."

"You noticed and you didn't say nuthin? That's exactly what I expected from you. You rather get an attitude and shut down rather than check on yo man."

"What!"

"You noticed a drastic change in my behavior, and chose to be

175

withdrawn rather than be concerned enough to ask me if I was alright."

"What are we talking about? Jahi, you a grown man. I can't stop you from doing what you want to do, eating what you want to eat. If you not happy with how we chose to live our lives that's on you."

"You right. It is on me. It's my fault for trying to be what you need and give you what you want."

"Jahi, I didn't ask you to be anything other than yourself. If you didn't like how I was doing things, you shoulda said something. You had me thinking we were on the same page."

"I gave you an inch and you took a mile. You so full of yourself it's insulting."

"Full of myself, at least I'm being myself. You the one running around here scarfing down meat, gaining weight, missing church and eating swine. What you call that?"

"Tired."

"Tired!"

"Yeah!"

"Tired of what? Me? You tired of me?"

"I'm tired of you living single in a marriage. Not once did you ask me why I was doing what I was doing. This could have been over. I wanted to see how you were gon handle yourself. How you were gon take care yo man!"

"What I do? Fail the test? I didn't know I was being tested. What else was I supposed to do?"

"Boom! Care! You were supposed to care, that's what you were supposed to do. Like you out there caring for strangers. I needed you and you didn't throw a brother a bone. What I did is reversable. The neglect you showed me got me wondering why we together."

"How I neglect you, Jahi?" She responded in a softer tone

"If you have to ask me, do this. Call one of yo girls."

That was the insult she couldn't hear. Her girls should never come up in their arguments.

"Call up lonely Jules, yo professional buddy with all the advice and no man. Tell her what I was doing, how I was eating then ask her how she woulda handled it." She already knew.

"Better yet call your mother." Mecca always thought her mother spoiled Jahi.

"Bet money, both of em woulda been concerned. Aint no way Lala would have let me go a day out the box. While you telling Jules all yo business, she looking upside yo head wishing she was in yo shoes and had a brother to check on. At the end of the day, they woulda had the decency to sit down and ask me what was wrong, what I needed and how they could help. You didn't."

"What kind of games you playing Jahi?"

"Games? He laughed. "When you know me to play games?"

"Oh yeah you got games alright."

"I tell you what. You wanna go back and forward with me. Do it."

"Oh, now you issuing threats?"

"Promises Mecca. I promise you I'm not leaving the marriage. I'm not June Bug. I'm not that one. You don't get to play with my life. You not the only one in this marriage. I promise you gon be one unhappily married woman until you learn how to surrender. Just like I surrendered before I put a ring on yo finger."

"Surrender to what Jahi?"

"To each other! And we are, on the same page. Love make you want to do things to make each other happy. That's why I laid up in the bed reading books with you. I wasn't interested in them books. I was interested because you were interested. And you are gon be watered down and minimized; that's how we merge. That's how we do the thang, that's how we become one flesh. Trying to prove you can take it or leave it, that's not what you want. Sisters like that don't celebrate anniversaries Mecca."

"Is that what this is?"

"What you mean is that what this is?"

"You think I'm too independent? Is that it?"

"Nope!" He laughed, "You definitely not too independent, when you want something, you have no problem asking me for what you want and I deliver. Independent women go get it themselves. You don't do that, you come right to daddy baby. You come to me and I give you what you need!" He gloated.

"Well, what you sayin Jahi?"

"I'm saying to be in a marriage with me things gon have to change. My needs got to be met. Besides what you doing that's so important you can't give me what I need? I give you what you need. I handle my business."

"Oh, you think so?" She taunted. "Wouldn't I be the one to ask?"

"Right right right right. My bad, you would be the one to ask."

"Are you asking me?"

"Yeah, I'm asking you. Do I handle my business or not?"

Mecca backed down. "I'm glad you asked. Obviously, I did something to make you pull away from me."

"Oh, you see that huh."

"Yeah, I see it. I see it now."

"I'm listening. Have I been handling my business? That's what I'm asking you. I'm waiting on the answer."

"The short answer is yes."

"The short answer? What you mean the short answer?"

"The long answer is no."

"What's with this short and long answer stuff? You need to qualify that."

"I can qualify it. Yes, you've done everything a good husband do for his wife and family. Yes, you pay the bills, make sure we're safe, fix stuff. Yes, you do all the heavy lifting, shouldering responsibilities so I don't have to worry. You're a good father, not stepfather but a good father to Jobari you even try to understand his dad, who I never understood. You treat my family and friends good. Take me where I want to go, do what I like to do."

She retracted. "Well, you used to. You look dope all the time so my eyes don't have to wander. You all that!"

Jahi smiled. "Keep on, it's something you not saying. You giving me compliments not complaints but you doing good, you got my attention."

"I do have a complaint"

"What's yo complaint?"

"You stopped giving me you."

Jahi laughed. "I see you. Now here you go with the sweetness."

"You stopped being my man."

He laughed again. "I stopped being yo man?"

"Yeah, that's what hurt the most. I didn't fall in love with what you were doing for me, my family or my friends. I fell in love with yo essence. You definitely that alpha man. I'm into who you are as an individual, the way of yo swagger. I like it when you full of yourself, when you doing yo thang the way you do it. When you disagree, get on my last nerve and stand yo ground. All of that. Bae all I need is for you to be yo magnificent self not who I want you to be in a moment that may change like the weather. I need you to rock with me like you used to do. I like the zig and the zag, the ebb and the flow of us! Our differences got us equally yoked. See, you even got me rapping to you the way you used to rap to me. How I'm doing so far?" Mecca leaned back at gave Jahi the sly look JE gave the women.

"So far so good baby. I'm about to pop my collar. Uh huh, keep talking." Jahi pulled out his money clip. "I'm bout to make it rain on you girl. Keep talking."

"I want you to make it rain, gone throw them 20-dollar bills on out there; Ima pick up every one of em. But Bae, that's another thing. I miss yo rap. You don't rap to me no more. You not around here playing yo guitar, listening to yo loud music. You haven't worn yo shades and you know how fine you look in them shades. I aint even seen the bow leg walk. Where it go? How you been walking around here anyway I can't even remember."

"I see you. I see what you doing. You got me all frustrated then you stroke my ego. But that's alright. I like it I like it! And of course, I walk. What you mean how I been walking around here? What you want. What you want. You wanna see me walk like this?" Jahi got up and started walking around like Denzel. "Girl I'll walk all day."

"Yeah, that's it, you looking good, you looking real good to me. You think I'm playing but that's it." Mecca stood behind him to admire his walk around the living room. She touched his legs when he walked pass.

He jumped back. "Get back off of me! Don't get yourself in no trouble while you trying to rush up outta here. See, I'm still giving you what you want. What! You want me to rap to you?"

"Yep! That's how you got me in the first place. That's right, just like Bobby Womack. Bring it on back!"

He positioned himself like he was getting ready to get his rap on. He got right up in her face, looked in her eyes and angled his body. It made her blush, she pushed him away.

"See how you do. That's all I want. I didn't marry you to make you miserable Jahi. I just want my man back."

"I got you baby. I feel you. But it's hard to act like a boyfriend with no responsibilities when you carrying the weight. Cause that's exactly what I do. I carry the weight. But you say you want yo man back?"

"Yeah, I want my man back."

"I can do that. I can do that. Only one condition."

"One condition? What's that?"

"Give me my woman back! That's what you do! Give her back!"

"Come on now Jahi."

He laughed. "Come on now nuthin. It takes two to Tango. See you thought you had me going. Blowing me up with them compliments Game recognize game Mecca. Yo game is weak Mecca. Yeah, you betta go get yo girl to help you out with me. I liked her a lot more anyway. That woman I married. What you do, tie her up. You got her held hostage somewhere around this house; you didn't know you lost her huh. Yeah, that's right you! Became a nagging wife."

"No I didn't"

"Yes you did. Ask Jobari. You were on the phone nagging this morning. I heard you. Hollering. Calling me. I heard you when you fell yo behind on the floor too. I heard you slide across the floor. That's what you get for cutting up. And you hit the floor hard. Shook the bed. I almost got up but I didn't cause you had it coming. See God don't like ugly!" He laughed uncontrollably.

"You wrong for that Jahi. I knew you heard me. And I did hurt myself."

"Aww poor baby hurt herself while she was hollering." He laughed even harder.

"Keep laughing, we gon see who get the last laugh. And I got my girl right here. Just so you know, she aint went nowhere. You just saying that to get back at me."

"You wish! Baby that girl left with yo man. It got too serious around here so they got together and got up outta this piece. Yeah, both of em gone. Why you think I been walking around here like a mad man. A man's woman brings her best game to the table. You know why?"

"I know you talking crazy, I always bring my best game. But yeah, I wanna know. Why?"

"Because his woman wanna be his wife." Boom!

"See you got jokes!"

"So, you gon lighten up, be sweet, nice, kind and understanding like you used to be before I married you. Like yo momma? Lala. Her name even sings and don't be jealous that's my girl. Quiet as its kept, I'm waiting on you to turn into her."

"What! Boy my daddy will beat you down talking like that."

"Yo daddy the one that told me Lala was just like you and to be patient because it'll pay off in the long run."

"I gotta talk to that man. And I aint jealous, I thought I was already bringing my best game but I guess I can do better because I do not like getting into it with you Jahi. Besides, I got my work cut out for me. I gotta get you back right. Boy you need a detox!"

"Now that's what I'm talking about. That's my woman. That's right take care yo man girl." Jahi pulled his tee-shirt up and showed her his protruding stomach. "I'm all yours!"

Mecca patted his stomach. It sounded like a tight drum. "No you not. Look at this Jahi. My God, this aint nuthin funny. I'm telling you now, you gon need an enema so don't be trippin. I already know you full of cheese, you done built up mucus messing with that dairy. That aint nuthin but inflammation. I gotta massage yo stomach. You may be getting an enema every day for a week. I gotta put you on a juice fast till this go down. That's how sickness start Jahi. Between me and God you aint getting sick."

"I aint doing no enema Mecca! We gon start going back to the gym. Tomorrow."

"You gon start going back to the gym tomorrow. I aint never stopped. And it's gon take more than the gym Jahi so don't be being difficult."

"I swear you in the wrong profession. You worse than a doctor and you know I don't mess with them till I have to. Baby I'm tired! I feel sluggish. Look at me. You aint been taking care of me. I'm not gon be doing this with you. I'm too old for this."

"I know you tired and sluggish that's because you're full of undigested food Boo."

"I don't wanna talk about it no more, we gon do what we gotta do point blank period. Just do it and stop talking about it. Enough about me. Let me see what I need you to do."

"What you need me to do Jahi? Don't make it something crazy. We still gotta get to the anniversary."

"Say one more thing about…"

"Ok ok. What you need me to do Boo?"

"I need you to take yo little mean fine self back in the room and put on one of those dresses, I like. One of them girly girl dresses; the ones that move when you walk. The ones that flow. And don't forget them noisy dangly earrings and bracelets that make you sound like a toy."

"You talking bout my swing dress?"

"Yeah, yo swing dress. Whatever you call it. Put that on.

"You know you doing too much Jahi."

"No, I'm not. How I'm doing too much. You wore em when we were dating. And didn't leave till you had all them bracelets on. Came in the door jingling baby. Don't act like you don't know." He grabbed Mecca and put her in a fake headlock. "You had me out here acting a stone fool just to get this conversation."

He let her go and she laughed. "I know right? It shouldn't take all this."

"No, it shouldn't. And it bet not happen again. But look at you purring like a kitten. You like that don't you."

"I do. You know you got to stimulate my mind."

"Stop acting like I'm not the man."

"You the man."

"I'm the man?"

"You the man Bae"

"Now I'm officially Bae again huh"

"Yeah, you, my Bae. You aint never stopped. You gon always be my Bae. Ima do better. Ima be good because I need my friend back. Now that we talking, I can tell you."

"Tell me what?"

"What I went through. What happened when I hung out with Jules at her office last night."

"You know I don't get in woman stuff. I don't like that."

"I know but Jahi, I gotta tell you."

"What you got to tell me. What happened between you and Jules last night?"

Mecca took a deep breath. "Well, here I am thinking we was gon do our usual girl talk thingy and she was seriously slinging shade. I mean venomously. Something not right with her."

"Slinging shade? She wasn't her usual happy self huh."

"No, she wasn't."

"Then I guess you don't know?"

"Know what?"

"For one thing Mecca, you don't need to be telling Jules all our business. You go over there complaining about stuff she would love to be dealing with. It's not fair to her. The sister is lonely. You over there like Momma Howard say, crying hungry with a loaf of bread under both yo arms and she starving."

Mecca laughed. "Boy you crazy, you need to stop being silly

talking bout a loaf of bread under my arm and she starving. That don't have nuthin to do with what we talking about."

"How come it don't? It's the perception of lack. Crying when you already have what you need. I been to church now, don't mess around here and have me preaching."

"You know what, you right."

"But seriously, she is. She deserves a man in her life just like the next woman. You don't have to be a psychologist to know that. Next time you wanna complain go talk to a married woman. Go talk to yo momma. Betta yet, talk to my momma. They got husbands. Ya'll can get together and talk about us bad as ya'll want to; it aint like ya'll going nowhere."

"I didn't think about it like that. You on point. Only one thing Jahi, Jules is not desperate for no man."

"You think she not?"

"I know she not. She coulda been married."

"Yeah?"

"Yeah. You never met him but there's this brother, a real conscious type. A Muslim brother name Khalif, he come around from time to time. He and Jules had some *go'ins ons* in her sophomore year before she moved to Savannah. Her grandfather Franklin was all in, thought he was the best thing since sliced bread. They'd be having the radical black man talks, turning up. He was hopin they'd get married. But Mina. Jahi you aint met Mina. Jules's momma. Bae. She not nuthin to play with. She politely moved her right on down south with her daddy till she graduated college. Mina wasn't letting nuthin and nobody interfere with Jules's education, not even me."

"You think she broke that up?"

"Think! We know she broke that up to the extent Jules won't have too much to do with him today. The man been tryin to get back with her for the longest but she not having none of it. I'm surprised he still come around."

"Whoa. That's deep."

"Exactly. So don't feel too bad for Jules. And he's a cool dude, got his own business. Doing well for himself. And if you don't mine me saying, he's a good lookin brother. He don't have to chase no woman. For some reason, he just want Jules."

"Mecca, men don't hang around that long for nuthin. He got a reason; you just don't know what it is. Jules not telling you her business. But that's more reason to lean into her a little more. sound like she dealing with her own problems. You know how to be a good friend Mecca. She needs you more than you know. Don't be mad at her. I love her cause she loves you. I don't care what she said, she not trying to do you no harm."

"I know, you right."

"Look here, I got a buddy down in Savannah waitin to meet her. But later for that, we need to be getting outta here. We already late."

"Wait. You knew about her moving to Savannah?"

"Yeah. Obviously, her parents been talking about getting back together and her father is gon do whatever he need to do to make that happen. He wants his family in Savannah with him. He's opening a family healing center; the way I hear it Mina and Jules supposed to run it. So, he shutting this one down and it's not like Jules had a choice in the matter. You can't blame the man for wanting his family back. The brother not pulling no punches he pulling strange. Dr. Benjamin Rowe? That man's family pretty much own the county where they live. It's a prestigious black family and they funny about keeping things in the family. They own land, hospitals, and cemeteries. I heard Mina went to school on one of his scholarships; that's how they met. Why am I telling you this, you know the story. She didn't tell you about the move because she don't wanna go."

"No, it's all good. I only know bits and pieces of the story as a child. Franklin and Mattie not nuthin but secret squirrels, they may know your business but they not telling you nuthin about theirs. And I was ready to go off on her. Ima miss my girl!"

"They not supposed to tell you all their business. Sometimes, you just gotta take the ride. Give em the benefit of the doubt. Don't be so quick to assume the worse. You and Jules girls, she wouldn't do nuthin to hurt you, that's all you need to know. We talking third generation friendship that's why we need to get to that party."

"Thanks for getting me straight Jahi. I don't know what I would do without you."

"Long as you not trying to live single in the marriage, you don't have to find out."

"Ok Bae. I don't wanna talk about that no more. I got it. Bae, can you bring yo bass and sit in on the jam session with dad like you did last year?"

"Oh, you wanna hear the bass man play?"

"Got to have it."

"You got it. I'll do my Larry Graham thang. Ima funk it up like I did when you met me!"

Mecca's cell phone rang. It was Layla.

"Mecca!"

"Hey Ma, what's up? What you doing?"

"What you mean what's up? What ya'll doing? When y'all coming? Chile it's a mob of people over here, people we aint seen since who knows when. How you find everybody? The only person I haven't seen is Esther."

"I been planning for the longest, dad and Grandma Honey helped but Esther couldn't make it."

"Leave her to me, I aint bit more worried about Esther than the man on the moon. I'm dropping in on her on the way home. Aint nuthin wrong with her, she just trying to avoid Carl. Enough about Esther, I love my surprise, I knew that man had something to do with it; trying to act like he didn't know nuthin. Ima get him." Layla got distracted. "Girl Franklin and Mattie just walked in. Lord have mercy Mina and Benjamin? Jules's daddy done came all the way from Savannah. Wait till y'all see him. Mecca, he looks so scholarly, like a Cornell West! Girl people pouring in here, let me get off this phone. What's taking y'all so long? Jahi got you hemmed up over there. I done told you bout yo mouth. What you say now?"

"Why you have to say that momma?"

"Look Missy, you don't fuss at me. I know you wanna act like everybody's momma but I had you, you didn't have me. Put my son on the phone. I know you over there mistreating him."

"I don't have to put him on, you on speaker he heard what you said."

"Good!" She sweetened her voice and drag his name. "Hey Jaaa--hiii! You know the party can't start till you get here don't you. These old boys need some help. You know what I'm saying? A little bass in the place. Luv you, gotta go! "

"I got you covered ma. Love you too Lala."

"Hey, tell yo wife she betta be glad I didn't invite none of my cougar friends while she over there playing childish games."

Jahi laughed. "Nawl ma, I'm waiting on her to turn into you."

"See there you go son, that's wise. Good things come to those that wait. Stay on in there for the long haul. But I gotta go, I love you more and don't hang up yet ya'll son wanna tell you something." She yelled out. "Come on Jobari, she right here on the phone." Layla gave Jobari the phone and went back to the party.

"Hey Ma, where y'all at? Man, they turned up, the place is lit. Anyway, I wanted to let you know I apologized to Diamond, and Pops let me propose to her over the microphone. Of course, she accepted, cried and now she over there with your grands sucking up all the attention. So, get ready to try on dresses, we're getting married next June. Hey where's the man of the house?"

"Wow Jobari that's beautiful. I'm proud of you son. Jahi is right here listening, we're on speaker."

"Jobari my man congratulations. A good man always steps up to the plate and take care his responsibility. You already know how we feel about Diamond."

"Yeah. Y'all always treated her like a daughter. I appreciate that. Take yo time black man, we'll be here. Lala got y'all seated next to Uncle Myles and his wife. Ma, wait till you see Kato he's dreaded up with a full beard. Him and Myles look like two black Jesus's in the flesh. Just so y'all know the cousins coming over to me and Diamond's later to talk about the *go'ins ons* around here. Hey Ma!"

"What Jobari?"

"No disrespect but if it's not too much to ask, can you lighten up, not be so serious, maybe have some fun. Hey ma…"

"What Jobari?"

"And you please not wear a church lady suit and put on one of yo pretty dresses like you used to?"

"Jobari!"

Jahi stepped in. "Don't Jobari him. Hey son, I said the same thing. Now that she got me in church, she acts like she don't know how to be just plain ole pretty and have fun."

"Yeah, that's all I'm saying ma."

"Ok Jobari. Ok Jahi."

"Hey Jahi you know we need you to bring some noise right."

"I hear you. I got all that covered my man. I'm packing up now and I'm gon personally make sure your momma have a good time."

# CHAPTER SEVENTEEN

### *Reality Checks*

*"I aint mad but one day you and Carl gon have to be in the same place, in the same room at the same time.
I know that's why you didn't come."*

Esther opened the door. Layla was standing there with the *I know what you did* look on her face. Champagne in one hand, two glasses in the other. They hugged and she walked inside talking like it was an ongoing conversation.

"Anyway, thanks for getting everybody else there even though you didn't come. I saved one for us. Got you a glass, got me a glass so we can have a toast." Layla poured their drinks. "Drink up its nonalcoholic. Everybody was there, Smooth and his wife came through. We got our *Step* on til Mal cut in."

Esther put her hands on her hips. "Are you kidding? Don't tell me he still jealous of Smooth. He too old for that kinda mess."

"Oh no he not too old. He betta be jealous. You shoulda been there. We had so much fun we making this anniversary month, so you aint get outta nuthin. Oh, you gon celebrate. I didn't dance that much when I was young. Mal got on his saxophone broke me off some *"Let Me Love You"* came back with *"Boo'd Up"* and them little Yahoo's went crazy. They crack me up acting like we don't know nuthin. All they living on is samples of ole school music. Oh yeah, Jobari proposed to Diamond and set the date, we gotta go dress shopping. They think it's something new but me and Mal was Boo'd and pensioned up before they were born. I don't know what came over him, but Jobari had something to do with it. He had his earring in his ear, haircut, shaved down in the front. I call it man baby hair. He looked good to me! Ima have him stick his head in the door when he come to get me so you can see; he not gon keep it like that long. When the DJ took over, we snuck out! But I had to come by and see my girl."

Layla knew Esther staying home couldn't stop the intervention. She eased into the conversation.

"Last weekend Jobari and Diamond was visiting. Mal and I was hugged up on the sofa watching a movie enjoying ourselves, minding our own sweet business. They walked pass us, came back, stood in front of us and laughed. I asked em what was so funny, they were cracking up a little bit too hard for me. Diamond said they were laughing cause me and Mal was Boo'd up. That's why he did the song. Mal wasn't paying attention, he kept watching the movie while they laughed, but I was offended. They looked crazy when I told em to get their unmarried behinds outta our house."

"Boo'd up?"

"Yeah, that's what they call it when you got a significant other, that's what Mal and I want for you."

"What?"

"A significant other. Friends are alright but we want you Boo'd up!"

"Tonight. Layla, really? Would you please enjoy yo anniversary and stop worrying about me. Please Mrs. Miller."

"We not gon keep doing this."

"I done told y'all at this point in my life..."

Layla interrupted. "I am not trying to hear all of that! At this point in yo life you should be living yo best life and you not!"

"I'm serious, I'm not gon be nobody's nurse maid. I just got my freedom."

"Girl stop playing. You been had yo freedom. You got yo freedom when Carl walked out, when Jade went to college, when she got married and when she moved out yo house. Exactly how much freedom you trying to get? Meeting somebody don't take away yo freedom. Every guy we introduced you to Esther is just as free and healthy as you are."

"You can't know that. You been married so long you don't know what's out here. I have to review a brother's health history before we can even talk about a dinner date, and they not gon tell the truth. Ever gone to dinner with a man that had *Gird* or irritable bowel syndrome? No, you haven't. Let me tell you it aint nuthin nice, I couldn't even eat the meal from all the noise coming outta his body and the discomfort on his face. I was embarrassed for the man. How I'm supposed to act like I didn't hear it. These old dudes want you to be perfect when they all jacked up. I'm not going through no man judging and summing me up knowing they done had heart attacks, strokes, high blood pressure, prostate cancer and sugar diabetes. They ran the streets all their young life, got old, found themselves alone; now all of a sudden, they wanna do right, they wanna settle down. Girl Boo! I guess so, it's not much else they can do. You know what, it reminds me of *the Color Purple* when that fool kept trying to find a woman to take care his no-good kids and a dirty house. Only now it's five grandchildren. Talking about find the right woman. The right woman to do what? Knowing full well they having difficulties.

"No, you didn't. Oh my God, you know you one angry woman. Don't be so mean. You crazy for real."

"I may be mean. I may even be crazy but what I'm not is stupid and I aint desperate. Not for no trouble. I know like they say, the *go'ins ons*. Most of em done messed themselves up with the liquor."

"Emma everybody not messed up. Not that its yo business but aint nuthin wrong with Mal."

"And that's cause you got him out the street 43 years ago."

"Whatever. Any who, they want the right woman to sit up at home and watch a movie like me and Mal. So don't be throwing shade honey baby, we enjoy our old movies. Last weekend we watched *Three Faces of Eve.*"

That's fine for you and Mal. The way I see it, everything already been done, aint nuthin left to do but die and if you get with the wrong one you won't even be able to do that in peace."

"You know you got an answer for everything don't you. You wanna make me laugh."

"You wanna laugh? I know it sound funny but I'm serious, it's different when you have a history with the person Layla. I don't have a history with nobody but Carl. And you bet not try to sell that no-good cheater back to me cause I aint buying. It don't make no sense to come to a relationship falling apart at the seams, knowing you gon be a liability and a burden in five more minutes to somebody you don't even know."

"Esther you too much. You sound defeated like it's the end of the world. This is the perfect age; these brothers got a lot to give without all the mess. But you can't be bitter, you gotta have room in your heart for a companion. That's where it begins. When it's in yo heart you not gon be worried about all that foolishness. You'll love and accept his love. Not every man looking for his granddaughter; the ones I know don't want to be bothered. They want somebody that grew up with them. Somebody they can relate to, talk about old stuff, listen to the dusties, not explaining em like a history teacher. Yeah, it looks good when the man 50 and the young lady is 25 but baby when he turns 75 and she just pulling up on 50; he betta hope she love him! The handwriting gon be all over the wall. Ima leave that alone cause that's not what I'm here to talk about."

"That's about the smartest thing you said tonight. But some of em do alright. See. Men are different, they'll pay the money to keep somebody; they not stupid. They will pay for what they need cause they know they gon need somebody to take care of em. We just suffer for no good reason."

"I'm sure some do fine but you always talking about me and Mal. How you admire us. How good we look together. It's not us you admire, its God in us and time working on the relationship, scramble it together and Wa La. We got flaws, bumps, bruises like the next couple, it aint no fantasy. We accept and love each other despite everything we been through. He's my buddy now. We can't stand to see each other in pain. If I'm crying Mal gon make it right. If I'm hurting and its Ben-Gay, he got it. If he needs his ego stroked, Ima do that too, it's probably the only time lying is not a sin. If it's quiet he needs I'll shut the house down like four flat tires aint nobody coming over. Pop Pop need rest, it's my job to make sure he gets it. We take care each other. We trying to stay alive and well. Both of us think you deserve the same thing. It's not always romantic, sometimes it's plain ole boring and that's ok too."

Layla stopped placating Esther and told the truth. "Esther. Esther."

"Yeah? Why you looking in my face calling me twice like I can't hear you? I'm not hard of hearing. I'm looking right at you."

"I'm calling yo name because Ima tell you something you don't want to hear and I'm not playing with you no more. You haven't moved on Esther. You still walking around here hurting. You gotta forgive Carl even if you don't take him back. Forgive him. That! You do for yourself. We gon have this conversation whether you like it or not. On my anniversary. That's the gift you gon give me! Some straight talk sister girl."

Esther teared up. "Don't you think I know I should! But the way he did things Layla. The way he flat out turned his back on us, make me angry all over again. He ruined our lives. Whenever I think I'm over it, something reminds me and I get mad all over again."

"That's because you not over it. You need to let that go! You talking like yo life is over. Why would you make every man pay for what Carl did? Esther it's some good men out here ready to love you right. You giving what happened between you and Carl too much energy. He's only one man."

Stop trying to make sense, stop trying to understand it. It aint gon make no sense. Forgiveness afforded us 43 anniversaries, not making sense. The only thing I know is one day Ima leave here, and Mal is too, and it can come sooner than later. I aint wasting no time being unhappy and I aint letting nuthin on earth make me lift up my eyes in hell. I been there and I didn't like it. I never talked about his infidelity to anyone but my grandmother; it wasn't nobody's business; I didn't even mention it to Honey. I never got so close to hating and wanting to kill somebody till that night. I was angry, ready to wreck my family, I didn't care. I was hurt, that's all I knew. Mal wanted a son and I refused to have another child. I told him, he betta go somewhere else and get one and I meant it. While I was busy not forgiving, I found out I wasn't supposed to have children at all."

"What?"

"Yeah. The doctor said Mecca was a miracle baby. When I was a teenager, a boy kicked me in my back and apparently did some damage."

"Kicked you in yo back!"

"Yeah, dead square in my back. I thought it broke, it had me cramping for days."

"Seem like the doctor woulda said something back then."

"Yeah, But I never got checked out, I never told."

"Layla, sweetheart, you never told?"

"Nope, somebody else told but I kept my mouth shut. I was doing something I had no business doing. Never mind that's water under the bridge. Anyway, the point is I let unforgiveness get in my head so deep my grand momma had to come to Chicago and lay hands on me. I was dead to that man. I didn't want him to touch me. When I tried to let him, I couldn't. I screamed and hollered like I was losing my mind. I couldn't stand the sight of him. The smell of him. The sound of his voice. My grand momma said I never conceived again because I spiritually rejected him and that it had nuthin to do with what the doctor said, that explains how I got pregnant with Mecca. I trust what she say. By the grace of God, she brought us through and we're here today celebrating…43 years."

"Layla, I don't know what to say. I feel like I been gut punched."

"You don't have to say nuthin. I'm telling you; I know hurt. Baby I know. I was still going to church with a murderous spirit, I coulda killed my husband. I wished he was dead, and still loved him at the same time. How demonic is that? That's why I don't play with the devil, I don't give him no room to play with me either. I got delivered. Now, I'll forgive in a New York minute. Aint nuthin that serious."

"Layla."

"Yes?"

"I never woulda thought y'all had differences."

"What couple don't have differences Esther? That's why I'm telling you somethings going on, you won't let another man in yo life. Talking bout aint nuthin left to do but die, you not even old enough to retire yet. Esther it's been over thirty-six years. You letting the devil rob you blind. Jade is grown and married. Y'all grandchild going on sixteen and we having the same conversation. Come on now you talking crazy. We celebrated today and Mal still think I don't know what happened that night in that car. And it takes everything in me not to tell him to his face. But that's my test. I'm leaving it at the alter and I'm taking it to the grave."

"I thought you said you forgave him."

"I did but it still comes back to try and hurt me all over again. I just keep beating it back till it go away. Let me tell you, it got better over the years. I don't feel it as much now. Somethings you don't get over; you learn to bear it like death, the bible says.

*"Then when lust hath conceived, it bringeth forth sin: and sin when it is finished, bringeth forth death."*

Unforgiveness not nuthin to play with. It's way outta our league. Elderly couples abuse one another over old stuff that made em resentful. Mecca told me about a woman that was abusive to her 86-year-old husband who used to cheat on her. She was pinching the poor man. The only way they found out is his skin was so thin the bruises start showing more and more till it look like he had been beaten in one spot. His skin was light, it turned him black and blue. God only know what else she was doing to him. And they raised a God-fearing dignified educated family."

"Oh my God! Now that don't make no sense."

"And what you doing do? Don't none of it make sense. What challenged me, is that the woman stooped so low as to describe a scar on Mal's body from when his appendix ruptured. That's when I knew.

It wasn't an old scar, it happened after we were married, it's close to his private. Go figure. Would you believe I had to pray for the woman Mal and myself to get past the madness and heal?"

"All I can say is you a better woman than me."

"No, I'm not! I realized the woman didn't know any better. Wasn't nuthin to convict her of her wrong doing. She use to date him, he wasn't no stranger to her. But it was different for Mal. The guilt ate him up. He blocked it from his memory; he thinks he ran away, and I leave it

just like that. It already cost us children. Like my grandma say, you don't get the big years without trouble. Esther, I wouldn't let another day go by; I wouldn't lay my head down on the pillow tonight without forgiving. If you don't forgive, you can't be forgiven. Look at how the Lord restored us. I'm praying you let HIM restore you too. I care too much not to tell you what God love. Because aint nuthin worth going to hell over."

"One thing I don't do is turn down prayer."

"That's good. So, let's pray. Bow yo head. Father God in the mighty name of Jesus…."

# CHAPTER EIGHTEEN

❧

*Esther*

*"Her momma's picture was on the refrigerator; she talked to her each time she opened and closed the door."*

Esther smelled like bergamot, made by Wilson the oil man over on the corner of 50th and Cottage. Saturdays in front of Walgreens parking lot he customized and sold oils. He prepared Esther's in exchange for lunch. A container with sauteed kale greens, cornbread, chickpeas, wild rice, yams, and a large glass jar of fresh grapefruit juice; straight from her juicer.

He made her essential oils for medicinal and spiritual purposes. Bergamot kept her energy high and immune system strong. During challenging times, pure Shea butter with Lotus oil kept away negative energy. Getting dressed in the morning was a ritual with deliberate movement. Sitting and moving her sterling silver ankle bracelet out the way with oiled hands long enough to rub the mixture down her shapely legs, that left her standing all of five feet five inches tall. Focusing on her bare manicured dainty feet making sure she was well covered before accessorizing her toes with rings; the Ankh and a Daisy, her favorite flower.

A face full of interest. Smooth caramel skin with warm undertones. Hundreds of thin brown locs that met her hips twirled into a messy bun on days she didn't wrap her head to protect her crown. A wide smile that made her eyes swint. She looked like laughter behind iridescent eyeglasses resting purposefully on the tip of her keen nose secured by a rhinestone chain. Esther loved talking to people and leaned in to listen.

A cultural beauty that came in the game teaching fifth-grade students Kiswahili. She draped herself in Kaftans and at times wrapped her curvaceous 140-pound body closely in sarong skirts. A woman of femininity that honored her temple. She wore lleke, Jigida, Lagidigba, waist beads made from glass, nuts, wood, and metal as an expression of femininity and protection under her garments. Her dressers piled high with Mud, Kente cloths and layers of cotton fabric to execute designs in Batik when she wanted to create garments that bartered well.

A craftswoman, she worked skillfully with her hands. Made garments, jewelry, ceramic pieces, pots, stuff and things. She lived with her in-laws Rufus and Emma on the 1st floor of their Greystone on 43rd and King Drive. She met Carl in church and became their spiritual daughter when her parents passed. They moved in when they got married. After the divorce she and their daughter Jade stayed.

The back door led to a cozy courtyard fenced on both sides where she kept her Kiln, and Jade played. There was enough grass to plant flowers, grow vegetables and on a warm evening, no later than 8PM, sit chaperoned on hand painted benches to enjoy the company of male acquaintances that stop by checking to see if she was ready to date.

She engaged them with pertinent conversation, once she discovered the brother was a carnivore, or smoker looking for a woman to attend to his self-inflicted poor health or didn't know Jesus as his personal Lord and Savior, the visit was over. There would not be a second. Esther guarded her heart. Emma said, "When they not suitable, don't go another further." First Lady Beulah told her, "If they don't know the Lord when you meet em don't make the introduction. That's not yo woman place, take him to a man. Stay in your lane lest you be tempted."

Church mothers like her grandma was always speaking in the scriptures. If you asked them what they thought they'd say, "It don't make no never mind what I think. What the word of God says that's what's important. Do that!" And it was settled.

Carl was conservative, Esther was radical, she was into black culture and sacred space. Artsy space full of character. She believed the home should reflect the woman and be regenerative. It had to give back. It had to nurture and serve. When they divorced her home became her place of business. The items toward the front of the apartment were staged for sale with interesting handmade price tags hanging waiting to be bought.

Visiting was a cultural experience. She stained the imperfect plastered walls orange, red, turquoise, and gold. Warm island colors that adapted well to the changing of Chicago's seasons. Colors that made friends come and sit a spell with their thoughts. Freed eyes to roam, discover and learn. Esther mounted memorabilia on the walls.

Signs that read *"Colored Section, US Route 66, Steak & Egger"* and a large green wooden whipping paddle with a lady riding a bike on it that read *"The Hurrier I Go, the Behinder I Get."*

The vintage red and chrome kitchen table, the red rooster dish towels that hung over the handle of the vintage stove was her favorite, they belonged to her mother. The black and white checkered linoleum floor that led in from the hallway invited Jade to play hopscotch while she cooked. Esther took old *Folgers Coffee* and *Clabber Girl* cans, punched a hole in the top, strung wiring, and created chandeliers that hung over her table like they were supposed to be there.

She kept family and friends close. Not caring for photo albums, she displayed their pictures. Jade's pictures graced the hallway walls, chronicling her age with measuring tape that marked her growth spurts. Family members, friend's past and present had a special place. But her momma's picture was on the refrigerator; she talked to her each time she opened and closed the door. Jade basked in Esther's creativity, their way of living in a home that had meaning. Things told stories that never ceased to amaze her, it was their history, a family museum. She took friends on tours, articulated their history from Mobile to Savannah where Great Grandma WeBee was known for her fried green tomatoes, shrimp & grits, pralines, and peaches.

Sneaking Jules and Mecca in Esther's bedroom to look at the pictures that sat on her dresser was their sacred secret. The first time they entered, they cut their fingers and mingled blood promising to never tell. They were mesmerized by the handmade frames bedazzled with gems, cowrie shells, brown twine, and speckles of rice that represented the Gullah people; each frame uniquely different captured the light from the window and the mirrors on her walls making the room look magical.

As a little girl, Jade learned to climb on the high-sitting four poster bed to bury herself amongst the soft pillows and printed throws that smelled like her momma. Esther kept sage and a basin of water in her bedroom to bless their heads. And started the day with a bible scripture to be read by Jade; the first book she learned to read reciting one scripture a day.

There were so many things to remember about the time she and Jade cocooned in their home, making it nearly impossible to leave. But her needs were not the same. Jade graduated Howard, created *Hair Song*, a line of natural hair care products, and went into business.

She married the contractor. He won her heart when he renovated the storefront, she purchased exactly the way she wanted it. Jade was preparing for her daughter Crystal's sweet sixteen party. Esther was the grandmother of a teenager. She hadn't noticed teaching, crafting, hosting *Djembe* and *Shekere* classes, cooking, and volunteering at the museum was how she lived life. Time moved on but she didn't. She didn't want a second husband. Her deceased parents believed as long as the spouse was walking on top of the dirt, there was a marriage. She didn't want to go against what her parents believed now that they were gone.

# CHAPTER NINETEEN

### *The Millennials*

*"Just call my attorney and bail me out cause I'm going to war."*

Jade remembered but it wasn't about memories anymore. She was tired of the unforgiveness that held everyone hostage. Concerns mounted bordering on neglect and elder abuse. Confronting Esther was heart wrenching but it had to happen; it had to be done, there was no way around it. They were living in a house on fire. Esther's fears blocked the door, no one could escape. Rufus dream about going back down south fell on deaf ears so he just stopped dreaming. When she was a child, the apartment was warm and full of wonder. As an adult it looked like a public storage unit housing vintage items.

Esther went from selling to hoarding. She filled every spot with something till it was hard to visit, moving items out the way to sit down took time. Rufus and Emma got lost somewhere in the shuffle. Nobody, not even Carl noticed the apartment was a hot box. The temperature was set at 80 degrees; early Fall, it was sweltering. Everything was captured in time; it looked the same way it did when she was a child. The dining room was complete with a place setting for a family of ten; as if someone was coming to dinner. The curtains were heavy and drawn most of the time blocking out the sunlight. Dust was settling, Rufus was falling and Emma was forgetting.

One night he fell out the bed and the ambulance came to help him up. The next time he fell outta his chair, the ambulance came and wasn't so friendly. The EMT said non-emergency calls took them away from life-threatening situations. That he should see a doctor and stop wasting their valuable time. A white shirt came out personally to document and issue the recommendation.

Jade knew it was a matter of time before he would fall and hit his head on the sharp edges of the huge cocktail table. A houseful of rugs was the perfect trip hazard. Forgetfulness reared its head. Emma forgot when she had a pot on the stove or food in the oven; the fire alarm was sounding off all the time. They were losing and misplacing keys. Esther compensated keeping extra sets in her unit which was a fire hazard in and of itself. There was no way they should be living there. Jade had no choice but to expose what was going on at the Greystone. She couldn't bear the thought of a tragedy.

Jobari worried about Honey living alone in a four-bedroom house in the city. Coming and going as she pleased like nuthin changed in the last thirty years. Carrying a handbag with every piece of ID she owned, cash money and important documents strapped around her body.

The neighborhood changed. One day she came home and her driveway was blocked. She looked at her camera to find the house the person entered that parked the car, when she rang the bell a woman, she didn't know answered the door. Her friends had moved and rented their house. When she asked the young lady who was younger than Jobari to please move the car with a smile, she was cursed out and had the door slammed in her face. Honey went home broken, no one ever spoke to her that way. She was embarrassed, she didn't want to report the incident, she didn't want the police involved, she didn't want to alarm Mal and Layla. And she didn't want to risk losing her freedom so she didn't tell nobody. Honey parked on the street figuring they would stop but they didn't.

♣

The talks intensified, there was an urgency in the air. Jobari had enough, he was getting mad just thinking about it. He took a thoughtful toke off the joint, poppin his lip inhaling on the 4 2 4 count he put the eighth blunt in a clockwise rotation and went on a rampage as he stood up fanning his hands.

"Man! I'm done talking about it. Now what we gon do! All I know if somebody hurt GGMa Honey it's not gon be good y'all. Call my attorney and bail me out because I'm going to war. I'm going all in, it's not gon be no future for me. I'm telling y'all it's not gon be nuthin nobody can do or say to stop me. These teenaged thugs out here putting hands on elderly people. I don't wanna hear nuthin about what they don't wanna do. No disrespect but they don't have no choice in the matter as far as I'm concerned. We gon have to run this train like the *Underground Railroad* with a shotgun. It's time for us to make decisions for them, now. Because I'm ready to die for em so they gon be free or we all gon die. And that's real talk, it's bad out here!" he threatened before he took a breath, lit the ninth blunt and put it in rotation.

The grands grew up different. Free thinking radical, solution focused and tech savvy, they did business and went for the money. Having loyalty only to themselves and opportunities, they knew how to collaborate and make things happen. Wasn't no waiting 30 years on a pension. They made money from home, handling business walking around with ear pods in their ears, sitting in computerized meetings. Getting together during the anniversary gave them a chance to discuss things that were obvious to them but escaped their folks. They left the celebration, met up at Jobari and Diamond's house, smoked weed and laid it all out on the table puff puff passing the *Loud*.

Kato leaned in hitting his fist in his hand. "Straight facts man, these lil snot nose dudes running up on old people carjacking and beating em up. I mean they literally fighting old dudes that can't even defend themselves. Breaking their spirit down to nuthin. Making em feel worthless. I'm talking about men that raised whole big ole families cuz. Respectable men. Grand dads, veterans like Big Pops that fought in the war, snatched us up in the collar and made us do right. You don't beat up no old man. That's messed up son! I mean back in a day we weren't perfect but we most definitely weren't putting old people to sleep, runnin up in churches robbing the preacher and shooting the people. Even the gangs left something sacred."

Jade got upset. "That's because they're not teenagers. Stop calling em teenagers. Call em what they are. You have to be a beast to do something like that. I know one thing, when they start holding their mommas accountable, I bet it stop then. I betcha that much."

Her comment shocked Al. "Jade! Baby listen to you listen to you. What you mean the mommas? What about the daddies?"

Jade fired back. "What about em?

"What you mean what about em? It's time out for that invisible man crap. Mommy you gon have to rethink that. It's brothers out here making moves, paying child support, pushing strollers and taking care their babies every day. While the mommas spending money on fake nails, fake eyelashes and hair weave. Don't' tell me because I know that for a fact so don't be so cold my sista! Yeah, the way I see it you either a part of the problem or a part of the solution. Right now, you talking like you part of the problem."

"How am I part of the problem?"

"You sound like an undercover agent. Like you getting paid to sit amongst the people poisoning minds with that dangerous talk."

"Paid? What are you talking about Al? You must be outta yo mind. How am I getting paid?"

"You getting something the way you talking. You got me side eyeing you. Don't tell me I been sleeping with the enemy." He said passing the joint back to Kato. "Don't forget we started Green Construction Initiative to put young black men to work. Why you beating em down? You wanna beat em down further than they already are? You met em. The same ones that went to jail, did good on the construction site. All they need is a chance. Give em something honorable to do and they'll do it. They not lazy they wanna work. But the mistakes they made is keeping em blocked."

The blunt came back to Jade. She took a few small shallow tokes, held her breath, crossed her legs and leaned back on the sofa. "I never said they were lazy Al. I never said that. Hey y'all Al over here getting paranoid putting words in my mouth knowing full well I give them jobs at *Hair Song* warehouse whenever I have openings.

"What you holding yo breath for Jade? I told you about that! And I'm not paranoid and I'm not putting no words in yo mouth. I'm looking right at you, reading yo mind girl, sounding like a spy. I hear everything you thinking before you even think about it. I see you flashing yo eyes at me, looking like a video vixen in them tight jeans."

Jobari introduced another blunt. "Boy shut up man. We were smoking weed before it was legal, we smoking ole school. See that's why you straight trippin man. You need to slow that down cuz. He done read all the rules of smoking week now he flying too high, you getting outta pocket man, you gon regret all that talk you doing tomorrow."

"Man, it's a science ok. Aint no too high? "Dude if I'm high I'm high on facts. I'm cracking atoms, I'm talking brass facts right now son and aint nuthin you can do with that. You can't deal with this re-al-ity. Getting these brothers hired is almost impossible. They don't have no faith man! They lose faith every day. They get angry, then here comes the trickle-down, ripple down effect, here they come. They start knocking our grandparents in the head and taking their cars. And you know why?"

"Why? I wanna know what could possibly justify hurting senior citizens."

"It's not about justifying Jade; it's about understanding why they do what they do and then coming up with a solution to stop it. They do it because they don't know the value of earning nuthin for themselves, they can't conceive of buying nuthin the right way and the rest is the perpetuated history of the slave mind. Think on that my sister!"

"See I told y'all! Y'all always talking about good ole Al. Y'all just don't know. See how he gets when he high. He turns into radical man. He done called me everything from video vixen to mommy to sista. Ima need y'all to miss him on the next round."

Jobari stood up and start hitting himself in the chest hard. "What makes us any better? Just because we're not knocking senior citizens in the head don't mean nuthin. Listen to what Jade just told us. How long we gon sit down rationalizing, extrapolating and letting this happen? How many times Rufus got to fall? How long we gonna let Esther create a fire hazard? And GG Ma Honey get punked out by thugs. Huh? Ima tell you this, let me say this. If they try to break in the crib I don't care if they never learned the value of earning or buying nuthin, its gon be one less person on the planet. That's it, that's all. God knows I wanna be prayerful and do the right thing. I'm getting married. I have children to raise and I don't need no trouble. I work hard but when you come for my family, I'm turning up like a street thug! Man, I'm telling you the thought of it is too much, know what I'm saying! You feel me! I put a camera on the doorbell for protection and she coulda got killed going over there. How you think that make me feel man. On my life man! On my life! I'm going out blazing! That's all I'm saying!"

Al stood up. They were standing face to face. "Forget that man! You know what? You know what? Y'all up here talking like y'all want some jail time. And I can't be in the house too long so miss me on that! You and Kato need to breathe. Take a deep breath because y'all aint killing nobody, aint nobody giving up their future, aint nobody dying, you hear me though. We gon handle this business respectfully like three intelligent black men. These fears and emotions got to go; it's got us talking crazy. Going off about stuff that aint even happened and may never happen. Blowing stuff outta proportion. I'm listening what she said, she's scared for her mother and grandparents. And for that matter I'm scared too. I don't even know why I'm scared.

What I'm doing scared. I'm sitting over here on the edge of my seat like something bout to jump off, like I'm under a microscope, like somebody watching me. My face feels tight like it's about to split open and my eyes hurt. Man! What you got us smoking Jobari!"

Al looked at his cell phone. "Dude! It's almost 2 o'clock in the morning. We been smoking weed since 10 o'clock, that's four hours. I don't even know what happened to the music. What's wrong, what's up with you? What you the dope man or something?"

"Nawl I aint no dope man. I just keep a stash around the house for me and my woman. Man, y'all just gon have to stay and sleep it off that's all that is. We can convene this meeting in the morning." Jobari stood up and start barking out orders like he was holding them hostage. "Hey hey, y'all hear me though. Don't nobody move, stay right where you are because aint nobody leaving this piece. Try to leave and I'm sending Max and Bella to stop that action so I'm telling y'all don't try it. If you do, you gon have two bullies coming yo way and I aint calling em back, you feel me. So don't get no big ideas, you feel me. Now! Listen up. Aint no need to panic. We got plenty of room, plenty of orange and grapefruit juice in the Fridge; you feel me. Just don't mess around and drink the brown juice. That's all I'm saying. You feel me."

Kato laughed at Jobari. "Man, you bugging! I didn't know you was this crazy cuz. You real crazy. You betta be glad Diamond wasn't around when you start talking all that stuff about not having no future. And you need to hurry up and get married man. You need somebody to hold you down. I aint never been this high in my life! I don't believe this! Man, where you get this stuff from? You got us out here messed up! Man! We straight twisted!"

"I know. I know. I shoulda called it a night when Diamond put the kids to bed. That's what I shoulda did."

❦

Morning came with foggy heads and a good breakfast. Diamond was up cooking and looking refreshed. She looked around at em and laughed. "Man! What ya'll do last night, y'all look tore up from the floor up! If I knew y'all was gon spend the night I woulda pulled out some pillows."

"Nawl Bae, we aint need no pillows. We shoulda called it quits when you did. Look at my baby she done got up and cooked us breakfast.

"Yeah, and y'all bet not leave till you eat. I don't wanna hear nuthin about not having time to eat, where you gotta go and what you gotta do. You wake up in this piece, you eating. Point blank period.

"Nawl Bae, everybody's hungry, you don't have to worry about that."

"Y'all know what, I was laying in the bed last night thinking, we really gotta be careful about how we do things, know what I'm saying. You feel me? We can't just bum rush our parents. Think about it, Pops and Lala really believe everything is alright. They have no idea how we feel about bringing the kids over there. Every time we visit, I have to figure out a polite way to move things without hurting their feelings."

"That's because they got a full fledge dining room set. A 60-pound China cabinet full of glass that's not attached to the wall, a buffet, and a long table with sharp edges. They don't even go in there; all Pops do is toss mail on the table. I have to stop CJ from running so he don't end up with a big gash in his head and Cherish pulling up on everything, it's not safe. They don't need no dining room; we don't gather to eat on holidays no more. They spend the holidays visiting people."

"The first thing I tell my clients before they consider selling their home is to update. Dining rooms can be wasted space or they can serve a better purpose. Jobari knows. I had to get my parents right. Once we sent them to one of our Airbnb's for the holidays they got with the program. Especially Thanksgiving and Christmas; they act like they supposed to be somewhere on an island. They don't miss us coming over and they don't miss the house. My dad said the days of getting pimped out by a house are over."

"Diamond been trying to convince Lala and Pops to do the same thing but I don't know if they're ready for all that. They home bodies. Al, I think all they need is a quick fix. A simple renovation. You know, something like that."

"Most definitely. That's easily correctable man. I can open a few walls, enlarge the rooms and give em more space. That's what most of my clients want. Like you said, that's a quick fix. But first we got to get Rufus, Emma and Honey situated. Any work that needs to be done; Green Construction got that covered. You don't have to worry about that, we'll work out the financials, they won't have to come out of pocket. Because what we not gon do is relive last night."

"Not relive last night? Whoa, what y'all fools do. I know y'all was loud as all get out. I don't even remember when the noise stopped."

"You don't even wanna know Bae."

"Nawl cuz, you really don't wanna know."

Jade felt relieved. "Thanks Al, we appreciate you."

"Jade, we talking about family, life and safety. If I can't do that for you, what kinda man would I be?"

"Whoa. I musta missed something, Al over here looking all serious and Jade is extra appreciative. Anyway, I don't know if I mentioned it but the properties in demand are sprawling or small raised ranch houses, and let me tell you they not going cheap. Seniors want to enjoy life, not be stuck in a big empty house with a dangerous staircase. I did a back-to-back last month. It was a legitimate swap and a sweet deal considering the strain on the housing inventory. The parents bought their son's condo in Hyde Park and the son bought their house in Homewood for his growing family. They got the best of both worlds. Seniors are downsizing, they're letting these large houses go. Some of em not nuthin more than death traps."

"My sentiments exactly. That said, the expertise to move things forward is sitting right here at the table." Jobari you're a tech man. Diamond can look into the real estate. I can be the general contractor and Jade can be my project manager if she can find the time."

"Oh, don't worry about that. Ima find the time."

"Good. We got power couples in the family. The only person coming up short is you, Kato. Where yo woman man? What's popping with you?"

"I see you Al. We over here chopping it up and you turn right around and make this about me huh. That's cool. I see you slick. I don't know where she at? You got one for me?"

"I just know you not saying you can't find nobody?" Diamond chided.

"Yeah, I found mad bodies but yo, a sister gotta bring more to this table than a body. I'm looking for substance. I need a woman that can come through. I like that cerebral, Indie Arie type.

"Jobari!" Diamond whined

"Yeah Bae." Knowing she was up to something.

"We just gon have to make it happen. I know too many black women that got the whole package. Two of em live in Atlanta managing our southern properties but they travel back and forward to Chicago all the time. They'll be at the wedding. We gon hook it up. Aint that right Boo?"

"That's what's up. See, Diamond looking out for you and her girls already. Before it's over, she gon make everybody get married."

She pushed Jobari's head. "Boy shut up!"

"All I can say is make it happen. If one of em can rock with me, we can move it forward. I been out here long enough. I'm getting old and being single getting old too."

Al got up from his seat. He was ready to go. "I heard that. One of the perks about having a significant other is knowing when it's time to leave. We been here all night. Me and Jade gotta go. Thanks for breakfast Diamond."

"Ok, I see. First y'all was talking bout hooking me up now y'all putting me out?"

"Well Kato, it's about that time. Me and Diamond got things to do. When you get booed up you won't mind leaving."

"See y'all got jokes. Y'all not nuthin right."

# CHAPTER TWENTY

♣

### *Won't HE Will*

*"It's alright Mecca! God knows. While you were taking care other people families, He was taking care of yours.*

Jobari and Diamond met with Mecca and Jahi. "Thanks for sitting down with us. After the anniversary we had an overnight meeting and we have some concerns."

"Have some concerns? About what?"

"GG Ma Honey, Rufus, Emma and how they living."

"That's a whole lot of concern. GG Ma Honey, Rufus and Emma? What about how they living?"

"Well Ma, you're a social worker so we need yo expertise."

"Alright. What's the concern about how they living? Let's start there."

"There's some *go'ins ons*, that no one knows about and put it like this, it's not good."

"Ok Jobari you got my antennas up. What's going on that we don't know about that's not good?"

"For starters let's talk about GG Ma Honey."

"Let's! And let's stop beating around the bush. What's going on!"

"Is there a reason she's living in the old neighborhood in a four-bedroom house alone?"

"Jobari, you know as well as I do, GG Ma Honey is extremely independent, she don't invite us into her business and we respect that. She's been in the neighborhood since Lala was in high school and her friends are there."

Jobari and Diamond looked at each other with *we knew it eyes*. Jahi gave him a nod to keep talking. "Had, friends, there. Her friends moved away. And GG Ma Honey. Was independent. Emphasis on was. From now on she needs to keep us informed about her whereabouts and *go'ins ons*."

"Moved away?"

"Yup! As in rented their homes and got out. Aint no friends next door. Aint no friends down the street or around the corner; they been gone." Jobari raised his eyebrows, smiled and leaned into Mecca. "Uh, they moved out a long time ago."

"Momma Dae. The neighborhood is a hot spot for Section 8 and renters. That's what happens when no one wants to invest in the community; nobody's buying over there. Diamond Realty is overwhelmed with listings. Stores and businesses closed their doors. Renters are even moving out. It was a food desert till they finally opened an *Aldi's*. Outside of that, you have to go to another neighborhood to shop."

Jahi chimed in. "Let her sit with that for a minute Diamond. That's a lot to take in."

"Thanks Bae, it's a lot to take in but I need to hear it, like you said earlier everything is not about me. I'm leaning in now. What's going on?"

"When Diamond told me how the area was going down, I installed front and back doorbells with cameras."

"You sure did Jobari. I remember you doing that. She musta said something to Lala and Pops."

"Ma, I don't know if she said or what she said but what she didn't say is that these new neighbors, with their disrespect, been blocking her driveway. She can't pull in so she can't put her car in the garage, she's been parking on the street. When she asked the neighbor to move the car, she got cursed out. Now they block it all the time. I drive by to see and they still doing it. And its plenty of parking available on the block. But she's not gon say nuthin and she's not gon report it to the police. Because she don't want no trouble, she don't wanna move and she don't wanna lose her independence."

"Gotcha! And knowing Honey she's one tough cookie, she probably thinking this is my house and I'm standing my ground. You know how she feels about property. When did you find this out Jobari? Why didn't somebody say something to me?"

"I don't know if y'all noticed but nobody talks around here. Everyone is in their own silo on the strength of respecting and minding their own business. Living independent gon get somebody hurt if not killed. Ma, we need to get her outta that neighborhood like yesterday."

"Oh, say no more; it's a wrap! Diamond you may as well get ready to list it because we're not renting nuthin. We're done with that. And her pension is not gon be wasted on senior living, it's too invasive and it's too expensive. Find her a nice two-bedroom condo out this way, closer to Flossmoor."

"Momma Dae, we already worked out some ideas we'd like to run pass you. But for the sake of this conversation, do she need two-bedrooms? I've saw some nice sized one-bedroom units."

"Yeah, she's gon need two. She used to living in a house, used to having space, and we don't know what's coming down the pipe. If somebody have to stay overnight, she can accommodate them."

"She'll need a two and two. Two bedrooms and two bathrooms. That way she won't feel cramped, and have to share with company. Now that we're talking about it, she's definitely gonna need a balcony or patio so she can sit outside, get some fresh air and have a container garden. She can create a nice outside space to enjoy without leaving her unit."

"You know exactly what to do Diamond. We trust you with all the particulars. We want her to feel good about the transition. Y'all know it aint gon be easy. It wouldn't be easy for me either. I see too many seniors slip into a deep depression because well-meaning family members snatched their independence. One family threw out their mother's furniture, bought everything new and she couldn't stop crying. They weren't thinking; she had an emotional attachment to her furniture. You gotta think about how hard she worked to buy a house and it wasn't just for us; it was for her too. We're not gon disrespect her life. When the time comes, we can get her a live-in homecare aide so she can live independently for as long as possible. Then she's moving in with Lala and Pops or us."

"See that's the social worker coming outta Ma. She jumped on that with both feet. I like that enthusiasm, but we may not have to do that. Let's just list for now."

"I know y'all been discussing it. Sounds like you got something in mind?"

"We do. She getting ready to live. You know how she always wanted to travel, she gon travel. We gon make it happen. She'll hang out in some of our Airbnb's. Me and Diamond got that end covered."

"Look at God! Who knew the great grands were gon come through? You right Jobari, we're planning for her life not her death. She's got a whole lot of living to do! She dreamed of traveling ever since she was a child because her mother traveled. And it's getting ready to happen for her now; what a blessing! See how God set you back for a come up and He don't forget the desires of yo heart either. She probably gave up on traveling but He didn't. You never know how God will move and it'll mean more now at this age. Sometimes we're so busy dealing with babies and young people we neglect our precious seniors that cut a path for us. They're the ones that sacrificed and gave it all. They didn't know nuthin about being selfish. They may not have had a coat but they made sure the children had one. And a lot of times they were the last ones to eat to make sure it was enough for the children not to just eat; but have seconds. That's a whole different kinda mindset. And now they get beat up, carjacked and overlooked. Not on my watch!"

"Like Rufus and Emma."

"Alright Jahi! I'm all in. What's going on with them?"

"And Esther"

"Esther too Diamond? O.k. I'm good with that. We just gon do what we need to do!"

"It's a long story Momma Dae."

"Well start talking!"

"Jade can tell you better than we can. Suffice to say Rufus is falling, Emma is forgetting and Esther is hoarding. Momma Dae, it's a fire hazard over there."

"Lord have mercy Jesus! He don't put no more on us than we can bear. I know what to do but I'm upset with myself. I'm so upset with myself! Jahi, where have I been?

"It's alright Bae, this what you do all day, you got this, and I got you. What you wanna do first? We following yo lead."

I'm getting a team out there tomorrow! We need to stop by Jade and Als'. I want to get over to the Greystone tonight and see exactly what's going on. I saw good people with capable families get caught in the system. We not going out like that. There is no neglect. Jobari call GG Ma Honey tell her we dropping in on her tomorrow, so she needs to be there. We're doing a wellness check whether she wants one or not. I don't care nuthin about nobody's rights. We're going in. Better yet, set up a family meeting. I'm running around here like a chicken with my head cut off taking care everybody's family while mine is going down the drain! No more."

"It's alright Mecca! God knows. While you were taking care other people families, He was taking care of ours. And nobody does it better than HIM. Nuthin happened. We on top of things. Charity will begin at home, that's what it is."

"That's what it is Jahi?

"That's what it is."

"Man, you over here preaching! Momma Howard always said, everything happens for a reason and a season. It's a reason we got together and talked after the anniversary. It's time to pour into our family and take care, our legacy."

"Jobari. What's going on with mom and dad? Ten minutes ago, I woulda told you if it was something crazy, to just throw me down a flight of stairs. But I'm ready. What's going on at the big house?"

"Just kill you huh, Ma. Nawl, we not throwing you down the stairs. And we not even talking like that. Like Jahi said, we got this. Pops and Lala are in decent condition but we do need to get that dangerous furniture outta the dining room and do some minor upgrades for safety. Diamond, can you run down the plan we outlined?"

"With pleasure." Diamond started her presentation. "So, we collaborated and put a lot of thought and consideration into being sensitive to everyone's needs. First things first. Rufus and Emma will relocate to Mobile. Rufus been talking about going home for the longest so that's an easy win. We suspect he may have issues with circulation, so he can't sit too long. If his doctor clears him to fly, we flying them out in two weeks. If not, it'll be a slow road trip with a lot of stops so he can stretch along the way. That'll stop blood clots from forming in his legs and anywhere else for that matter. Carl is going down early to get things together before they arrive and he'll stay with them for two weeks to help get them settled.

The Greystone will do the heavy lifting. Their pensions are not large so it'll put some money in their pockets. Actually, they'll do better than when they were working. We ran the numbers; the Greystone has the potential to generate a substantial stream of revenue. On the low end it could rent for $2000 a night with a 3-night minimum, earning them $6000 per visit. If the Greystone was rented once a month at that rate, again a low-ball projection, it would gross $72,000 annually.

At any rate, it will increase their income exponentially. They aint never made this much money. So, this is a good thing. However, Diamond Realty, that's me, plan to market it in a way it'll have regular use. We'll market to Work Groups, Social Groups, Weddings, Reunions, Corporate Meetings, Staging for Movies, Family

Vacationers and Holiday traffic." The cost will be offset by their grandchildren Al and Jade through Green Construction. They'll pick up the tab until closing.

"I like that, Diamond."

"We thought you would."

"What about GG Ma Honey?"

"We glad you asked. Now. Moving forward. She's going on an extended vacay. She'll have her choice of stays in our Airbnb's in and out of the states. Maybe starting out with my parents so she can be comfortable. They already set up three Airbnb's of their own and they love it; they can help her get acclimated to the idea. And Jobari working some other ends to sweeten the deal. He's keeping it a secret but trust, it'll be all good. Continuing. The Sheldon Heights property will be renovated by Green Construction as in Jade and Al Green and be listed with me, Diamond Realty.

Comparables are $200,000. The property is in good condition. We budgeted for $60,000 in renovations with a minimum scope of work. Basic kitchen and bath upgrades are the fastest way to increase property value. Al will frame and drywall the basement, polish the concrete floor to add to the square footage of living space. Pluming is already roughed in down there so we'll install a four-piece bathroom. A toilet, a sink, a bath tub and a shower. The more bathrooms the better. There's a potential profit of $140,000 to get her invested in two condo properties in two states one in Chicago and one in Mobile or Savannah to be set up as Airbnb's. She can reside in one during the winter and the other during the summer months and still be close to family. It's her choice."

"Diamond, that sounds good! I wouldn't mind doing that myself."

"And you know whenever ya'll ready we can do that. Well Ma, we need to sit with an attorney, ours preferably and deal with everything legal from living wills, to trust. You know, tie up the loose ends."

"Makes sense to me and I know Jahi was involved that's why he sitting over here holding my hand like I'm gon spaz out. How about adding some wrap around services? I'd like to have them work with a private Gerontologist for health, lifestyle consultation and referrals. Maybe even some environmental consulting."

"Sounds like a plan Ma."

"Well then, like y'all say. Let's go get it!"

# CHAPTER TWENTY-ONE

♣

### *Esther's Place*

*"Esther my love it's not a discussion. Sweetheart you have to move. Tonight"*

Diamond handed her the listings as Layla spoke. "The Greystone is slated for rehab early Spring. Moving with Al and Jade will give you time to find something nice before school starts in September."

Layla was nominated to tell Esther in no uncertain terms that she was a burden, a danger to herself and those she loved. Unforgiveness had them all dying a slow death. Hearing it from the family was one thing but from a team of social workers, and a friend from the fire department was the absolute bottom. The system needed to be silenced, Esther would leave immediately and transition to a new residence from Jade's home. She packed the one bag she was allowed to bring; the other items would be picked up only as needed.

Rufus and Emma suffered through brutal winters as medications thinned their blood. It was senseless when they could spend their remaining years with his family in a warm climate. Three of his eight siblings were alive with a reasonable portion of their health; a brother and two sisters; Rufus was the youngest. When they spoke on the phone, he ended the conversation with, "Save a seat for me." It was a Howard salutation. Growing up across from the train tracks reminded them one day they would all board the train to heaven.

♣

The transition went well. Carl flew to Alabama with his parents to get them situated. The property was empty and ready to be rehabbed for the June wedding. Esther planned to spend more time at the museum once she retired and wanted to live close by. Walkability was important. April came, it was getting warm, June was coming, school would be out in time for the wedding. After a Saturday event, she crossed the park and strolled block-to-block rediscovering the neighborhood. She walked down Langley, there was a Classical Revival style two-flat Greystone that pricked her heart, it was the only house on the block for sale. Similar to Rufus and Emma's Greystone but smaller.

The limestone-façade and bricks were in excellent condition. The front porch, doors and windows, were refreshed and original. The large bay windows were reminiscent of days she looked out to watch girls play Double-Dutch in the narrow street afterschool. Esther was surprised the property ignited her interest; she called her agent. Diamond instructed him to give special consideration, and to steer away from properties she would not approve. He was relieved. He was tired of looking. Nuthin, he found was suitable. Late April, Esther found what she wanted in a good community.

From the front porch she could see the museum, the park, the hospital, the university where she spent time in the library. The Midway where she attended summer festivals and a church on the corner of Champlain. She could thrive there, everything familiar was in walking distance. Esther visited the property different times of day, different days of the week, weekends even Sunday mornings to study the beautiful hats the women wore. Watch the girls' swinging handbags in white ankle socks and to hear the sound of black patten leather shoes clicking against the pavement.

Boys behaving like little grown men brought back childhood memories when she went to church with her family and later Carl. It was community. Even though there was one neighbor that refused to extend a gracious welcome but stared with a meddling eye and watched closely with wrong intent; the neighbors that welcomed her long before the showing was more than enough to fill her with good thoughts.

A two-flat with a basement would bring revenue, provide space to continue the *Djembe* and *Shekere* classes once she retired. Although she'd be sweeping chicken bones from the front steps until the neighborhood shifted, she wouldn't need to sub teach to afford vacations. A couple of colleagues came along to support her decision. When the agent opened the door, she crossed the threshold alone and stood wait for the space to welcome her. Once accepted she turned, opened her arms invitingly and said. "Welcome to Esther's Place!"

They were anxious to see. While they waited, they peeked through the door's stained glass window and saw the deacons' bench in the vestibule. Once invited, they rushed inside. The mahogany floors, quarter-turn staircase with wainscoting, antique mirrors, and 8 feet pocket doors that opened to a parlor were breathtaking. The living, dining space was perfect for entertaining. The nice sized kitchen was roomy enough for more than one cook. The back porch was newly built. The small backyard was fenced and had room for her kiln, a garden, sitting chairs, and the two-car garage backed up to the alley with a front door courtyard entry sorta like, *Jaden's Court* at the big Greystone. The warmth that greeted her at the door sealed the deal. Esther was home. moving was simple. She brought only the basics, her bed, kitchen table and sofa. Everything else would come in time as she healed.

♣

Weeks later, Esther found herself preoccupied with Sundays, watching congregants park and walk from cars became a pastime. People entering one-way and exiting another. Sounds of the service washed over the community as only Sunday mornings could do. She was beckoned. Sunday after Sunday watching the parade of marching beautiful huge, ornamented hats with elaborate features go by. They were more than hats; they made a statement. Like a glorious crown.

Women dresses sweeping ankles, swinging just over the heels of colorful pumps. Shaved suited men, handkerchiefs in pockets, matching ties, clips, bibles in hand walking with wives. Children mimicking adults. Girls' skirts below knees. Boys with fresh haircuts, shirts tucked, ties, dress shoes, carrying instruments, opening doors for girls and women. Sounds of praise, lifted voices emanating, vibrating down the block from the church on the corner. She watched distracted by its presence.

In her mind, it seemed like the church could be seen from every angle, as if that was possible. When she found the Greystone, it was there, she saw it, the church on the corner, but it hadn't spoken yet. Now it had much to say and wouldn't stop talking. Esther was restless knowing she hadn't been living life, hadn't forgiven Carl and found reasons not to focus on her personal needs. Afraid to trust she buried herself under everything creative, community, educational, and cultural. The teachings of church mothers who spoke in the scriptures were mere memories. She prayed, meditated, read scriptures and watched Rufus and Emma leave out the door every Sunday for more than thirty years, refusing to go to church. The best she could do is send her child, her tithe and her offering.

Esther was angry, she blamed God for the divorce and blamed HIM for the loss of her parents and blamed HIM and blamed HIM and blamed HIM for everything that hurt in her life. A young Christian she vowed to keep herself pure until she married. After witnessing Carl give his life to Christ during a summer revival, she claimed him for her husband. During the time they dated she lost her parents, Rufus and Emma took her under their wing, and she drew close to the family.

Their second year in college Carl fell out under the anointing and got up speaking in tongues. After they became intimate, Carl felt compelled to get engaged. The family couldn't be happier. The pastor approved. Rufus and Emma counseled them about the sanctity of marriage leading up to the wedding. They never mentioned a baby was on the way.

They looked beautiful in their sacred attire, church members were excited, showered them with gifts and prepared a delicious meal for the reception in their honor. Six years into the marriage, Carl was not pleased. They had nuthin in common, he was discontent, and his eyes wandered within the church. Esther remembered the special attention he gave a choir member leading a song. Long conversations after rehearsals. Eyes meeting when she sang, and he played. How little Jade was when he walked out, moved on and began a new life with the choir member; shamelessly staying at the church as if nuthin mattered. Jade's birthday was a constant reminder of how quickly her life changed. She swore she'd never return to his uncle's church that was a part of a district, that was a part of a jurisdiction. There was nowhere to go. Esther sent Jade to worship with Rufus and Emma. Covered herself from head to toe and attended Mosque.

Church was different from the Mosque. The church had a pull, a constant nudging that brought her to a complete halt, till she stopped going to the Mosque. Sundays drew her closer wanting to hear the loud uninhibited sounds. The *"Well Bless the Lord's, and Won't He Will's,* in conversations women had on the way to cars.

Sundays came with good feelings. One Sunday she heard the singing, got excited, rummaged through her closet tossed around sarong skirts, headwraps and belly beads. Found the perfect Kelly green, pink and yellow floral linen dress, the one Emma gave her to wear on a date with Carl before Jade was born. She gently dropped her head, sorted her locs with her fingers pulled them up to create a messy bun, hooked on her ankh earrings, dressed her wrist in bracelets, bangles, put rings on fingers, oiled her legs, slid on a pair of green kitten-heeled slingback pumps with no stockings, and grabbed an oversized straw bag. Keys in hand she walked out the door, swiftly down the stairs and over to the church on the corner not quite ready but determined to get there.

Anticipating a closer look, promising herself to go in only if led and not before; she stood idly by. Within seconds she got caught up in a vortex of people and pulled inside. An usher escorted her to a seat at the front between two well dressed women with huge hats smiling at her with a knowing. A knowing that something was gon happen. She knew it too; an unction was stirring inside her; she'd been there before but not all the way. The anointing hadn't fell on her like it did Carl. Sure as the saints of God waved their arms, danced and shouted thank you Jesus to the quickening sound of Deacon Johns guitar, she knew she would give up and give over. She had to surrender. It was in her to do it. Time and chance waited for it to happen.

The music seeped down in her soul. The sister to her left couldn't stop quickening, shouting. "HIGHER! High ya ya ya ya!" The one on her right, arms kept rising up over her head, hands grabbing a quick fist. Snatching like she caught something in the air. Turned her head speaking mightily in tongues. Stomped her foot sending shock waves through Esther's body and down the aisle. One by one the whole pew of people went up in unquenchable praise. Esther jumped up outta her seat like something was wrong in her stocking the way she kept stooping down and standing up. Jerked her way in the aisle and took off running like her feet were burning and she was stomping out the fire.

The ushers, in white uniforms, white gloves, white stockings and white shoes full of the spirit covered her, one on each side, running alongside her praising God. Keeping pace like *Tennessee Walking* horses trotting with two beats suspended in moments. The music got louder, the aisles filled with people shouting and dancing. Esther made three rounds. Stopped at the altar fell on her knees, wrapped her arms around her body, rocked back and forth like a baby soothing itself. They covered her with a white crisp sheet, missionaries came, wrapped their bodies around her putting her in a circle, shielding her from the crowd. The musicians locked into a perpetual beat that intensified. The pastor came down from the pulpit, stood in front of the alter and proclaimed with God's authority.

*"A move of God is going on! God is moving by his power; He's moving by his spirit. If you want something from the Lord, get it on your mind and make yo way to the altar. The setback was a setup, you coming out today. God's breaking yokes off backs. Get ready for yo breakthrough. Tell yo neighbor when you come out you bringing em out with you. "*

It seemed the pastor was speaking to Esther. She stayed on the altar, broken, talking to God.

*"Lord, I'm so tired. I'm tired of the hurt. Tired of feeling let down. Tired of being disappointed. Tired of being angry with you and the church. Tired of living in the past. God I'm just sick and tired of being sick and tired. I'm tired of myself. Tired of walking in my own way. God, I want you! If I have to give up everything that's alright too; I just want you! I'll stay here on the altar, lay here on the floor, I'll get up under the floor; just give me you!"*

Esther's confession went on and on, not knowing the crowd had cleared. There she was alone at the altar. As she was receiving the Lord as her personal Savior, she began speaking in unknown tongues into a microphone before the congregation. Carl was standing at the back of the church.

*"I came hoping we could talk about reconciling"*
*"Really and why would we do that?"*

Esther let go. Thanked the Lord for the time he blessed her to be there, walked out the Greystone for the last time with only a bottle of lotion in her hand, didn't look back not once. Keeping a few items donating the rest to charity, the hoarding stopped. She had a new home new community, new church, a new life. The future was intoxicating. She spent time wisely *tending* to herself. Not wanting not longing not anxious for nuthin. In whatever state she found herself she was content. Embracing her singleness, fasting, praying, reading, writing and listening to the sweet sound of silence resonating in her soul. In need of self-love, the kind that take time. Uninterrupted time. She went inside and nursed the wounds herself; she became responsible for her life; it was up to her to live and not die. She became the place of worship, the worshiper, and the minister. Ministering to her spirit through the gospel. The thought of putting on her robe telling the story how she made it over, opened a flood gate of tears held back way too long.

    She cut her locs. Addressed the needs of her dry skin, buffed her feet, painted the toes Carl said looked like little M & M's and thanked them for carrying her through the trying times. She found peace in the center of God's Will for her life. And it felt good not being defined by anything and anybody. It felt so good she made dates with herself. Went to the lakefront, vegan restaurants and ate healthy meals with herself. To the theatre, enjoyed black culture and jazz in the park with herself. The chance to live again was a blessing. She wanted to give her whole heart. All of who she was to a man.

    She desired a man. A man that could get a prayer through, have a good discussion about the good book. A man that could relate to her God-given creativity. Share perspectives over carrot juice and morning glory muffins at the corner cafe. Listen to Saturday morning dusties in the backyard and probe the depths of her mind.

    And they came. Spiritually conscious black men walking, talking, living and breathing, in good healthy places. The church, mosques, gyms, museums, cafes, bookstores, festivals. Playing chess and congas in the square. Riding bikes, doing Tai Chi on the lakefront; holding the ball, inhaling the good Chi exhaling the bad. Like minded men committed to a life's work. Everywhere she went they boldly presented themselves; she never saw them till she was made ready. They were beyond potential and engaged in purpose.

    Energies met and greetings, Jambo, Habari gani, Assalim Lakim and Good Morning ignited a connection making them interested. Making them want to share, making them want to talk and listen to one another. Men that embraced their heritage, honored their role as black men. Men that conversated and collaborated one with another.

Respected and protected the sanctity of women, children, family, and community. Esther was content. Carl wasn't.

# CHAPTER TWENTY-TWO

♣

*Crossing Over*

*"The only thing demonic is your ignorance. Your self-hatred is pitiful and your verbal abuse can't penetrate y heart."*

Almost a year later, a man was made. Jobari, the fifth generation of the Howard family stepped to the plate and committed to marry the mother of his two children. Wedding plans filled the atmosphere with the newness of hope. Teamwork brought family together. Everybody had something to contribute to the wedding and the launching of the Airbnb. It was a time of celebration. All they had to do was rest easy, the wedding coordinator was in control. The doorbell rang, it was Carl.

"Aren't you the frequent visitor. What's going on Carl?"

"You what's going on!"

"Uh. Me?"

"It's good to see you Carl, but I'm on my way to the Greystone. Rufus and Emma are doing a walk through. I promised to be there. Al and Jade picked em up from the airport this morning."

"Is that how you greet yo guest. You opened the door telling me you on your way out."

"Carl you not a guest. I didn't invite you and like I said I'm on my way to meet Rufus and Emma."

"That's nice. You going to meet Rufus and Emma. Those are my parents. My family. Listen to you talking to me like I don't know what's going on. They weren't lying when they said you were the daughter they never had. I didn't know I married my sister."

"Carl why are you here? I didn't open my door to contend with you. Just so you know, they are the parents I lost. We been together a long time, it's strange not having them above my head like the angels they are. If it weren't for those two, I don't know where I'd be."

"You know you one interesting woman Esther. Are you aware of yo tendency to speak to me about my mother and my father as if I'm not their only son, their only child? Don't forget, I brought you in this family!"

"And don't forget you standing on my door step, so be careful. Are you aware when I talk about your mother and father it has absolutely nuthin to do with you? It's about our relationship and how God brought them in my life when I lost my parents. Get that in your head Carl. God orchestrate lives not you and not me. So anyway, yeah, I can see how I could be coming across that way. It might have something to do with how you walked out, left me, our six-year-old daughter and got too busy to check in on as you say, yo mother and father and married the woman that's cheating on you now. I can see how I could be coming across that way. But that's unnecessary talk that I'm not revisiting in my home. Arguing don't live here Carl. Again, what brings you to my door? I haven't been here two months and you done dropped by three times in one week. Excuse me for not inviting you inside but as I said before I have to go and then I have to get to the museum."

"Dig that! I guess I had it coming, huh. I didn't know you were that busy. I guess you in demand. Far be it for me to impose. You still volunteering at the museum?'

"No no no no. I'm not volunteering and yes, I am in demand, and you are imposing. I have a date for Jazz on the lawn and you wouldn't know how busy I am because we don't talk. We don't have that type of relationship. I don't discuss my business with you Carl and you know this."

"Dig. I didn't mean to pry."

"And I didn't mean to tell you, my business. I don't mind us getting together for family functions. All of us are excited about the wedding but Ima need you not to drop by my home unannounced. I don't see the logic. Jade is at home with Al with our granddaughter and yo parents live in Alabama."

"My apologies, I didn't think it was a problem."

"Well, it is a problem. How could it not be a problem? You a married man and I'm a single woman. I'm yo ex-wife, you have no business here, this is my new home. I'm a Christian woman, I have a reputation to protect and a nosey neighbor always looking for something to gossip about. Let me go head on and shun the appearance of evil. I need you to stand back outta the doorway, we really should be all the way on the front porch."

"Was. A married man. Me and Karen is getting divorced."

"Again, that's not my business but who didn't know? You married the woman you cheated with; that's what you do. Cheat. She just so happens to be cheating on you this time."

"Do I look worried?"

"Uh. And that would be too much to ask me."

"Is that all you have to say?"

"Why should I have anything to say? I'm the last person you should be talking to."

"Why?"

"Cause what's going on with you has nuthin to do with me. I moved on; I'm gone. I'm glad I'm gone, proud of myself. I'm focusing on my life and I like it. I never courted I married. Now I'm learning to court. Meeting brothers that enjoy my company, and doing things with me. I went out for a morning coffee the other day. Something we never did."

"Coffee? You don't even drink coffee."

"Of course, I don't but the brother that took me to breakfast do. I had my usual. Bottom line. It felt good to be appreciated."

"Well, it certainly shows. You look good. You cut yo locs."

"Thank you. I did."

"I like this look; it softens your face."

"Thanks. And you looking very unattractive ignoring what I said twenty minutes ago. For the third time I have things to do Carl."

"Can I tell you I was wrong?"

"You can tell me whatever. I already forgave you so what we talking about right here right now?"

He got angry. "You know it wasn't all my fault. You crash landed on me and you weren't saved. Got into that demonic stuff, leaving food for the ancestors. Going around them Muslims. Running around with strange friends, talking about Ah shay. Buying fake oils from that bum over on the corner, cooking for him. Had all that junk in our house you call yourself making and cut off yo beautiful straight hair to put them things in yo head."

"Would you be referring to locs?"

"Yeah, them things make people look like troll dolls and them big clothes that turn a man off. We were unequally yoked but I had no right to walk out. I was wrong. Notice I don't have no problem admitting when I'm wrong unlike you."

"The only thing demonic is your ignorance. Your self-hatred is pitiful and your verbal abuse can't penetrate my heart. It's clear, I was wrong, and I sincerely apologize. When I lost my parents, I drew close to yours, they drew close to me, and I married you. I ask yo forgiveness; I had no right. So now we realize the marriage was a mistake."

"I forgive you."

"Bless you. Who we are as individuals, our personalities our interests how we see the world, our energy is not compatible. Your inability to give back escapes me. Nuthin originates with you, you graft onto others, and take what they give to move your agenda. For you it's get and gain and wanting to be seen. The disrespect you have for our culture saddens me, that's why this conversation has nowhere to go but down. Did I know the Lord like I do today? No, I didn't and neither did you that's why we were pregnant with Jade before we got to the alter and cut the cake. We were going to church not living a dimes worth of nuthin. My God, you take me places I don't wanna go! Ima need you to step all the way back outta my doorway Carl! You so disrespectful. You the father of my child and granddaughter so I will not be rude and shut the door in yo face but I'm shutting this door so move yo face."

Carl kept his foot on the threshold. "Wait a minute Esther, I came here hoping we could talk about reconciling."

"Are you kidding me right now. And why would we do that?"

"I saw you."

"You saw me?"

"I saw you at church. I stopped by to talk, you weren't here, I heard music coming from the church over on the corner. I went to the service to clear my head. I saw you surrender yo life to the Lord. I saw when you ran, fell on your knees and I heard you repent, cry out and speak in tongues. It was confirmation. God told me to come home. Esther, you my first wife and I'm yo husband. Whether you like it or not, we're married as long as we living. Remember, it was till death do us part."

"And you felt my experience with the Lord was confirmation for you to re-enter my life?"

"What else could it be?"

"You tell me. Because the last time I checked with my pastor, yo marriage was a public display of adultery. That would be the death of our marriage."

Carl stepped back and Esther closed the door breaking their eye contact.

# CHAPTER TWENTY-THREE

♣

## *His Story*

*"The page flipped slowly followed by the words, "the Lord Giveth and the Lord Taketh Away."*

Standing in front of the Greystone was emotional but no tears were shed. It had been almost a year since they last been there. JE opened the door; the Greystone was not what they remembered. He attempted to show Rufus and Emma their old bedroom decorated in their honor. Where the kitchen butler pantry wall was removed to accommodate newer appliances. Explained how rooms were combined to make larger bedrooms and open living spaces. How they maintained the original integrity of the Greystone, but it didn't matter they were just proud to pass the property on to the children and keep it in the family. They hung out in the coach house with JE and Blue until it was time for the rehearsal dinner.

The Greystone could sleep twenty people comfortably. Honor was given to all the grandparents. They were assigned the 1st floor to be attended by bridesmaids. JE and the groomsmen setup the theatre room on the lower level for the surprise viewing and the coach house for the after set. The bridal party arrived, it was old times when Mecca, Jules and Jade hung out in Esther's kitchen helping her cook.

Mother Howard made homemade biscuits that melted in mouths like butter and passed the recipe down. Honey cooked for two days. A health-conscious generation no one ate pork. She jerked, smoked, rotisserie and barbequed chicken and Tofu. Smothered cabbage, sautéed kale greens, made a side dish of roasted brussels sprouts with red bell peppers in olive oil, spicy rice, potato and macaroni salad, and a gang of *Milnot* milk drenched bean pies. The wedding menu was similar.

Diamond's coordinator captured her imagination. Both families milling around, mixing and mingling. The rehearsal dinner would not be in a restaurant and the bridal party would not stay in hotels, everything revolved around home, family and friends.

The oldest, Daddy Howard sat at the head of the table, JE sat beside him and Mother Howard at the other end. He blessed the food and the hands that made it, broke bread, talked and reminisced. Myles and Layla laughed about the day she met Malcolm. After dinner, the coordinator escorted them to the theatre room for the presentation. Daddy and Mother Howard were seated in two large hunter green leather recliners with the family wrapped around them. Diamond left no stone unturned. The Howard Family journey was memorialized. Emotions unleashed, and the room became a sacred space. The lights dimmed down and the DVD started.

Chapter one opened with the caption, *The Fighting Black Devils*, a picture of Daddy Howard standing in front of the Victory Monument in Bronzeville, in his Army uniform with a group of friends from the 370$^{th}$ Regimen. The next picture was Daddy Howard hugging a woman, holding a baby. The room stirred, Mother Howard patted his knee and explained what they were forbidden to talk about. It was his first wife Adeline and their seven-year-old son Junior before a fatal car accident took both their lives. After they died, he left Chicago moved back to Mounds with his family where he met Mother Howard. The chapter closed, followed by the words, *All Souls Belong to HIM - Blessed Be the Lord that Giveth and Taketh Away*. And the page flipped slowly.

The second chapter opened with an upbeat gospel song, *"I'll Take You There"* by the Staple Singers. The caption read *New Beginnings*. Daddy and Mother Howard's wedding picture appeared, then the house he built with their sons, all eleven of the Howard children sitting on the front porch holding their baptism certificates. The Howard girls cooking at the church picnic. JE in his Navy uniform at the train station coming home on leave. JE in his Army uniform returning trying to stuff Myles in his duffle bag like he was taking him back with him. A Caucasian baby girl with curly blonde hair in a sailor dress. Pastor Jones and the church they attended. Lovejoy high school. Class pictures of Honey and Addiemae. The Spence family, their house, car and barbershop. A picture of Angie sitting on Honey's lap with ribbons on the end of her braids. The girls collecting sticks of gum from the railroad tracks in Sunday dresses. Mother Howard picking berries and pole beans. The girls running from chickens. JE and Myles brushing Maggie. Rufus in Mobile with his family. Rufus, Emma, and friends at the *Club DeLisa*. Rufus and Emma dressed to the nine walking the Stroll. Rufus and Emma Standing on the front porch of the boarding house where they met. And it closed with Carl standing in front of his school with Rufus and Emma on his first day of kindergarten.

The third chapter opened with *"Keeper of the Castle"* by the Four Tops. The caption read, *Chicago*. There were pictures of JE and Honey downtown when they arrived, ABLA projects. Mattie and Franklin pregnant with their first child; the one they lost before Mina. JE and Franklin in the maintenance room. JE showing off his muscles looking like Popeye, Franklin holding up his dog tags with one hand, and a black power sign with the other. Marcy Newberry Center, Fosco Park, Medill and Smyth class pictures. Layla and Mina playing at their new house in South Shore. The house in Roseland. Honey in her mail uniform, Honey sitting down in her new office behind her desk, and Honey's diploma. Myles band *Undercover Funk* in the garage with a yard full of teenagers, the guys on the front porch and Layla's eighth grade graduation Standing in front of Lilydale Baptist church with Mina and Jade. The movie ended with pictures of the house in Roseland and Shelton Heights. JE's home in Indiana with Blue. Esther's Greystone in Woodlawn and the renovated Greystone on King Drive. There were recorded well wishes from family members in Mobile and Savannah. Rufus' siblings, dear friend Momma Alice, cousin Indigo, Boaz and her fiancé Jaffar.

The last chapter opened with NeoSoul music *"Never Give You Up"* by Raphael Saadiq and read, *May Gods Prayers Travel Beyond the Fifth Generation and Bless You to Stay for the Long Haul.* There was a picture of all the grand and great-grandchildren sitting on the front porch steps of the Greystone. A tape of information crawled at the bottom, *"Please be sure to leave your emails and mailing information."* When it ended Diamond told everyone. "Be sure to keep taking pictures, and recording the history of the next generation."

Diamond looped the song making it play over and over and over. Everybody felt good just grooving to the music, listening, and singing the words till the DVD finally ended and the screen went blank.

❧

Jobari looked across the room at Daddy Howard sitting quietly. He stood still and called out. "Daddy Howard. That was powerful! All this love and happiness is because of you…one man that stayed committed to his family. Look at yo history! It's alright that we feel good and celebrate. No disrespect, we don't mean no harm. We just love you. We know you a man of few words but please bless us with yo wisdom." He sat down and everyone clapped to encourage Daddy Howard. He stood, bowed his head and offered a spirit-filled, humble prayer.

*"Lord forgive us. Thank you for this my family you saw fit to give me. How you kept yo hand up on us, walked with us, talked with us down through the years. Thank you Dear Sir! You the power and the glory. All glory is thine. Thank you for reaching out yo hand when we were disobedient. Lost in foolishness, unforgiveness, and sin. Make us whole. Save us from ourselves. Sanctify us wholly. Fill us with the gift of yo precious Holy Ghost and that with a mighty burning fire. Let it burn up everything that's not like you. Save us from the gutter most to the uttermost. Touch us from the tops of our heads, to the soles of our feet. Teach us humility. Teach us how to suffer. Teach us to know you in the fellowship of yo suffering. Make our souls worthy of the cross. Seal us before the appointed time. Amen."*

A hush came over the room. He sat down, crossed his hands, bowed his head and kept saying, "Thank You Father" over and over again. Mother Howard latched on. Told everybody to take the hand next to them as she led them in the prayer they learned as children. They prayed in unison:

*Our Father, which art in heaven,*
*Hallowed be thy Name.*
*Thy Kingdom come.*
*Thy will be done in earth,*
*As it is in heaven.*
*Give us this day our daily bread.*
*And forgive us our trespasses,*
*As we forgive them that trespass against us.*
*And lead us not into temptation,*
*But deliver us from evil.*
*For thine is the kingdom,*

*The power, and the glory,*
*For ever and ever…Amen.*

    And when it was over, they knew not to quench the spirit but to wait and allow God to move. The prayers touched Jobari. Within seconds he ignited. "I want blessings' on our lives. I want what Daddy Howard gave us. I want to continue the legacy of prayer and righteous living. I want my household to serve the Lord. I want a real relationship with God." He called Diamond over to him and held her hand. "Diamond, we went to church every Sunday, but we weren't living righteously. Are you willing to give your life to the Lord? Because I am and I can't go into this marriage backwards. I already know its gon take faith in God for us to do this the right way Bae."

    Diamond's family stirred with excitement while she spoke. "Yes! It's what I wanted. My family and I been praying for this for a long time."

    Daddy Howard lifted his hands in praise, everybody followed while Bishop Turner led them to the Lord, spoke a word over their lives, the lives of their children and their future. Right after, tributes testimonies and confessions poured out around the room and they had church. Rufus testified of their gratefulness. How he hadn't fallen since they moved to Mobile. How blessed they are to sit on their front porch, walk the property with his sisters and his brother. Visit Momma Alice a friend that looked after Indigo, his brother's great granddaughter and her son Boaz. How she asked him to walk her down the aisle at her wedding next summer at 80 years old. How they were going to Savannah to meet her fiancée, and visit his art gallery that was near the healing center Jules's parents were opening. And how they were looking forward to getting back home. They invited the family to visit, and wished Jobari and Diamond well. "May you and Diamond enjoy yo years together. May God bless yo union to stand the test and trials of time."

    Then the tributes started, Myles spoke. "I'm blessed to be a Howard, to carry on our belief and tradition of prayer. My wife and I pray for our families every night before we close our eyes. We do it because prayer works, it travels, and it follows you everywhere you go. I know it do. Coming up in a houseful of females I was frustrated and resentful. Impatient. I swore I wasn't gon never get married. I wanted girlfriends but wasn't gon commit to nobody and lived that way for a long time. I was a womanizer. I went around hurting good women that deserved more than I was willing to give. I see Layla and Mal laughing they know I made Layla's teenage years miserable."

"To say the least!" Layla added laughing

"But it was all love right Layla?"

"Yes Carl, it was all love. He did what big brothers do." She laughed again. "Drive little sisters crazy!"

"What can I say. I was living a fool's life. I was heavy handed with Layla and she checked me at sixteen. But the change didn't come till I met my wife. God chose the most unlikely people to cross paths. Momma Howard, you told us He knows who we are. He knew what it was gon take for me. When I think about how my mind was twisted to do harm, it humbles me. It took someone different."

Before he could finish someone yelled, "Different is good!"

He agreed and repeated. "That's right. Different is good! I met her recruiting young men and women for the Army at the community college. I noticed this beautiful sister that said nuthin as she walked by on her way to a classroom. Turns out she was teaching African American Studies. Out of curiosity, I peeked my head in her classroom and she invited me to observe. I found I had no knowledge of self; I was ignorant of my history as a black man. I was oppressing my own people. The lesson broke my heart so I kept coming to class and the queen graciously enlightened me. The way she spoke, wore her natural hair, clothes made with her own hands covering herself. Jewelry that meant something. The smell of sacred oils radiating from the heat of her body."

Jobari yelled out. "Watch out there now Uncle Myles!"

"Yeah Jobari, you know what I'm talking about. I was taken. Just like Diamond took you. She didn't force me, she inspired me to do it different. To eat healthy when I was killing myself, eating swine, smoking, drinking hard liquor, staying out all night and laying down with strange women. It's a scary thought! But I found her in her commitment to the black community and it blew my mind. Even her students honor her presence. Girls covered their young bodies because she covered hers and held it sacred. And when we had our son, she named him Kato, because he's, our perfection. When you see us presenting bearded, bald or locked, know it's Hadassah. Why am I saying this? Because I'm proud. One more black man stepped up to the plate, and honored the mother of his children, the keeper of his future and he's a Howard. Congratulations Jobari and Diamond, you have blessed yourselves. May you both learn and grow together in every way imaginable and keep prayer not at the center but at the head of your lives."

Hadassah stood graciously while Myles spoke of her, when he finished, she covered her heart with her right hand and responded.

"Alhamduliallah."

Carl blurted out. "Are you Muslim?"

Myles and Kato sighed at his ignorance knowing she would give him a worthy response. One he might not be ready to receive.

She responded. "I attend services and go where my husband leads. I submit to God as do you. Why do you ask, my brother?"

"Your name. And I noticed you use Arabic terms. Esther does that too. She attended Mosque. I was wondering if you did."

"Oh, I see. So, you assume when we use terms other than the King's English that was forced upon us, the person leans toward a specific religion or belief?"

"If I'm honest, I would say that's my assumption."

"Then I thank you for your honesty. Let us learn today. I may say Ah-Shay a Yoruba word that may be your Amen. I may use the expression Hotep, bidding you peace. To me personally whether its Arabic or Kiswahili it feels natural to my tongue and bless my spirit when I open my mouth to speak. Speaking of blessing, I find it most interesting that your wife speaks Kiswahili fluently, has taught the language to young children and that we share the same name."

"Share the same name?"

"Yes."

"You don't share the same name!" He said emphatically. "Her name is Esther."

Kato called out. "Teach Mother." Myles knew what was happening. He leaned in. "Be cool Kato, she got this. He needs this encounter; we been praying for him. Watch it happen. She gon put something on his head like she did me. He'll be alright."

"Yes, her name is Esther. In the bible, there is the Book of Esther, as a Christian I'm sure you're familiar with it. You read it." She stated carefully, not to question him.

But Carl didn't make matters better for himself. He was resentful, even jealous of Myles new disposition and answered self-righteously. "I grew up in the church. I read the bible many many times."

"Then you would know the *Book of Esther*. Chapter 2 verse 7. *"And they brought up Hadassah, that is, Esther, his uncle's daughter: for she had neither father nor mother, and the maid was fair and beautiful."*

"I'll stop right there. I find it prophetic that this would be her experience. And I like to believe the Lord gave Rufus and Emma to her for such a time as this. If one continues to read one would see that she was found worthy of honor. She saved her people."

Carl went silent and Hadassah had more to say. She paid special tribute to Daddy Howard in a brief colorful lecture about the 370th Regiment that amazed them all.

※

Jobari moved by his Uncle Myles public display of admiration and his aunt's graciousness followed suit. "Uncle Myles that was beautiful. I got it from you too huh. The men in this family got passion. I like the way of our swagger. If it weren't for the family, the men and women that shaped me, I don't know where I'd be. My dad is coming for the wedding, but I appreciate the relationship Jahi was man enough to build not only with me but with my dad like a brother. He's been in my life a short while, but he's been a father too." Jobari shifted his attention to Jahi. "And I appreciate you."

Jahi placed his hand over his heart, "For sure, I love you too it's my honor and it's my responsibility to you."

Jobari went on. "I see wasn't nuthin perfect. Daddy Howard lost his first family but found the strength to keep going. Big Pops had to make the decision to leave a child in Germany. GG Ma Honey stood on her feet eight hours a day, delivering mail until she could save enough money to buy a house and get us out the projects. Cousin Emma cleaned the Greystone till the owners gave it to her and we're celebrating in it now. Look at our history! We came full circle."

"Talk about it Jobari!" Mecca called out proudly. He shook his head. "That's my momma, y'all know how she is. She don't cut no corners. Anyway, I'd just like to say, we wouldn't be getting ready for tomorrow. There would be no wedding if there were no men to lead the way. I was looking for perfection when I wasn't perfect. We look at elders like y'all were born grown, like y'all didn't have a past, didn't go through unforgiveable stuff but like Momma Howard says all the time, you don't get the big years without trouble. Being here today on the eve of our wedding looking at my woman. How she hung in there with me, what she did for my family the day before her wedding. The sacrifices she was making, I knew nuthin about to get this done reminds me why I'm making the commitment tomorrow. But that aint nuthin new, I knew what kinda girl she was when I met her. She's always been that type of woman. Never selfish, always coming out the bottom of her heart and giving from her abundance. And wasn't no question in my mind if she was gon accept the Lord with me. She's a ride or die kinda girl like Momma Howard. I'm thankful for this rehearsal dinner that let us get it all out on the table, and strengthened us for tomorrow."

Diamond hugged Jobari. "Y'all, know I love this man and can't wait for tomorrow. That's why we got to shut this puppy down and get some rest, we wanna look good in the morning. God bless everybody! We prepared for you to enjoy the rest of the evening. The coach house is good to go if you're not ready to retire. Help yourself. Have some fun and we'll have breakfast together in the morning."

The grandparents and the bridal party retired for the evening. But the night was far from over, they went to the coach house and played Bid Whist. Calling the trump suit. Three uptown, three downtown, three no trump. Strategizing, bluffing, making books, reneging on bids, slapping cards down hard on the table with every winning hand with the Jazz Crusaders *"Way Back Home"* skipping around in the background. By 10 o'clock everybody was Boo'd up. Even Carl and Esther, seem like they were finding forgiveness in each other's eyes.

JE sat next to Honey, leaned in and got to Talking that talk. Gave her that sly grin and stroked her cheek with the back of his hand. Told her his life was empty without her and how things would be different. That wasn't nuthin in the way, that they were older, wiser. That they knew what they had, what they wanted and needed. That there weren't no surprises, no pretense and that these were the best years. That 78 wasn't too old to begin again. Not with each other it wasn't.

"Honey, our grandchildren are grown. I'm a faithful man. I'm not out there in the street and I'm ready to take you home. Can we go home now? I'm tired of this I need my wife with me."

Honey looked perplexed. She could see that JE was serious but wasn't exactly sure what he was proposing. She smiled. "Jay, you know you too much for me! You and that sly grin get me every time. What you talking bout being faithful and going home? What you trying to say?"

"I mean go home. I never got over not being able to get my family out the projects. Thank God you had the strength to do it but it nearly killed me. It tormented me until I bought the house. I had to do right by you Honey."

"Jay…we're good, we made our peace. Everything is alright between us. You don't owe me nuthin. You know that."

"Woman, I need you to listen to me. Listen to yo husband. I'm a man Honey. I'm trying to tell you something. The house in Indiana, belong to you. I bought it free and clear with my money. Money, I got from working with my own hands and the sweat of my brow. That's how I made peace with God and everything that hurt in my life, the Navy, the Army, being away from you."

"And the children."

"I didn't say nuthin about the children. I said, being away from you! Understand. I love our children but this wasn't about them. You see they grew up and moved on. It was you and me before it was them. Let's get back to us."

"But Jay…"

"Listen! I'm talking to you woman."

"Ok. I'm listening."

"Good. Now the way I figured with the neighborhoods changing, you done moved two times trying to stay ahead of the game. Trying not to relive the hell, you went through in them projects. But you never left the city. Honey, we come from a small town but we not small-town people. So, when I boiled it all down, I figured you wouldn't mind living somewhere with a small-town feel, something in between Mounds and Chicago. You know not too rural but not too city either. That's why I bought the house in Indiana that's close to Chicago. Somewhere to come back to when we not traveling."

"I'm listening. You sho put a lot of thought into it I know that much. You must be serious."

"I am serious. I need you to come home to what, I provided.

"Really?

"Yeah. Really."

"What about my house?"

"What about it? It was a nice house; it served its purpose but it came between us. I saw the neighborhoods coming down around you. I watched the children grow up and move on with their lives. I know what's going on over there now. I see people blocking yo driveway, you sleeping with the lights and the television on all night. A couple of times you left yo keys in the door. You didn't know that did you?"

"Oh my God Jay! I left my keys in the door?"

"Uh huh. More than once. Girl, you don't know how many nights I slept in my car watching that house. For a minute, I thought I was gon have to pay yo neighbor a visit. But Jobari just so happens to call me and got to talking. Turns out we were on the same page. It was time to put it on the market where it should be and get you out of there. No matter how much I wanted to be with you, keep you safe; I couldn't. My daddy fooled around and raised men. I couldn't have spent not one night let alone moved in yo house."

"I know. That's why I never asked you to stay when things got better between us."

"See I like that. I like how that sound. Us."

"And I like how you Talking to me. I missed that. And I think I missed something else. You been laying down some heavy talk, you got my mind racing. But did you say, when we not traveling?"

"Yeah. Seems our grandchildren want us to travel."

"Are you kidding me?"

"Nawl nawl. Why would I do that? Look here." JE showed her the tickets Jobari and Diamond bought. "Here's the tickets right here." he gave em to Honey and she stared at em. "Go ahead. Open the packet, it's got a whole itinerary. When we leaving, where we're staying, what we gon do while we're there and when we coming back. After we rest up from the wedding, we getting outta here. We got yo passport. First stop, Paris France. You been imagining long enough, now you get to see with your own eyes."

"I don't. I don't know what to say."

"Since it's getting late, you probably need to be saying goodnight. You can go lay down but me and the guys need to put things away and setup for the morning. Somehow the family decided I was gon be the maintenance man. And to make sure I stayed around they gave me the coach house, so we gon stay here tonight. Enjoy the wedding tomorrow and then we going back to Indiana."

"Jay, don't tell me we got a house in Bronzeville too."

"Well, I won't tell you Rufus and Emma put a deed on it and gave it to me. So, I guess you do. That is, if you taking this old man back."

Honey leaned her forehead into her hand, on the tips of her fingers, like she was pondering. Closed her eyes went quiet and start rocking. She couldn't talk. Then JE saw the tears coming down.

"I know it's a lot. Kinda overwhelming, I know it seem like it's coming fast. But it didn't happen overnight, it was in the works for a long, long time. You know what I realize?"

"What Jay?"

"Most people really don't believe the bible. No matter how much we read it, we don't believe it till it comes alive in our lives. When it gets really real. When prayers are answered, things start turning around and the lights start coming on." JE stopped, took a deep breath. "Well, Honey all I can tell you, is this right here. What's going on is what the bible was telling us when HE said yo cup will overflow until you won't have room enough to receive."

Honey clamped both her hands together like she was praying, covered her mouth, opened her eyes, nodded her head slow and spoke. "Jay, I'm not sure where it is, I'm not sure of what it all mean. I don't claim to be no bible scholar but somewhere in that bible, God said He would restore the years that was eaten up and that He would make your latter greater. I read it many times. And prayed things would get right between us. But I didn't believe. I just never thought about it and how it would happen, or if it would happen for us at this time in our lives. I guess I'm saying, my hope was for the children. I thought we were all said and done, that our story was written."

"Is that right? Well, I learned a long time ago, faith in prayer is not enough, you gotta do the work. Remember that night I told you God was gon give you everything you wanted? I was talking about us. I put that prayer on the road, and I went to work. My parents taught me that.

"I remember. How we went to Mounds without the children; planning to get a divorce. I was angry I swore fore God I was through. Told Cousin Emma I was done. But pastor prayed. I thought he was gon ask us not to divorce but he didn't. He was too wise for that. He knew my heart was hard. He asked us to just put it off, to stay separate for as long as we needed and then he prayed. I think he knew what he was doing."

"That man pastored my mother and father. How you think they stayed together this long. She told you, you don't get the big years without trouble. They had trouble and plenty of it. You didn't know my dad when he was younger, he wasn't no different than me, Myles, and Jobari. That's why we gotta keep our arms around CJ. Keep him in church. See they had a good shepherd. A pastor that wasn't caught up in foolishness; his desire was to watch for their souls. He asked the Lord to show him everything that was coming up the road in the lives of all his members, so he could guide them.

The Sunday I walked down that aisle to meet the Lord at the altar for myself, he put prayer on my road. See prayer just like time never stops, it keeps, traveling, steering, leading and protecting us. Prayer rides right alongside the bad derailing it with faith that take works to get us to our God-ordained destination.

May that old preacher's soul rest in peace. If I could go back and shake his hand one more time, I would. Now it's up to the next generation to keep the faith, be willing to do the work and if God says the same; they'll make it. But Honey we know sure as they walking in sinful flesh, they gon have trouble in their bodies so we got to get them prayers on the road. We got a whole lot of children out here." JE and Honey joined hands, bowed their heads and JE led the prayer.

*"Father God in The Mighty Name of Jesus…*

*"And I will restore to you the years that the locust hath eaten, the cankerworm, and the caterpiller, and the palmerworm, my great army which I sent among you. And ye shall eat in plenty, and be satisfied, and praise the name of the LORD your God, that hath dealt wondrously with you: and my people shall never be ashamed."*
*– Joel 2:25-26*

# CHAPTER TWENTY-FOUR

## *The Greystone*

The Greystone was in reasonable shape. Al played a pivotal role as general contractor. He met with the architects, reviewed the building footprint and finalized the scope of work. The Greystone would keep its integrity, the original character that made memories sacred. The rehab addressed foundational work. The opening of masonry walls, roofing, mechanical, electrical, plumbing. The works. Mechanicals were relocated to the North wall.

The weathered exterior brick walls were removed, flipped, and laid back where possible. The bricked patio extension created a nice courtyard they named *Jaden's Court*. It provided the perfect curb appeal for entering the coach house where JE and Honey stayed when they were in the city or when things needed to be maintained. The 19th Century American Victorian Era, black enameled ornamental wrought iron was carefully removed, repaired, and reassembled. Additional fencing was added to match the existing ironwork. Three fireplaces were inspected and serviced. Back porches were rebuilt to enhance outdoor livable spaces. The full walkout basement was made accessible to the 1st floor unit. Windows were swapped out for egress windows for safety, increasing the flow of light and function. Window parts were fully reconstructed including sash, sill, stool, jam, stops, side casing, counterweights, and aprons. Panes were removed and reglazed. Broken windows were replaced with double-strength glass to match the original thickness. The front porch remained prominent. Exterior sconces were reconditioned and replicated where needed.

Oak hardwood floors were sanded and stained. Original woodwork, transom, pocket doors, interior doors, molding, door trim and quarter-turn staircase was cleaned and polished. The 2nd floor was shored up with beams. Lead pipes were replaced with copper for excellent water flow.

Cast iron radiators were serviced and reconditioned for efficiency. Several perpendicular walls were removed to enlarge square footage in bedrooms, living and closet space. Additional bath and restrooms were installed on wet walls with the exception of the kitchen area. Butler pantries were opened extending kitchen space to accommodate an island, and a graciously scaled dining room. Existent arches were widened to open the floor plan. A landscaper was contracted to complete the exterior enhancements. Concrete flowerpots and plantings were installed. Layla staged the space to perfection. It took less than a year to complete the work.

The Greystone was ready, the wedding plans aligned perfectly. It was warm, June came, school was out, *Robyn's* sang, and the family was remembering. Remembering how they ran through the water that *Jett* from behind planked fire hydrants, and played in the streets on hot summer days in Robert Brooks extensions. Bronzeville found its way into all the wedding pictures posted on the website.

CJ started school in September and went to church on Sundays.

# CHAPTER TWENTY-FIVE

*Bronzeville*

The Black Metropolis. A Mecca of business, black culture, commerce, art. A narrow strip of land spanning seven miles. Stretching along 22nd to 63rd streets between State and Cottage Grove. The Black Belt, where Chicago's black population at its peak of 300,000 coalesced. Fused, blending prosperity and poverty, professionals and laborers.

Where jazz, blues, gospel, artist and black intelligencia mingled. Where the *Chicago Defender* editorials rebuked oppression and lynching's in the South and summoned blacks to come North.

Where black preachers, Imams, politicians, labor, civic rights leaders, writers and poets, boxers, heavy-weight champions, dancers, social activist, singers, composers; lived, moved, and had their being.

The Greystone stood as a testament to the history of the Howard family in Chicago and the prayers like time that never stopped traveling. The wedding was a culmination of the past, present and the future. A celebration of architecture and urban renewal in the community. A social and political movement. A lesson in history reinforcing black family values and beliefs. Undergirding the tradition of securing the *Chicago Defender, Muhammad Speaks, The Final Call* and keeping the *AM* radio dial locked on *WVON 1450*, the *Voice of the Negro* for generations. The wedding events followed suit. Family and guest dined, toured, used resources and spent their money in Bronzeville.

Welcome to the Wedding of

## *Jobari & Diamond*

Celebrating Love & Heritage
Mount Pisgah Church Chicago
Officiant, Bishop Turner
June 28, 2019

♣ ♣ ♣ ♣

Instrumental Prelude – "Back at One" Brian McKnight

Seating of the Family |Procession of Attendants

Entrance of the Bride

"For You" Performed by: Tenor Saxophonist Malcolm Miller

Poem Performed by: "Ancient" by Hadassah

Bride & Groom Bow Down at the Alter

"I Give Myself Away" & "Give Me You"
Performed by: Soloist Lily Rose

Exchange of Personal Vows
Jumping the Broom Ceremony, Minister Kwame Daniel
Presentation of Bride and Groom, Bishop Turner

### Jobari & Diamond Steele

Recessional - "Way Back Home"

Parents of the Bride - "Jean & Paul Thomas"

Parents of the Groom - "Mecca & Jahi Dae"

# Wedding Coordination Services
## Provided By: A Good Thing Wedding Planners

The Colors: Rose Gold, Black & Ivory

The Groom's Ring: A tri-colored wide band of white gold, with a smaller band of rose gold, and a layer of black diamonds set with black rhodium. The Bride's Ring: A half eternity diamond halo band crafted in 14 carets, rose gold with nine diamonds in a row. Rimmed with diamond accents arranged in a scalloped pattern.

The Calla Lily Cake & Rose Table: A 3-Tiered Lemon cake filled with Swiss Meringue buttercream to cleanse the palate. The square cake contrasted the shapes of flowers displaying a mixed group of roses and lilies resting on a white linen cloth trimmed and set in green lemon leaves.

The Wedding Gown: An ivory fit and flared romantic floral lace gown that led into a soft tulle train with lace straps that cap the shoulders and frame a V-Neck low back. Complemented with a stunning gold vintage wedding shoe with 3-D embroidered gold lace in the body of the shoe. The heel featured crisscross gold leather straps, gold leather piping and an open toe. The hairstylist created a high long ponytail for a youthful clean look.

The Bridesmaids Dress: A satin rose gold one-shoulder dress, with a trumpet skirt line, faux wrap detail with a twist bodice, and empire waist. Complimented by rose gold stiletto heeled shoes draped in lustrous silk ribbons that wrap around the feet and ankles in a crisscross and oversized bow at the back of the heel. The hairstylist fashioned a messy bun ornamented with Baby's-breath.

The Flower Girl Dress: Ivory, rose gold with black embellishments. Satin polyester, crinoline netting and illusion tulle. Tie closure. Petticoat. Ivory poly satin bodice, decorated waistline black hand tie sash with rose gold flower pedals wrapped in fluffy tulle. A back zipper closure and black-tie bow with a double layer of fluffy tulles with rose gold petals around the bottom of the dress. The hairstylist fashioned a girlish messy bun with a full bang.

The Ring Bearer: Dressed in groomsmen attire

The Groomsmen Tuxedo: A black tuxedo modern and slim linen with matching vest and satin trim accents. Flat front pants, a white classic collar shirt with folded back French cuffs and monogram cuff links. rose gold ties, vest and suspenders complimenting the bridesmaids and Christian Louboutin red-bottom shoes. The groom accentuated his look with black and tortoise eyeglasses.

The Walk Down the Aisle: A long, dramatic walk. A larger number of smaller pews began immediately at the back door, stopping just short of the alter yielding to longer pews on the front row to accommodate parents and grandparents. Decorations were scaled to prevent the blocking of sight lines of the ceremony and cameras. Diamond's father met her at the 50-yard line and walked her to Jobari.

The Seating Arrangement: Great grandparents, grandparents, parents and stepdad filled the first row on the right side. Aunts, uncles, cousins, and siblings that were not in the wedding party sat in the following two rows. Diamond's parents were seated in the first row on the left side of the aisle along with additional family members to comprise two rows. The wedding party stood with the bride and groom throughout the ceremony.

Prior to the processional Jobari's great grandparents and grandparents were escorted first followed by Diamond's grandparents. Then Jobari's parents and the mother of the bride and groom were escorted to their seats.

Guest with children were seated on the end of the row furthest away from the aisle and, when possible, closer to the back of the ceremony so they could exit quickly if needed. The wedding was beautifully governed and concluded with the Jumping the Broom ceremony.

Exchange of Personal Vows: The couple in its dedication to family beliefs bowed at the alter during the singing of *"I Give Myself Away & Give Me You"* as an act of surrendering their lives to God and one another.

Jumping the Broom Ceremony: *We conclude the sacred ceremony with the African American tradition of Jumping of the Broom. Honoring black slaves unrecognized as whole persons and not permitted to marry. African people, a resourceful people, a spiritual people, jumped the broom as a ceremonial uniting of man and wife. Today it reminds us of the past and the pain of slavery which will never ever be forgotten. As Diamond and Jobari jump the broom, they physically and spiritually cross over the threshold into holy matrimony to begin making a home together. The broom symbolizes the sweeping away the old welcoming the new; energy. Clearing the path for all things good and honorable to enter their lives. Witnessed by the community of family and friends charged to speak life into their union thereby strengthening a nation. Diamond and Jobari can begin their life together with a clean sweep!*

Jobari and Diamond were handed the broom to make sweeping gestures. Diamond placed it in their path and together, they jumped and the reception began!

The Reception: Gospel, Jazz, R & B, and *Steppin* Music

The First Dance: Jobari & Diamond *Stepped* to "Change Places' by Jeffree followed by a Steppers line - (*guest waited in line to step with the bride and groom*).

The Wedding Menu: Tasty, summery and health conscious. Jamaican Jerked Chicken, Rosemary and Black Peppered Rotisserie and Barbequed Chicken, Barbeque Tofu Skewers, Grilled Tilapia with Smoked Paprika, Louisiana Red Beans, Jamaican Steamed Cabbage, Sautéed Kale, Southern Collards & Mustard Greens with Smoked Turkey, Roasted Garlic Parmesan Brussel Sprouts (laced with red bell peppers drenched in olive oil) Spicy Jambalaya Rice, Potato, Macaroni, Caesar Salad and Fried Sweet Plantain.

"Airbnb Website Launch"
Content Created & Published By: Kel

A Bronzeville Greystone Perfect for Weddings,
Large Family Vacations & Reunions
Group Gatherings & Company Meetings
3 Night Minimum – 2 Week Maximum - $2,000/Night

Newly Restored Greystone in Chicago's Historic Bronzeville community on tree lined boulevard. Hotel perks. Private suites. Minutes to downtown. A rare find and great base for your Chicago visit. Occupy the entire 5000 sq. ft. Three levels of indoor and outdoor living space. 8 bedrooms and 2 family rooms sleep 20 individuals comfortably with recreational space. Panoramic views of the city. The Greystone boasts a hidden private backyard and courtyard, 2 porches, an oversized 2nd floor balcony and bricked patio.

Private front door with CODED door lock and security system
Five (5) Step Enhanced Cleaning
Allergy friendly oak hardwood floors
Leather seating throughout
Fully stocked kitchen, stainless steel appliances, granite countertops
Microwaves and coffee makers
Breakfast island seats 8 people
Graciously scaled dining room seats 12
4 Queen and 4 Full sized beds, 2 sofa sleepers
Clean fresh, sanitized sheets and pillows
Bright airy bedrooms with blinds and room darkening curtains
Built-in closet organizers, hangers, (2) irons and boards
2 full and one-half baths on each level, double sinks, fully stocked
Extra towels, hair dryer and basic toiletries
3 LG 90inch 4K televisions. One on each level.
Bedrooms equipped with 47inch TV- Comcast, Netflix, HBO, ESPN

High speed secure wireless and wired Internet.
2 Dedicated workspaces for laptops
Theatre/Recreation room -Pool & Ping Pong Tables -Arcade
2 front load washers, 2 dryers, hamper, folding table w/supplies
Jaden's Courtyard
Outdoor gas grill & patio furnishings
Great Location to enjoy activities:
Ample on street parking -public transportation assessable
Quick access to Downtown and Lakefront
Close to Lakeshore Drive and Dan Ryan Expressway
Millennium Park – *The Bean*
Art, Field and Museum of Science and Industry
5-minute Taxi, Uber, Lyft ride to Michigan Avenue
Magnificent Mile
Short train or bus ride to Chicago downtown
Shared Divvy bike (rental) across the street
Short walk or drive to trendy restaurants, and coffee shops
Shopping and exercise clubs
Umbrellas provided
Bike storage in garage
Guest Access: Entire Greystone

*JE Howard Property Management & Maintenance Services*
*Monday through Friday*
*7a to 3p.*
*Readily accessible for emergencies.*

# EXCERPT FROM UPCOMING SEQUEL

## DOWN SOUTH SUMMERS
"Where Seeds Were Sown"

A Novel of Confessions

❦

Layla Patrice

A Black Pearl Literary Perspective
Generations Series

*Things could be a lot worse was Jules's personal calling card for dealing with stuff that messed her head up. Becoming a psychologist was her way of making peace with the world. Rationalizing took the sting outta hurtful things. She hated confrontation, avoided it at all costs. If someone told her to kiss where the sun don't shine Jules pretended, she didn't hear a word they said.*

"Honey, I wasn't paying no attention to what she said. She'd go on and. I'm not one to get stuck, I believe in moving forward, onward and upward. I will not become the monster I despise. And so, you were saying?"

*Jules would reason that the person who slapped the daylights outta her was simply acting out of anger.* "You know Mecca, sometimes you have to take things with a grain of salt, we're emotional beings and subject to do things we don't mean to do. I refuse to make a spectacle of myself. That's why we have the police."

*True, but she never called the police, instead she punished herself for not having the guts to set boundaries. And she punished herself severely. Cried ugly tears, slobbed and snotted all over the place till her eyes were swollen shut and when her po body couldn't take no more, she gave herself the pep talk.*

"Alright now Jules." *She would say referring to herself in third person.* "Get it together, just get it together, things really could be a lot worse, and they not as bad as they seem."

*She had a ritual. Jules wiped her eyes, smooth her clothes out with her pretty little hands, looked in the mirror, gave herself a big smile* and it would be business as usual. She'd walk right outta of her beautiful restroom and give good counsel.

"Is that it, Jules? Mecca challenged rising up from the chaise making herself less comfortable. Is that yo answer? She repeated circling Jules's chair then stopping in front. "Is that all you got to tell me? Not being physically abused or cheated on should be reason enough to die in a marriage. Huh?" She said walking away from Jules and over to the window sensing her discomfort.

Jules got up from her seat and followed her with a pathetic attempt to assert herself. "Now you know I don't believe that." When Mecca turned to face her, she retreated, went and sat behind her desk to finish her comment. "And don't go putting words in my mouth. Expressing myself is not a problem."

The moment the words left Jules lips; an urgent hush loomed throughout the room locking them in a thick undercurrent of silence. Jules felt her body tensing, it was the silence before the storm. Mecca slowly turned away from the window with a look of disgust possessing her face, stared straight at Jules, eyes bucked, nose turned up and tight jawed.

"Since! When! Jules? Since when did you not have a problem expressing yourself?"

Jules knew exactly when. She struck the desk with the palms of both her hands and hollered. "Mecca!" Not wanting her to continue the probe.

"Mecca what! Don't tell me you didn't hear what I said either. You know what I'm Talking bout. How long Jules?"

"How long what!"

There she was again acting as if she didn't hear what was said. She grabbed and began rolling the three metal Chinese balls in her sweaty palms. Mecca made her feel belittled just like Mina did.

"How long you gon be in denial? You do have a problem expressing yourself ever since you been going down south in the summer. I don't know what happened but it's time you stop playing healer and get healed! You take too much crap. If I can be vulnerable, why can't you? I just sat here and spilled my guts and you wanna keep acting like you in control of every situation and circumstance in yo life when you know you not. What's going on with you Jules. You may as well tell me because whatever it is, I'm telling you now. It stops tonight!

Made in the USA
Middletown, DE
28 September 2022

11459226R00139